All the News...

All the News...

JAMES F. LYNCH

DODD, MEAD & COMPANY · NEW YORK

ISBN 0-396-06333-0
Library of Congress Catalog Card Number: 74-147132
Printed in the United States of America
by Vail-Ballou Press, Inc., Binghamton, N.Y.

To E. D....as ever

All the News...

Chapter One

"IT LOOKS almost antiseptic," Bob Davis said, nodding through the glass at the block-long city room.

The gray-haired receptionist looked up from his paper. He wore a neatly pressed linen jacket with the words *The New York Record* in red on the left breast pocket.

"I don't think I've ever seen a newspaper more neat," Bob continued when it was obvious the receptionist would not comment. The eerie light of the fluorescent fixtures, the dully painted walls and the tombstone appearance of the sound-absorbent ceiling tiles created the image of still life caught by a flash camera. It was June, though slight hint of it came through the sealed windows and the giant air-conditioning plant perpetuated the autumnal chill *The New York Record* engineers found kept the staff most alert.

So this is *The New York Record,* Bob mused, straining in vain for a glimpse at a famous face, a by-line name, a sign of animation. Only the top editors, their secretaries and the clerks were in so early. The neat stacks of copy paper laid out around the horseshoe desks told where the copy editors would sit in the late afternoon as the paper slowly came to life and the process of printing the next day's news began. The desks of the reporters were still clear, their tops shining dully beneath the cold light, their drawers bulging with clippings, source books or trash quickly cleared off the top before quitting time.

Through the glass partition at the receptionist's back, the men in the news room seemed to be moving in slow motion with an exaggerated show of decorum. "I guess it wouldn't be dignified if anyone on *The New York Record* ran," Bob said to himself, shaking his head at the sight of the clean floors, the empty wastebaskets and the lazy curl of cigarette smoke that

1

was dissipated quickly through the noiseless air ducts. It was far different from the *Fort Wayne Item,* Bob conceded, even though his pride at being assistant city editor of the *Item* would have made him defend the paper even against *The New York Record.*

Bob was waiting in the reception office for a job interview, one that he thought he had manipulated rather skillfully and well. He had somehow been able to convince the assistant managing editor of the *Record,* Zachary A. Zugsmith, that he didn't want to work on the paper and that was tantamount to a challenge to Zugsmith. Everyone in the newspaper business, Zugsmith thought, wanted to work for *The New York Record.* It was up to Zugsmith to get the best of them, to keep the standards of the paper high and to convince the top candidates that there was no other paper to work for in the whole world.

"Mr. Zugsmith will see you now," a fat woman in horn-rimmed glasses said, holding the door of the city room open. Bob followed her through the door and then past some desks he hadn't seen before. They were larger than the others and faced in the opposite direction, just like the set-up at the Columbia School of Journalism. These, Bob reasoned, were where the executives sat. It seemed only natural for *The New York Record* to have the desks arranged so the editors could watch the city room without appearing the slightest bit interested.

As his guide waddled past desk after desk, Bob began to wonder where Zugsmith sat. Even as his professor in editorial writing at Columbia, where Bob first came to Zugsmith's attention, the assistant managing editor of *The New York Record* seemed a little like a god, and indeed he was considered such in some circles. Many newsmen agreed that Zugsmith was the cleverest newspaper man in the country. But Jim Reynolds, Bob's city editor in Fort Wayne had spoken less kindly of him, warning that Zugsmith was always on the alert for talent and used his classes at the university to recruit some of the best men from other papers attending seminars or special classes. Bob Davis received his warning about Zugsmith before leaving Fort Wayne on his sabbatical. "Stay away from Zugsmith," Reynolds had said, "he'll fill your head full of nonsense or hire you away at twice our pay."

The "nonsense" was Zugsmith's way of doing things on *The New York Record.* He was responsible for the day-to-day handling of the news and he turned the function into a major exercise of power. He was the acknowledged master of the city room, bringing favored people into the close circle of important jobs on the paper and banishing others to the farthest reaches of the cavernous room where the exiles performed tasks little resembling newspaper work except in the direst emergencies. Like any feudal system, the city room was rift with jealousies, frustrations and plots, all of which Zugsmith reveled in as sort of a healthy malignant brew that brought forth the best efforts on the part of the most people. The results, he would often say, are undeniable and few could argue with the enormous success and prestige that the paper enjoyed.

Millions regarded *The New York Record* as *the* paper of record. Many people didn't even believe there was such a thing as the atomic bomb until they read about it in *The New York Record,* complete with a diagramed chain reaction and a précis of Einstein's theory that made it all possible. The paper was the most widely quoted, most powerful, most feared, hated and respected in the country. Its crossword puzzles were the hardest, its sports coverage the most esoteric and its over-all national and foreign coverage the most complete almost to the point of saturation. A whole cult had sprung up about the paper, with radio and television personalities asking their listeners or guests: "Did you read that article in *The New York Record?*" The basic appeal was one of simple snobbery, with people carrying the paper even if they didn't read it and pretending to be part of the great "in" crowd *The New York Record* supposedly catered to with sociological features and featured society news. The advertising volume testified loudly to the faith of big business in the message *The New York Record* was trying to get across. Despite its archaic type faces and stiff, formalized make-up, hundreds of papers throughout the country could have survived on advertising *The New York Record* turned down or held out each day.

Many critics said the success of the paper was largely attributable to its past publishers' knowledge of real estate values in the city and it was true that four previous sites had been sold at huge profits. A block away at the old office *The New York Record* had occupied for twenty years, an electric sign still ran around the building, the last relic of the newspaper and its growing prosperity.

With prosperity came prestige and an imperious operation of almost grandeur. *The New York Record* carried no comics, no gossip columns, no coupons. Bob wasn't sure if Zugsmith reflected the paper's personality or it reflected his. He tended to doubt it, though, since the smugness, the dullness, the dedication to giving all the news, at least about the subjects it deigned to cover, had been entrenched in *The New York Record* before Zugsmith ever appeared on the scene.

"Come in, Davis, come in," Zugsmith called from behind his desk as Bob hesitated at the doorway. He was a short, intense man, with a thin fringe of hair running around his bald head like the mark of some ancient monastic order.

Bob shook hands with Zugsmith self-consciously. He had never been one of the students who stayed after class for long discussions or accompanied Zugsmith for a drink at the nearby bars. Bob had spoken to Zugsmith about his editorials, but he had no idea of trying to ingratiate himself since his honest intention was to return to Fort Wayne. It was Zugsmith who sought out Bob, perhaps out of a sense of curiosity why Bob wasn't interested in *The New York Record* or perhaps because he liked what he saw in the editorials or the quietly competent way Bob handled himself in class.

4

Seldom was one of Zugsmith's campaigns launched with more cunning. Bob never knew how well planned his appearance in Zugsmith's office had been; it was no accident, nothing casual. Zugsmith had found Bob's weakness with the aid of Bill Stewart, a reporter who was taking the same course while working on *The New York Record*. Stewart, fresh out of the university, where he had been the correspondent for the *Record,* had been encouraged to make friends with the handsome midwesterner and to show him around the city.

When Zugsmith learned from Stewart that Davis was the type who had to respond to a challenge, the assistant managing editor's strategy was clear: Stewart had to impress on Bob that not everyone could make the grade on *The New York Record,* even though he held a high position on another paper. At first Bob laughed at the suggestion that he wouldn't be able to make it in the big city and then the reaction set in that Zugsmith was hoping for: Bob being equally determined to get a job on *The New York Record.*

Diane Reilly wasn't part of Zugsmith's plan, but she helped, too. Diane, a singer in a Greenwich Village nightclub, had gone to high school with Stewart and it was natural that the club was one of the stops he made in showing Bob the city. When Bob saw Diane, the rest of the city's attraction dwindled to zero.

"This is Bob Davis," Stewart said when Diane came to their table after her act. "This is my favorite high school classmate, Diane Reilly," he said turning to Bob.

"I can see why," Bob said.

There was something about him Diane liked. "Are you a newspaper man, too?" she asked.

"Yes," Stewart put in, "but Bob is from out of town. He's the assistant city editor of the *Fort Wayne Item.*"

"Assistant City Editor? Aren't you rather young for such an important position?" Diane eyed him with respect. All she knew about editors was what Stewart had told her and all the editors he spoke of on *The New York Record* had been there at least thirty years.

"I'm probably not as young as you think," Bob said, pleased with the compliment. "Besides, it's not like *The New York Record*. The *Item* is a much smaller paper and it's a lot easier to get ahead."

Stewart smiled. "That's what I've been telling you all along. The competition is a lot tougher in the big city. I don't think you'd be an assistant anything on my paper at your age."

Bob ignored the young reporter, turning all his charm on the girl. "You sing very well."

Diane smiled her thanks, her brown eyes twinkling. She wore little make-up because her startling white skin and long raven hair needed no highlighting. Her breasts moved rhythmically against the top of the low-cut gown she wore and a slit in the skirt showed that her legs were as sensational as the rest of her body. Diane's ambitions to sing in the better clubs uptown had long ago been dampened by her refusal to meet the demand of agents or managers that invariably were part of the offer. There was a sensuousness, a fire, an air of desirability about her that made Bob vaguely uncomfortable.

"Diane's brother is a priest," Stewart put in, filling the void that had developed as the two looked at each other. "Did Tim graduate from Notre Dame? No, it was Fordham, wasn't it?"

"Did you go to Notre Dame, Mr. Davis?" she asked, her interest evident.

"Bob was a big football hero at South Bend," Stewart said. "He's not a Catholic, though."

Bob smiled broadly. "Do I have to be?"

Diane shook her head, her eyes searching his, "Not so far as I'm concerned. Bill always teases me about my brother being a priest and refusing to talk with any of the customers here. He says I want to see everyone's baptismal certificate before I speak to them."

"But that's not so?" Bob asked.

She wrinkled her nose at Stewart and turned back to Bob.

"Don't believe anything Bill says. He always tells the wildest stories. That's why I tell him I don't believe everything I read in that paper of his."

"*The New York Record?* That's heresy," Bob said with a smile. "Bill, why don't you call in to see if you have an early assignment tomorrow."

"I already . . ." Stewart caught himself, or at least the look that Bob gave him. "I'll do that," he said, "don't you two go away."

By the time Stewart returned, he had lost his job as guide to Diane. It was a natural for her since she had mornings and afternoons free and Bob's classes didn't start until three each day. In three weeks, they had covered most of the tourist attractions and Bob had become convinced that New York wouldn't be too bad, after all. With Bob, the challenge that Diane represented tied in with the challenge of *The New York Record.* He was confident he could make the grade on both counts.

"You've had an interesting life, haven't you?" Zugsmith asked, glancing up from the resume Bob brought with him.

"Not really," Bob answered, honestly.

"Football and track in college, a member of the 1948 Olympic team. How did you make out in London?"

Bob smiled. "I didn't go. I was celebrating making the team with a bunch of my fraternity brothers and I broke a bone in my ankle. I missed the trip."

"That's too bad," Zugsmith said drily. "I see you were in the Korean War. Were you the command pilot on a B-25?"

"Yes, I was a command pilot, but that's not saying much. They were pretty short of pilots in those days."

"I envy you. I was 4F in World War II, although later the paper said I was essential. Of course, I was too old for Korea." The statement was only half true, Zugsmith knew. He had always hated violence and his nervousness at the thought of being drafted led to his 4F rating. He was essential to the paper because so many men on the staff were enlisting. As a

7

result, World War II was the time of Zugsmith's greatest triumphs. He worked long hours and came in close contact with all the top men on the paper. He rose rapidly, leapfrogging over the places held by others who had gone off to service.

Looking back, Zugsmith was certain he would have moved ahead even without the war. He realized, though, that he always felt uncomfortable in giving orders to those he had superseded. He was hard-driving and intense about the paper, but almost shy about himself. The paper was the god; he was merely the high priest seeing that proper reverence was paid and due respect rendered. His zeal confused many. It wasn't clear if Zugsmith made *The New York Record* or *The New York Record* made Zugsmith; they were virtually an entity.

"What do you think of our little shop?" Zugsmith asked Bob.

"I had always heard that the *Record* was big . . ."

"*The New York Record,* if you please," Zugsmith said almost curtly. Bob recalled a speech in class: "There are many *Records* in the newspaper field, but there is only one that is *The New York Record.*"

"Of course, *The New York Record,* I'm sorry," Bob said, surprised that Zugsmith carried his classroom manner into the office.

"I think the whole city room of the *Fort Wayne Item* could fit into one corner of the city room."

"Yes, that's right. You're the assistant city editor of the *Item,* aren't you?"

"I was when I left. You never know what happens in the newspaper business when you're away."

"Do you like what you're doing?"

Bob hesitated as he groped for an answer. He felt his job lacked challenge.

"I like the paper all right," he conceded, "but being assistant city editor out there is really nothing much. I miss the excitement of the early days when I started on the paper."

"Do you think working for *The New York Record* would excite you?"

Bob smiled. "I think it would certainly be challenging."

"How much do they pay you out there?" Zugsmith reached into the drawer of the desk and pulled out a long cigarette holder.

"I'm supposed to get a raise when I get back that should put me at $150 a week."

Zugsmith smiled as he put a cigarette into the holder and lighted it. He watched a smoke ring start to the ceiling and then disappear in the air-conditioned air currents. "Our assistant city editors made more than that before the war. Today, copy editors start at $140 and reporters get that after three years. It's not a very exciting 1958 salary, is it?"

Bob smiled wanely.

"What would you say to starting here at $175?" Zugsmith spoke with the cigarette holder thrust upward from the corner of his mouth. Bob thought he resembled or was trying to resemble the cartoon he had seen of Franklin D. Roosevelt. The cigarette holder, in fact, was Zugsmith's personal vigil light to Roosevelt, according to Zugsmith second in greatness only to Moses (and not Robert, he hastened to tell his classes).

"That's not a bad starting salary. What would I be doing? Writing editorials?"

"No, I admit your editorials were good for Journalism 28, but I don't think you have the background to write editorials for *The New York Record*. All our editorial writers are specialists—in government, politics, social service or the like. What would you write about?"

"Begging your pardon, sir, but I think I could write editorials on par with those of *The New York Record*. From the ones I've read, they seldom take a positive stand. You yourself said my writing was incisive."

Zugsmith tapped the cigarette holder on the desk like a proctor calling an unruly class to order. "Those editorials were written in the abstract; they would never do for *The*

New York Record. Yes, they were frank, mainly emotional stands on one issue or another. But they were your thoughts, not the thoughts or the aims of *The New York Record.*"

He turned in his chair and looked out the window at the soot smeared theater wall across the way. Zugsmith could remember when the building was new, when he, too, questioned the editorials and wondered why they didn't hit harder or generate more enthusiasm.

"You say our editorials don't take a stand? Why then are we accused of being anti-Catholic, pro-Catholic, Zionist, anti-Semitic, Rightist, Conservative, Leftist, and Communist? How can we be all these things if our editorials don't take a stand? It takes skill to be all things to all people. We stand on both sides of a question and don't move unless we are absolutely forced to. And then we do it so imperceptibly that no one remembers where we were."

Bob was unconvinced. He rubbed his hand over his chin stubbornly. "Don't you think it would be better for *The New York Record* to take a stand at the start, to be a pacesetter?"

Zugsmith smiled. Once again he was the professor straightening out a student's logic. "Why argue with success? *The New York Record* is the most powerful paper in the world. The President reads the paper to find out what our foreign policy should be. The Russians read it to evaluate their own foreign policy."

"That has a lot to do with the play of the news, the reporter's evaluation of events and your headline treatments," Bob persisted. "The editorials are not the sole reflections of policy, I know, but evidently editorial writing wasn't what you had in mind for me. Frankly, though, I would prefer straight reporting; I could get to know the city better." Diane was the principal New Yorker he wanted to get to know better. A reporting assignment would at least let him finish about the same time as Diane's last performance.

"Bob Davis, Bob Davis," Zugsmith repeated half to himself

as he gazed at the ceiling. "But I don't think that's a by-line name for *The New York Record*."

Bob could feel the hair tingling at the back of his neck. "I won several prizes on the *Fort Wayne Item* under that by-line."

"Bob Davis in Fort Wayne; yes; Bob Davis in *The New York Record,* no. It's too small townish, too Middle Western." Zugsmith could see Bob's face flushing. "Don't get angry. I was told by the publisher that Zugsmith wasn't a name to be managing editor. *The New York Record* needs prestige, or a name to sound like prestige. That's why Beaumont Phelps Manley is the managing editor."

"Just because of his name? Wasn't he a famous correspondent during the war?"

"Yes, I guess that was part of it, too." Zugsmith was sorry he had let his own frustration show in seeking to soothe Bob. "I guess Robert Fulton Davis could be a by-line, though."

"Unfortunately, it's Bob, not Robert. My father named me for an old friend and his name was never anything but Bob, not Robert."

"Well, how about B. Fulton Davis?" Zugsmith persisted. "You do have a middle name, don't you?"

Bob shook his head. "No, just Bob. Bob Davis. That's it."

Zugsmith frowned. "It really doesn't matter. I have a much better job than reporting in mind for you, Bob. It's something where your incisiveness will come in handy, where your penchant for asking questions will be appreciated."

Bob smiled. "I hope you don't mind, but I'm always suspicious when a job is built up that way. What did you have in mind?"

"I thought you'd make a valuable addition to one of our desks. We always need copy editors and I think you would do well. That's how I started."

Bob knew copy editors worked roughly the same hours as reporters. He would still have time to meet Diane after her last show.

"At what salary?" he asked offhandedly.

Zugsmith was taken back. He thought Bob would jump at the chance. "At $175, the figure I mentioned."

Bob knew Zugsmith seldom interviewed applicants himself. He knew the mention of being passed over for the managing editor's job had put Zugsmith on the defensive and Bob had no compunction in pressing his advantage. He shook his head. "As an editorial writer or a reporter, $175 would be fine, but as a copy editor, no."

Zugsmith crushed the cigarette into an ash tray on his desk. He put his chin in his hand and looked out at last season's posters fluttering on the theater wall. "Why do I always want the difficult ones?" he asked himself. "Davis has talent, undoubtedly, but his attitude seems so hostile. I wonder if he'll really make a *New York Record* man." Turning slowly to Bob he said:

"I told you our copy editors start at $140. I'm willing to start you at thirty-five dollars above scale. After all, you have no big city experience."

Bob shook his head stubbornly. "You said I'd be a valuable addition to a desk. All right. I know the Guild is asking for two hundred dollars for copy editors in the negotiations now under way. If all copy editors, in the eyes of the union, are worth two hundred dollars a week, I certainly think a 'valuable addition' should be, too."

"Two hundred dollars a week?" Zugsmith leaned over the desk, an incredulous look on his face. Suddenly he smiled. "All right, agreed, on one condition."

"What's that?"

Zugsmith walked to the door and closed it. Bob wondered what the conditions would be.

"You must never tell anyone you are getting two hundred dollars."

"I never tell anyone my salary. I don't expect to start now."

"But you don't know how the grapevine works in this place. If it gets out that I started you at two hundred dollars, there will be a line of men asking for a raise. It's bad for morale."

"Not for mine, it isn't," Bob said, smiling broadly.

Diane was pleased when Bob told her he wasn't going back to Indiana.

"*The New York Record?* Bill says it's the greatest paper in the world. Congratulations," she said after hearing of the interview with Zugsmith. "Will you be a reporter like Bill?"

"No, I'll be on the desk, a copy reader, or as they say on *The New York Record,* a copy editor."

"What's a copy editor?" Diane was interested mainly because it was obvious that she had to know more about newspapers if she was to keep him interested.

"A copy editor gets the story from the slot man and . . ."

"What's a slot man?" Her puzzlement was growing.

Bob smiled. "He's like the chief copy editor. He's called a slot man because usually he sits in the middle of a horseshoe-shaped desk so he can reach the men working for him more easily. Anyway, he gets the stories from the reporters or the rewrite men or the news services and passes them out to the copy editor. The copy editors correct any grammatical or spelling mistakes, try to check on the facts, supply any needed explanations, smooth out the sentences, cut out unnecessary words or paragraphs and then write a headline."

Diane's eyes widened. "All that? Will you be handling any of Bill's stories?"

"No, I'm going to be working in sports at first."

"Sports? I guess you'll get to see a lot of games. I'll be looking for your name on the stories."

Bob shook his head. "You don't understand. The copy editors don't go out to games; that's the job of the reporters. And the copy editors don't get their names on stories either; that's for the reporters, too."

"You mean to say that you do all that work and don't get your name on the story? That's not fair."

13

"That's the way it works. Besides, it will probably only be for the summer."

"A temporary job?"

"Well, I figure I'll be fed up with the paper by then and be ready to go home."

"Don't you want to work in New York permanently?"

"Not really, no. I'm only taking the job to prove I can do it."

"Is that really important to you?"

Bob sighed. "Yes, I'm afraid it is. It's been that way so long as I can remember. In sports you always want to play against the best and in the war it was always the toughest missions to fly. I can't help it, I guess. *The New York Record* is the best paper in the world, according to a lot of people, and I wouldn't feel right if I didn't try to prove to myself that I could work there if I wanted."

"And that's the only reason you're taking the job?" There was a note in Diane's voice that Bob caught quickly.

"Well, no, not the only reason. I thought that working here this summer would give me more time to get acquainted with you and the city. I really look forward to our sightseeing each day."

Diane looked at the hem of her gown. Suddenly she raised her head and asked, "Are you sure you don't have a wife or fiancee you're hiding back in Fort Wayne?"

Bob laughed, picking up her chin and holding it cupped in his hand. "Would you be jealous if I did?"

"Jealous? No, I just wonder why you want to work for a small paper when you could be working for a big paper. Surely they must pay you more here, don't they?" She had grown fond of Bob, fonder than she wanted.

"Money isn't everything, besides this place is so big that you feel lost. You have no identity. You're just another cog in a big machine."

"But couldn't you get to be a reporter and start writing?"

"No, I'm not likely to be writing. Bob Davis, I'm told, isn't a proper by-line for *The New York Record*."

"I still don't think it right that you do all that work and don't get your name in the paper."

Bob laughed. "No, the cogs are anonymous. That's another reason I want to go back to Fort Wayne. At least I'm a bigger cog."

"Couldn't you become a big cog here?" Diane persisted.

"I'm afraid that would take more than three months," Bob said.

The sports department was the stepchild of all the departments on *The New York Record*. Zugsmith was never interested in sports and he derisively referred to sports as "fun and games." To him the department was valuable because advertisers were willing to pay extra for advertising on sports pages. For that reason, sports received as little space as possible, but on as many pages as possible. The result was something incongruous, with whole pages devoted to agate results or racing entries.

All the dregs, the survivors of merged papers, the old-time sports editors, the kids out of college and the not too bright reporters were assigned to sports. Zugsmith's theory was that the editing was easiest there and the headlines the simplest to write. Somebody was always beating somebody else. He wanted Bob to start there until he became familiar with the paper. His sports background would be valuable and in his case it wasn't a dead end. Zugsmith had plans for him.

"You're the fellow Zugsmith hired, eh?" Emerson Norbert, the sports editor, said when Bob reported.

Bob was surprised to learn Norbert was the sports editor. Like many others he always assumed that Zane Redfield, the columnist, was the sports editor, too. There was no reason to think otherwise: Redfield was the expert on everything. It would be difficult to visualize him subordinate to anyone.

If Norbert was Redfield's superior, though, he seldom asserted his authority. Norbert was a firm believer in not rocking the boat. He had been a schoolteacher before joining the paper and had risen to his position through attrition and industry. At a time when salaries were less impressive the paper had a system of paying ten cents an inch for everything printed in the paper. Since Norbert was on make-up, the material he had pilfered from magazines and other papers was always in type. When it came time to end the space rate pay, the publisher had to make Norbert sports editor to give him a salary comparable to what he had made on space alone.

Zugsmith made all the policy decisions, even making suggestions, which were really fiats, about which reporter should cover an event. Norbert acquiesced meekly, though the department thought the decision was his. Actually, about the only decisions Norbert ever made was who was to get tickets for the various sporting events, and what should be said to readers who wrote in for information or to complain. Norbert handled all the mail himself, looking up the clippings of the article cited and then sitting down with his secretary to dictate a reply. It was the same way with tickets. He kept them in a locked steel box in his desk. Tickets had introduced Norbert to the better things in life. They were good for steaks and gasoline during rationing, for opera and theater tickets when traded to the heads of other departments. Usually every one could get tickets to sporting events except the members of the sports department. After all, Norbert felt, what can they do for me?

Norbert spent his usual five minutes with the new man, waiting for Joe Herman, the head of the desk, to arrive. Joe was a horseplayer and he might be a few minutes late during the season if the fifth race was delayed.

While he was waiting, Bob was issued a paste pot, a supply of pencils and a pair of shears. "Sign this, if you will, please," the clerk said as Bob took his stuff to the desk.

"Do you sign for pencils here?" Bob was surprised. He had heard *The New York Record* was generous with its men.

16

"No, just for the scissors. We've been losing a lot lately. Once, though, you had to turn in pencil stubs before you could get new ones. It was a habit the sports editor picked up when he was a schoolteacher."

When Herman arrived, the others had moved into the desk at either side of the center, where a huge pile of copy sagged. The introductions were a kaleidoscope of names and faces. It took most of the night for Bob to sort out the men. Herman, the desk head, was a cigar smoker, dark and dour. Roger Webster, who sat next to Bob, had recently been promoted from copy boy. David Osborne, a former sports editor of a paper long dead, wore an eyeshade that left his red-vein-choked nose protruding into the harsh overhead lights. Dave Marx was a tall, thin man who wore a vest. He seemed more occupied with word games throughout the night than with reading copy. Mike Corry was shifty-eyed like Clements, but he did seem to be doing most of the work, which Herman kept piling on him. Rex Bloom was a toothless cigar chewer, rolling the tobacco over his gums until it was reduced to a soggy mass that he spit out bit by bit.

The most impressive thing to Bob was the silence with which the desk worked. There were a few muttered curses as one of the more experienced men struggled with a particularly difficult writer, but Webster, sitting next to Bob, never said a word. Bob was also surprised to see how heavily edited the stories were. He assumed that the staff, the largest in the world, would be competent. He didn't know that many of the men were still holdovers from the days of space writing, when the accent was on quantity, not quality. Oh, some of the writers were leaders in their fields, but others had little going for them except the prestige of appearing in *The New York Record,* a sugar-coating that seemed to gloss over many faults.

As the copy flow subsided, the silence became more noticeable. Only an occasional growl of "copy" from Herman broke the stillness. After lunch, Bob heard the squeak of a chair as David Osborne rocked himself to sleep.

17

"Doesn't that squeak annoy you?" he said to Webster.

Roger looked startled. He scribbled furiously on a piece of copy paper then passed it to Bob. "Joe doesn't like talking on the desk," the note said.

Bob crumbled the paper into a ball and dropped it into his wastebasket. He wanted to laugh, but something in Webster's face made him turn to his style book and start reading through it.

Working on the desk was different from what Bob imagined. If this was the easiest desk, what was it like on the other desks? He busied himself with his style book, counting the hours until he could see Diane. In that respect, the job was fine. He saw Diane nearly every night. They could go to more places now that his income prospects had improved. The work on the sports desk was not hard, but Bob noticed Herman was changing many of his heads before sending them to the composing room. Bob knew there were nuances he still had to learn. He studied the changes and by his second week Herman was no longer changing his heads.

"You're catching on good," Herman said the third week. Bob was so surprised by the sound of Joe's voice and the compliment that he didn't reply.

He had another surprise while drinking coffee at the counter of a small luncheonette near the paper. Some one slipped into the seat near him and said, "How's it going?" It was Roger Webster.

Bob started to laugh. "You know, Roger, your voice startled me. I don't think anyone has spoken to me in the three weeks I've been on the desk."

"It is a strange place," Roger agreed. "I've only been on the desk a little over a year. I was a copy boy for ten years."

"Ten years a copy boy? Why?"

"Ten years isn't bad, some fellows were copy boys for fifteen years. It's just a matter of timing, I guess. That and the fact that *The New York Record* never fires anyone. It takes a long time for jobs to open up."

"Why didn't you go to another paper? Surely you could have landed a job better than copy boy."

"Jobs haven't been too easy to find in New York. Besides, I was going to school for four years and I didn't mind it. You were lucky catching on the way you did."

"But I've been on the *Fort Wayne Item* for six years," Bob protested.

"Still, where would you be if you didn't have Zugsmith at the School of Journalism?"

Bob smiled over his coffee. "You know about that?"

Roger lighted a cigarette. "The only thing more efficient than the news operation at *The New York Record* is the grapevine. Everyone knew you were Zugsmith's boy the minute you walked in."

"Zugsmith's boy? Is that good?"

"Outside of being an illegitimate son of the publisher, there's nothing better. Star-crossed, special-blessed, what have you."

The next week Bob assumed he had arrived when David Osborne borrowed a dollar. David liked his liquid lunches and he seldom had enough of the allowance his wife gave him to get through the week. Any glow that David's touch might have given Bob soon disappeared, though.

It was after the papers had been delivered to the desk and the late copy was just starting to arrive. Bob, sitting next to David, was bending over some copy while the old man rocked on his squeaky chair. Suddenly Bob heard a crash and sensed David's disappearance from the chair. He had slipped from the chair and sent the wastebasket skittering across the floor with an extra crash.

None of the others moved, but Bob leaped from his chair and helped the old man up. He sat David down and loosened his tie.

"Are you all right?" he asked solicitously.

The answer was the greatest stream of profanity Bob had ever heard, in the service or out. "Jesus Christ," David concluded as Bob's ears, then his neck, then his face turned crimson. "Haven't you any goddamned work to do? Why the hell can't you mind your own business?"

Bob dropped into his chair openmouthed. He turned to the others, but they were all busily bent over copy, trying desperately to fight off smiles.

Roger scribbled a note and passed it to Bob. It read: "Don't let it bother you. The old man still has a lot of pride. We all pretend that we don't see it when he falls."

David wasn't the only one with pride, Bob found. Joe Herman was proud of his knowledge of racing, the only sport he truly followed. He'd go to the world series once in a while and a football game once a year, but every day the horses were running in New York he was at the track. Because he was a turf fan, he was careful in giving out racing stories for copy reading. Bob knew it was a compliment when Joe gave him the big racing story of the day.

"I'm not too sharp on some of these terms, although I used to pick a lot of horses," he explained to the desk chief.

"If you have any questions, ask me," Joe said comfortingly.

Bob read the story. It was like every other story on racing in the paper since the racing writer believed in sticking to one formula unless something most unusual took place.

"I don't think this horse's name is spelled right," Bob said, taking the copy to Joe. "I think it should be Rhododendron, but it's not spelled right."

Herman looked at the copy. "Those horse owners don't know how to spell. Look in the entries this morning."

Bob went to the dictionary to check on the spelling of rhododendron.

"What are you doing?" Joe wanted to know.

"Looking up rhododendron."

Joe looked at Bob in disgust.

"No, look in the racing form," he said. "Horses' names ain't in the dictionary."

Chapter Two

BEAUMONT PHELPS MANLEY was the perfect choice—
or so the publisher thought—as managing editor of *The New
York Record*. He had the right name and, most important, he
was around at the right time. His associates on the paper
called him B.P.; his intimates knew him as Beau. He was one
of a long line of brilliant reporters who had been transformed
into an incompetent executive. His rare combination of Old
World charm and political contacts solidified his hold on the
job and he emerged as a leader in the field of journalism, a
paragon of professional excellence.

There were few outside the *Record* who realized Zugsmith
was the power behind Manley's throne. The managing editor
was the public relations figure, the image-maker the publisher
needed. His appearance at social functions was impeccable,
his speeches at conventions flawless and his decorum before
the public beyond reproach. Beau's first contact with Bob
Davis was a result of his two great weaknesses—liquor and
horses. He had been around drinking with old friends and was
in the sports department for racing results when he walked up
to Bob.

"I beg your pardon, young man," Beau said to Bob. "I
don't believe I've met you." Despite his drinking, Beau seldom
lost his sharpness. In fact there were some old-timers on the
paper who said that the drinking and the horse playing were
Beau's ways of trying to preserve his links to the times when
the by-line B. Phelps Manley was appearing regularly on the
front page at the top of stories from the capitals of the world.
That was shortly after World War II when Beau returned with a
chestful of medals to his place on the city staff. Beau was no
Sergeant York, but his instinct for news and his persuasive

talk led at one point to a town where he convinced the German garrison that the smart thing to do was surrender.

Besides the medals, the surrender of the town brought Beau a colonelcy and a chauffeur-driven staff car that toured the battlefronts to inspire the troops in the last drive against the Nazis. The car also made frequent trips to Paris to recharge Beau's source of inspiration. A strong bond grew between Beau and Charlie Azzarow, his chauffeur. Charlie was about the only one of a gang that had grown up on 127th Street that didn't end up in Sing Sing or on a slab in the morgue. He insisted that was because he always stayed out of trouble, but others said it was because of his skill in moving a car through the city streets and out-distancing the police.

The rough New Yorker and the polished Bostonian were an incredible pair. It wasn't only their speech or their manners that contrasted; it was everything about the men. Beau had the good looks to go with his good breeding and Charlie was so slovenly that even the tailored uniforms Beau insisted on buying him did little to take away his appearance of a gauche, furtive man. Perhaps the men recognized a kindred spirit in each other: Beau was going places and nothing was going to stop him; Charlie could get places and no one could stop him. They both had a fierce loyalty and when Beau returned to *The New York Record,* Charlie went with him.

Beau was convinced he could mold the rough-talking Charlie into an acceptable reporter. The copy desks soon convinced him of his error. Fortunately, Beau started his foreign reporting soon afterward. He was able to convince the publisher that Charlie should go along as an interpreter. The only language Charlie spoke was Bronx, but the subterfuge at least satisfied the auditors. Beau was happy and the publisher pleased because of the series of exclusives that came off the wire from the *Record*'s roving correspondent. Charlie was more than a companion, though, for whatever capital he landed in he managed to make contact with elements that provided valuable news tips. Sometimes it was the porters at the hotels, the bartenders in the cafes or the whores and their pimps. Many of Beau's exclusives sprang from his talks with Charlie over coffee in the morning.

There are some who say that Charlie really got Beau the job as managing editor. He did propose the selection to the publisher, but Beau's selection was another instance where he was in the right place at the right time.

Sanford Miller, III was on a tour of foreign capitals when the old managing editor died. Miller was having breakfast with Manley and Azzarow in Vienna when word was received of the death in New York. Although it was not unexpected, the death left a gap that Miller had not planned to fill. After the usual review of the man's career by the breakfast guests, Beau turned to the publisher with a question.

"Who will you name to replace him?" he asked innocently.

"How about you, Beau?" Charlie shot back quickly, almost as if they had rehearsed it.

Beau laughed. "I'd be no good in an office."

"Why not?" Miller asked. "I think you'd make a damned good managing editor. You've got all the talent, all the looks, all the charm. How about it, Beau, would you take over for me?"

For once Beau was lost for words. To his credit, he blushed. He looked at Charlie, then he turned to the publisher and laughed nervously. "I don't know what to say," he said. "If it wasn't morning and I didn't know that you'd been up only a short while I'd swear you were drinking."

"Say you'll do it. Your writing has given you the prestige for the job, I'm sure it would be a popular choice."

"Not with some of the assistants back in New York."

"The hell with them. I'm not running a nursery. If I see a man I think can do the job, he's the man I want."

"How about Zugsmith? He's a comer, or so everyone said. I know I always thought he'd be your next managing editor."

"Zugsmith? He doesn't have the grace or the name for the job. I want Beaumont Phelps Manley. What do you say, Beau?"

"It's a helluva name to get on an office door," Beau said with a weak laugh.

"All right, already," Charlie put in. "Just make it B. P. Manley and forget about it. I want to get back to New York."

It was Charlie, too, who got Beau started playing horses. There wasn't enough excitement for Charlie waiting around as a chauffeur, even as a chauffeur for a managing editor. He kept trying to quit the *Record* for more interesting work, but Beau would have none of it. He considered Charlie his good-luck charm and set him up at a desk in the corner of the city room. Charlie would read out-of-town papers for items the *Record* might follow up. There wasn't much excitement there, either, but Charlie was happier because he became the bookmaker for the entire paper. Press men, printers and porters, as well as men from the news room would drop by his desk for whispered consultations. There was no need to hide, for every large building in New York had its own bookmaker. With more money, Charlie was happy and Beau soon became a racing follower and his good-luck charm's best customer.

"I'm Bob Davis," Bob said shaking the proffered hand warmly.

"Davis? Oh, yes, Davis. Zugsmith told me about you. I thought I'd run into you sooner or later."

Bob was flattered that the managing editor had heard of him in such a short time. He knew men had been on the paper for years without meeting Beau. He went back to his copy reading as Manley went to look at the copy coming off the teletype machine.

"Does he always come in like that?" Bob asked Roger after Manley had left.

"He's a great horseplayer. He doesn't win much, but he'll never be cured. I think he just does it to keep Charlie Azzarow around."

"Azzarow, the office bookie?"

"That's right. Charlie and Beau were in the war together."

"If he's so lucky, why doesn't the boss win more often?" Bob asked with a smile.

Bob seldom played the horses, but he became more interested in the form charts when he learned of Beau's hobby. Handicapping came easy to him because it was pure science to Bob, with none of the emotion-swaying that would have arisen had he been betting actively. He did it for his own amusement, often filling dull spots during the night by picking from the previous day's entries and checking his percentage when the paper came up. Because he had a mathematical bent, he soon found he had a better percentage than any of the regular handicappers. He knew, though, he would never be able to duplicate the showing if he had to.

Bob soon had a chance to test his theory. He was going out to lunch when he met Manley walking back toward the sports department.

"Hello there, Davis," Manley said. "Who won the big race?"

"Echo Lake, sir," Bob said, surprised that Manley had stopped to talk.

"Echo Lake, eh? What looks good for tomorrow?"

"Jones Boy in the fifth," Bob said, remembering his perusal of the form before the luncheon break. He said it casually, almost automatically.

"Too much distance," Manley replied, moving past Bob regally.

Bob forgot all about the incident until early the next night, when Manley sent for him. The managing editor's office was elaborate, with framed copies of prize stories and reproductions of historic front pages on the walls.

"I owe you an apology," Beau said in his most charming

manner. "Jones Boy won by four lengths and paid eight to one. My horse was fifth, about twenty lengths back. I should have taken your advice."

"I haven't seen the results yet. I didn't know who won."

"Don't you play the horses yourself?"

"Not very often. I guess its sort of a midwestern morality." Bob knew horseplaying was endemic on *The New York Record*. He was eager to explain his disinterest.

"Well, you certainly can pick them. I don't think a single racing expert in the city figured that horse better than ninth. How do you do it?"

Bob was uncomfortable. He knew the *Record* needed a racing writer, but he wasn't interested. He didn't want to get involved for only another month. "It's a mathematical formula I've worked out. It's pretty complicated."

"Mathematics? That stuff never works. I guess you just happened to hit a lucky one."

"They're all lucky," Bob said, relieved.

"Don't suppose you could do it again. Pick a long-shot, I mean."

"I haven't looked at the entries, yet, but I'd be glad to try."

"Don't bother. I'm really not interested. I just thought it was odd the way you came up with that one." Beau had seen too many one-race experts to get excited.

Bob went back to the desk. He had a press of work waiting for him and he didn't get a chance to look at the entries until just before the first edition. When he did sit down with the form, he could feel the pulse pounding in his temples. He knew he had to prove himself and he knew that pressure could throw off all his calculations. Still he went on, checking all the major tracks. There was one horse, a rank outsider, that might have a chance if it rained. On a dry track, though, there wasn't a chance and the forecast was for good weather.

He had another horse in mind for Manley, but he didn't want to volunteer the name unless he was asked. That way, the onus would be on the managing editor. Still, Bob was determined to let Manley know his first winner was no accident. He decided to serve indirect notice of his handicapping ability by leaving a twenty dollar bet for Charlie.

He was on his way out after leaving the bet, when he met Manley coming off the elevator. The managing editor's coat was sprinkled with rain, his hat dripping. "I'd wait before going out if I were you," he said. "It's a regular cloudburst."

"Yes sir, thank you sir," Bob stammered, striving desperately to recall the name of the mudder. "Pot Luck!" He shouted as the name came to him with a rush. "Pot Luck in the eighth," he said, smiling knowingly.

Manley looked at him oddly. "Pot Luck? No one rates that one. He should go off at fifty to one or better."

"He's a mudder," Bob said doggedly. "I would have played him myself if I'd known it was raining."

"Fifty to one? It's worth a ten dollar bet, anyway. Good night, young man."

Bob felt cold before he hit the rain. He knew his calculations were right. He hoped Pot Luck, his jockey and trainer knew it, too.

Pot Luck went off at sixty to one, assigned the feather weight of 108 pounds but burdened down by the gumbo-like track and, in Bob's mind, Manley's ten dollar bet. Fortunately, the horse didn't know about the added weight and got up in the last eighth to win by a head.

Charlie Azzarow was in the sports department a half hour before posttime, nervously checking the ticker and the teletype machines. He peeled off $94 from a huge roll of bills when Bob's twenty dollar horse came in at little better than four to one.

"You're pretty good for an out-of-towner," Charlie said flatly. "How do you think this pig in the eighth will do?"

"It's still raining. He . . ."

"Rain? Oh yeah, Beau told me you said the horse was a mudder."

"Can't miss then," Bob said confidently.

"Yeah, that's what they all say."

"I picked one already," Bob said fingering the $94.

"Beginner's luck," Charlie said, turning back to the teletype.

His cigar-chewing tempo picked up as the teletype began to chatter out the first line of the eighth race. "He win it," he half shouted, still peering intently as the payoff odds were tapped out. "Holy Cripes! One twenty-seven sixty!"

One twenty-seven sixty! Bob did some rapid figuring. Manley had won $638. He should have played the twenty dollars on Pot Luck himself.

Charlie was working furiously with a pencil by the teletype machine. "Six thousand bucks," he muttered happily. "Six thousand three hundred eighty bucks."

"Aren't you making a mistake? I figure Mr. Manley won $638," Bob said, shouldering his way to Charlie's side.

"Manley? Beau? Yeah, he won $638. I played one hundred dollars myself. I get $6,380."

"One hundred dollars?"

"That's right, how come you didn't play it yourself?"

"I didn't know it was raining when I left you the note. If I had . . ."

"Brother, you sure can pick 'em. Wait'll I tell Beau."

Charlie took off for the managing editor's office, the eddying grapevine almost keeping pace with him as news of the big hit flashed through the office. Charlie and Manley had had big winners before, but nothing like this. One twenty-seven sixty! The payoff figures were repeated over and over like an irreverent chant or slogan.

Manley sent for Bob as soon as the daily conference with department heads was completed.

"Young man," he said, sticking out his hand and guiding Bob to a chair, "You certainly know your horseflesh. I can't remember when I last won six hundred dollars on a race. I think it was on a daily double about ten years ago. How do you do it?"

Bob was pleased. He exulted in the warm glow of his success. "I told you, sir, it's mathematics and a little knowledge of horses and track conditions."

"Mathematics, eh? It never changes? It never fails?"

"I don't say it never fails, I just say my formula works out to a better percentage than any handicapper's in town. It . . ."

"Better percentage? You mean you've been handicapping horses for comparison with the other papers and yours have come out better?"

"That's right, sir, I had .804 percent last week and . . ."

"Eight oh four? The best handicappers are lucky if they hit sixty percent. How would you like to be our racing writer? We haven't been publishing selections, but we could start. You might be the sensation of the city."

Bob could feel the veins tighten in his neck. He never liked racing, but he didn't want to appear unappreciative of the opportunity. He knew there were at least thirty men on the paper who would jump at the chance.

"I don't mean to sound ungrateful, sir, but I'm really not interested in racing. I wouldn't want to get into that if it's all the same to you."

Manley's mouth was agape. He never thought he would hear anyone turn down the racing job. It meant short hours, mixing with the wealthiest and best families in America, going to Saratoga during the heat of the summer and to Florida during the cold of the winter. It was a job Beau might have wanted himself if he hadn't been managing editor.

"Not interested in racing?" he roared. "How the hell can you pick the horses like that if you're not interested in racing?"

Bob was taken back by the vehemence of the managing editor's tone. "I mean I'm interested, sir, but not *that* interested." Suddenly Bob thought that the only way out for him was to tell Manley the truth.

"I really plan on going back to Fort Wayne in September, sir."

"Fort Wayne? What the hell have they got in Fort Wayne? Leave *The New York Record?* What's the matter, aren't you happy here?"

Bob almost regretted having decided on the honest approach. "No, it's not that, sir, I'm really very happy here. I just . . ."

"Oh, you have a girl in Fort Wayne, is that it?" Manley asked, smiling in understanding.

Now that it was out, Bob decided to keep going. "As a matter of fact, I have a girl here, sir, but . . ."

"Then why the hell do you want to go back to Fort Wayne? Aren't we paying you enough?"

"Oh the pay is fine, sir. I . . ."

"How much are we paying you, by the way?"

"Two hundred dollars a week."

"You realize that's above the scale?"

"Yes sir, but I couldn't have taken less."

"Oh, then it is money, eh? All right, starting next week you're getting $250. How does that sound?"

"Two hundred and fifty dollars a week? Is that for the racing job?"

"No, damn it. Don't take the racing job. Just keep on doing what you're doing. Be a copy reader, if you want, but let me know what your daily longshot is."

Bob suddenly felt a surge of power shoot through him. He sensed that the managing editor was in the right frame of mind for more acute bargaining. "For $250 a week?" he asked archly.

Manley looked at him in horror for a moment, then averted his gaze. "All right, damn it, three hundred dollars a week, but that will make you the highest priced man in the sports department."

"That's another thing" Bob said, savoring his moment of triumph. He still was not keen on staying in New York, but *The New York Record* held a lot of appeal and at three hundred dollars a week it held a helluva lot more appeal.

"I'm not too keen on staying in sports. I know it's looked on as the fun-and-games section here, but I was never fond of fun and games. I'm on to the style of the paper now; I'd like to go to a more interesting desk."

Manley's face flushed. "Are you sure you don't want to be my assistant? You know you're pretty god damned fresh for a punk from Indiana. . . ."

"Mr. Manley, you sent for me. When I started to work here, Mr. Zugsmith sent for me. This whole thing wasn't my idea. No, I don't want to be your assistant. That is, not yet." Bob smiled inwardly at his nerve. He felt somehow he was really hoping to get fired so he would have the two weeks' salary given to a discharged employee. "I do think I might be more useful to the paper on some other desk."

Manley's anger cooled at the mention of Zugsmith. "Yes," he said, "Zugsmith did tell me he hoped to move you up to the foreign desk after a few months. You say you're ready now, all right. We'll see."

"At three hundred dollars a week?" Bob asked.

"Yes, at three hundred dollars a week." Manley started to laugh. "At least I won't have so far to walk to get your daily tips," he said.

The arrangement worked out beautifully so far as Bob was concerned. The foreign desk was much more interesting than sports, the work more of a challenge. For Manley, it was more natural to stop to speak to Bob at the foreign desk because he had to pass there to get from his office to Zugsmith's cubicle. Charlie's desk was next to the foreign desk, so Bob began to play the horses he picked himself. He had an agreement with Manley that he would not be asked to pick more than one horse a day, but that one had to be a long shot, where the odds were at least four to one.

Because things came easy to Bob, he didn't mind sharing his selections with others. As a result, there were multitudes of two dollar bets riding with Bob, Manley, and Charlie each day. As his streak of winners continued, the electric current of excitement increased in intensity. There was always a crowd around Charlie to get a bet down and the sports department had to erect barriers around the teletype machines to keep the anxious punters away. Only Zugsmith was free of the betting fever that swept through the building. He looked on disapprovingly at the knots of people around Charlie's desk and he did his best to have Bob kept busy so he wouldn't have time to study the past performances.

Charlie Azzarow, too, was becoming alarmed at the increased rate of play and the large number of winners. "Hey, Indiana," he said to Bob one night in the lunch room, "Can't you stop giving those horses to all the printers?"

"If I give them to the managing editor, why can't I give it to the printers? You know the paper's slogan: Equality for All."

"Sure, sure, but I'm being killed. My banker says that something has to be done pretty quick. Some days he pays as much as ten thousand dollars just to this one building. That's getting a little too steep."

"What do you want me to do, pick losers?"

"That wouldn't be bad. A lot of guys have been betting against your picks lately because they figure you can't go on. Twelve out of twelve, though. My banker must've lost over a hundred thousand. Of course, he'll get it all back, but he's getting sore."

Bob wanted to laugh, but Charlie looked too pitiful. "Why don't you stop taking the bets. You . . ."

"But Beau's a friend of mine, I couldn't do that to him."

"All right, stop taking the printer's bets. Say the managing editor has ordered a crackdown on gambling. It is illegal in this state, isn't it?"

Charlie bit deeper into his cigar. "Certainly it's illegal, you know that. I couldn't refuse the printers, though, they're the backbone of the business. 'Equality for All,' you know."

Bob smiled. Charlie was a likable hypocrite.

"Why don't you stop betting my selections? I understand you're one of the biggest winners."

"I'm nearly twenty grand ahead, Indiana, but that's another thing. I've stopped giving my own action to my banker and he's complaining that I'm taking my business elsewhere. I'm in a spot."

"Charlie," Bob said, blinking his eyes at the cigar smoke, "I'd like to get out of this thing just as much as you would, but there isn't a thing I can do about it. If you think of anything, I'd be glad to cooperate."

Of course, Bob did nothing. He was too new to the *Record* to know how the inner machinery worked. Charlie was familiar with every tick, every cog, every bit of oil necessary for the *Record* to function. It had to be timed just right, it had to reach the right people, Charlie knew. Above all, he realized, no one must ever know.

It was the first week in October. Bob had picked five winners a week every week for nine weeks. The favorite office pastime had ceased to be crossword puzzles and word games. Virtually every man in the place spent his idle moments figuring out what a parlay of all Bob's selections would have paid. It was a fruitless exercise for no bookie would have handled the action. As it was, Charlie's banker had limited the odds he would pay to forty to one and large amounts of cash were being pushed through machines at the tracks to push down the odds on Bob's horses.

Charlie was still having troubles with his banker, but he was unruffled. He had something going for him and it paid off. The timing was perfect—the city election was less than a month away and Beau was on the Coast at a convention. The setting was right, too: the letters to the editor column of *The New York Record* and the top position on the editorial page. For those on the staff who missed reading the editorial page, the editorial and the letter were reproduced on the bulletin board along with a memo from the publisher. The letter decried the widespread gambling in the city and asserted that bookies operated in every commercial building in New York, "probably right in your own newspaper." It was signed: "Erate Citizen." The editorial was signed, too, something unusual for the publisher. Although the prose was unmistakably that of Zachary A. Zugsmith, the editorial and the memo were signed Sanford Miller, III, effectively cutting Manley off from any appeal when he returned.

The memo read:

"It has come to my attention that organized and unorganized gambling is taking place during working hours on the property of *The New York Record*. As a leader in the community it is up to *The New York Record* to set the proper moral tone for the community so it is ordered that all organized and unorganized gambling cease at once under penalty of discharge from employment. This is not to be construed as to include bridge or penny ante poker, as traditionally played by the late crew. All other gambling is to cease at once."

"What the hell am I going to do now?" Charlie said to Bob as they read the memo on the board. "This puts me out of business."

"According to that, you could get a deck of cards and stay around late."

Zugsmith had come up behind the two men while they were talking. He heard Charlie's remark, but said nothing until Bob walked away. "You know this whole thing was triggered by a letter to the publisher," Zugsmith said.

Charlie felt uncomfortable as Zugsmith pointed to the reproduced letter with a pencil. Zugsmith underlined the signature: "Erate Citizen." "You never could spell, could you, Charlie," he said walking away with a quick glance over his shoulder.

The cigar fell from Charlie's mouth as he stared at Zugsmith's peculiar bouncy walk. He looked quickly to see if anyone was watching, then took down the reproduced letter to the publisher and tore it to bits.

Chapter Three

BOB WAS glad the horseplaying was over. Charlie would be back in business soon enough, but at least he was out of it. His bank balance was up, his place on the paper secure, his reputation with the other men established. It was better than ending on a losing note, something that always haunted Bob. He could concentrate on his work now and enjoy the foreign desk. It was a big change from sports: more interesting, more challenging, more demanding and more rewarding. In the two months since his transfer he had learned a lot, but his real education was still to come when Tom Crum, the slot man, returned from his sick leave. While Crum was away, Bob found the working conditions more relaxed than under Joe Herman. The fill-in slot men were careful not to jeopardize their standing as "one of the boys" and they permitted jokes or even got off a few themselves during the night.

Tom Crum would tolerate jokes, but he seldom could see any humor in them unless they were his own. He was close to being the typical *New York Record* man, Bob thought, from what he had heard. Crum threw himself into his work so completely that he seldom talked of anything else when he was at home. He'd leave the office and call before going to bed to make certain everything was all right. The two months on sick leave was the hardest time of his life, not because of his illness, but because his wife wouldn't let him call the office or even dissect the paper with her each morning.

In Crum's mind, he was the only one who understood what Zugsmith was trying to do on the paper. He knew Zugsmith had been head of the foreign desk and Tom envisioned himself following Zugsmith into the executive circle. He was a small, wiry man, with a sharp face and a large mop of unruly hair. He moved and spoke quickly, but his thought processes were slow and his hesitancy in answering the copy editor's questions about editing or headlines often created embarrassing lapses.

Tom was hesitant because his objections were seldom self-inspired. They were usually based on some dictum of Zugsmith's everyone else had long forgotten, and Tom would search his memory for the specific reason for the objection or strive for a solution he thought would be acceptable to Zugsmith. His memory was so faulty that Tom would bar the use of a word outright even though Zugsmith had objected only to a specific context or usage. To Crum, it was all the same: Zugsmith had objected to the word; it was not to be used.

This hampered the headline writing, but it was all part of the foreign desk tradition: the headlines were the hardest to write because they always had to be attributed or limited. It wouldn't be proper for the copy editor to write a headline that could start a war or cause a diplomatic flap. It had happened, of course, but not when Tom Crum was in the slot. He was too cautious, too careful, too scared to pass anything he wasn't absolutely sure of. His caution was also based on what Zugsmith would favor and sometimes Tom outguessed himself by trying to find the Zugsmith approach to a story or headline.

Crum knew that Zugsmith's current accent was on color and background in stories. If a man came off a desert island and picked up *The New York Record,* he should be able to understand every article in the paper. Each story should be self-contained and complete within itself. That was Zugsmith's aim; it became Tom Crum's creed.

If the correspondents had been informed of the aim, it would have simplified matters on the desk considerably; the correspondents would have continually supplied both the color and the background. But like so many things on *The New York Record,* the correspondents were never told. Zugsmith thought such an order would hamper them in collect-

36

ing and reporting the news. It was up to the desk to supply the background, the bridges to the past.

This was something new to Bob. It hadn't been that way on the *Item* and it wasn't that way in sports. On a continuing story, such as the Algerian crisis, Bob thought the system wasteful and unnecessary since the same basic background facts were repeated day after day. But he dutifully sent for the clips on the stories he was unfamiliar with and supplied the desired background, always striving to keep it shorter and less obtrusive.

The first night Bob worked under Crum was memorable. Seldom had any of the slot men on the foreign desk rejected a head by Bob, but he had been warned that Crum was hard to please.

"I think you can sharpen that head a little," Crum said, giving the headline back to Bob.

"I'll try something else," Bob said pleasantly. He knew Crum resented his links to Zugsmith, for in Tom's eyes, Bob was a rival.

The second head was rejected and the third and the fourth. Finally, Bob was getting angry. "What do you think I should say?" he asked Crum.

Tom scratched his head and looked over the top of his glasses. "I don't know, but leave it with me. I'll work something out."

Bob sat down and looked over the four heads he had written. He thought the first one was the best since it caught all the new elements in the story from the lead. He realized he had tended to get more interpretation into his subsequent heads to satisfy Crum. About twenty minutes before the deadline, Crum threw a head to Bob. "We'll go with that," he said. "Would you schedule it, please?"

Bob thought the headline missed the whole point of the article, but he knew it was worthless to argue. He erased the earlier entry on his work sheet and wrote out the new headline. He turned the headline back to Crum to be sent to the composing room, then put the rejected versions on a spike holding duplicates of the dispatches and reference material.

When the paper came out, Bob noticed that the headline on his story was different from the one Crum had written.

"That isn't your head, is it, Tom?" he asked innocently.

Crum looked over the top of his glasses at the large type. "No. I guess Zugsmith rewrote it in the composing room. It's a better headline than mine, though."

Bob went back to his seat and rifled through the paper on his spike. He found the sheet he wanted and then went back to Crum. He put his headline on the desk alongside the headline in the paper. "That's the same thing I said in the first head you rejected," Bob said, hiding a note of triumph in his voice.

Crum looked at the sheet of paper and then at the printed page. "That's right," he said, taking Bob's piece of paper and crumbling it into a wad. "It sometimes happens that way." To Crum, the incident was closed. He tried hard to find fault with Bob's heads the rest of the week, but he had to concede that Davis had the happy knack of finding the right combination of words to convey the meaning of a story in a headline. It was a rare talent that seemed to be eluding Crum in recent years.

Tom's insistence on trying to get something different into a headline or on filling out the background of an article was not motivated by any sense of pettiness. He truly believed *The New York Record* was the greatest paper in the world and had a reputation to uphold. Perhaps if he had been allowed to develop on his own he might have done things differently, but Tom Crum was too much a product of the system to be different. He had started as a copy boy and worked his way into Zugsmith's good graces by spotting errors that copy editors missed. It didn't matter that the errors were missed in the rush of working long hours during the war; Zugsmith recognized in Tom a kindred spirit who would sacrifice everything for the paper.

With Bob, though, it was different. He was secretly pleased that in a short time he was one of the highest paid men on the desk. He knew working conditions had been far less attractive before the Guild grew in power and forced the publishers to grant the men something close to a living wage. But his pleasure in his job, his satisfaction with work well done and his knowledge that Zugsmith was pleased with his showing were only superficial. If it weren't for Diane, he would just as soon be back in Fort Wayne. The pulse of the city, the excitement he had read about, the sense of being a vital part of history eluded Bob. But then he was seldom excited by anything; he fought against admitting to himself that even the parade of history under his eyes each night was boring. The events in Europe or in Africa seemed little related to Bob Davis, particularly when he wasn't seeing Diane. She had a taken a winter job at a resort hotel and their dates were few over the long weary winter in the city, and after she returned to the city, their relationship seemed unnaturally strained.

"You're very quiet tonight," Bob said stroking her hair as she lay back against the couch in his apartment. He had taken the apartment to be close to the club where Diane worked, but it was weeks before he could get her to visit it.

"I'm just tired," she said, gazing into the fake fireplace where a swirling drum gave an illusion of flames.

"Tired of me or just tired?"

Diane turned wide-eyed to Bob, but then she shrugged and smiled enigmatically.

"I guess I haven't been the sparkling host," he conceded, "but just watching the light play on your face is so much better than any conversation."

"Or kissing me?"

"Oh, I didn't know you objected to that. Do I have bad breath or something?"

Diane laughed. "No, do I?"

Bob cradled her head in his arm and kissed her long and

passionately. "No, matter of fact, you don't. But something is definitely wrong. You stiffened when I kissed you just then. Before you went south for the winter you seemed to enjoy kissing me. What's changed?"

She sat upright on the the couch, moving away slightly and looking into the swirling light again. "It's different kissing a man in your hallway and kissing him in his apartment."

Bob smiled to himself, reaching out to touch her hand in the semi-darkness. "If I disappointed you in any way, I'm sorry. What do you want me to do, throw you down on the bed and rape you?"

"You're twisting what I'm saying," Diane protested. "You know I like to have you kiss me, that's the trouble. I know, too, you'd like to go to bed with me. That's the trouble, too. I realize I'd like to go to bed with you, too, but I can't."

Bob moved closer, his face in her hair, his arm around her waist.

"No," she protested, pushing him away. "Now that I've started, let me finish. You know how many job offers I've turned down because agents wanted to sleep with me. Now, I ask myself, why should I go to bed with you? You can't help me with my work and for all I know you still have a girl back in Indiana."

Bob moved to the far end of the couch and lighted a cigarette. He blew the smoke to the ceiling in a long sigh. "The trouble with you is you're afraid to live. You've been thinking like Diane the club singer and Diane the priest's sister so much you're all mixed up. Certainly I wanted to sleep with you the first minute I saw you. Any normal man would. Let's face it, girl, you are sex personified. That gown you wear, those songs you sing, those looks over your shoulder are right out of Salome. I know it's all show business, but the responses are all there, panting, longing, dreaming. There's nothing wrong with that, I know, but then you come out after the show in your going-home-to-mother dress and your East

Bronx morality and I'm left panting in the hallway like a horny dog."

"I know it's hard on you," Diane said, then she started to laugh. "I didn't mean that the way it sounded."

"I know what you meant," Bob said glumly. "But you're right, I'm a victim of your split personality. So what do I do?"

Diane stood up and walked to Bob at the end of the couch. She kissed him then offered no resistance as he pulled her down beside him. "Maybe I better be going," she said.

"Why? You said your mother no longer waits up when she knows I'm going to be bringing you home. It's only 3:15."

"It's such a long ride back for you on the subway."

"I don't mind it. I sleep most of the way anyway."

"Even so, we better be going."

He kissed her again, his tongue darting between her lips, his hand pressed on her breast. His pulse quickened as she melted into him, offering no resistance and half moaning softly to herself.

"Bob, Bob," she whispered hoarsely, "we have to stop."

"Why?" He covered her throat with kisses moving toward her lips once more. He could feel his own tumescence straining against his trousers and he half turned to press into her.

"I'm afraid," she protested, but her hand brushed over the hard knot pressing into her, more in exploration than in rejection.

"Relax, relax," he whispered slipping his hand under her skirt and pressing his way to her thigh. Suddenly Diane stood up, her eyes flashing, her lips trembling. She looked at Bob an instant, then kissed him deeply. She broke off his embrace and turned away. Then she walked into the bedroom.

She was just slipping under the blankets when Bob entered the room, kicking his shoes under the bed and clawing at his zipper to drop his trousers. He looked silly, he knew, with his shirt tail flopping about his naked loins and his socks around his ankles, but Bob wasn't intent on appearances just then. He

41

was frantic with desire as he crawled in beside the girl, his lips pressed on hers and his knee forcing open her legs. She, too, was ready, he could tell, the honey of her almost setting his skin on fire. He rolled between her legs and pressed toward her. But it was too late as all the strength left his arms and his body trembled. He lay for a moment against her warm flesh, working spasmodically and then rolled to the side, breathing heavily and cursing beneath the gasped breaths.

"I'm all wet. Am I bleeding?" Diane asked innocently, the fright evident in her voice.

"No you're not bleeding," Bob had to struggle to keep from laughing.

"Is that all there is to it? I really didn't feel anything. I wanted to feel something, Bob, honest I did, but I just didn't. I'm sorry." She began to weep silently into the pillow, turning away from him with her hair over her shoulder the way it fell when she sang.

"It's not your fault, darling. It was me. I just wanted you so badly I went off before I was ready or before you were ready. There wasn't anything for you to feel, really, just let me rest a minute though and I'm sure that will be taken care of."

"You mean nothing happened? We didn't . . . didn't have intercourse?"

Bob nodded contritely. "It was more like external-course. You're still a virgin."

Diane sat up in the bed, clutching the sheet around her exquisite form. "I am? Nothing happened? I better get out of here right now. I feel so cheap and I'm all messy. Do you have a towel or something I can use?"

Bob slid out of the bed and put on his trousers with one motion. He took a robe from the closet and held it for Diane to slip into. "Put this on. There are towels in the bathroom. I'll wait on the couch."

Diane had a curious smile on her face all the way uptown on the subway. She held Bob's hand and seemed to be hugging herself with some grand joke. He knew it was useless to

42

shout above the clatter of the train, but he could hardly wait until they were on the street to find out what seemed so funny.

"It's really nothing," Diane insisted, smiling more broadly and squeezing Bob's hand against her waist.

"You're probably laughing at your great lover. That hasn't happened to me since I was a kid."

"What has happened since you were a kid? Anything? Or . . ."

"Premature ejaculation, I think they call it. I . . ."

"Is it serious?"

Bob began to laugh. "It really isn't anything. It won't happen again, I promise. It's just that for all these months I've been thinking about that moment and then when it finally arrives I'm gone."

"That's what I was laughing at really, darling, but don't get mad. I was thinking about my great big football hero and Air Force captain, how you must have felt let down. At first I thought it was my fault."

"Your fault, what do you mean?"

"Well, this friend of mine had an awful time after she got married. It took months before she really got together with her husband. She was always an athletic girl and she said her doctor told her that her maidenhead was so thick and tough from all the exercise she did he might have to operate."

Bob smiled broadly. "What was the doctor going to operate with?"

Diane looked at him crossly. "No, I mean it. Her husband used to wear himself out for months and she was still a virgin. She only told me, she said, because she had to tell somebody."

"Now you have something to tell her back."

"Bob!" The hurt in her voice was evident. "You know I'd never tell anybody about us."

They had reached the apartment where Diane lived with her mother. "That's good," he said, "I never could stand those girls who kiss and tell."

She kissed him passionately, pushing her body into his until he could feel the knot rising again. "Do you think it will take us months?" she whispered.

Bob was off the next day and the hours seemed like months until he could see her again. He almost wished he had gone to work to have something to occupy his time, but instead he busied himself about his apartment, going out to buy wine and fresh flowers for the table. Their date had been arranged or at least taken for granted for more than a week. Diane always arranged to skip her last show when Bob was off. They had more time together that way. But tonight was not an ordinary day off; not after last night. All doubt about where he stood with Diane had vanished. Suddenly it was all worth while; this is why he wanted to stay in New York.

She was shy coming into the apartment, but still eager, like Eve reaching for the apple: convinced it was wrong, but determined to taste it.

She sat on the couch with one leg curled beneath her like a little girl. She sipped the wine slowly, savoring the scene and Bob's look.

"I always thought I could never look anyone in the face after doing something . . . you know, like last night."

"Drink your wine. Don't think about last night. Tonight it will be different."

"It's different already. Wine, flowers, that music on the phonograph. This is more like the seduction scenes I've read about."

"Seduction? Yes, I guess you could call it that, but you don't seem to be protesting."

"That's what I started to tell you about last night before you got all excited. I decided you were right. You and that woman in Florida."

"What woman?"

"Oh some woman I met. She was married five times and she told me she didn't regret any of them, even though none of them lasted. 'Love is giving,' she said. That's when I de-

44

cided I wanted to give myself to you. I once swore I'd never sleep with a man unless we were married, but maybe that's too old-fashioned. You've never mentioned marriage and . . ."

"You know I'm crazy about you. No one has ever done what you have to me. I just count the hours until I can see you. My time with you is the only time I'm alive."

He kissed her tenderly, but she pulled away as the champagne from his glass spilled on her dress. "I'm sorry," he apologized, wiping her dress with his handkerchief.

"I think it's the perfect solution," Diane said calmly. "I've been sitting here wondering how I could go about taking my clothes off without seeming so brazen. Why don't you put some more champagne in your glass and bring me some more, too. I'll be in the bedroom."

Her calm detachment vanished as Bob slipped into bed naked. He knew he had to be more relaxed and he moved deliberately, kissing her neck, her breast, her stomach and then moving back to her lips. He played her like a virtuoso, pressing against her gently until she could stand it no longer.

"Put it in," she said hoarsely, her finger nails digging into his back.

He met some resistance, but he held firm against her contortions as Diane swung her hips into his. Their bodies blended as one in a flash and then Diane took command. Bob was the slave now, his hands holding her buttocks to keep from being dislodged as she moved violently under him, alternately kissing him wildly and then biting his ear, tearing at his back and moaning softly. "Love me, love me," she whispered.

"I do, I do," Bob replied, his words trailing off as the explosion arrived and swept him off the heights he had longed to scale for so long. Again he lay trembling astride her, but this time it was different. She moved her hips expertly and the contractions were like electric fingers running up Bob's spine. She was the most wonderful woman in the world. If this was her first experience, Bob thought, my God! She was a rare gem, each time better and better until Bob was exhausted and all the sparkle had gone out of the champagne.

"Now it's your turn to be quiet," Diane said on the walk from the subway station to her apartment.

"I just don't know what to say. I never met a girl like you before. You're absolutely fantastic. If I didn't know better I'd swear you were the one who had been married five times."

Diane smiled happily. "You mean I was good? But maybe your standards aren't very high."

"After you, there are no standards. You are absolutely in a class by yourself."

Chapter Four

EVEN TOM CRUM was bearable now. Bob never felt so good in his life. His days were filled with Diane—walking in the park and visiting any number of sights he had never bothered with before. Suddenly the city was new beneath its crusts of dirt. The ugliness of the night disappeared when he was with her and everything seemed worthwhile.

There was still much about *The New York Record* that Bob questioned, but he was less militant now, more tolerant and more inclined to find a laugh in situations that might have angered him at one time.

"You have to have a sense of humor to work on this paper," said Howard Tucker, the star of the rewrite battery. Tucker was in his early forties. He was a short ugly man, with a long crooked nose, a drooping lower lip and uneven teeth. His hair was white, prematurely, he hastened to tell everyone on first meeting them.

Tucker was the philosopher on the staff. He could quote from Shakespeare, Virgil, the New and the Old Testament, Dr. Conant's entire five-foot bookshelf of classics, or the latest science-fiction novel. Howard came to *The New York Record* from Trinity College, where he was an assistant professor in the English department. He was seeking a medium of greater expression than an assistant professorship and he thought he had found it in *The New York Record.*

Bob found Tucker a delightful companion on lunch hours at Curry's, the bar across the street from the paper. He never tried to keep up with Tucker in drinking, however, for Tucker had a capacity for liquor almost as great as his capacity for philosophy. The esoteric nature of his philosophy grew in direct proportion of the number of drinks he put away. After six drinks, Tucker was back before his class at Trinity lecturing on good writing, bad women, and indifferent success; he was an expert on all three.

"You know," Bob said during a lunch-hour talk with Tucker, "I would never have believed that the writers could be so bad in the raw if I didn't see it myself. I thought only the ones in sports were bad, but evidently it's that way on the whole paper."

Tucker sipped his drink with a twinkle in his eye. "Are you sure you're not saying that because you're a frustrated writer?"

"But I'm not a frustrated writer."

"No? I thought all copy editors were frustrated writers, just as all rewrite men are frustrated reporters or correspondents."

There was no denying that Bob's role was a new one for him. In high school, in college, and in the service he had always been the hero: the team captain, the Olympic athlete, the hot pilot in command of the plane. On a newspaper, the reporter was the hero, the copy editor merely a supernumerary performing behind the scenes unknown, unsung, and unenvied. He was barely tolerated by the reporters, who were convinced the copy editor was part of a conspiracy to ruin all their bright leads, take out precious color, and cut their epics to length without feeling for the nuances the writer had woven into a story so painstakingly. And yet Bob felt he was or could be just as happy as a copy editor as a reporter.

"When I came here I thought I was going to be a reporter, but Zugsmith told me that Bob Davis wasn't a by-line name for *The New York Record*."

"You, too, eh?" Tucker drained the last bit of whisky from his glass and signalled the bartender for a refill.

"When I first came here," he continued, "I thought I was going to be a dashing correspondent, traveling all over the world, visiting the famous people I had read about, and being caught up in the thick of the human comedy."

Tucker was regarded as the finest rewrite man on the paper. He was fast and accurate and had a flair for the language. He could take the dull facts of a routine police report and convert it into a sparkling account of life in the city merely by talking to the man who had culled the facts from headquarters and then called them in to rewrite. The articles by Tucker were never signed, but his touch was unmistakable on a story, and he was a far better writer than ninety percent of those covering the city and more than half of the staff overseas.

"I always wondered why they never sent you out on a story," Bob said. "I know you've won prizes for your stories, but I never see your by-line. Don't they ever give a rewrite man a by-line?"

"They do sometimes, it depends on the rewrite man. The big thing is whether his name will look good in the paper."

"What's the matter with Howard Tucker?" Bob asked, mystified.

"Too common. At least that's what Zugsmith said. No, I can't say he ever said it, but I know that's what it is."

"If he didn't say that to you, how can you be sure?"

"Well, I came here during the war. I was mustered out early because of malaria and I thought I would rather be in a newspaper office than in a college classroom when all the excitement was going on. Well, when I wrote for the interview, the resume I sent in was in the Army style. It was pure fiction, the way most resumes are, but I never had any compunction in stretching things a bit when I was looking for a job. I always felt it was up to me to prove myself after getting the job and I knew I'd be able to do it here.

"Well, it worked and I got a telegram to start work. They were desperate in those days and if you had any background at all you were grabbed, especially if you had been in the service. At any rate, I had to report to Zugsmith. 'Mr. Howard,' he said, 'I think you'll make a fine addition to our staff.'"

"He said the same thing to me."

"But don't you get it? He called me Mr. Howard. I didn't think much about it at the time because a lot of New Englanders use that form of address, your first name with a Mr. in front of it. Well, I went to work and after a few days of rolling around the office to get the hang of things they sent me out on a story. It was a fire and I got a lot of good solid information on it because I ran into a fire captain who was looking for publicity. I turned the story in and the city editor took it in to Zugsmith after he had finished reading it. I knew this was done because the story was on Zugsmith's desk when he sent for me."

Tucker sipped his whisky, letting the suspense build for Bob like a master story-teller.

"When I walked in the office, Zugsmith stood up and shook my hand. 'Mr. Howard,' he said, 'this is excellent. We usually don't give new men by-lines, but we're going to make an exception in your case. See?' He held up the first page of my article and there on the top was 'By Tucker Howard.' Then it came to me: 'Tucker Howard.' 'Mr. Howard.' Zugsmith had my name turned around."

"How did he do that?" Bob asked. "Zugsmith is pretty sharp, I can't understand that."

"What he had done was to pick up my resume, which was done in the Army style. You know, last name first, then your first name. Evidently he didn't see the comma because he was convinced my name was Tucker Howard. 'Do you have a middle initial?' Zugsmith asked as I stood there with my mouth open. 'No, sir, I don't, but you have my name reversed. It's Howard Tucker, not Tucker Howard.'

"Zugsmith looked as if he had been slapped. 'Howard Tucker? Are you sure?' he said. All I could do was nod. Zugsmith went back to his chair and looked at the story once more. 'I don't think there will be anything more, thank you,' he said, sounding as if he was going to get sick."

"Did they run the story with your by-line?"

"They ran the story without the by-line. I was assigned to rewrite after that and I'm still there. I guess I always will. I've developed roots."

"But what about your prizes? I should think the by-line would be acceptable to the public; it never seems to worry the contest judges."

"As a matter of fact, that fire story won two prizes for me. One from the firemen's union and the other from some insurance company. Of course, I thought that was my passport to being a reporter, but Zugsmith told me I was too valuable to go into the field. 'Anyone can report,' he said, 'it's only the true craftsman that can turn all those facts into the wonderfully smooth prose that you do.' So I was trapped. I made the mistake of being too good."

Bob nodded. The mistake was a common one on *The New York Record*. The men who did the best work got the most work to do, whether it was on rewrite or on the desk, where one man would be asked to read as many as ten feature stories a night while others would be capable of handling only three or four at the most. The same was true on reporting assignments. The reporters who could handle difficult stories were constantly being called on for the extra effort that was needed on these jobs. The incompetent ones usually received the more routine or easily handled stories to cover and these were often the most desirable assignments, involving meetings with leading government figures or celebrities, all of whom had press agents to render the assistance a good reporter would have shunned, but which was eagerly accepted by the incompetents.

"I know what you mean," Bob said. "I've seen it on the desk. I know many of the copy editors have a lot more talent than the correspondents, but they'll never get off the desk because desk men are hard to find. Good men die on the desk, they say."

"You probably do as much rewriting on the desk as I do. I only get about three calls a night."

"Only three calls?" Bob was surprised. "It seems every time I see you you're busy writing."

"That's true, but its not all for *The New York Record*. I do a lot of pulp work, mostly science-fiction."

"Say, that's great. What magazine does it appear in?"

"Most of the far-out ones. I don't know whether you've ever read any of them but if you should, look for my by-line."

"Do you use Howard Tucker?"

"No, Tucker Howard. I though that was a nice twist so that I could shield my identity in case anyone should ask. I think Zugsmith was right, it has been lucky for me. I've sold a lot of stuff under that name."

"Have you reached the point where you could get by just by writing science-fiction?"

Tucker signalled for another drink. He looked at the amber liquid for a moment and then tossed it off in one motion. "I could if I weren't trapped here."

"What do you mean trapped? I should think you could go any time you want."

"That's the difference between youth and age." Suddenly he was beginning to feel very philosophical as the liquid warmth crept up from his stomach and lightened his head. "We're all trapped whether you know it or not. I'm trapped because my work is so easy and I can get paid while I am writing this science-fiction junk. You're trapped because of the money they're paying you, or maybe because Zugsmith has told you he has big plans for you."

Bob shook his head. He was a good two drinks behind Tucker, but he, too, was beginning to feel the liquor. "I don't buy that. Yes, I'm making big money, but there are times when I feel the whole thing is ridiculous. The nit-picking that goes on, the chicken-shit. I still don't think *The New York Record* is the great be-all. It might have been a great paper once, but I don't see how it can still be great with all the incompetent people on it and all the mistakes that are made."

Tucker smiled broadly. "That's heresy, young man, you realize that? You could be burned at the stake for that. You're not entitled to those thoughts until you've been here longer. Now if I said that, it would be all right, but you're only a rank newcomer."

"You don't have to have it rubbed in your face to know horseshit when you see it."

Tucker laughed so loud the others at the bar turned away from the television set briefly. "You know what *The New York Record* reminds me of? It reminds me of that fairy tale where the two tailors swindle the Emperor into thinking they are using such fine cloth for his new clothes that only the just can see them. Do you remember that one?"

"The *Emperor's New Clothes?* Where he walks down the street naked?"

"That's right. Everyone calls *The New York Record* the little old lady, but I call it the Emperor. The swindlers have convinced everyone that in looking at the paper they are looking at greatness personified. It's fashionable to quote it and some of those Park Avenue dowagers don't believe they're dead unless they read it in *The New York Record*. To us on the inside, though, we can see all the warts, the varicose veins and everything. That's why when I really get mad at the system, I think, 'hasn't the Emperor got big balls.'"

"But if you don't like it," Bob protested, "why don't you just kick him in the balls and quit. I would."

"That's where the trap comes in. Look, I'm paying alimony to my first wife and I have a wife and a daughter now. That check every week means a lot to me. It's a higher pay than a lot of full professors get in a small college, so I wouldn't want to go back to teaching. Of course, I'm getting to the age where another link in the chain is being forged. I'm too old to start a new job. Other men on the paper are in the same spot. Some of them actually hate what they're doing, but because of the money, or the security, or their age, they can't go elsewhere or they're afraid to go elsewhere. So they just sit here and vegetate."

"I know what you mean, but I've never seen it in that light."

"Certainly, look around you. There are plenty of vegetables on the staff. *The New York Record* seldom fires anyone, except for drunkeness and there isn't too much of that any more. Now the damned paper is put out on coffee. In the old days, everyone used to have a bottle in his desk or his locker, but I guess the college-training calls for drinking on a more genteel basis—in Curry's, for instance."

"Does the drinking make you feel less trapped? Or is that a trap, too?"

"Now who's being the philosopher? I suppose it could be a trap, too, but I consider it insulation. I think it softens the blow when you wake up suddenly and find you're not going to be the Pulitzer Prize correspondent or the assistant managing editor and you're fifty years old and still on rewrite or the desk and good men die on the desk, you said it youself. And your college bills are still coming in and your kid needs braces on her teeth or a birthday party or a wedding reception and your mortgage is due and wouldn't it be nice if you could start over again and all that bullshit."

"I'll drink to that," Bob said, motioning to the bartender and pulling out a bill to put on the bar.

"No," Tucker protested. "You can't drink to drinking; it's too repetitious and remember we don't, don't, don't like repetition on *The New York Record*. Let's drink to the Emperor, *The New York Record.*"

"To the Emperor's balls," Bob agreed giddily, his laughter blending with Tucker's in a hollow echo within his numbed brain as if he were hearing it from a great distance.

Tucker's soul-baring solidified the friendship between the rewrite man and Bob. Tucker would sometimes go with Bob to catch Diane's last show and sometimes take the two of them to offbeat restaurants he had discovered. He was witty and pleasant and gave a new dimension to Bob's relationship with Diane, which neither of them wanted to deteriorate into a constant falling-into-bed. There were still Bob's nights off to look forward to each week, and each one was more precious, more tender than the last. Bob didn't feel trapped on *The*

New York Record, but he was beginning to feel trapped, although willingly, by Diane. Without her and the reality she represented Bob knew the things about his work that struck him funny or absurd would have been annoying; other copy editors had developed ulcers over the same things. But Bob had his release and his escape: The thought of seeing Diane made the hours pass quickly and Tucker's philosophy of irreverence lightened his time of trial. Whenever he might become discouraged or angry or disgusted, Bob would mutter "balls," then start to smile as he remembered Tucker's imagery.

Much of Bob's rebellious spirit could be traced to his logic, his love of order and common sense. His father had instilled in him the need for direct action in achieving these goals, and Bob had to catch himself repeatedly from rushing head on into battle with Tom Crum and even Zugsmith, whose doctrine Crum enforced.

One of Bob's chief objections, and that of all the men on all the desks, was the length of the dispatches filed by the correspondents and the constant cutting that had to be done as the story was shaped to the news hole. The system on the foreign desk was particularly grating to Bob's midwestern sense of economy because the cable charges on many of the dispatches ran as high as eighty-five cents a word. At that rate, Bob felt, each word should be golden, needing only slight burnishing by the copy editors to bring forth all its blazing glory on the front page.

Despite the high cable charges, the correspondents made little effort to keep their stories short except by dropping the articles and using a cablese shorthand for titles or other well known phrases. Each day the correspondents would send a summary of the stories they would file, with the approximate wordage incorporated into the message. When the wordage seemed excessive, the correspondent would be told to cut his file, but the only effect was to make the writer lose all sense of length. Virtually every one of the correspondents filed longer dispatches than promised in their summaries. The irony to Bob was that the stringers, those men who worked for European or Asian papers and filled in when there was no *New York Record* correspondent in the area or on the scene, could write precisely to space, seldom overfiling and frequently giving more details in their precision than a staff member could supply in twice the space. Unfortunately, Bob felt, the long suit for many of the writers was length, with clarity, coherence, and unity as absent as conciseness.

"Couldn't we ask the correspondent to file less?" Bob asked Crum one night in the middle of a lengthy dispatch from Algeria. There had been a late battle between the French and the rebels and Bob was clearing the copy as it was received from the wire room. By sending each page to the composing room as he received it, Bob could only guess about cutting the article. It did no good to arbitrarily cut the correspondent off when his word limit was reached, for frequently the material in the last paragraph would be deemed important by Zugsmith or one of his assistants and that material had to be kept.

"He's on the scene, maybe he thinks the story is worth it," Crum said, seldom varying his defense of the writers. Crum knew the story would probably have to be cut, but that was up to Bob. He had to get the whole story before he could evaluate any of its parts. That's what copy editing was all about. He had learned, let Davis learn, too.

"Half the material is local color or background we could do without," Bob protested.

"Color and background are very important to a story. Zugsmith is always asking the writers to get in more color, and background places the news in perspective."

Bob shook his head stubbornly. He knew Zugsmith's insistence on background was motivated by a false premise. He wanted to be sure that some one picking up the paper for the first time would be able to get all the news and learn its significance by reading just one issue. It was a good thing, Bob thought, that *The New York Record* had not covered The

Thirty Years' War or The Hundred Years' War. The background information would have filled the whole paper.

At eighty-five cents a word, Bob thought, each word should be a gem. At eighty-five cents a word, Crum thought, as few as possible of the words should be changed or rewritten. Even when the dispatches were poorly organized or badly written, they would not be turned over to the rewrite staff. This was a sort of class distinction since Crum, as instructed by Zugsmith, believed the foreign correspondents were the cream of the crop of *The New York Record* reporters. They had served an apprentice period, in most cases, on the city staff and when they were sent overseas they were assumed to be capable of handling every situation. As a result, any rewriting had to be laboriously scratched out in long hand by the copy editors, preferably between the lines of the material sent from the wire room.

In sports, the desks were equipped with typewriters and when Bob wanted to smooth out a lead or put in an insert he merely had to flip up the desk. On the foreign desk, though, there were no typewriters and Bob had to walk to the rewrite bank whenever he wanted to touch up the stories of the correspondents. While Crum was out for his operation, none of the men who filled in for Tom complained about Bob's habit. They were more interested in seeing the copy he turned in and there seldom were complaints about that. Crum was different, though, he operated straight by the book—Zugsmith's book.

"What are you doing?" Crum demanded when he found Bob on the rewrite bank at the typewriter.

"I'm just fixing up Lexford's story a bit."

"You're not rewriting him, are you?"

"No, I'm putting in some background and smoothing out his transitions. I'm not doing anything I wouldn't be doing at the desk. The only thing is, it goes faster by typewriter. It is easier to read, too, than my Chinese scrawl."

"You're not supposed to use a typewriter," Crum insisted. "If Zugsmith saw you, there'd be hell to pay. We pay as much as eighty-five cents a word for Lexford's stuff, you know, so Zugsmith doesn't want him changed a lot. He can't be that bad that you have to rewrite him."

Bob grew angry. "What the hell difference does it make how much we pay for the cable charges. If it's bad, it's bad even if it was two dollars a word. It still has to be fixed."

"But not by typewriter. Take it back to the desk and edit it, but don't rewrite it."

The sublety escaped Bob. He knew, though, that the belief was widely held on the paper. It was all part of the cult of the gigantic: If the story is long enough, it is good enough; if the correspondent is highly paid enough, he must be incapable of writing poorly; if a statement is repeated enough, it must be true. He wondered how the tabloids and the news magazines were able to present the same stories as *The New York Record* in half the space. He made the mistake once of making that observation to Tom Crum.

"The tabloids used only four paragraphs on this story," Bob pointed out. "Is there any reason why we have to use a full column?"

"You can't judge *The New York Record* by tabloid standards," Crum said with the same inflection Zugsmith used in the classroom. "We are the paper of record. We have to present the full story regardless of what the tabloids do."

To the copy editors, it was an impersonal thing, since they held no brief for the correspondents, whom they seldom saw, only when a correspondent was on home leave or on vacation would he stop in the office. To the correspondents in the field, though, the editing was all motivated by hate for the country he was covering, or, worse, for the correspondent himself.

Many of the correspondents would suffer if they saw how their lovely dispatches had been changed and tailored to fit a much too small a hole in the paper. Some took it stoically as another blow to their egos and their ulcers, but some complained bitterly in messages that night after seeing the paper or in letters to Beau Manley or even to the publisher. The letters would set off an investigation to find who had edited the story. Then the copy editor, found guilty without benefit of a trial, would have to write a detailed explanation of why the changes had been made. Bob thought the system was stupid. "Obviously," he explained to Crum, "The changes were made because they were intended to improve the sentence. The way Lexford had the sentence was awkward. I seriously doubt he had any rhythm to his piece as he claims. To say that changing one sentence and preserving the original intent of the original sentence ruins the whole piece is ridiculous. I think Lexford should be told so."

Lexford was Lewis L. Lexford, a small Englishman who had been on the paper since the war. He was a charming fellow, with a tiny pencil-line mustache, and he wore the best clothes in whatever climate he was working. He was the perfect picture of a very proper foreign correspondent and remained so until he sat down at the typewriter. Undoubtedly Lexford had wonderful sources and obtained top-grade information, but his Oxonian training clashed with his journalistic instinct whenever he filed a dispatch and the results were often cloudy. He relied on the desk to catch factual errors as well as grammatical lapses. He never noticed those changes in his copy; he never sent messages of thanks, only of complaint.

Crum knew Lexford was not the best correspondent on the paper so he liked to give his dispatches to a copy editor he could trust. He knew the assignment was not an envied one since the man selected had to sweat over each line, each paragraph, often rearranging large segments of the story to put the news in proper perspective, or at least what Zugsmith thought was proper perspective. Bob was fast and dependable. His speed enabled him to read each story twice. He went over it quickly for the obvious editing changes the first time to get the sense of the whole dispatch. Then he would read it word by word or almost letter by letter to be sure that his eye had not trapped him into reading over a mistake. The background material was furnished by the clippings from the morgue, although Bob was so familiar with Lexford's area that he had evolved a capsule updating to be slipped in easily and quickly without bothering to send for the clips. This, too, was fine with Crum so long as he didn't realize the capsule told in fifty words what Lexford ordinarily would take five hundred words to communicate. He caught on when Bob cut a long-winded explanation of the situation by Lexford in favor of his own concise and perfectly readable version of the same events.

"You can't cut Lexford that way," Crum protested, giving the copy back to Bob, who was starting to write the headline.

"Why not? We don't need that long-winded background he gives. It gets in the way of the story too much."

"Background is the story in this case. The murder of the policeman by the South African doesn't mean anything in itself. We have to get in the background about the pass laws and the riots and everything else that Lexford has there."

"But the space is only six hundred words. If we use his background, we'll have only about one hundred words of new material."

Crum was adamant. "If that's the way it works out, fine. But we have to have that background."

Bob sweated over the story some more, striving desperately to save words so that more of the new material would be usable. He thought the facts were interesting, but their presentation was poor, almost as if Lexford had taken the report straight off the police blotter. With his fine honing of the phrases, the rearrangement of paragraphs, the breaking up of the quotes into more dramatic conversation snatches, Bob tried to bring some life into it.

When the paper came up, Crum turned to see how much of the Lexford story had been put into type. Lexford was always the last to file, even though he had the advantage of a five-hour time difference. Getting the copy at the last minute would have been easier if the writer were better, but Lexford could not be induced to get his material in early. He claimed that the Government censor was slow in giving the copy back

60

to him before he could have it transmitted, but that was only the crutch he used. Actually, Lexford preferred to wait until all the services and other correspondents had filed their dispatches. By looking at the copy in the cable office, he could tell if he was on firm ground. Frequently he would have no idea of what to make the lead of his story until he saw what his rivals were writing. Sometimes, he would ignore their line of attack completely, happily putting "Exclusive" at the start of his dispatch when he had something none of the others did.

Unfortunately, Lexford's news judgment was not from Zugsmith's school of journalism. When Lexford's exclusive seemed too frothy or of too little consequence, Crum would dash off a cable pointing out that both the Associated Press and Reuters had different angles for their file than Lexford. The correspondent then would reword the duplicates of the dispatches he had bribed from the telegrapher and send off the story New York wanted.

It was only Reuters and the A.P. that Lexford had to worry about. He knew the executives of *The New York Record* did not trust United Press International and there could be a wide difference in the U.P.I. dispatch and Lexford's without any questions being raised. The distrust of the wire service sprang from the fact that many of the men had worked for the Associated Press and the publisher was a member of the board. It just wasn't politic for *The New York Record* to carry too much U.P.I. material. Frequently, Lexford would append a note to his dispatch warning against believing the U.P.I. and then a week later he would come through with the same dispatch under a new lead that made it appear he had another exclusive.

Because he was a fast reader, Bob kept up with the other papers. This helped in his work on the desk and enabled him to pinpoint facts quickly and accurately when something had to be referred to or checked. The background he wove into Lexford's stories, the polishing and the honing of the paragraphs soon stirred notice throughout the office and outside.

"Lexford had a good story tonight, didn't he?" Crum would say after checking the paper. Bob would nod, "Not bad." He could expect nothing more from Crum because Tom really didn't see the copy in the raw; he read only the edited version and in some cases he seldom had time for that since Lexford's file was frequently late. The situation was such that Bob joked that the LLL signed at the bottom of the dispatches meant long, late, and lousy. It was a typical copy editor's joke, but Crum was not amused. To insult a correspondent was to insult *The New York Record;* foreign coverage was the paper's long suit and Crum didn't like any reflection on that even in jest.

All through the long winter Bob had a steady diet of Lexford's dispatches. Only his dogged determination to handle anything Crum put before him prevented him from complaining. Only his nights and his days with Diane carried him through the desolate season in the city. There was encouragement from Zugsmith, too, and that helped Bob's morale at least. Zugsmith received copies of all dispatches unedited and he was therefore able to appreciate the work that had gone into the stories on the various desks. Zugsmith was like a good football coach, keeping a constant check on his players and dropping a word of encouragement now and then through a monthly newsletter he circulated within the paper.

But Bob's work was more than craftsmanship recognized only by the men on the paper. Lexford's dispatches took on a new dimension under Bob's skillful editing. The pathos inherent in the stories was brought to the top and dramatized or emphasized by the proper placement of modifier or punctuation. Further, the stories screamed for attention through the headlines Bob wrote. They were generally sensitive and compelling within the narrow limits of the one-column letter count.

Bob knew copy editors were the workhorses like the lineman in football. It was their job to clear out the obstacles to perfect rapport between the reader and the reporter and then when that was done to see the writer lionized just as was the halfback who ran off the block made by the guard for a touchdown. It had always been the other way around for Bob, but he didn't mind it now. "That's my job," he'd say to Tucker when the rewrite man would comment knowingly about Bob's contribution to Lexford's dispatches. "That's my job," all through the long winter, from South Africa to Algeria, to Morocco to the Congo as Lexford moved around so the paper could capitalize on the new favor he was finding with the public. Wherever he went, Bob was there, figuratively, standing at Lexford's elbow or looking over his shoulder. There was a noticeable slackening of Lexford's appeal on the nights Bob was off, for other copy editors would merely put in the paragraph marks, convinced like the people in the fairy tale that they couldn't see the fine weave of the whole cloth in the Emperor's clothes because of some weakness in themselves. The magic that was in Bob's editing wasn't there for the others. To them Lexford could not be improved; he must be great; everyone was talking about him.

In the spring, Bob was slaving away on one of Lexford's dispatches and cursing liberally to himself when Crum approached with a short piece of wire copy in his hands. "You say Lexford isn't a good correspondent?"

"Not our best, I don't think," Bob said mildly.

"I guess your opinion doesn't rate so much," Crum said triumphantly, putting the wire copy on the desk before Bob. "Lewis L. Lexford of *The New York Record* has just won the Pulitzer Prize."

Chapter Five

EVERYONE ON the paper knew of Bob's contributions to Lexford's Pulitizer Prize except the publisher and his top aides. They lived in another world, more interested in the lineage figures and the net revenues than the daily routine of the city room. Tom Crum refused to concede that Bob had been a factor in the prize. He knew who had handled the stories, but he was convinced Bob's contribution had been minimal.

Zugsmith knew, of course, and it made him happy in two ways: He was right about Bob showing promise, and it was another Pulitizer Prize writer on the paper. Lexford was one of his boys, too; that made it all the more sweet.

For Bob, Lexford's prize meant a new identity. He was no longer "Zugsmith's boy"; he was the one who won the Pulitizer Prize for Lexford. He preferred the new designation even though it brought with it a role as a critic on numerous articles that were slipped before him when things on the desk were slack. Reporters, the news clerks, and even the copy boys were constantly asking his advice on features or on some outside writing they were doing. Within the office, he enjoyed the same hero status he would have if he had won the Pulitizer on his own. Only Tucker was unimpressed.

"I've seen how they pick these things," he said to Bob in Curry's. "One year I had gone back to teaching at a school that awards prizes only a bit below the Pulitizer in prestige. Because I was on the paper and the faculty, too, I was picked as a juror."

"Did some one try to bribe you, or something?"

"No, but it was a revelation about how the prizes are given out. I was told to report to the judging room at 3 o'clock in the afternoon after my class. I got there about 3:10 and I was

64

the only one there, except for the curator for the awards. The room was about ten by twelve and there was a long table piled high with entries in the prize contest. 'These are only a few of the total we received,' the curator said, 'but I thought I could weed out some to make your task easier.' At any rate, I started to read the entries and after about an hour, two more of the jurors arrived and they started, too. By about 4:15, all but one of the jurors was there and finally the last one arrived at 4:30."

"How long was the judging supposed to take?"

"That's the whole point. At five, the curator said it was time for cocktails and we drank until about six and then had dinner. At seven o'clock we started looking at film clips of television documentaries. Hundreds of entries had been received in this category, too, but the curator had cut them down to about two or three minutes each. At any rate, we looked at film clips for two hours and then went back to the jury room. It was time to vote, the curator said."

"But how could you possibly vote when you hadn't read all the entries?"

"Exactly. Well, the curator brought out the ones he thought were the best and asked us if we didn't agree. We were so tired and bleary eyed from looking at all those TV films that we nodded dumbly, I guess, and that was it. Of course, the national news reporting prize and the foreign news prize went to the *Record,* so I couldn't say too much, I guess."

"But you hadn't read them, right?"

"Well I had read them in the paper, but I don't think I read them that day in the jury room. The funniest thing of all, though, was that one of the nominees for the local reporting prize was really outstanding. It was a series on crime by Harrison Brown, a damned good reporter who died about three years ago. Actually, Brown's piece was better than the foreign or national entries, but the curator said that three prizes couldn't go to *The New York Record* because it would look like a monopoly. So we gave the prize to some one on the

Herald Tribune who happened to be in the right place at the right time. Conceivably the same thing happened to Lexford. In fact, I'll bet that half the twenty or so Pulitzer winners on the paper were in the same boat: they were either lucky or they were helped by the desk."

"And the other half?"

"They were hired away from other papers after they won the prize. You wouldn't know that from the promotional ads we run, but that's the case. Probably the same thing applies to them, but I don't think any other paper could operate the way we do. For one thing, they don't have the big desks we have, and for another, they don't have the budgets to be able to afford a really bad correspondent."

"*The New York Record* technique is sort of strange, isn't it?" Bob asked, half musingly.

"At least it's effective. Good copy editors are harder to find than writers, so it's smart to put the accent on editing."

"I wonder why there's such a shortage of copy editors. The money isn't bad, but I guess the reporting jobs are the glamorous ones. The hours are probably the worst thing about it. I'm lucky having a girl who works nights. I can see her in the daytime and after work. Some of the other fellows, though, particularly the married ones, seldom see their wives or their kids. They might just as well be merchant seamen. You know that yourself. It's the same thing with rewrite."

Tucker nodded understandingly. "It's tougher on the wives than on the men, I think. At least there's some comradeship on the paper, but the poor wife is alone so much. She seldom can go anywhere because her husband is working. That's why I'm always shifting my days off so I can go to P.T.A. meetings or something with my wife. On the desk, though, it's a lot harder to shift days off, isn't it?"

Bob nodded.

"The ones I feel sorry for," Tucker said, "are the young unmarried kids. Not you, you're different, but just look at some of the kids on the other desks. How do you take out a girl if your days off are Tuesday and Wednesday? I think the prospect of marrying anyone working nights would be enough to discourage any girl."

"Undoubtedly the reporter with a regular beat—the court, or politics, or something like that is better off. At least he works in the daytime since that's when the government agencies are open."

"But reporters work at night, too, don't forget. The police headquarters men work at night and those in Washington never know when a story is going to break. You're right, though, the reporters are a definite social cut above both of us. It's part of the deification process carried on here. Zugsmith was never a reporter, you know, so he thinks they're something special."

"Is that why none of his directives about keeping the stories short or the sentences simple are passed on to reporters?"

"It could be. I guess Zugsmith doesn't want the reporters to have fettered minds. He wants them to get in as many facts as possible and all the local color around. Then it's up to the desk to sharpen it. You think the stuff is tripe because you see it in the raw, before the magic formula starts to work."

"Magic formula? I've never heard of it, what is it?"

"The prestige of print. Certainly you've noticed it, but you've been only half aware of it. Haven't you ever wondered how a story that is all marked up and botched up comes out so neat and clean in the paper. You send it to the composing room as a mess, convinced it's one of the worst stories you've read. When it comes out in the paper, with every line justified and neatly set under a headline, it doesn't read half bad."

Bob had seen the system work many times, but he had never thought of it in that manner. Sometimes, when he was angry or bored or tired, he would put in the paragraph marks on the copy of the worst writers on the paper and send it to the composing room with virtually no editing. He felt the result would expose the writer for what he truly was: a hack, but it seldom worked that way. When Bob read the article in the paper, the transitions seemed smoother and the sentences seemed to flow more easily than when they were just received from the telegrapher.

"I've never thought of it that way, but it's true. In effect, I guess it represents a succumbing to the fable of the Emperor. Because the words appear in the paper, we think they're well chosen words, proper words."

"It might work that way, but I've known writers who complain when they're edited too much and then when they're not edited enough. Once the desk just put in the paragraph marks on one of the poorer writers and he complained that they had ruined his story. When the copy was retrieved from the proof room and he saw that the copy hadn't been touched, he complained that the desk wasn't doing its job."

"I've noticed that around here, the desk is blamed for everything. The reporters are never told of their mistakes so far as I know."

Bob hadn't been on the paper long enough to get to know many of the correspondents, but he knew that there were favorites and fallguys. The favorites could not be touched. The fallguys could virtually be rewritten without any complaint from the slot man.

"I don't think I've ever let any feelings toward the writer affect my editing," Bob said. "I haven't been here long enough to really get to dislike any of the writers."

"You're lucky. You've got honesty working for you. Some of the copy editors, I know, get their hackles up as soon as they get the copy from a particular writer. It would be all right if they improved the story, but too many times they tend to put everything into the stereotyped style of the wire services."

"I know. I think it's a defensive formula. Time pressure tells on different men in different degrees. The formula, the pat statement is safer, tried and true. There are bad editors as well as bad writers."

"The thing that amazes me," Tucker said, shaking his head,

"is how come *The New York Record* seems to have such an abundant surplus of both?"

The remark was only half in jest. Both Tucker and Bob had agreed many drinks ago that the paper was overstaffed. There were two reasons for the large staff: the refusal of the publisher and his predecessors to fire anyone and the dedication of the paper to give all the news on any major event down to the most exhausting detail. *The New York Record* grew as its circulation grew because some ancient sage in the business or the editorial office had once equated a large staff with success. The formula had worked in the early days of cut-throat competition between papers in New York since the *Record* frequently outflanked or outhustled the other papers through sheer weight of numbers. Some long forgotten disaster was the first event to receive the detailed treatment for which *The New York Record* had become famous and the standard joke in the business was that the oversized staff was sitting around awaiting another disaster.

As communications improved, the need for such a large staff diminished, but still more reporters were hired and more copy editors sought. The problem was that so many of the older men were being promoted into higher positions that the number of employees could hardly keep up with the number of executives. Each department had supernumeraries whose functions were ill-defined. The result was a budget that was constantly strained by the costs of gathering news and hard put to have anything left over from advertising and circulation revenues for profit. In the early days, the paper showed a profit in its real estate transactions, accurately forecasting where the new growth in the city would be, moving to that site until the parade had almost passed, and then selling the land at a handsome profit.

The other profits were from the affiliates of the company, a paper-producing plant, for which *The New York Record* was its own best customer, and an import-export business that operated in connection with the nations where the paper had correspondents. The export-import business showed only tiny profits, but it was a handy tool for piling up currency reserves to pay off the staff in countries where the paper's correspondents were operating.

Most of this Bob learned from Edith Miller, the publisher's young daughter. Edith was following a long family tradition by getting to know the business by working on the paper. Her mother and grandmother had done the same and the publishers of *The New York Record* always had a strong sense of history. She had noticed Bob even before Lexford's Pulitizer Prize had brought him general recognition. There was something different about Bob that intrigued Edith Miller.

Edith knew most of the people she was writing about on the society page. She had developed a pointed style that slaughtered most of the sacred cows of the four hundred, but they loved it because she was one of them, or so they thought. Edith was something of an anomaly; she was one of the few members of the publisher's family who had a real feel for the newspaper business. The others had a feel for business, which was only natural since her father's background, like her maternal grandfather's, had been Wall Street. The annual reports showing the spiraling profits and the growing dividends were the well written stories to the Millers; at least to all of them except Edith.

If she had gone to any other college except Sarah Lawrence, Edith would have been a rebel, railing against war, injustice or the mess the older generation had made of the world. If she would have inherited anything less than three million dollars, she would have been a Communist, a Zen Buddist, or whatever was popular at City College that year. But Edith Miller was none of these. She was a sensitive, level-headed young woman supremely confident of her future and well aware of the power of her position. Her money, she knew, made up for her lack of outstanding beauty, although she could not be called unattractive. She had wispy brown hair, olive skin, a rather large nose, but not too large, and deep brown eyes that seemed always to be looking through Bob whenever he walked through the city room and nodded to her. Her eyes seemed almost calculating and they were, for Edith had already checked Bob out with personnel to make sure he was single. A little more calculating enabled Edith to be on Tucker's usual stool at Curry's bar when Bob walked in one night.

"If you're looking for Mr. Tucker, he isn't here tonight," she said, smiling brightly. "He left word that I should buy you a drink and he'll see you tomorrow."

"There must be something wrong. He's always here at this time of the night."

Edith smiled again. "I know, but I had someone call him back to the office."

"You did? Why?" Bob was flattered. He knew Edith could be helpful to him.

"I wanted to get a chance to meet you." Edith turned her eyes on Bob and smiled.

"But we've met. I say hello every time I see you." He climbed onto the stool next to Edith and looked at her quizzically then signalled to the bartender for a drink.

"But you don't really know me, except that I'm the boss's daughter." There was a little toss of her head as if she had made an announcement.

"Isn't that enough?" Bob couldn't figure out what she was driving at.

"No, I don't think so."

"In that case, let me introduce myself," Bob said with a smile. He looked at Edith for the first time. She had the confidence of money, good grooming, the right clothes but without the detached air that seemed to hint there was only ice beneath it all. She lowered her eyes in the face of his stare.

"You have a nice smile. That's why I wanted to meet you.

Most of the men on the paper sort of drop their eyes when they see me. They give a sickly grin and say, 'How are you, Miss Miller?' or 'How do you do Miss Miller.' "

"Don't I?" Bob knew his openness was unusual on the paper. Men had worked there for twenty-five years without nodding to anyone outside their departments.

"You smile and say 'Hi,' just as if I'm any other girl."

"To me you are a girl, aren't you?"

"You mean, you're not impressed because I'm the publisher's daughter?"

"No, I'm sorry, I'm not. I'm more impressed with what you write. Some of it is really brilliant. I'm impressed with that and that you are the publisher's daughter writing that. But so far as just being the publisher's daughter, I don't think you're even impressed with that, are you?"

Edith hugged her drink in a delicious feeling of understanding. She sipped lightly, then smiled over her glass at Bob. "Touché," she said, "Or almost touché. No, I'm not impressed by being the publisher's daughter, but I'm impressed by the money that means, the doors it can open, the things it can get me."

"And what might that be?" Edith turned to him and stared just as he had done. He was better looking up close than at a distance.

"That's the trouble, I'm not sure. Oh, ultimately, it means a man, I suppose, but he has to be the right kind of a man."

"One with money so that you won't think he's more interested in your bank roll than you?"

"No, he doesn't have to have money; there aren't enough men like that around anyway. When I say the right kind of a man, I mean one who wouldn't let my money stand in the way. I'm not fool enough to think money wouldn't have a lot to do with attracting men, but you can tell what's more important, me or the money."

"It's an interesting bit of tightrope walking."

"There's one thing," Edith said almost as an afterthought.

"The man I marry, I think, has to be familiar with the newspaper business, or at least willing to learn. It's sort of a family tradition, you know. My father got to be publisher by marrying my mother and my grandfather by marrying the boss's daughter and so on for a couple of generations back. The only thing is that the men have been from outside the business. I think it would be good for the paper if the next publisher really had an understanding of the business."

Bob smiled to himself. "I thought the policy on the paper was don't rock the boat. If it worked all right last year and the year before that, why not do it again. Would you want to change that?"

Edith looked into her drink. She paused before she answered. "I think we're living in a world of change. *The New York Record* has to change with the times. Take the stuff I'm writing, for instance. Probably, if anyone else was writing it but the publisher's daughter, it would never appear. But the important thing is that it is appearing in the paper. It shows the society hypocrites for what they are, but that wouldn't have been possible years ago on the paper even by the publisher's daughter."

"Perhaps you're right. The funny thing, from what I understand, is that the society people love it. They think it's a great privilege to be harpooned by you. But you take yourself pretty seriously, don't you?"

"Me? I wouldn't say that, but when a girl gets to be twenty-five she starts to wonder. In my case, it's more than just me, it's the paper. My father is still a comparatively young man, but I know he'd like to see me married before long. He wants to start training his successor."

"When I came here," Bob said, a broad grin splitting his face, "Zugsmith told me that I could go far. He didn't say the publisher's job was going to be open, though. Where do I apply?"

Edith looked at Bob, her lips unsmiling. "If you apply yourself right," she said, "you just might fill the bill."

Bob was kidding, but there were more drinks, more talks and more understanding with Edith in the next three months. He enjoyed her company and the crowd she traveled in, but he missed Diane, too, and there was just so much he could do with his two nights off. Edith had a sparkling wit, her conversation was intelligent on whatever subject they got on and she was good company, but it wasn't the same. Edith was more demanding because she knew the office routine perfectly and she usually managed to be around when Bob was getting ready to leave. His visits to the Village became fewer and fewer and Diane's greetings after canceled dates grew cooler and cooler. Being with Edith was fun, but it was also a drain on his physical and financial resources. He tried working overtime to discourage her, but that only made her wait longer and become impatient.

"Why are you working overtime again tonight?" she asked finally, her annoyance clear.

"There are some big stories breaking and besides, I can use the money." Bob was only half truthful.

"If you're not making enough I could speak to my father about a raise."

Bob realized he had said the wrong thing. "No, please don't. I'm making more than a lot of the fellows on the desk. It's just that all those places we've been going to cost money."

"I told you I'd pay for it, but you wouldn't let me."

"After all, I'm not a gigolo, you know." Bob thrust out his chin stubbornly. Edith laughed.

"Sometimes I wish you were. At least when gigolos work overtime, it's a lot more interesting than what you're doing."

"Is that what you learned in society news?"

"I don't know where I learned it, but I know Uncle Zach doesn't appreciate my hanging around here late. It cramps his style."

"Zugsmith? Uncle Zach?" Somehow Bob could not think of Zugsmith as uncle anything.

"Yes, he was almost my father, you know. At least he had a terrific crush on my mother, but her father wouldn't let her marry him. He still thinks of me as his daughter, though, and it bothers him to see me around. He doesn't like to walk out at the same time as Helen Crawford when I'm around."

"Helen Crawford? You mean Zugsmith . . ."

"That's the lay of the land." Edith started to giggle. "I guess she's slept with just about every one in the city room, but Uncle Zach thinks she's all his."

Helen Crawford was a good reporter whose once fabulous beauty had been artfully preserved through the years. She was outgoing and friendly, widely respected for her ability to wear clothes that showed off her still attractive figure to its best advantage. She had started as a secretary to Zugsmith, but her ambition and his conscience had landed her a job as a reporter. She didn't have to be good, but she was, writing tight, readable stories on the most complicated subjects and covering the roughest assignments with the top men in the field.

"You know her, of course," Edith said half accusingly.

"I've met her, but not, shall we say, socially. I'm funny that way. My father had an old saying: 'Never get your meat where you get your bread and butter.' "

"The hell with this overtime. Let's go out and have some fun."

Bob shook his head, his defenses destroyed. "For a young girl you certainly are determined. If we go out tonight, though, we're going to the Village. There's someone I want you to meet."

"You mean the singer?"

"Yes, how did you know?" Bob asked, surprised. He knew Edith had checked his personnel file, but he didn't know she had gone beyond that.

"I'm a reporter, remember. When I want to find out about some one, I do some digging. You'd be surprised how much I know about you. I can even figure out your motive in taking me to the Village."

"You can? Well, tell me. I just thought of it on the spur of the moment. I didn't intend to ask you at all."

"You think that after I've seen this gorgeous girl, and I understand she is really stacked, that I'll stop chasing you around."

"Will you?"

Edith looked deep into Bob's eyes. "I might," she said blowing smoke in his face from her cigarette. "Would you want me to?"

"I might," Bob said imitating her archness then sticking out his tongue at her.

Diane and Edith Miller hit if off like oil and water. Diane's suspicions about Bob's absences were confirmed.

To Edith, the club was cheap, with a tiny stage and a three-piece combination that served as the backdrop for Diane's songs. The six-foot square dance floor was choked by tables that were seldom filled, except on Saturdays, when the tourists streamed into the area in search of excitement and thrills. The La Strada was like hundreds of other small clubs in the area, struggling to get along with a cheap menu and a minimum of entertainment, attracting the overflow from the bigger clubs, the strip joints, and the better restaurants.

Nick Politis, the owner, often told himself that he really couldn't afford Diane, but her beauty, her voice and the debt Nick owed to her father, the late Captain John Reilly of the Police Department, made him forget the economic realities. Besides, her salary was low and she was willing enough to fill in as a hatcheck girl or the hostess if the need should arise.

She sat at the table in her costume, without bothering to pull her robe over her as she usually did. Her heavy breathing moved her breasts up and down so bewitchingly Bob had trouble keeping his eyes level.

"And what do you do, Miss Miller?" she asked icily.

"Edith is a society reporter," Bob cut in quickly, noticing

76

the edge in Diane's voice. "Her father is the publisher of the paper."

"Oh, isn't that nice. Now I can see why you decided to make the job permanent."

"Permanent? Wasn't it always?" Edith asked, turning to Bob in surprise.

"Well, I did plan to go back to Fort Wayne at the end of the summer when I started work, but I changed my mind," Bob said.

"Obviously," Diane said, finally pulling her robe over her breasts. "It's so cold here, I think I better get dressed."

"Should I, should we wait?" Bob said. "We could get a cab and . . ."

"No, don't bother," she said, her eyes snapping at him. "I'm pleased to have met you, Miss Miller. Good night, Mr. Davis."

Bob stared at her exquisite body moving in a swirl of robe through the tables to her dressing room. "Let's get out of here," he said to Edith, his throat dry, his palms wet.

"She's a lovely girl," Edith said, breaking the moody silence on the way to her apartment.

"She is," Bob agreed, not really wanting to talk. He wondered how he could repair his blunder. Taking Edith to the club wasn't such a good idea.

"I'm surprised she's working in such a cheap club. Did you say her brother is a priest?"

"That's right, in the Bronx. Her father was quite a well-known police captain in this district from what I heard. He was killed about ten years ago stopping a holdup of this club. That's why Diane works here; the owner feels he owes the family something."

"She is good, though, isn't she?"

"How do you mean that? She's not the world's worst singer or the best by far. She could be working in better clubs if she was packaged right and if she was willing to play games with the agents or the managers."

"Is that really true? I thought that was only in the movies. I could speak to my father. He could probably arrange an audition for her in an uptown club."

Bob winced. He didn't think Diane would be receptive to such an offer. "That's very nice of you, but I don't think she's going to want to have anything to do with *The New York Record* after tonight."

He lapsed into silence again, troubled by the hurt expression in Diane's eyes. He resolved to stop seeing Edith, but he knew it would be difficult; she was so persistent and her friendship could be helpful to him.

"This is it," she said, nudging him from his reverie with her thigh as the cab stopped in front of a large canopy. He paid the driver and turned to say good night. "I'm afraid I haven't been much fun," he said dully.

"It was my fault. I shouldn't have barged in on you like that. I'm sorry." Edith looked at her nails and bit her lip.

Bob sighed. It was a long way from the Village to Park Avenue.

"No, I didn't have a firm date with her; it's just been a long time since I've been down there."

"Why don't you come up for a drink?" You'll feel better."

Bob was curious about the apartment, but he was hoping to head off Diane before she got home. "What about your father? He might be up."

"Father doesn't live here. He stays at the club. He and mother are just about going through the motions now. Not everyone knows it but Winchell and his millions of readers. I guess that was before your time in New York, though, wasn't it?"

"I'm not surprised, but I'm sorry." Bob had deduced that the publisher was not exactly the family type because of the numerous young show girls he guided through the paper at night. He seldom was seen in the office with Mrs. Miller. Edith smiled and tossed her head defiantly.

"Don't be sorry. It doesn't bother me and I guess they're both having more fun than if they were living together. Father has his show girls and actresses, mother has her painters. She collects them the way Hearst collected art. Right now it's a modernist out on Fire Island. She's out there now, so you don't have to worry about her either."

The doorman saluted smartly as they entered the lobby. Bob wondered how many men Edith had towed past him. He tried to tell himself he was going up only to see the apartment, but he knew there was more to Edith's invitation for a drink. His ego was bruised after Diane's coolness. He needed the drink and anything that might go with it.

The apartment was more than Bob could have imagined. There was a large sunken area facing a fireplace, a modern bar in one corner and a stairway leading to another level. The furnishings and the decorator touches suggested wealth subtlely, without being ostentatious.

"Not bad for a working girl, eh?" Edith said teasing.

Bob shook his head, the importance of Edith being brought home by a picture of the publisher on the mantel. "I really should be going." He suddenly felt uncomfortable.

"You haven't had your drink. Sit down, relax. I can start a fire if you want, it works by gas and starts right up. Should I?"

"No please don't. I'll just have a scotch and water and then I'll be off. It's getting late."

Edith went to the bar and mixed the drinks. She turned on some soft music then brought the drink to Bob.

"Cheers," she said lifting her glass.

Bob took a deep drink. He was pleased that she had not made it too weak, the way most women did. Suddenly Edith began to laugh.

"What's so funny?" he asked.

"I was just thinking how everything is turned upside down. When you usually think of drinks and soft music, it's the man who is trying to seduce the woman. And here . . ."

"Are you trying to seduce me?" He studied her carefully,

unsure of himself. She looked back at him, her smile fading.

"I don't know, really. I think it's a matter of ego. Just about anyone else would be working on me. I can't figure you out."

"Well, after all, you are the Boss's daughter, you know."

"But that's the whole point. That's why the others would be trying so hard to romance me. In the two months we've been going out, you've never tried to get fresh and we have hardly necked at all. It's just a very proper kiss goodnight as if you recognized your duty." She bit her lip again, a nervous habit from her youth. She could see Bob was stung.

"I don't think that's very kind, to you or to me," he protested. "There was no duty involved. I wanted to kiss you goodnight, that's why I did it. I've had a lot of fun with you and I like you a lot."

"But in a platonic way, is that it?"

"No, but . . ."

"Are you thinking about that saying of your father's about getting your meat where you get your bread and butter?"

"Well, not exactly. Well, yes, maybe I am." Bob had forgotten telling her that.

"That's nonsense. My father had a saying something like that, too. He said I should never go to bed with anyone on the paper, unless . . ."

"Unless you married him, right?"

"No, unless I could marry him."

"He sounds like an unusual man. I'm sorry I don't know him." Bob had seen Miller on his tours of the building, but had never met him.

"I can fix that very easily."

It was a tempting thought, but Bob thought there would be too many complications. He finished his drink and got up to go. "You probably could, but I don't know if it's such a good idea. I really better be going."

"But I didn't give you your present. That's why I brought you up here."

"What present?" Bob asked suspiciously.

"For winning the Pulitzer Prize. It's in the bedroom, sit down a minute, I'll get it. I have it hidden on my mother." She ran into the bedroom and closed the door. Bob sat down, wondering where she had put his coat. It had been so long since Edith had mentioned Lexford's prize, he thought she had forgotten.

"Bob," Edith called from the bedroom. "I can't reach it in the closet. Could you get it down for me, please?"

Bob got up from the couch resignedly. He walked to the bedroom door and knocked once. "All right to come in?" His pulse seemed to quicken at the perfume smell coming through the door.

"Come in, come in," Edith called.

Bob swung open the door. Edith's dress was on the floor near the foot of the bed. She was lying on the bed naked, her hair framing her shoulders, her arms raised to him.

"Come and get your present," she said, huskily, wiggling her fingers and twisting her hips.

"I wonder what Zugsmith, Uncle Zach, would say ·if he could see me now," Bob thought as he dropped his trousers. "It's cold," he said to the girl, "get under the covers."

Edith obeyed meekly, touching his smooth naked body as he slipped in beside her. He put his arm around her waist and drew her close, pressing himself between her legs but making no attempt to enter. She was smaller than Diane, her breasts a rank or two above nubility, her legs less shapely, her hips thinner. Bob was surprised that her opening was bigger; or perhaps it was Diane's movements, which could be perfected only in show business. Edith lay back unmoving as Bob worked over her, carefully supporting his weight on his elbows. He slowed his movements as he realized she wasn't responding. With a quick movement he rolled on his back, holding her close and never losing contact. Now his hands were free and he gently squeezed her breasts as he kissed her and began a slower movement that grew more rapid as she at last started to respond. His hands moved to her hips to guide her movements and to keep her from ejecting him by the wilder and wilder rhythm of her body. As the climax arrived, he pressed her buttocks together as if to draw off the last drop and she continued to move, entreatingly looking for more as he fell back on the pillow.

"You are different, aren't you?" she said, with the pleased purr of a new experience. Bob snorted.

"It's something I picked up in Korea. An old Navy man told about that. He said it used to get the twelve-year-old whores going when nothing else could. It changes the angle of approach or something."

"It certainly does something. But twelve years old, did you ever?"

"I never asked any of the girls for their birth certificates and when you're out there I don't think it much matters. I think most of the girls I had were older, at least sixteen, but you can never tell about an Oriental."

"Is it true that they're different?" Edith giggled, biting Bob's shoulder as she teased him.

"I never found a cross-way one yet. I'm still willing to look, though." Edith shook her head determinedly.

"You're going to be too busy to do much looking from now on young man. A man with talent like yours should go far. You really made me feel . . . made me feel, you know?" She stretched her arms to reach out to the new vistas Bob had opened for her.

"I'm glad. I was beginning to think you were just doing it out of sympathy. It was a very nice present, though." He smiled at her and kissed her on the nose. She was more attractive with her hair mussed.

Edith leaned over to kiss him, pressing her breasts against his chest and smiling wickedly. "I wanted to make up for your doing all the work and Lexford getting the prize, but now you had to do all the work and I got the prize." She shivered as the memory tickled her.

"If that was to make up for the Lexford thing, you must be pretty mean."

"Mean? How can you say that? I don't understand." Edith looked hurt, but then Bob smiled.

"It's the first time I've been screwed to make up for a screwing. Is that fair?"

Edith hugged her hand to her breast deliciously as she rolled with laughter. "I think it was better than fair, it was great. Would you like to try again?"

Chapter Six

BOB RESENTED being taken for granted by Edith. He enjoyed her company, was impressed with her good looks and witty conversation, but he found her sorely wanting when compared to Diane. But there was no way, it seemed, for him to escape. Night after night Edith would ambush him, causing tongues to wag and speculation to mount about his future.

"He's got it made," the office gossips said. "He comes here as Zugsmith's boy and now he has the publisher's daughter after him. He'll probably wind up the next publisher."

That was in the back of Edith's mind, for she had never met anyone like Bob before. He was less possessive and more self-assured than any man she had met. She knew quite well that like many a headstrong rich girl she was the aggressor, but that only made their relationship more dear since she realized Bob was not after her money, or interested in the position he could obtain through her.

She was often tempted to speak to Uncle Zach about Bob's schedule so he wouldn't have to work late, but she knew Bob would resent any favors. She was content to wait for him at least two nights and usually had something planned for his days off. Bob didn't mind at first, but he missed Diane. He didn't want to hurt Edith or his standing on the paper because of his friendship for her, but he was glad when she took off for a tour of the fashion centers of Europe.

Diane had missed him, too. Then her anger returned as she counted the weeks since she had seen him last.

"I thought you had married the boss's daughter," she said when she finally came to his table.

"Not yet, I'm still thinking about it." He was pleased that she cared. Her pleasure at seeing him was apparent, though she tried to appear cool and merely friendly.

"Are you still seeing her?" Diane asked too calmly.

"She's in Europe for a couple of weeks. I might see her when she gets back, though."

"I'm sure you will. Meanwhile, I guess I'm supposed to be grateful you're here."

"I've missed you," Bob said, putting his hand on hers across the table. Her hands were cold and a little shiver ran up Diane's spine as he touched her. She hadn't been prepared for that.

"I missed you, too," she said, her eyes misting as she looked across the table into his eyes. "Oh, Bob," she said, fighting back a sob, "you don't know how I missed you."

He moved into the chair next to her and put his arm around her, his lips touching her cheek. "I really didn't want to bring her here that night. I just didn't want to insult her. After all, she is the publisher's daughter."

"Let me have a handkerchief," Diane said, turning away so Bob wouldn't see the tears in her eyes. She took the handkerchief he offered and wiped her eyes. The mascara came off in a dark splotch.

"I'm sorry," Diane said as she handed back the handkerchief, but she was smiling broadly. "I have to go for the last show. Can you wait?"

Bob squeezed her hand as she got up to go. "I thought we could celebrate tomorrow night on my day off. Do you think you could miss work?"

"Certainly," Diane said quickly, "but what are you celebrating? A birthday?"

"No, an anniversary. I've been a year on the *Record* tonight. I guess I have the job, because everyone is on trial for six months. If they haven't fired me now, I guess they're not going to."

"On trial? For six months? I never heard of anything like that. Either you can do the job in two or three weeks or that's it from all the places I've heard about."

"But *The New York Record* is different. Some men have

been there for twenty years and they still haven't been told they've passed the trial period."

"What about that girl, the publisher's daughter. Did you pass your trial period with her?" Diane's eyes flashed.

"I don't think that's very kind. You know how I feel about you. If it wasn't for you I wouldn't even have taken the job on the *Record*. I didn't stay in New York because of Edith Miller."

"I just wanted to hear you say it; wait for me," she said, bending and kissing him quickly.

Edith's trip to Europe led to a promotion of sorts for Bob, although it was by pure coincidence. Crum needed a man to fill in on the late shift and there was no longer the problem of having Edith hanging around the office waiting for Bob to finish. In effect, his choice of Bob was a vote of confidence and something Zugsmith had wanted for some time. The late man was not chosen lightly. He had to be fast, accurate and dependable. The late shift functioned with one-tenth of the staff working on the early shift and sometimes was called on to perform miracles at the last minute as late news came flooding in from overseas or from Washington.

Bob had heard about the late news breaks. Frequently copy editors had been called back from Curry's to handle a momentous story that appeared in a late extra that went to press at five A.M. Normally the paper would be shut down at three o'clock, but the extra two hours could be gained by rerouting some of the trucks and shipping the papers by plane instead of using trains for the out of town points. As a late man, Bob could go home at three or three-fifteen usually, which meant Diane would be already dressed and waiting for him when he got to the club. She was suspicious at first, since she suspected Edith might be somehow involved.

"Are you sure you aren't spending these extra hours with Miss Publisher and then coming down to see me?"

"You give me credit for more than I deserve. If I could

work all night and then keep two women happy, I'd really be something. Besides, she's still in Europe."

"I thought she was only going to be gone a week. Didn't you tell me her father had an apartment on the top floor? You could take her up there or she could take you up there. It would make things easy for you."

Bob laughed. "I never thought about it, but that might not be a bad idea. I'll have to ask Edith when she gets back."

Bob liked the late shift, even though there were long hours of sitting around. He was on his own for most of the night and he didn't have to argue with Crum about headlines or editing. He knew the assignment to the late shift was a grudging accolade and he enjoyed the chance to get to know Zugsmith's assistants and the men from the other desks.

Much of the work was routine. Corrections had to be made, late inserts put into stories, dispatches updated. On ordinary nights, the volume of copy was never very great or the pressure intense. It was only when the big story broke that the tempo increased, the deadlines loomed faster, and the pressure mounted. For many of the men on the late shift, their presence represented insurance. They would not be needed for any demanding task only in the event of a major disaster, an outbreak of war in one of the new nations or some other event that did not respect ordinary working hours. For these men, many of the nights were filled with chess games, cards, or reading. When Tucker was on late, his typewriter would be going unceasingly, but Bob knew it was only another science-fiction opus in the works.

Bob was surprised to see Zugsmith around late one night. He realized later it was the same night that Helen Crawford was assigned to the late shift. That was it, Bob concluded, but he didn't know the whole story; he really didn't know Zugsmith.

The assistant managing editor was a creature of habit. He had to have so many cigarettes stuck into his long FDR holder before edition time, so many drinks after dinner, so many trips to the water fountain, the precise routine for saying good night to his staff. And with Zugsmith, Wednesday was the day for sex with Helen Crawford. It had been that way for years, for him a release from the tensions of the office and for her a meaningless reminder of her youth when she was filled with romantic notions about newspapers and newspapermen. Those notions had long since deserted Helen Crawford and she had run the gamut from publisher to copy boy in the search for the spark that would have meaning again. She didn't need Zugsmith now and he didn't need her as much as he needed a woman. It was easier for him than with the younger girl reporters or the others in the office. Helen didn't want anything, didn't expect anything.

Helen's late assignments once a month were the only complicating factor. They always came on a Wednesday and Zugsmith would be like a caged lion as he paced in his office or out in the city room while waiting for her to finish. He knew the hotels in the area would be filling up soon and the motels on the outskirts of town were getting very stubborn on accepting taxi traffic since the mayor's latest crackdown—inspired by a *New York Record* editorial. Zugsmith didn't drive, so a trip to Jersey was out; besides, Helen had to get home to the apartment she shared with her sister, and Zugsmith's mother would know he had been out all night. The solution was an accidental one, but it proved practical for Zugsmith, at least for a while.

He was trying to hurry Helen after she had finished her work and was preparing to leave.

"I just have to go to the ladies' room. I won't be a minute," Helen said.

"Hurry it up, will you," Zugsmith said, biting down on his cigarette holder. "The hotels will be filled."

Helen looked at him sadly. He seemed so helpless and weak. "Why don't you come in with me? There's a couch in there and it won't take that long." There was a note of mockery in her voice that Zugsmith didn't catch.

"That's right, but suppose someone comes in?"

"No one will come in at this hour. The cleaning women don't get here until six o'clock and the guards never come in. Come on, it'll be all right." There was a little of the coquette in Helen as she led him into the anteroom where the couch and the make-up tables were arranged around the walls. She thought this would be her final act of defiance of the great *New York Record* tradition. She smiled as she lay back on the couch and Zugsmith snapped out the light by the door.

It was a convenient solution, Zugsmith had to admit. From then on, the Wednesdays Helen had to work were a little more bearable. He didn't have to worry about the hotels, could save room rental, and that was important to Zugsmith, too. He hated paying for a hotel room when he didn't stay the night. It was contrary to the principles of thrift upheld by *The New York Record*.

There were suspicions about Zugsmith's arrangements with Helen, but no one bothered to confirm them. The ladies room was so far removed from the heart of the city room that it would have meant a walk through deserted offices to check on where Zugsmith was going. Besides, it was only once a month and by the third month he had the process devolved to the point where he would put an "Out of Order" sign on the door before going in to meet Helen. When they were finished, they could slip out the back door and get cabs to take them home. It was neat, it was quick, it was stimulating, as if both Helen and Zugsmith knew they were thumbing their noses at the Establishment they were both committed to serve.

Sanford Miller, the publisher, had an arrangement similar to Zugsmith's, but his was much more neat and cozy. With the penthouse apartment at the paper, Miller could entertain in style and frequently did. He could be seen on many nights during the theater season with one or two young show girls in tow, showing them the magic that transformed the written or spoken word into lead images and then into millions of impressions that ultimately would land on breakfast tables across the country. The massiveness of the plant, the work of the composing room, where the girls would have their names cast by an eager linotype operator, the roar of the press room were things to experience. By the time the girls reached the penthouse, their heads were whirling with the great bustling energy of the place that seemed contagious as Miller completed the tour with an intimate glimpse into how the publisher worked.

There were four entrances to the penthouse, each with a status and significance of its own. The first was through the main lobby of the building, where the guards would bow courteously and the elevator operator look straight ahead as the publisher and his guest or guests entered. This was the entrance reserved for large, but decorous groups, which usually stopped to see the city room and the composing room before going up to the penthouse, or, in the case of visiting dignitaries, to the special dining room.

The other entrances were through doors at the three other corners of the building, one leading to a private elevator that went directly to the penthouse, another to a self-service elevator that stopped at every floor, and the last to the freight elevator that would often be used to transport noiser, larger or drunken groups to the publisher's suite for a party that only the freight elevator operator, a faithful retainer well past retirement age, knew was going on, until the next morning when the cleaning crew moved in.

Invariably, Miller used the main lobby on his first tour with a new ingenue. After that, the entrance he used depended on the age of the girl he was with, the hour, his condition and whether he had sent his chauffeur home or not. Without the chauffeur, he would pull his Cadillac with the SM 3 license plate into one of the loading docks and go up the entrance with the self-service elevator that stopped at every floor. That way, the mailers and deliverers would know that the publisher was entertaining again and there was always the risk of running into a late-working executive on one of the other floors. With a special girl, though, and chauffeurless or not, he would leave the Cadillac someplace else and then take a cab to the private entrance lobby for an unheralded and undetected ride to the penthouse.

Mrs. Miller, as Edith had told Bob, seldom came to the paper, except when her vote was needed at board meetings or stockholders conferences. Like her mother before her she had yielded the reins to her husband when he ascended to the post of publisher, but she still retained stock and a large say in the management of the company. But Mrs. Miller was uninterested in the paper except for what it could bring her. She was there on election night, again on New Year's Eve and then infrequently if an outstanding personality was being entertained or shown through in the daytime. She never forgot her role and the Millers gave the outward appearance of the perfect couple when the occasion demanded. They didn't fight and they didn't argue, even when they were alone, which was seldom. They were too mature and both of them realized that theirs was a marriage of convenience similar to the ones that had united the old royalty of Europe. The marriage had given *The New York Record* a publisher with a keen business sense who drove the earnings of the paper to record levels. The record earnings enabled Mrs. Miller to indulge in her love of art and artists so it was really a wonderful arrangement. She sometimes wondered how many other wives who had been the vehicles to provide a publisher for the paper served as she did. The tradition was too rich to be besmirched; they also serve who only . . . only what, she thought, but then she couldn't be bothered.

On the night Sanford Miller's arrangement collided with Zugsmith's, Bob was the late man on the foreign desk. He saw the publisher come into the office, pointing out the various desks where the top writers sat. Bob nodded to the publisher respectfully, trying not to stare at the striking young blonde at his side. She was obviously fresh out of her teens and Bob almost felt sorry for her as she drank in the whole scene with wide-eyed wonder and juvenile exclamations. Miller was half drunk, which wasn't unusual, but that made him only more grand as the host and the guide on the tour. It was like a baron showing his latest courtesan the yard where the serfs worked, Bob thought, bending over a late dispatch from India studiously.

Miller swept the girl through the whole length of the room, all the way back to wire room where a copy boy was uneasily holding the fort. The boy eyed the girl greedily and then turned back to the Western Union ticker as it sprang into life with another inning of the baseball game on the coast. Miller guided the girl around the corner into the darker reaches of the floor, intending to swing around behind the empty departments and take the rear elevator up to the penthouse. As they passed the ladies room, the girl decided she wanted to renew her lipstick. She started to open the door when Miller noticed the out of order sign.

"It's not working. You'd better come upstairs to my apartment."

"I just want to use the mirror, to renew my lipstick," the girl said coyly. "I don't guess the mirrors are broken, are they?"

Miller smiled. She was so young, so delicious. "Hurry up," he said. "I'll wait."

"There's a girl in there with a man," the blonde said almost in disbelief as she emerged from the door almost at once.

"A man in the ladies' room?" Sanford asked incredulously.

He rushed into the anteroom where Helen was trying to pull a slip over her nakedness. Zugsmith had run into the main room, slipped into one of the booths and crouched up on the seat so his legs would not show beneath the partition.

"What are you doing here?" Sanford demanded of Helen. One breast peeked from beneath the slip she held before her. "Where did he go?" Helen said nothing and Miller ran into the other room, looking under the booths for a man's legs. He could see nothing and he walked back to the anteroom, where Helen was still lying naked with only the slip covering her inadequately.

"What are you doing in the ladies room?" she demanded, seizing the initiative. She had known Miller, among many men, years ago. She still was taken by his good looks, but she knew she had to be bold.

"The young lady said there was a man in here. I came to look."

"The only man I see is you. You are a man, aren't you? I remember you used to be, anyway."

"It's been a long time, Helen, how are you?"

"I'm well, but you always said I was good. Would you like to er—reminisce a bit?"

Miller looked at her, a sudden uneasiness stirring in him. He had been younger then and so had she, but she was not unattractive now. The tension he had built up on the tour of the plant with the simpering young blonde at his side was still in him and the sight of Helen on the couch made him more eager. After all, why not? It was his paper . . . .

"Stay right where you are," he said sternly but not unkindly.

Miller walked out the door where the young blonde was waiting. "I'm sorry, my dear," he said, "there's a slight disciplinary problem I have to attend to. It won't take a minute. Take the elevator up to my apartment. I'll be up directly." He walked back through the door as the blonde stared.

As he walked back into the anteroom, Miller snapped out the light. He fumbled his way to the couch in the dark and never heard Zugsmith sneak past from the other room. Miller was too busy, too preoccupied, but suddenly he gave a cry as if he had been stabbed.

"What the hell is that?" he said, his hands darting to the point of pain. "Oh," he said, "a cigarette holder, I might have known. Damn Zugsmith anyway."

93

Chapter Seven

AS LATE man on the foreign desk, Bob had a chance to become acquainted, in a distant way, with many of the foreign correspondents. *The New York Record* had built its reputation on foreign news and the paper was always boasting of being the first to get an interview with a revolutionary leader, the first to enter a city after a battle, the first to foreshadow the fall of a government. The foreign staff was huge, with full-time correspondents in sixty-two countries and part-timers, those who also covered for the Associated Press, Reuters or another paper, numbering in the hundreds. Because Bob was on when the flow of messages had dribbled to a trickle, he often received personal notes to be passed on to the foreign editor, to Zugsmith or even the correspondent's wife. He in turn communicated with the correspondents by letting them know what stories had been used on the front page and where their dispatches were used, with the type of a headline and the length. The system was like a Neilsen rating for the correspondent, with the eager ones striving to capture the office's eye with a page-one dispatch and the uneager ones wondering how little work they could get away with.

In many cases the correspondents were merely at listening posts, where news might develop. Here, though, Crum felt that they should be earning their money, too, and he would frequently lash them with abusive cables when he didn't think they were covering the beat. "Isn't there any news in all of Norway?" he cabled one correspondent, who was too busy chasing blondes to care much about keeping his ear to the ground. When the hard news was scarce, Crum wanted feature stories about how the people lived, what made their fashions, or the like. "If I were out there, I'm sure I could find something to write about every day," he told Bob as he left instructions to send another prodding message.

Bob wasn't surprised by the records of some of the men because of the selection process on the paper. He had assumed at first that foreign correspondents had to be proved internationalists with many contacts abroad to qualify to represent *The New York Record* overseas, but such was not the case. There were many men overseas who did have countless sources in the countries they covered, but their replacements or the men being sent to the many new trouble spots—for trouble was news to *The New York Record*—had no such background. The foreign correspondents were recruited from the ranks of the city reporters. Uusually it was those Zugsmith thought showed a flair for dramatic writing, but that was not the sole criterion.

The man's marital status—a bachelor was always preferred for overseas assignments—his language aptitude, and his willingness to go were the principal qualifications. According to Tucker, the language requirement was the most important, but if Zugsmith really wanted to send some one overseas, a cram course at the Berlitz School would usually get the correspondent by. There was no need to worry that all he might be able to do would be to order in a restaurant and find out where the rest room was. There were always faithful retainers around all the offices of *The New York Record* and these natives guided the men from New York and kept them informed of what was happening in the country. The correspondent was like the white man's presence in the outposts of the empire. He was to be obeyed and cared for, but respected? That was too much to ask when he could not read the language, sometimes could not even get a telephone number without the aid of the clerk or the secretary in the bureau. The aides would take care of everything except the filing of expense vouchers and the collection of the pay checks. This was one skill that all correspondents had carefully cultivated.

Of course, the selection of the correspondent depended on

the post, too. In the prestige posts, Paris, London, Berlin or Moscow, the requirements were more demanding. The correspondent had to look like a *New York Record* man and act like one, associating with the proper political leaders and keeping a pipeline to high places for the latest information. In some cases, *The New York Record* could not supply its own men for these posts and had to hire men away from other newspapers or the wire service to fill the role adequately.

For the smaller and less impressive posts, those without hot water or even running water, the principal characteristic seemed to be stamina. These were the hardship posts where a man would stay only a year and then get three months at home. The plushier posts were two-year assignments where a man could take his family with ease and expose his children to the broadening element of a foreign culture, a school in another land. These posts had all the conveniences of civilization: press aides, news conferences, briefings, and numerous government officials to quote. The hardship posts had terrible communications, local press censorship and uncooperative officials. To many of the nations, the reporters were intruders to be tolerated, but nothing more. The result was that frustration was often evident in the unintelligible gibberish the cable operator sent over the wires to the dispatch point. When the gibberish of the reporter's frustration combined with the errors of the operator and then the shorthand of cables, the result was like a riddle that defied solution.

In most cases, the wire services—United Press International, Associated Press and Reuters—would be available to check on the intent of the story. But the wire services often got their information from the same source as *The New York Record* correspondent and the added material proved little help.

Rules of thumb helped the men on the desk, Bob learned: When in doubt, take it out; always go with our man, even if you think he's wrong. When the dispatch of a *New York Record* correspondent differed from that of one of the news services, the second version would be appended to the first so that the reader might decide for himself which was correct. The problem was that the headline would be based on the correspondent's idea of the news. Headline readers who did not pursue the length dispatches to the end would receive an entirely different version of the news than might actually be the case.

This was playing it safe. If a decision was made by Tom Crum, Bob knew, Crum would run the risk of using the wrong dispatch. If he used both dispatches, he could always shift the blame to the correspondent or the wire service so long as no decision had been made. Inaccuracy was never entirely the fault of the correspondent. Frequently, the correspondents were deliberately fed the wrong information as some source tried to launch a trial balloon or sought to achieve some end. In other cases, the correspondent would get a story from a translator who could not find the exact nuances for the English meanings and therefore distortion would be introduced. The correspondent, even if he had the language facility, could not check on everything himself, even in the top posts, where all of the press aides and government contacts spoke English.

Errors in the stories were seldom blamed on the correspondents, though. The desk was the scapegoat under Zugsmith's system. If a date was wrong or a fact mis-stated, Crum would receive a memo asking why the copy editor hadn't checked the story. In Zugsmith's view, Crum was responsible, but Tom quickly shifted the blame to the man who had handled the story. When praise was due on a story, the praise would go not to the copy editor, who like Bob had fleshed out Lexford's dispatches and breathed life into them, but to the writer who only vaguely recognized the sentences cited or the paragaphs praised. Lexford wasn't the only one who was saved or helped by the desk; there were few writers who required only the insertion of the articles and the marking of the paragraphs. The men on the desk had to know how to fill in the holes in stories, how to strengthen a lead, when to let the story run and when to cut. Unfortunately, their professionalism was tempered by the cult of length that often demanded even the most insignificant foreign dispatch run at least a column.

Stephen Farrington Barnes was probably destined to be a foreign correspondent because his name fascinated Conrad Clements, the editorial personnel man, but Bob helped things along, too. Barnes' name caught Clements eye on his letter of application and all Clements could see was that great by-line name for *The New York Record*. Stephen Farrington Barnes! It was a name that spelled class, it was a natural for the paper. Clements hardly glanced at the rest of Barnes' application. It listed service on some of the top small papers in the country, but significantly each of the jobs Barnes held was for a short time. Clements would have been unconcerned, even if the warning had been more apparent: the trial system would wash him out if he wasn't capable; but how could a man help but be capable with a name like that.

Because he was from out of town, Barnes was assigned to start on the city desk. "It's just until you get to know the routine and learn a little about the city," Clements assured him. Barnes was undisturbed. He had been an assistant city editor, a wire editor, a feature writer, a columnist, he said; one more new job would not make any difference.

Barnes was a wizened little man with a rat-like face. He was scarcely forty, but his weathered skin made him appear older. His small bright eyes were constantly shifting behind the huge glasses he wore. His sharp nose, tiny chin and thin mustache added to the rat-look characterized by the quick twists of his head to see if anyone was listening as he talked. To hear Barnes talk, Bob found, was a revelation. He had been everywhere, seen everything, and done everything and better than anyone else. He never smiled; everything was a smirk or an exasperated obscenity. He didn't last the full time Clements had planned on the city desk for the slot man thought Barnes's knowledge of languages would be more helpful on the foreign desk.

For the first few days, Barnes was reserved as he was introduced to the routine of the desk. He seemed nervous and unsure of himself when reading copy, but Bob knew this was common with new men. It was only after a week on the desk that Barnes began to relax and to accompany the other copy editors to Curry's for lunch. It was in Curry's that Bob first learned that Barnes was the greatest athlete, the greatest newspaperman, and the greatest lover in history. He had a way of emphasizing his statements that made them unforgettable.

"I speak six fucking languages and look at the shit they got me reading," Barnes said to Bob on his second week on the desk.

"Any fucking ass hole with a high school diploma could read that shit," Barnes persisted. Bob grew more uncomfortable. He was afraid to say anything for fear of prolonging the conversation, which Barnes had initiated in the first place.

"Well, it's all part of the routine," Bob said. He wondered if Clements had gone beyond Barnes's resume; if he had really spoken to the new man.

"They call these fucking guys correspondents? I could write better shit than that fucking stuff when I was in grammar school."

None of the crowd from the paper was exactly prudish, but Barnes used the words with the relish of a seven-year-old scrawling them on the side of a building. He evidently thought the language of the gutter was the accepted one in Curry's. Naturally, the words were not unknown there, but Barnes was right in one thing; he was the best, or at least the most adept at using them. Hardly a sentence of his could be uttered without one or both of his favorite words. They became his trademark on the desk and many men believed that the initials in his name: S. F. Barnes, stood for something other than Stephen Farrington.

But Barnes attempted to dominate every conversation, no

matter who had started it or chosen the topic. If some one on the desk was talking about sports, Barnes would recall that he had once played golf, (played football, played baseball, bowled, skied, or whatever) against "that fucking guy and I beat his ass off." According to Barnes, he could have been a golf pro, a tennis pro, a boxer, a baseball star, a football star or anything else. He had all the qualifications of a superman, he didn't hesitate to tell the men on the desk, but he just couldn't stand "that professional shit."

Bob in his thorough midwestern way attempted to pin Barnes down to dates and places for the triumphs he scored, but the man was too elusive for that. Anything that could be checked was glossed over as a mistake. "There's so much fucking water over the goddamned dam that I don't remember all that shit," he'd say.

If it had just been a question of Barnes's modifiers, no one would have minded too much. The problem was that Barnes's dislike of work was as deeply rooted as his repulsive personality and it soon became apparent to all the men on the desk that Barnes was not doing his share. Just what a man's share was on the desk was hard to determine because some could work twice as fast and turn out three times as much copy as others. When it came to the point where Barnes was taking two hours for one story and a headline, though, Crum realized he could not be counted on to produce anything. The copy he did edit had to be gone over carefully. He still hadn't caught on to the style of the paper and the many nuances in Zugsmith's memos escaped him completely.

"What's all that shit?" Barnes asked when Bob showed him the stack of Zugsmith's memos.

"It's a series of notices Zugsmith has put out on ways to improve the editing and writing. It's like a brickbat and bouquet thing; if you rate a bow it's a puff; if you boot one, it's a fluff."

"There must be two hundred fucking pages there. It seems like an awful lot of chicken shit to me."

"Some of it is pretty hair-splitting, but at least you might get an idea of some of the ways we do things here."

"Yeah, what the fuck? I thought you guys just had to put in the fucking paragraph marks, but some of those sorry bastards write awful shit."

Bob had no idea if Barnes ever read the memos. His copy editing didn't improve and Crum soon relegated him to the reading of the one and two paragraph shorts used as fillers. There was little background to be lost on such material. Accuracy was almost automatic since few things could go wrong in two or three paragraphs. The system gave Barnes considerable time to sit around and read the paper or do crossword puzzles. This meant the rest of the men had to work harder to take up the slack that Barnes represented. On the table of organization he was a copy editor and the formula was that x number of copy editors could read x columns in a night regardless of whether "the best fucking copy editor on *The New York Record*"—as Barnes regarded himself—was working or not. At first the men were amused by the situation, but Crum realized he was running into a morale problem.

He complained to Clements, hoping for relief, but Crum had the reputation for complaining about so many men he wasn't taken seriously. Clements had long realized that many of the complaints Tom made sprang from his inability to handle men properly. Besides, *The New York Record* never fired anyone, except for drunkenness. Stephen Farrington Barnes certainly was no drunk. Next month, Clements thought, Crum will be complaining about someone else.

Things got so bad that Crum confided in Bob.

"How is Barnes late at night?" Tom asked as he was briefing Bob on the later stories to be expected.

"I try to keep him busy with an advance that doesn't have to make the edition. That way he doesn't have a chance to talk and then I can go over the editing when he goes home."

"That's a good idea, but it wouldn't work on the early shift. He's awful, you know and all that talking he does. It's driving

101

a couple of the men to stop drinking. They don't go to Curry's any more because they think they might run into Barnes."

Suddenly Bob had an inspiration. "Didn't I hear that Collins was sick in the Congo and had to have a replacement?"

"Yes, why?" Crum asked. "Are you interested in going out there?"

"No, I'm not, but how about Barnes? French is one of the languages he says he speaks, so why not suggest to Zugsmith that he would be a good one to send. It would be a great by-line and he might not be too bad, if he really has some of the experience he says."

"He knows the language," Crum said, half to himself. He was toying with the idea and weighing the disadvantages of having a poor correspondent against having trouble on the desk. "It might just work. He can't be much worse than some of our other stars and it has a certain enchantment to it."

"You mean the by-line, Stephen Farrington Barnes?"

"No, the fact that he'd be five thousand miles away."

Bob had the assignment of selling Barnes on the plan. Crum was certain that Zugsmith would agree because of the understandable shortage of correspondents willing to go to the Congo. Clements, of course, would be no problem; he could hardly wait for the Barnes by-line to appear.

Despite Barnes's desire to get off the desk, Bob didn't have an easy job. He started slowly, with stories about the glamour a foreign correspondent enjoyed. Then he started telling Barnes about the lovely young Belgian girls in the Congo. When he saw a spark of interest begin to glow, Bob added that unfortunately the assignment would involve two weeks of indoctrination in Paris.

At last Bob moved Barnes to the point where he agreed to ask for the job. "After all," he said, "with your command of language, you should get along great over there. You'll probably show up the other men the first month."

"Yeah," Barnes agreed innocently, "I might even get the fucking Pulitzer Prize."

His departure from the desk was hardly noticed. Usually when a man left there was a small party in the office and then some more drinks at Curry's until early in the morning. Barnes just slipped away, the sudden silence in Curry's the next night being the only barometer of his departure.

When he started filing his dispatches from Leopoldville, they weren't bad; not good, but not bad. "It doesn't read like Barnes without all those four-letter words," Bob said to Crum.

The principal shortcoming with Barnes' dispatches was that they were usually a day behind the wire services. That wasn't unusual, but to be a day late consistently made Zugsmith wonder. He had Crum prod Barnes daily with messages urging an earlier filing time, but there was no reaction. The prodding grew more intense, with a message going out from New York every day for a month. The times when Barnes would reply he would blame transmission troubles, but he was at a loss to explain why the wire services and the other papers with correspondents in the Congo were able to get their stories in on time. The mystery deepened when Barnes suddenly stopped filing. After two weeks of using the services, Zugsmith called Crum into his office to tell him that a new correspondent had been hired in the Congo. The new man was ending a tour for Reuters there and would report to New York for a short course in procedures before returning.

"Whatever happened to Barnes?" Crum asked, uncertainly.

"I got a telegram with his resignation yesterday," Zugsmith said. "He's out on the Coast now working for some radio station."

"Why didn't he wire that he was quitting before leaving the Congo?"

"I don't know. Perhaps when Schmidt comes in for his indoctrination you can ask him."

Schmidt was a pleasant Swiss national who whistled his "s" sounds. Bob introduced him to the crowd at Curry's on his first night on the desk. Bob was eager to find out what had happened to Barnes.

"Barnes?" Schmidt said, the word ending like escaping steam. "Oh, yes, that was that crazy man you had out there."

"He was sort of wild, wasn't he? But he could speak the language, he said, so we thought he'd turn out to be all right."

"Speak the language? Not French, or at least not that I heard. The only French I heard Barnes speak was the profanity he used in trying to get the Telex operators to send his dispatches. I remember he said to me: 'You have to let these fucking wogs know who's boss or else they'll shit all over you.' He didn't know that the Telex operators all spoke English."

"So what happened?" Bob could visualize the scene as the little rat-faced man flayed away at the natives.

"Nothing just then. The Telex operators always put his dispatches on the bottom of the pile. Sometimes he wasn't filed until the next day."

"That explains how his file was always late," Bob said with a smile. "I thought that he was cribbing from the other dispatches and that was why he was late."

"No, he insisted on getting his own stuff and wouldn't take any tips from any of us. Out there, you know, it's pretty much a cooperative thing. We trade notes and quotes and everything, but not Barnes. His insistence on looking for a scoop was really what led to his exit from Leopoldville."

"Do you know why he left?" Bob had been waiting all night to ask.

"It was a very big story. Barnes learned there was a cult of civil servants who were interested in purging the country of what the members called 'bad elements.' The plan was for when the Congo is independent. It's sort of like a Belgian version of the Mau Mau, I suppose."

"Did Barnes ever file the story? I don't remember reading it?"

Schmidt smiled benignly. "No, he never did file the story. He left in too big a hurry. He found out the cult had a list of those who were to be killed on freedom day. He contacted a member of the organization and right after that he took off.

He flew into the hotel, packed his bag, and caught the afternoon plane out. I understand he is back in this country now."

"But why did he leave? It seems sort of strange."

"Well, when he looked on the death list, the first name was Stephen Farrington Barnes. He turned so pale and ran so fast I don't think he even let the office know until he was back in Paris."

"He should have filed the story from Paris. He was safe."

"By that time Zugsmith had the whole story. He knew all about it."

"He didn't print it, though. I wonder why."

"It's simple," Schmidt whistled. "There was no cult. It was made up by the correspondents and some Congo officials to frighten Barnes. We never expected him to run so fast or so far, though. We were just trying to shut him up. He had an awful mouth, you see."

Bob laughed quietly to himself. "That's why we maneuvered him into the Congo job. We sort of worked a hoax, too. How did you know so much about it, though. Were you in on the plot?"

"Not really," Schmidt said, "I only typed the death list."

Chapter Eight

BARNES WAS an accident, Bob knew, and the paper could really not be blamed. Strangely enough, though, the best correspondent *The New York Record* ever had was no longer writing. Eliot P. Lowell had won two Pulitzer Prizes for foreign reporting before he was thiry-five. He was the epitome of *The New York Record* man, dedicated, hard driving, and competent to an almost unctuous degree. He should have won a third Pulitzer, but he caused the paper so much embarrassment over the way his potential prize-winner turned out he was not nominated. Instead he was banished to the frigid inner reaches of the editorial board, where he was assigned a meaningless research task for a book that would never be written. *The New York Record* wanted to keep Eliot P. Lowell far away from the pickets calling him and the paper Communist. The publisher hoped the pickets would go away or that Lowell would rebel at the make-work project he was on and resign. But no such luck.

"Why doesn't he resign?" Bob asked Tucker in Curry's one night when they were discussing Lowell.

"He's too proud," the rewrite man said. "He's convinced he was right despite public opinion and is determined not to quit so long as one voice or one picket sign is raised against him. I guess you could say he's stubborn, too, but I think he's just too much *New York Record*. He's never worked any place else, although he's had a lot of offers. He's too young to retire, too."

"I wonder if any other papers would really want him." Bob knew the correspondent had cost the paper many readers because of his support of a Latin American government that turned Communist. Lowell was widely attacked as an agent of

Moscow and seldom a week went by without some demonstration against him and the paper or a series of scathing letters to the editor.

"Yes," Tucker agreed. "That Communist thing has hurt him a lot. Communism wasn't too popular at the time."

"Was it ever?"

"It used to be with the college kids when Lowell was going to school. All the kids wanted to save the world. You know, join the party and free the masses. I doubt that Lowell ever joined the party, but there were quite a few Communist cells in his school and certainly active interest."

"You sound as if you knew him pretty well."

"I did. I still do. He left me far behind so far as writing goes, but we still get together for a drink each Christmas or New Years."

Bob was interested. Tucker was obviously in a talking mood and Bob had another hour before he could meet Diane. "Tell me about him, what sort of a man is he?"

"If I tell you that, I'd have to tell you the whole Eliot P. Lowell story. I don't think you have time for that."

"I'll buy the drinks while you do the talking. We can quit when I run out of money or you pass out."

"It's a long story," Tucker said quietly, his jaws snapping together firmly. "If you're going to buy the drinks you better start now."

Eliot P. Lowell started on *The New York Record* as a City College correspondent. He had a flair for writing and his accounts of the weak City College teams competing against superior rivals made good copy. The writing gave Lowell a certain status on the campus and the extra money provided him with the accouterments to go with that status. He wore a beard long before beards were common on campus and carried a gold-headed cane he found in a Bowery junk shop. The cane was more for protection than show, for Lowell was always frail and the target for toughs on the campus and at night, when he patrolled rough neighborhoods in search of items for the three papers he represented while still in college.

There was no doubt in anyone's mind that Lowell would go to work for *The New York Record* when he was graduated. He started in sports because his links from college had been mainly to that department, but few people expected him to be confined to the world of athletics. In the few years he worked in the department, though, he set a standard for excellence that still hadn't been matched. If he was writing about football, he would don a uniform and work out with the team; or if he was writing about a star pitcher, he would try to bat against the pitches that baffled the professionals. He sparred with boxing champions, sat as a co-driver in an Indianapolis racing car, braved the dangers of the Olympic bobsled run to bring life and vitality to the sports pages that no one else could.

When he was transferred to the city room, the pattern was repeated. Lowell had a new angle on everything, politics, labor, crime or whatever he was sent to cover. His writing was bright, his stories never dull even though they ran for columns and columns as was the style in those days. In Europe, Africa, and Asia it was a string of more triumphs for Lowell. The stimulus of new places, his inherent curiosity, and industry spurred him on. The two Pulitzer Prizes were only some of his rewards, for Lowell wrote scores of articles for magazines and three books and was in heavy demand as a lecturer. In the end, though, it was his early link to sports and sports heroes that proved his undoing.

The sports hero Eliot P. Lowell was closest to was Carlos Guzman Leche. Carlos was a happy-go-lucky Latin who had been rescued from washing dishes in a Broadway hash house by a scholarship to City College arranged by the wrestling coach. The coach had seen Carlos eject two drunks from the restaurant with almost embarrassing ease and he dreamed of making the short round youth with the arms of steel a great wrestler and football player.

Carlos was great in wrestling, where it was man against man, strength against strength. In football, though, where his savagery was curbed by the rules and, where psychology played such an important role in the fakes and feints of the ball carriers, Carlos was lost. One memorable varsity game in the record books tells of 120 yards of penalties assessed against Carlos for gouging, punching, or kneeing his opponents. That marked his retirement from football and the beginning of his concentration on wrestling.

But even great wrestlers had to pass the minimum number of courses. To help Carlos get through, the coach arranged for him to room with Lowell, who loved sports and was particularly fond of Carlos. Carlos was a mass of muscle, with a broad, ugly, friendly face. Lowell was almost gaunt, handsome, even in his beard, with an inquisitive look that seemed to challenge the world to give up its secrets. Although Lowell tried hard to drill Carlos before each test, he flunked out after the wrestling season and turned to the professional sport.

Lowell followed his career through the preliminary events to the main contest at the Garden, when the "world championship" was at stake. Then there was a period of eclipse because Carlos could not be persuaded by the promoters that it was necessary to lose once in a while, to "arrange" things, so the gates would get bigger and the sport could grow. After his money ran out, Carlos was convinced and soon he was in the spotlight once more, winning more than he lost, taking the falls and dishing out the punishment, raking in the money and spending it even faster, enjoying the good life with not a thought of home or his people clouding his own good fortune.

Carlos had been retired a long time when Lowell met him on a Latin American tour that the correspondent specifically planned to include Carlos' country.

"Amigo," Carlos called happily as Lowell walked to his table in a small sidewalk cafe in Carlos' hometown. He sprang from the table and buried Lowell in a bear hug that made his ribs ache.

"Take it easy," Lowell said, struggling to get free. "I know you're glad to see me, but you don't have to put me in the hospital to prove it."

Carlos put him down gently, his eyes beaming. The years had been kind to the old wrestler, his stomach was not as flat as it had been and his hair, what little there was left, was white, but the mark of strength still shone on Carlos' face and his body.

"I am sorry, amigo, forgive me. It has been so long since I have seen you. I have read of you much, though, all the time. You are even bigger than when you were covering my wrestling. You are number one in the press, just as I am number one here in my hometown."

Lowell looked Carlos over carefully. "The years have been kind to you, my friend. You look as if you could still take on Londos or any other of your old rivals. What are you doing now?"

"Oh, I still wrestle a bit, but only against local heroes. Some are pretty strong, but they are no match for old Carlos. The way they wrestle in the states is different from the way it is done here and there are many tricks the young foxes have to learn before they can beat Carlos with all their strength. I do it really to make people laugh. I don't need the money, *el Presidente* has made me commissioner of sports and my salary is good. I referee the boxing bouts once in a while in the capital and settle arguments among the promoters and the boxers, but that is all. Mostly, I am retired. I drink when I want to, sleep as long as I like and make love when I can. It is a good life, no?"

Lowell was disappointed. He always thought Carlos could accomplish great good among his people. He was a natural leader and the hero worship could have easily led to a position where Carlos could lift the country into modern times.

"It is a good life for another man, perhaps, but not for Carlos Guzman Leche. For the Carlos I knew, it is an empty life, a bad life, a wasted life."

"Why do you say that, amigo? Ah, I see. You are up to your old tricks again. There is something on your mind, something you want me to do. What is it, my crafty amigo?"

"If you can honestly tell me you are happy with this clown's life, I would not speak. But I am thinking of you, my friend, and your pride. Wrestling local strong boys is no work for Carlos Guzman Leche, the greatest wrestler in the world, the world champion . . ."

"World champion, ah yes," Carlos said, his eyes brightening even more. "I remember how happy I was that night. A man gave me a great jewel encrusted belt and the pictures were in all the papers the next day. After the pictures appeared, the man came and took back the belt. I thought it was mine to keep: I was the champion. But champions were not always true to the pictures in the paper or to the jewels in the belt. I was honest, you know that, but they told me there would be no work for the wrestlers, the arenas would be shut and people would go hungry if the bouts could not be arranged, as you say, fixed. I would not let them do it to me, I fought them and went on winning. But finally no one wanted me. There was another world champion and then I knew things had to be arranged. I learned to lose, or at least to make it appear that I had lost. True, some of them were younger and meaner than I, but . . ."

"Meaner? Who ever said Carlos Guzman Leche was mean? Rough, yes; mean, no."

"But I was mean, amigo, don't you see. I often think how mean it was of me to waste all that money. I had fun, I bought cars and clothes and girls and threw the money away while back here in my land babies were starving, people were going hungry. That money could have helped my people. I learned, too late, how mean I had been. Alas, there was nothing I could do."

Lowell looked at Carlos intently. He could see the old wrestler was sincere. "I am glad to learn, my friend, that you have a conscience. There is much you can do; it is not too late. That is what I meant when I said wrestling was not the job for you. There are better things you can do to help your people."

Carlos rolled his eyes and shook his head hopelessly. "Where are those jobs? I would like to have one, but they are not in my country, I fear."

"What I mean is that you should go into politics."

Carlos started to laugh, quietly at first and then uproariously as his whole body shook and the glasses on the table bounced.

"But I am in politics. I am the sports commissioner. Thanks to *el Presidente*. That is as high as I can go."

"Not an appointment. I mean run for mayor. As mayor there is much you could do to help the people in your town. Maybe later you could be governor of the province and help still more people. Then, the people might decide that Carlos Guzman Leche has helped so many of us he should be president."

"Oh no, amigo. Please do not get me started laughing again. No one gets to be Mayor or Governor unless *el Presidente* wants him to be Mayor or Governor. And no one gets to be *el Presidente* until this one dies, you know that my friend. You have written much about my country and her neighbors."

"Yes, Carlos, but you have the leadership these people need. You could do so much for your people that the President has refused to do. You know as well as I that he is stealing from the taxes and not putting the money to work as he should be doing. He . . ."

Carlos held his finger to his lips, looking over his shoulder before speaking in a low voice. "*El Presidente* knows you do not like him, amigo. He thinks you are here to write bad things about him and our country. He even asked me to speak to you and ask you not to be too hard on him. *The New York Record* is a powerful paper. He fears it will cost him some of the money he gets from your government. Your paper is not government-owned, amigo, is it? No, good, but down here we think it is like *Izvestia*, the Russian paper. Whatever *Izvestia* says, the Russians do; whatever *The New York Record* says, the United States government does, too."

Lowell was surprised that Carlos still clung to that notion after having lived in New York. "It's not that simple; sometimes I wish it were. But I'm afraid the government does what it wants regardless of what *The New York Record* says."

"Mr. Hearst's war with Spain made us afraid of newspapers in your country. We do not want another 'Remember the Maine.' We must be careful not to anger the Gringos to the north. That is what *el Presidente* told me. He asked me to do what he called public relations. He said: 'You must convince Eliot P. Lowell that our people live happily in a democratic state.' He said that, but I cannot ask you to do that. It is too much like 'arranging'; it is not honest. It is not honest for me to ask or for you to write something you do not believe."

"It is good to see you have lost none of your honesty. It will stand you well in politics."

"Please, amigo, do not make jokes. Politics are foreign to me; I am not like *el Presidente.*"

"But that's precisely the point. You are not like him, you are so much better. The people love you, you know that. *El Presidente?* He's tolerated merely because he has the guns, the army and the money. He is no worse than his predecessors, not that he wants to be worse, but the world has changed. You can't steal a million a week today. The world is watching and even Uncle Sam wants to see where some of his money is going. Trade agreements can be cancelled, loans ended and grants changed unless there is some semblance of democracy here. But you know, my friend, it is just a pretense."

Carlos was rapt. He did not speak for a moment until he was sure Lowell had finished. "Amigo, you have the magic of words, whether you write them or speak them. It was as if we were back in college and you were telling me about the many things wrong with the world. But your world, it is good. You

113

are at the top and still rising. What do you do next? Already you tell presidents and emperors what to do. Where do you go from here?"

"This is my last stop and then it's back to New York. I hope to write a series about Latin America. When I come to the article on your country I hope I can write that Carlos Guzman Leche, the great champion, has started a new career. He is working to free his country from dictatorship; he has entered politics."

"You cannot write that, amigo. *El Presidente* a dictator? I know and you know it is the truth, but if you write that after talking to me, *el Presidente* will say I failed in my public relations. It would be very bad for me."

"Why do you fear him? You once told me you feared no living thing. Is *el Presidente* some sort of an evil spirit?"

"Times change, amigo. The fire of our youth is replaced by the fear of our old age. The no living thing that is feared in your twenties becomes only a few living things in your thirties and then not very many living things in your forties. Besides, *el Presidente* has always been good to me. He has the money and the troops and the guns, as you say, but he has been good to me."

"Tell me, my friend, which comes first: The money, the guns, or the Army?"

"Eh? Of course, the money. That is our tradition: if you have the money, you can get the Army and if you get the Army you get the guns. The man who rules the Army rules our country."

"So all you need is money? Where did *el Presidente* get his money from? I thought he was just a poor farmer."

Carlos scratched his head, trying to recall *el Presidente's* rise to power. He was in the United States then and the details were not clear. "It is true he was a farmer, but a most wise farmer. He saw how bad things were under the old *Presidente* and he warned the big farmers the people would revolt unless there was a change. The big farmers knew this smart farmer could make big trouble, so they gave him money. The big farmers wanted to be on the right side if there was a change in government and there did seem to be restlessness among the people."

"Why don't you go to the big farmers and tell them the same thing. If *The New York Record* says that the people are restless, won't the big farmers believe it more easily?"

"Yes, it is true. But I am not the one to go to the farmers. I do not have the magic in my voice *el Presidente* does. My strength is in my arms, in my body. I cannot go to the farmers and say, 'I'll break your arms unless you give me money to help our people.' They would call the militia and everyone would say, 'Carlos is going mad; I knew it would happen some day from all those blows on the head.' "

"My friend," Lowell said kindly, "I think you underestimate yourself. You could find the magic in your voice if you wanted. The Carlos Guzman Leche I knew always could find a way to do things if he really wanted to do them. Are you different now? You are heavier, true, and balder, but your heart is the same, you have shown me this. The only magic you need comes from within you, where truth is shaking your soul in an effort to get out."

Carlos shook his head sadly. "It is nice to dream of a man on a white horse armed with the lance of truth and slaying the fiery dragon that keeps people in misery. But these are North American dreams. They are impossible here. You call us Latins dreamers, but it is you who are the dreamers; you are not practical. Here we live within the framework of our limitations. We do not expect miracles or hope for the impossible."

Lowell knew how to play Carlos like a violin. "You are hopeless, then? Dispirited? Defeated?"

"No one defeats Carlos Guzman Leche," he said, his eyes flashing, his face flushing. "You remember that from many years ago, do you not, amigo? 'You can beat me, but not defeat me.' You yourself said that when I left the college. I have remembered it always."

"But if you're not defeated, you can do what I suggest. You can get the money and then the Army and then the guns. You can be *el Presidente* and help your people instead of stealing from them. Would you deny your people their chance?"

Carlos rubbed his chin reflectively. He thought he was no longer interested in risks or in being anything more than a former hero. But Lowell's words made sense and held out the promise of greatness Carlos never imagined. "Eliot P. Lowell, you are a voodoo man. You take a man's words and thoughts and twist them and rearrange them until they come out the way you want. This must be your genius at work. You have made me think my friend, think hard. But there are people I must see, friends I must talk to before I decide. I will let you know what my decision shall be. If it is the right one, I shall need your help; if it is the wrong one, I shall need your protection."

Lowell was back in New York writing his series when the news services flashed word that Carlos Guzman Leche had robbed a bank in his native land. Leche, the dispatch said, had been pursued into the hills by government troops. Lowell had no difficulty in slipping away from his Army guide when he arrived to search out the hiding place of Carlos. After that it was easy. All the natives seemed to know Lowell and they speeded him along from clearing to clearing in relays, almost as if they had been expecting him.

At last they arrived in Carlos' camp, a high mountain glen approachable only through a narrow path winding down from the steep sides of the mountain. Carlos was sleeping in a hammock strung between trees when Lowell walked into the glen, his clothes stained with sweat and caked with mud.

"Amigo," Carlos exclaimed, his feet swinging down from the hammock gracefully as he glided forward to meet Lowell. His stomach was flatter and his movements smoother than the day in the sidewalk cafe. "You did come," he said, "I was afraid the troops would keep you away. Many troops have tried to find me, but all have failed. Perhaps it is that my friends do not give the troops so good directions as they give you."

Lowell was angry, or at least half angry. "When I told you to get the money, I didn't mean to rob a bank. Now you're nothing but a common thief. You've done yourself more harm than good."

"How can you say that, amigo? Have you not heard of Robin Hood? And what of Jesse James, your own western hero? Did he not rob banks?"

"Yes, but Jesse James never ran for anything except away from a sheriff. And Robin Hood never won anything except an archery contest."

"But they were heroes, no?"

"Yes, they were heroes, but how does that help you?"

"You said yourself I was a national hero, no? Well, I am still a national hero. The money I took from the bank I have given to the poor, just like Robin Hood. Now if I need an army, the people will be my army."

"But you're a fugitive. You'd never be able to unseat the President from out here in the mountains. Half the Army is looking for you. How do you expect to win over these men who have been sent to track you down? Besides, if you've given away the money, what can you use to buy the Army?"

"This is where you come in, amigo," Carlos said steadily, his voice calm but commanding. "Remember my job of public relations? Now you must write in *The New York Record* that Carlos Guzman Leche is raising an army with the money he has expropriated from the National Bank. Already some of the Army have come to me and told me that they want to help me. See? They think I have the money. Your story will convince them and others, too."

Lowell looked at his friend dumbfounded. "I couldn't write that. It isn't true. Wait a minute, did you say some of the Army has come to you, deserted the President?"

"It is true, I swear it. Many of the men you see around my camp here were in the Army last month. Now they are with me. I told them that when we overthrow *el Presidente,* I will promote them all to sergeant and give them raises. They like that. They were tired of *el Presidente's* Army anyway. Some of them haven't had their shoes off the way you see them now for years."

"Not all these men were in the Army, were they, Carlos?"

"No, some are from my village. They are the ones who helped me rob the bank. It was not supposed to cause so much trouble as it did. We had made arrangements that we would walk in, everyone would lie down on the floor and we would walk out without any trouble. The day we had planned, though, the manager became sick and a replacement was sent down from the capital. He was not one of us and he would not lie down when he was told. Naturally, he knew me and we were hardly out the door before he escaped from his bonds and called the militia. That is why I had to hide in the mountains. I could not let your plan be destroyed before it was even tried."

"My plan?" Lowell was stunned. He rubbed the back of his hand over his three-day stubble of beard. "I guess I did get you thinking, but Carlos you have made a mistake. You don't have the guns or the men to depose the President. He could let you rot out here in the jungle and just go on doing what he is doing."

"No, amigo, you are wrong. Each time he sends out a patrol, some of the men do not go back. Some think I still have the money and some just want to stay and see me wrestle."

"Wrestle? What the hell are you doing, still taking on the local strong boys?"

"I make a deal with the soldiers. I say that if their best man can pin old Carlos, I will go back with them. If I can pin their best man, he must stay. We do this once a week. We get many of the peasants off the farms, too. They know when Carlos wrestles and they come to watch. So, you see, amigo, they will be with us, too, when the time comes."

118

"But the guns, Carlos, you don't have the guns," Lowell protested.

"This is true, amigo, *el Presidente* is too smart to send mortars or field pieces with the men who search for me. All we have are the rifles they carry, a few machine guns, some hand grenades, many Molotov cocktails, and thousands of machetes. Is that not enough?"

"Against tanks and planes? Against artillery? I know you are a great hero to your people, Carlos, but you could not get them to throw themselves on tanks and against the strong defenses of the capital with machetes and rifles."

"Perhaps in your story you could say that foreign powers are supplying Carlos Guzman Leche with armaments to end the oppression of the fascists. Perhaps you could buy us some weapons in the Army surplus stores."

"Carlos, have you gone mad? Even if I could buy arms for you, or even if some government, maybe not the United States, but say some friendly government were to offer you arms. How would you get them?"

"Amigo, if the government were really friendly, it would arrange for me to get the arms. Parachute drop? A landing from a submarine? There must be a way that friends could get together."

Lowell regarded his friend with new admiration. "You have given this some thought, haven't you. I don't know if it would work, though. I don't know if my editors would let me write such a story."

"Let Eliot P. Lowell write a story or not write a story. My friend, you underestimate yourself. You know anything you write will be on the front page. And if it is in *The New York Record,* the world will know that Carlos Guzman Leche is fighting tyranny."

"Fighting tyranny? You seem to have caught the magic in your voice. Have you been taking lessons?"

"Ah, yes, amigo, as you said, you can find the magic if you

have the courage to look for it. There are men who have helped me in my speech, who have encouraged me to let my voice do what I thought only my arms could do: defeat a man or win him over. It is a heady wine, this power you have started me seeking."

"But Carlos, there is one thing you forget. I cannot fabricate a story for you or for anyone else. No matter how much I want to help you, I deal with facts. I must have facts to weave the bare bones of a story around. Unless you can show me you have the men, I cannot go back and write that you are anything more than a fugitive with a gang."

"Men? How many men do you want? A thousand? Ten thousand? You tell me how many and I will have them here on Saturday, the next time I wrestle. More than that, I will let you count them yourself. How many do you want?"

"Did you say ten thousand men," Lowell asked, obviously impressed. "If you had ten thousand men with you in this short space of time you might do what you plan at that. All right, if you can show me ten thousand men by Saturday, I'll write that you pose a serious threat to the President. But wait a minute, what about the arms? How can I handle that?"

"Could you not say, amigo, as you have done in many dispatches that I have read, that unconfirmed reports say foreign governments are to supply Carlos Guzman Leche with arms; could you not say that there is talk about such things?"

"Talk? Between whom?"

"Between you and me, is it not true?" Carlos said archly, his hands patting his stomach, harder and flatter than Lowell had seen it in recent years.

If Carlos' stomach had hardened a bit, his resolve had turned to concrete. Ten thousand men by Saturday! It was no easy task. The jungle clearing where he wrestled could accommodate little more than two thousand and it was doubtful that many more would come on such short notice, even if they had a chance to see the action. Suddenly it dawned on Carlos that

120

two thousand might suit his purpose precisely if the matter were handled correctly.

Saturday was bright and clear, though Carlos had hoped for rain. A storm would have suited his purposes better, but he felt he had planned well enough to ignore the weather. Lowell arrived well before noon. He wore knee-length boots, jodhpurs, an Eisenhower jacket, and a pith helmet he had picked up in India. Only the swagger stick was missing to complete the picture of the perfect *New York Record* foreign correspondent, or at least what the readers of *The New York Record* thought the correspondents were like.

Lowell sat beneath a tree on the trail leading to the large clearing where the wrestling match would take place. Lowell wanted to sit in the clearing, but Carlos convinced him snipers sometimes fired on the crowd from the nearby mountain. Lowell was easily persuaded to remain under cover. Lowell placed a pad on a box set up as a desk and counted the stream of men moving past him into the clearing. It was steaming in the dense underbrush despite the shade. The dark, sweet native drink a lissome young girl brought Lowell tasted good and refreshing. The drink, Carlos said, was made from sugar cane and bananas. It had the smoothness of rum, but it packed more of a wallop than vodka. By the third drink, the white-clad natives streaming by Lowell were becoming blurred. Some of the men carried weapons, others machetes and still others long pointed sticks they shook at Carlos in salute. One toothless farmer passing in the second hour seemed somehow familiar to Lowell.

"Say," the correspondent demanded, turning to Carlos, "Didn't I see that man before?"

Carlos laughed. "Amigo, it is the same with you Yankees among my people, too. They think all Yankees look alike. You are probably finding the same thing. Have some more refreshment. How many men have you counted so far?"

Lowell looked at the marks on his paper. They seemed to

blur together the way the white shirts and trousers of the men passing by were merging into one mass.

"I don't know. I can't read my own writing. What does that add up to you Carlos?"

He handed the pad to Carlos, who made some rapid calculations and then said: "Eight thousand, amigo, if each one of these groups represent fifty. I don't know if we will have ten thousand. The farmers might have stayed to work in the fields, it is such a nice day."

"Carlos, my friend, two thousand men more or less does not matter to me at this time. I am impressed. Still it would be nice if you could get the ten thousand. Five figures! That is an army by anyone's imagination. What time is it? When do you wrestle?"

"It is still early, Lowell, amigo, but I could start at once. We have another hour until the time I said I would appear. Perhaps, we will get our two thousand more in that time. Meanwhile, have another drink."

Carlos beckoned to the young girl and spoke to her intensely for a moment out of Lowell's hearing. "Tell those idiots in the clearing," he said, "to stop sending the same men back through here so fast. The American is suspicious. Tell the men not to look at the American as they pass. Have them wave their hats before their faces or bow their heads. And tell them to send everyone back once more."

The news brought a cheer in the clearing. Carlos' lieutenants were ushering the peasants out of the clearing as fast as they poured in, sending them back through another trail to pass the checkpoint again and again. One more trip and the wrestling could start. The men fairly ran through the brush, laughing behind their hats as they rushed by Lowell, now slumped over the box, his eyes glazed as the hordes of white shirts and brown faces rushed past in a kaleidoscope of motion that seemed to keep time with the throbbing in his temples, the double-time movement of his eyes from his notebook to the trail, to the lissome girl with the rough mugs on the tray, to Carlos standing behind him tapping out the number of men with his fingers on his belly, to the sun . . . the sun! God it was hot. "Carlos, get me another drink, will you?"

Lowell's account of the growing army in the jungle created a sensation. It set off repercussions in Washington, in Peking, in Moscow, in Bucharest, in Belgrade, in Cairo, and in the capital of Carlos' island. The C.I.A. sent a mission to offer financial aid, guns and advisers, fearing the Communist countries would be too strongly entrenched if they were the sole source of Carlos' strength. Peking sent a trade mission with the same guarantees, but the added offer of volunteers to throw out the Fascist dog in the President's palace. Moscow matched the Chinese offer and threw in a military training mission. Bucharest and Cairo both sent emissaries with token amounts of money and pledges to make their aid more meaningful in the future—meaning if Carlos' revolution was a success. And in the President's palace, a messenger left with three million dollars (American) for deposit in a Swiss bank.

Carlos made certain Lowell knew of all the offers of aid, of all the arms promised and delivered. *The New York Record* had a virtual monopoly on the news out of Carlos' jungle camp and even the wire services would rewrite their leads after the first edition came out. The Hearst papers accused the *Record* of warmongering, but the publisher was undaunted. "They had their war," Miller said to Lowell in his office. "They're just jealous that you have Leche all tied up. It reminds me of Pancho Villa, when I was young."

As the money flowed into Carlos' retreat, the number of recruits swelled. The first shot with a new Czech anti-tank gun disabled a government tank moving up the mountain road to Carlos' hideaway and brought the remainder of the tank company to Carlos' side. The dispatches said that Carlos had taken towns and finally provinces, but the more accurate report would be that the towns and the provinces took Carlos to their hearts, where he had always been. The years of oppression under *el Presidente* were heavy on the people; the coming of Carlos was like the fresh winds after the rain, the laughter of the fiesta, the stirring feeling of his great triumphs in the wrestling ring. The President appealed for help to the United States, but dictators had become unpopular that year; after all, *The New York Record* was against him. The winds of change had started blowing; almost before *el Presidente* knew it he could feel the chill.

All through the spring Carlos' success multiplied. He had the men and the equipment to risk battles now, but *el Presidente's* troops had little stomach for warfare in a countryside suddenly turned hostile. The government troops continued to fall back on the capital, fighting only when there was no choice. Only the Air Force gave Carlos' men trouble and the marksmanship of the pilots was so bad that the few casualties from the air raids were almost accidents. A representative of Carlos had visited the Air Force general and convinced him his men should not be too accurate in their strafing and bombing. The general had not yet decided whether he would fly out *el Presidente* or if he would stay and throw his support to Carlos. There was a question of a million dollars or so holding up his decision, but history moved too quickly for the general.

July 4, the date the Americans first freed the country, was always a big holiday. It was a double celebration for the Yankees and the islanders. *El Presidente* knew the emotional heights people reached on the holiday, knew the tremendous quantities of native beer that would be consumed by soldiers and civilians alike. In theory, July 4 represented the perfect time for a counterattack against Carlos' men. They would be relaxed, their guard would be down, they would consider the holiday inviolate. But *el Presidente* was more of a realist than a strategist. He knew it would take all of the millions he had cached in Switzerland to stem the tide or at least to try to stem the tide. Even then, it was a gamble. He, too, had admired Carlos for his wrestling, for his honesty, for his kindness. Compared to Carlos, *el Presidente* admitted he left much to be desired. A braver man, a wiser man, perhaps, or a more stubborn man would have stayed to fight. *El Presidente* was brave and stubborn, but most of all he was wise. He boarded his private plane at midnight July 3 and the holiday dawned bright and cheerful with the capital, the whole country Carlos' by default. He had won, just as Eliot P. Lowell had said he could and would. It wasn't a bloodless revolution, but more money was exchanged than firepower. The nation had been split almost amicably, with only the members of *el Presidente's* secret police and his thieving tax collectors the sadder.

Lowell wasn't on hand for Carlos' triumphal entry into the capital only because events moved so quickly, so unexpectedly. He was on a plane before the day was out, though, and that night dined with Carlos in the President's palace.

"So now I, Carlos Guzman Leche, am *el Presidente*. Does it not make you proud, Eliot P. Lowell, my friend?"

"It's a long way from Madison Square Garden, isn't it?"

Carlos laughed, spilling the wine he was drinking. "The Garden? I think winning the championship was more difficult than winning this fight. The money, Lowell, amigo, the money did everything. It was all arranged, almost from that first story you wrote about me. Without you, Lowell, Carlos would still be doing public relations for *el Presidente*. Instead, because of you, I am *el Presidente*."

"You have it in your power to do much good, President Carlos. When will you have your elections?"

Carlos appeared shocked. "Elections? I have just taken office. We cannot have an election now. The people are too upset. They must calm down before we have an election. I must know who should run."

"The people should decide who is to run. But it is true, the country must calm down. It will be months before you have an election, I'm sure."

Lowell stayed for a week, until the patrols on the streets were thinned out, the barbed wire around the city rolled up and put away. Back in New York, he stayed in constant touch with Carlos, suggesting programs, reforms, and legislation

125

that would help the people of the island to enjoy a better way of living. Lowell was an idealist of the highest degree. He saw in Carlos' triumph the chance for an honest man to take over the government and to bring real democracy to the Caribbean. Too many of the republics, Lowell thought, were merely fronts for dictators. He was confident that Carlos, his friend, would avoid that path and bring truly representative government to the island at last.

Six months after the end of the revolution, Lowell was back in the capital, still wondering about elections. "Carlos, my friend," he said, "I am disappointed in you. It is six months since you took control and you still have not set a date for elections. From what I hear out in the country, it is the same now as it was under your predecessor. You have done little in six months except to clean out the jails of political prisoners. Where are the reforms you said were needed here? Where is the great Carlos Guzman Leche the people loved and who in turn loved the people enough to risk his life, his reputation for them?"

"I am here, amigo, right besides you."

"No, Carlos, it is not you I see. It is your predecessor. Being *el Presidente* has changed you. You think not of the people, but of yourself. Your supporters, your Army have all the cruelty of the old Army. There is still hunger on the island and yet you and your men eat like kings. You have changed Carlos, you have changed."

Carlos looked unhappy. "It is not so, amigo. I am still the same Carlos you saw in the jungle. There is much to do, but we must move slowly. The people are not ready for a change. They have always had one-man government; they have always had hunger. Do you think a full belly would make a man love me if he did not already do so? No, amigo, there are some men who will never love me, some who are saving and thinking and plotting how they, too, can be *el Presidente*. Remember our traditions."

"Traditions be damned," Lowell said heatedly, slamming his glass to the table. "I say people all over the world are striving for democracy today and unless you give the people more of a say in the government, unless you make their lives fuller, you will never rest easy."

"I rest well now, amigo, there is no one who could supplant me now."

"I don't mean fear of a rival. I mean dissatisfaction with yourself. Remember how you hated 'arranging' the wrestling matches? Well, it is the same thing. You have 'arranged' your thinking so you are just as bad as your predecessor, but you are convinced you are still the great hero. Look at yourself, Carlos. There is greatness within your grasp if only you will let the people give it to you and not take it by bribery or by force."

"Bribery? 'Arrange?' " Carlos stroked his chin reflectively. "Eliot, amigo, you speak harsh words, but I know you say always what is in your heart. Still, your words trouble me. I must have time to think, I must speak to my aides."

"Carlos Guzman Leche has always held his own council. It is for you to decide, for you to act." Lowell was pleased to see Carlos disturbed. He knew all that was needed was time for Carlos' goodness to manifest itself.

Carlos snapped off the stem of the wine glass he held. "I must think, amigo, think hard. I shall give you my answer before you leave. If there is to be a change, it is only right that you and *The New York Record* should be the first to know."

Lowell went to bed satisfied that he had shamed Carlos into calling elections. He knew Carlos' candidates would be safe at the polls, but the elections would convince the world the revolution was really of the people. When Lowell awoke, he was summoned to Carlos' quarters for breakfast.

"Eliot, amigo," Carlos said cheerfully as the correspondent entered, "you have tortured my soul with your talk of the people and democracy and hunger. You have made me ashamed and, as you know, that is not an easy thing to do."

"I'm sorry if I caused you pain, my friend. It is really you and your place in history I am thinking of."

"History, ah yes. I shall have all the history books rewritten and it shall be told how you, Eliot P. Lowell, have helped me. It shall be told how you convinced me that what I was doing was wrong. Some day, perhaps, they will be calling you our Patrick Henry."

"Then you will call elections, Carlos, my friend?"

"I shall do better than that, amigo. I shall install a system where no man goes hungry, where no one has more than another, where all men are truly equal, just as your country preaches, just as you yourself have preached."

"No one has more than another?" Lowell said, almost rising from his chair.

"Yes, amigo, the purest form of democracy. Do you not remember City College? My country shall be Communist. Is that not wonderful?"

"So it was Lowell and not the Russians who sold Leche on Communism," Bob said, sloshing the last of his sixth drink in the bottom of his glass. The story had been so absorbing that he hardly felt the effect of the alcohol.

"Oh, I think the Russians moved in pretty quickly right after that and the pure Communism Lowell was talking about in City College and the kind Carlos thought he was going to install never came about. As you know, the prisons are pretty full down there now, and that wasn't the way Leche intended to operate. I think that after Lowell left, the Reds moved in and took over."

"But Leche is still in control. Couldn't Lowell get through to him to show him how he's being used?"

"The State Department hopped all over Miller when Carlos made his big announcement. The official version never mentioned Lowell, but Carlos said to a lot of people that he had got the idea from his good friend from *The New York Re-*

cord. Consequently, the paper wouldn't let Lowell go back and he's been the scapegoat for something that started out as a noble deed."

"But couldn't he talk Carlos out of it right then? He seemed to be able to manipulate him right along."

"If he had more time, he could have," Tucker said with a ironic grin, "But as soon as Carlos told him, a *Herald Tribune* reporter was ushered into the room and Eliot had to rush out to file the story before he got scooped on his creation."

Bob smiled. "Always, the newspaperman, *The New York Record* comes first, eh?"

"I guess so. Lowell was in a spot. He had to file or be beaten by the *Trib*. When you work for a demanding mistress like *The New York Record,* you find there are guys like Lowell who put the paper first before everything."

Chapter Nine

ZUGSMITH WAS undecided about Bob. He still considered him a rising young star to be watched, but he didn't seem to have the necessary drive for power. The assistant managing editor knew he was a favorite of Edith Miller and this, too, made him wonder if Bob was playing his own game of office politics. There were some men who could be depended on to wait until the normal rotation came around to them, but Bob did not impress Zugsmith that way. He seemed so independent and his strong link to Manley heightened that feeling, at least in Zugsmith's view. Although Bob was still a copy editor, exactly what he started at, he had come a long way in his short time on the paper. Being the late man on the foreign desk gave Bob prestige, if not more money, but then he was close to being the highest paid man on the desk anyway.

Tom Crum had ceased to complain about Bob's tendency to act quickly without calling Crum at night and Zugsmith didn't know if that was a good sign or not. He didn't know that Tom and Bob were fellow conspirators in the Barnes transfer to the Congo. He knew that a normal amount of sniping accompanied the rise of most men on the paper and he was reluctant to expose Bob to that because he felt Bob might leave before putting up with innuendoes that he did not deserve promotions. The mark of the true rising star on *The New York Record* was the number of men critical of the star's performance or his abilities. The more snipers, Zugsmith found, the more likely the man was to succeed. It might not work in Bob's case, though, since virtually everyone in the city room liked him. His easy-going manner, his mixing with the boys at Curry's and Lexford's Pulitzer Prize all helped to set Bob aside in the minds of the men.

Eventually, Zugsmith envisioned Bob as his successor, although Bob wasn't the first man who had been so designated. The others had left the paper or turned out below expectations. That was what troubled Zugsmith about Bob: He had refused to consider going overseas, which to Zugsmith, was the prize assignment on the paper. He thought Edith Miller might be the answer because Bob had explained that his refusal was based solely on personal reasons. Sanford Miller had the same idea. His daughter had mentioned the handsome young copy editor more times than Miller would have liked, but he knew that his best course was in keeping his own counsel so far as Edith was concerned. He had tried to appear interestedly disinterested when Edith spoke of the boy, but he knew that wouldn't last. He'd have to find out something about Bob Davis for his own and his daughter's protection; the only one to ask was Zugsmith.

"What do you know about this fellow Davis?" Miller asked on a special trip he made to Zugsmith's office.

"He's bright, a war hero, good worker, and looks as if he can handle himself and men, too."

"And women?"

Zugsmith smiled. "You mean Edith?"

"Obviously I mean Edith. You know they've been seeing each other and she's mentioned him more than she has any other member of the staff. What do you think is going on?"

Zugsmith shrugged. He enjoyed the publisher's uneasiness. He thought back on his own courtship of Edith's mother and he smiled. "What can be going on? Edith is a smart, good, upright girl. Of course, Davis is a goy, but he is of good character and I don't think you have anything to worry about."

Miller shook his head impatiently. "Look, Zach, I'm not worried about her going to bed with him; that's her own affair. I'm thinking about their getting married. Now, she hasn't said anything yet, but the signs are all there, the interest and her prying into how I'd feel about it. I have to know what the man is like. What does he think of her? Is he interested in Edith Miller or is he interested in *The New York Record?*

You know where the publishers come from around here; why should he be any different. Of course, I wouldn't want my daughter to marry a Christian, but if that's what she wants, I wouldn't stand in her way mainly because I couldn't. But I want to know the man."

"He's sitting right out there. Do you want me to bring him in?"

"No, I see him. He's a handsome devil, isn't he? I can see what Edith sees in him. He's strong enough, all right, but is he right? That's what I'd like to know."

"How are you going to find out?"

"I was hoping you could help me. I know that you've probably never spoken to him about Edith, although she tells me that you know she's been dating Davis."

"It wasn't up to me to stop her."

"No, I'm not saying that. I'd just like to talk to the boy, but I don't want it to be a summons before the Royal High Executioner. Isn't there any way you could arrange for me to get to see him?"

Zugsmith took out the long cigarette holder and put in a cigarette.

"I thought you had lost that cigarette holder," Miller said, recalling his episode with Helen Crawford.

"I always keep a couple on hand. Why?"

"Nothing. Well is there anything you can think of?"

"Harry Brennan, the Brooklyn man, is retiring at the end of the week, as you know. He's been here forty years or more I guess, as long as I can remember. Anyway, the reporters are giving him a party in Curry's on Friday and I thought that I might go. It would be a nice touch if you dropped in, too, and I could arrange to have Davis there. That way you could get him off in a corner without making it look too obvious. What do you think?"

"Friday night? I did have an engagement, but I'm sure it can wait. I think this is more important. I'll be there."

Brennan's party was like many others at *The New York*

132

Record. The men retiring had little to look forward to in the way of a pension or a full life. They had spent all their fire on the altars of *The New York Record* and the parade had passed them by in a flash, leaving only a few old jokes and repeated anecdotes to be dispensed with before they faded from sight. The presence of Sanford Miller at the party gave Harry's affair a bit more class and the committee of reporters pressed the publisher into service to present the gift they had bought.

Miller was gracious and charming, joining in the laughs and telling a story of his own in the spirit of the ribaldry. He was nervously waiting to get together with Bob, however, and had to stay later than he planned before he got his chance.

"I've heard a lot about you," he said, when they were finally seated alone at the end of the bar.

"Thank you, sir," Bob replied, assuming that Zugsmith had told the publisher about him.

"My daughter tells me you're quite a man."

"Your daughter is a wonderful reporter and a fine woman, but I'm afraid she has her reporting mixed up in this case."

Miller smiled. He liked the boy inspite of himself. "No, I don't think so. You're good looking and intelligent. A lot different from the society snobs that Edith is used to. I can see where she'd be attracted to you."

Bob really didn't know what to say and he let Miller carry the ball.

"Tell me, Davis, what do you think of my daughter?"

The question was so direct that Bob smiled. "Truthfully, sir, I don't think that's any of your business. I realize, of course, that you're my boss and all that, but you must realize that under the circumstances you couldn't expect any answer except she's a fine girl and all that. But I think you have something else in mind and I don't think I should answer."

Miller's knuckles grew white as he squeezed his glass. "Why not? After all, Edith is or is going to be a very rich girl. The man she marries . . ."

"Marries?" Bob ejaculated. "Did she say that?"

"Not in so many words, perhaps, but that seemed to be the idea behind all her talk about you. She seemed to be feeling me out about you. That's why I wanted to meet you."

Bob smiled. "And now that you've met me, what? Am I good enough for your daughter? Is that the question?"

Miller's discomfort was evident. The boy had guts, no doubt about it. He might be right for Edith after all. "Something like that, but you're as bad as she is; she won't be pinned down, either."

"I think that's the way things go. If I wanted to marry Edith and she wanted to marry me, do you think that anything you'd say would make any difference?"

"Probably not."

"Then your question was out of line, wasn't it?"

Miller was taken back. He looked at Bob for an instant, studying him intently. "You know, Davis, you remind me of a boy I knew in college. He was much smaller than you, but he had the same cut of the jaw the same go to hell attitude. He called me a no good Jew and I beat the hell out of him. I knocked him down eleven times I remember, but each time he got up. Finally some of the other fellows stopped the fight. Do you know what he said? He said, 'You can keep knocking me down, but I'll always get up.' That's the way I feel about you. I could fire you or send you away from Edith, but you'd always come back."

"Thank you, Mr. Miller. It's very nice of you to say that. I don't mean that sarcastically either. I respect you for what you are and for your interest in your daughter . . ."

"And in my newspaper."

Bob smiled, raising his glass in tribute to the publisher's acuity. "And in your newspaper. But you have to realize that the relationship between two people is just that: between two people."

"And the girl's father, or a million dollars or two doesn't make any difference?"

"Not to me, it doesn't; only the girl."

Miller looked at Bob intently. He was strong willed for a goy, at that. He couldn't be bought any more than he could be frightened. Edith had something, but Sanford Miller still wasn't sure. Being on the foreign desk was hardly an acid test. Zugsmith had said Bob wouldn't go overseas, so there was only one thing left: assignment to Washington under the tyrannical but efficient rule of Webster Clayton, another of the paper's Pulitzer prize winners. It would be harder for him to see Edith, but not impossible. More important to Miller, though, if Bob could survive under Webster Clayton, he would truly possess all the attributes of a *New York Record* man. He might qualify at that; Miller would speak to Zugsmith as soon as possible.

Bob agreed to go to Washington for no longer than six months. He knew the assignment was a choice one, but he also had seen good men lose out on *The New York Record* by being away from the scene of the action when it came time for a promotion. Bob wasn't yet restless enough about the promotion, but six months of only weekends with Diane were all he was willing to endure; his dates with Edith could be had in Washington if he wanted. He had heard much about Webster Clayton and was looking forward to working with him. Bob, of course, said working with Webster, but both the bureau chief and Zugsmith felt Bob would be working for Clayton.

Webster Clayton, Web to presidents and all of official Washington, was the most feared man in American journalism. He not only directed a large corps of reporters as head of the bureau, but he also wrote a column on the editorial page three days a week. His columns were not as gossipy as Pearson's but there was more inside information in Clayton's columns than a whole issue of the most analytical magazine focused on Washington. Clayton had carefully built up his contacts over the years and was known to all levels of society. He got his information from shoeshine boys, beauticians, Senators and Cabinet members. When Clayton wrote that a "high source" had

135

given him information, he frequently meant the President, for no member of the Washington establishment outside the White House could get the President's eye or ear so quickly. Naturally, Web's columns caught the President's eye and he was proud that the President had said on more than one occasion the first thing he did in the morning was to read Web Clayton's column.

Not only was the President guided by what Clayton wrote, but the columns also were required reading for the C.I.A., the State Department and the Defense Department. The Russian Ambassador, of course, was a constant reader of Clayton, as were all of the diplomatic corps, their staffs and their secret operators. Web's power was recognized and exploited. The President used the column to launch trial balloons or to shoot them down. More than one Presidential appointment drew initial reaction by being mentioned in Web's column. If the name created too much of a stir, signals could be changed without any embarrassment to Web or compromising of the President. Of course, Web used the column for his own ends, too. He could make or break a Senator or a Congressman by close scrutiny of his record or by ignoring him completely. The system worked so well that official Washington was confused sometimes about whose trial balloon was being launched, who was doing the launching or whose ox was being gored.

Web relished his role in Washington, enjoyed the prestige and the social status it brought. He was really at his best socially, for Webster Clayton was a son of the old South, gallant, charming, and handsome and a perfect must for all the top social functions each season. He had a full head of steel gray hair, an almost invisible mustache that just softened the lines of his mouth and gave rugged emphasis to his strong chin and prominent nose. He was seldom seen without a cigar, except when he was dancing, invariably with the most beautiful, the youngest, or the most endowed woman in the room.

Web's appeal for the ladies was legendary. Although he had had six wives, all were on speaking terms with their ex-husband and only one was collecting alimony. If Web had a weakness, it was undoubtedly women, but that was his strength, too. His old-world charm, his wit and his ability to win their confidence gleaned more information from capital wives than any amount of torture could wring from their husbands.

In the office, though, Web's charm was usually submerged in the clouds of cigar smoke as he battered away at his typewriter or drifted in each morning at almost a trot. The staff was acknowledged with the barest of nods. Web believed that bosses were meant to be respected and obeyed, not liked. His brusqueness was almost unnoticed in the frantic pace of the bureau, with telephones ringing constantly, teletype machines chattering, and typewriters trying their best to keep up with the fervid pace. The routine was far different from what Bob imagined, but he liked the rapid pace in the afternoon and early evening, which gave him time to do research in the morning or to sample the night life. The break away from the late shift in New York also meant he could fly to New York on Friday night and return on Monday morning, spending three of his nights with Diane.

Bob's introduction to Clayton was brief.

"Davis, oh yes," Web said, rolling the cigar to the corner of his mouth. "You're Boland's replacement. That's your desk there. Clark will show you what to do."

There was no handshake, no small talk. Web was back in his office before Bob could say anything.

"He moves quickly," said Stan Clark, a thin, red-faced man. "Don't let it bother you. I've been here three years and I don't recall him saying much more than that to me."

"I've heard so much about him, his charm, his wit. Is it truth or fiction?"

"Oh, it's true, all right. He's a charmer, make no mistake about that. The only thing is he saves most of his charm for outside the office. He doesn't have to worry about us. We're supposed to be doing a job and he seems too busy to ask how you're feeling or anything like that. Jim Boland, that's the fellow you're replacing, had a theory. He said Web lived in a dream world where he wasn't a correspondent at all; he's the President or a Senator or an Ambassador. When he comes back to the office, he wakes up and realizes he has to work for a living and that's when the charm leaves him."

"It's an interesting theory. Did the theory have anything to do with Boland's quitting?"

"No, he got a job with the Government. Most of our guys wind up in some Federal job or something. Web spoke to Boland about as much as he's spoken to any one in the office, but now you should see them at parties. They're great buddies. In fact, Web's fifth wife was first married to Boland."

"That makes it cozy. Sort of keeping it all in *The New York Record* family."

"It wasn't cozy for a while here. While Web was married to Jim's ex-wife, Jim used to burst out laughing everytime he'd see Web. He didn't say anything and he tried to hide it, but it got under Web's skin after a while. No one down here laughs at the head of the Washington bureau for *The New York Record,* you know. Web sort of got the point after a while, though, and I think that was one reason why he divorced the ex-Mrs. Boland."

Bob was puzzled. He couldn't see the connection between Boland's laughing and a second divorce for Jim's former wife. "I don't get it," he confessed. "How was the divorce connected with the laugh?"

"Don't you see? If Web was too good to talk to Boland, how come he wasn't too good to marry Boland's ex-wife. The laughter was really sympathetic because the gal was really a bitch. Boland knew what Clayton was going through."

Bob liked Clark. He was a lot like Howard Tucker. He had a dry sense of humor and a dedication to duty sprinkled with a dash of irreverence that kept him from becoming rattled by big events or fast-breaking news. Stan was an education besides being valuable in breaking into the new job. He cleared up many of the mysteries about the Washington operation that had puzzled Bob while in New York. One of the most interesting points to Bob concerned the attribution of news breaks in Washington.

"How does an informed source differ from an authoritative source?" Bob asked one night while he was processing some copy with Clark.

"There is a difference, although you'd never know it from the way Web writes. An authoritative source is some one official, some one in the Government. An informed source is some one on the outer fringes, a lobbyist, a PR man for a Senator or some one like that."

"How about a plain source? I've seen that in the paper, too." 'Sources say that the United States will . . .' Who does that represent?"

Stan started to chuckle. "A source can be an elevator operator, a cab driver or whoever happens to overhear anything. This is a great town for gossip. Sometimes a source can be the hairdresser for a Senator's wife, a real estate agent or even the reporter himself. Frequently in Web's copy, 'source' means the boss himself. The other reporters do the same thing when the managing editor is hollering for a story. They come up with the story he wants."

"You mean fake it?" Bob was shocked. "I didn't think that they did that on *The New York Record.* I know it was done on the *Fort Wayne Item,* but I'm really surprised to find it here. I should think the news would be too important, have too great an impact to allow that."

"What makes you think *The New York Record* is any different from the *Fort Wayne Item?* They're both in business to sell papers and the reporters are interested in keeping the front office happy. The idea is to protect your sources and let the Government and the public think you have something even when you're only fishing. If you play it straight all the time, you'll have to use an awful lot of bunk that they give out at the White House and then you find that the President was faking it just as we were, but on a different tack."

"I don't think it's honest," Bob objected.

Clark smiled wanly. "Web calls it initiative journalism. It must have been pretty good to win him the Pulitzer Prize."

Bob remembered how Lexford's Pulitzer had been won, so he was hardly impressed. Everyone felt *The New York Record* had to be represented among the prizes regularly, as sort of a acknowledgement by the jury for the unique role it enjoyed in journalism. To Bob, the prize selections were similar to the Academy Awards, where sentiment, conscience and loyalty swayed the voters as often as true worth and quality.

He had a chance to see initiative journalism at work one night when he was alone late in the office awaiting a change in a big story. The phone rang and he hoped it was the reporter with the few facts he needed to wrap up the story and quit for the night.

"The New York Record, Davis," he answered crisply.

"This is the President," said the voice on the other end of the line. "Is Web there?"

"No, he isn't, sir. What company did you say you were with?"

"This is the President of the United States," the voice said sharply. "Can you take a message for Mr. Clayton?"

Bob almost dropped the phone. "Yes sir. Go ahead, sir. I'll take it down."

"There's something big going on that I'm sure Web is on to it or will be very soon. Tell him I called and ask him to hold off on any story until he gets the word from the Pentagon. I was going to call Sanford Miller in New York, but I thought I'd check with Web first. Do you have that message?"

"Yes sir, ask him to hold off on any story until he checks with the Pentagon. Very good sir. Thank you, sir."

Bob was still excited when Clayton walked in a half hour later.

"Any messages?" Web demanded brusquely.

"Yes sir, the President called. He said there was something big going on that you knew about or would know about soon.

140

He asked that you not write anything until you check with the Pentagon."

"He did call, eh? I know damned well something big is on, but no one will talk. I've been trying to track it down all day. I wonder what it could be."

"Nothing to do with the President's health, is it?"

"I doubt it. He looked great at lunch today. He knows I've been sniffing around for something, though, because all of my good sources have suddenly become very guarded. He must think one of the sources came through for old Web. Good. Get the White House on the phone. I want to talk to the President."

Bob handed over the phone as soon as the switchboard answered.

Clayton's face changed as he spoke into the receiver. "Clara? This is Web Clayton. How are you? The President called a few minutes ago and I just got in. Put me through to him, will you, honey? Thanks, sweetheart."

Bob could hear another ringing as Clayton waited on the phone. Again Clayton's face changed as he started to speak. "Mr. President, Web Clayton, here. I just called to let you know that I came in to start filing my story when I got your message. Naturally, I held off when I found out how you felt. I forgot about the whole thing. I didn't want to do anything to embarrass you, sir . . . What's that? . . . Oh yes, it certainly could embarrass the whole country. When do you think you might be able to give me the go ahead, sir? Oh, too many uncertainties? Yes, I can understand, sir. Well, rest easy, sir. Your secret is safe with me. Best of luck with your, er, little project, sir. Good night."

Web replaced the receiver of the phone in its cradle, then took a deep drag on his cigar.

"I take it, sir," Bob said, "that you know what the big story is all about."

"That's what I wanted the President to think. This way, he thinks I'm sharing a confidence and he's in my debt. He'll owe me a favor or an exclusive interview or something. Meanwhile, now I know something is really cooking, I can step up the pressure and try to find out what it is."

"Would you print it if you found out?"

"You damn well know I would. If I don't, somebody else would and being first is still what this game is all about."

"But you promised the President," Bob protested. He thought Clayton would be going back on his word if he succeeded in tracking down the story and then printed it.

"What do you mean I promised the President? When I spoke to him, I didn't have any story to sit on. As a matter of fact, I still don't, but I'll have it before tomorrow, you can bet. Besides, what are you concerned about? A promise to a politician is just like a campaign promise, they're not meant to be kept."

Bob was unconvinced. He shook his head stubbornly. "I'm sorry, Mr. Clayton, but I overheard you say the story could embarrass the whole country. If you went ahead and printed it in the face of that, I think you'd be compromising your position of trust and compromising the paper, too."

"Who the hell asked you in the first place?" Web roared, his face livid, the cigar waving wildly in his hand. "Down here, I'm *The New York Record,* you remember that. I don't care what your Mr. Zugsmith might do or even what Sanford Miller would do. I'm on my own down here, there's no one to carry the ball for me, no one to take the rap. I resent your insinuations that I'd embarrass the country. Goddamit man, I'm as patriotic as any of them. Sure, I'd look at the story in the light of security, but if the President has to ask that it be kept out of the paper, then it deserves to be in the paper. That's what I'm paid for and I don't plan on compromising our readers just because some politician is working on some angle."

Web stood looking at Bob for an instant, then turned and walked into his office. He closed the door and Bob could hear the phone dial start to spin as Clayton began to track down "something big." He never succeeded, and the story, a landing by a Marine force to bolster a shaky regime threatened by

Communists, didn't hit the papers until two days later. The landing had gone well, with no casualties. Still Bob's anger at Clayton would not cool down.

"Just suppose he had found out about it and printed the story," he argued with Clark. "It could have led to counter action by the Communists. It might at least have given the Russians enough notice to get in some propaganda licks. The whole operation might have been called off."

"Listen Bob," Stan said. "What you consider right and what I consider right are different from what Webster Clayton considers right. In his view, he is responsible only to his readers. Of course, I think it's largely a question of ego, too. He has to know everything, to print everything. There is a lot of stuff everyone knows that no one prints, but that's different. So long as there's a chance for Web to beat the others, to find out something no one else knows, though, he's like a bloodhound; he never gives up. I don't say he would deliberately hurt the country, but I don't know."

"Is it true he was a big factor in getting us into World War II?"

Clark smiled wanly. "He certainly didn't do anything to keep us out. Roosevelt used Web to carry the ball for him a lot on some of the difficult foreign policy questions. Like the destroyer deal and the British bases, you know, the steps leading up to our involvement. Web worshipped Roosevelt and he and Zugsmith certainly made no bones about it that sooner or later we were going to have to fight Hitler. Web used to drink a lot in those days. I remember one night in particular. He was saying 'his' war was going to make Hearst's war look like a riot at a bull fight. Lately he's been writing a lot of scarce stuff, the old brinkmanship from Ike's administration, you know. I'm not sure whether he's carrying the ball for the President and a lot of Senators and Representatives are in the same boat. That's why we've been getting so many calls from the Hill lately. The boys want to know just whose policy Web is making in the paper."

"It's sort of astonishing how powerful he is, isn't it?"

"It isn't just Web, it's the whole paper. You must have seen that in New York. What *The New York Record* wants, it gets. It may not be the biggest damned paper in the world or the richest, but it damned well is the most powerful. It's political endorsements don't mean too much to the people, but with the politicians it's dynamite. That's what really counts."

Stan was right, of course. Washington life centered on politics and some one from *The New York Record* was welcomed at every function with a slight deference usually reserved for diplomats of friendly countries. Bob could see it as he moved into the social whirl of the embassies through a young secretary he met. When he was introduced as Bob Davis, the handshake was perfunctory, the acknowledgement brief, as conversations were resumed or new contacts looked up. When he was introduced as Bob Davis of *The New York Record,* though, interest was immediately evident. Faces lighted up and conversations were sparked about what a great paper *The New York Record* was.

Bob seldom used his affiliation, but it became almost a matter of necessity since everyone in Washington was of something. Henry Smith of Agriculture, John Browne of O.A.S., Raymond Oates, of the Army. Bob found, though, when he met people on his own, he had a better time. He had a good personality for parties and was usually able to circulate freely, joining in the conversations he wanted to, listening at the fringes at some, and then completely dominating others if he so desired. He was mainly listening at a reception in the Soviet Embassy for a new Russian ballet troupe when Web Clayton walked in, his cigar clinched in his teeth.

"Hello, Davis," Web said, not bothering to look at Bob. "What are you doing here? I didn't know they sent more than one invitation to the office." He scowled briefly at Bob, then continued to look across the room.

Bob was amused. He knew Clayton usually planned his schedule to take in only the top affairs. He seldom invited any one from the office to accompany him, unless it was a working night when another man was required.

"I was invited by the secretary to the Ambassador, sir," Bob said. "I've become friendly with her in recent weeks."

Clayton smiled and winked at Bob. "That's it, Davis, don't let any grass grow under your feet. This town is full of secretaries. If I was younger, I'd give them a run for their money, too. Have a good time." He swirled away in a cloud of cigar smoke. He never acknowledged Bob in a half-dozen near encounters at the bar, at the buffet, and on the edges of the dance floor. Bob also had little chance to see his secretary since she was busy seeing that all went smoothly at the party. Bob was idly twirling his empty champagne glass and debating whether to leave when Valentina Blatinkoff, the star of the ballet company, returned from the ladies room.

"You look so lonely standing there without a drink," the girl said in faultless English. "Could I get you something?" Valentina was blonde, in her early twenties, with a supple body that had won raves in Europe. Her pale complexion was perfect, her face strong, her deep blue eyes mysterious and alluring. Bob was taken with her beauty at once.

"Miss Blatinkoff," he said with a solemn half-bow, "I'm Bob Davis."

"Oh yes, of *The New York Record*." the girl said with a radiant smile.

"How did you know that? The Russians really must have a very efficient spy network."

Valentina laughed, a low musical laugh that had caught Bob's ear before as she stood in the center of group after group receiving the homage of the men, the grudging admiration of the women and the rapt attention of both as she spoke of her love for America, her hopes to bring her country closer to the United States.

"No," she said, "it wasn't espionage, it was curiosity. I asked someone who the handsome red-headed man was and they told me."

Bob tried to hide his delight with the girl. He looked around comically and said: "Who was the handsome red-headed man?"

"It was you, of course, Mr. Davis. I have always liked red-headed men. They are so full of fire and determination. Is that you? Your face is strong, you are probably very determined. The thing to discover, then, is what you are determined about."

"I'm determined to get you a drink. What will you have?"

"Just a little champagne, if you please. Vodka and whisky are bad for the muscles. A dancer is like an athlete. You must always take care of your muscles."

"You do it so beautifully. I noticed as you were walking across the floor." Bob smiled into Valentina's eyes and the tempo of the evening picked up markedly. Bob dismissed all thought of leaving. He could see the secretary giving him pained looks, but Valentina was too charming, too attractive to leave even for an instant. By adroit maneuvering, he kept her virtually to himself for almost an hour. Valentina helped to steer others away and she seemed to be having a genuinely good time. Bob wouldn't dare dance with her because he knew all eyes would be on them on the floor and he did not think his style could stand the scrutiny.

"I'm all right on a crowded floor in a dark room," he apologized, "But I'm afraid dancing with the great Blatinkoff would be too much for me."

"Why Davis," Web said with unusual warmth as he edged next to Valentina. "You've managed to monopolize Miss Blatinkoff long enough. Why don't you introduce me and give us older fellows a chance."

"Why Mr. Clayton," Valentina said, coyly. "I've just been dying to meet you."

"You know Mr. Clayton?" Bob asked, not entirely surprised.

"Everyone knows the great Webster Clayton of *The New York Record*," Valentina said, her eyes on Web's face.

"Just as every one knows the great Blatinkoff. Davis, why don't you go and get us some drinks. I'll keep Miss Blatinkoff busy until you get back."

When Bob returned, they were dancing. Web moved with astounding grace for a big man. Valentina was impressed, too, Bob thought. She followed Web flawlessly, her eyes never leaving his face as he talked effortlessly throughout the dance with a steady stream of light banter that brought forth her musical laugh again and again. Suddenly Bob felt he might as well leave after all.

For two weeks after the party he read items in the gossip columns linking Web and Valentina. He smiled as he saw a picture of the two at a benefit luncheon for the U.N. and he reproached himself for feeling just slightly jealous. It wasn't that he was thinking of Valentina in the same way he did of Diane; it was just that Bob resented Web being first again, and at his expense, too.

"You know," Bob said to Clark, "there's some talk in the columns that Valentina is going to be the seventh Mrs. Clayton. What do you think?"

"It's just gossip-column stuff. Web isn't about to get married so quickly, particularly to a Russian ballerina. He frequently gives the foreign gals a big rush while they're here, but he's never been serious with any of the foreign ones I know of. Besides, you don't think the Russians would ever let a big star like that marry an American. Of course, stranger things happen in this crazy town."

"Maybe the Russians are getting Valentina to soften Web up a bit. He's been rough on the Kremlin of late."

"Web has received all sorts of offers, bribes, gifts, call them what you will to be soft on this one or that one. I know a lot of newspapermen on the take, but Web Clayton isn't one of them. No, I don't think that would work. You just don't realize Web may be a lot older than Valentina, but I bet he keeps her amused."

Bob was sorry he asked. He still wondered exactly what she

saw in the bureau chief. He found out the next night he was on the late watch.

Bob was checking over some copy when Web walked in in evening clothes, which wasn't unusual; he frequently stopped in the office on his way back from formal functions. The look on his face, though, was most unusual, Bob thought.

"Davis, come into my office," Web said as he lurched by Bob. He was clutching something in his hand and although he didn't look drunk, he didn't look well. Bob followed him into the office. He saw the thing Clayton carried was a picture. The bureau chief placed it on his desk face down.

"Is there something wrong, Mr. Clayton. Is there anything I can get you?"

"Wrong? Anything you can get me? You got me into a helluva mess as it is introducing me to the goddamned Russian whore. She's trying to blackmail me."

"Russian whore? You mean Valentina Blatinkoff, the ballet dancer?"

"Ballet dancer my ass. She's a secret agent. I should have known better. She was too friendly, too willing."

Bob was still unable to make sense out of Clayton's rage. "What is it she's blackmailing you about?"

"What the hell do you think? You know I've been blasting the hell out of the Kremlin lately. I've been raising hell with Communists ever since Whittaker Chambers. I hate their guts and they hate mine just as much. They . . . this Russian bitch wants me to change my thinking on foreign policy . . . 'Just a little bit,' she said, the no good bitch."

"But blackmail usually involves some sort of threat. What sort of pressure is she trying to put on you?"

"There's the pressure," Clayton said, flipping over the picture on his desk. Bob picked it up. The picture was evidently taken in a hotel room or a motel. Valentina was on the bed smiling in a thin negligee. Clayton was kneeling on the bed naked, but his face was turned toward the camera as if his name had just been called. The pose was ludicrous enough, but the picture had been skillfully retouched to introduce an even more ridiculous aspect. Bob had to look closer to make sure it was retouching and not printed on the photograph after developing. The figures were true, of course, but lettered across Web's buttocks like a gigantic tattoo was the legent: "Read *The New York Record.*"

"Well, say something," Web commanded when Bob remained silent.

"It's a very skillful job. I mean it's obvious that the picture has been retouched. No one . . ."

"No, no, no, you idiot. I don't have anything like that tattooed on my ass. But don't you see? That's where they've got me. If it was just a pose of me crawling into bed with some dame, no one would give it a second thought or a second look. All that anyone would think would be that it was about time that some one caught me in that pose. But with that big tattoo or what looks like a tattoo staring you in the face, the picture might be too good for some of the scandal sheets to pass up. They all have their knives out for *The New York Record* and Webster Clayton, too. They'd love to give it to us both."

"They're not really serious about trying to have the picture published are they?"

"Unless I slack off on my hard line, they say the print will be mailed to every paper and every wire service, magazine and weekly in the world. I wouldn't put it past those bastards, they'd stop at nothing."

"Do you think you could sort of write something else for a while rather than international stuff and call in the F.B.I. or the C.I.A. to see if they could track down the negative?"

"According to that bitch it's on its way back to Moscow. I offered her money, she refused. I even offered to marry her."

"You offered to marry her? What did she say to that?"

"She laughed. 'Put on your clothes old man, you'll catch cold,' she said."

"Then what happened?"

"I guess I got dressed. I'd been drinking and it took me awhile. I . . ."

"Was Valentina drinking?"

"She had champagne, but she wasn't drunk. She puts that stuff away like water. Well anyway, by the time I got dressed, the picture had been slipped under the door. I never saw the guy who took it and the motel manager said he hadn't seen anything either. They probably bribed him."

"Where was this?"

"A little motel in Gretna Green. Ye Olde something or other. It was her idea. I should have known better."

"Gretna Green? You could have been married there before you went to bed."

"I know. That's what started it. I said we should get married so long as it was so convenient, but she said she wanted to make sure we were sexually suited. Of course, that sounded great to me, and that's when she suggested the motel. I thought it was too easy. I should have known I was being had. Sexually suited my ass!"

Bob rubbed his chin reflectively. He was surprised that Web had even considered marrying Valentina, but then again he wasn't. She was really some woman. "Suppose you were married to Valentina? Would you object to the picture then?"

"Object? Certainly I'd object. What are you driving at."

"Well, just suppose you were married. Don't you think the Russians would object to having their star ballerina marrying a filthy war mongering capitalist newspaperman? Do you think they'd want to publish a picture that would make her look silly, too? And if you were married, the picture would lose a lot of its appeal for the scandal sheets."

"All right. Suppose all these things are true, how are you going to get her to marry me. I couldn't woo her now, she'd know what I wanted."

"The big thing is, though, do you really want to marry her?"

"I'd love to get that bitch in bed, really in bed, I mean. She owes me one, that's for sure, but she'd never marry me unless you drug her."

"Or get her drunk?"

"You'll never get that girl drunk. So long as she sticks to champagne, she'll drink you and me under the table every time. Besides, she'd be on her guard with me, figuring I was trying to pull something."

"No, not you. Me. I'd be the one who would get her drunk. I'd be the one who would approach her."

"And you'd marry her?"

"No, no. We'd work it out so that we'd be in close touch the whole time. Then when she passes out, you rush in with a co-operative Justice of the Peace. The next morning when she wakes up, she's Mrs. Webster Clayton number seven."

"She'd scratch my eyes out," Clayton said, his fear apparent. He licked his dry lips at the thought of Valentina in bed.

"I thought you said you'd like to get her in bed. Are you afraid to take a chance?"

"Damn it all man," Web said, the fire returning to his voice. "I've flown bomber missions, lived through the blitz in London, and had six wives. You ask me if I'm afraid of a woman who has been tricked? The answer is hell yes, but I don't have much choice. How do you suggest we go about putting our plot into operation?"

"I'll make a date with her, saying I have something important to talk to her about. I'll stick to champagne, too, so we'll be on equal ground."

"She drinks that stuff like water. I'm liable to end up married to you if you're the one that passes out."

"There's an old tried and true formula, drinking mineral oil before you sit down to a drinking match. The oil coats your stomach and the alcohol isn't absorbed into your blood. It passes right out through the kidneys."

"The diplomats used to do that with Khrushchev. That old bastard can really drink, too."

"Good, then we'll try it?"

Clayton shook his head with an air of resignation. "I have nothing to lose."

"There is one thing, though," Bob said.

"Yes?"

"You'll pay for the champagne, of course?"

Clayton smiled. "Put in a bill. We'll charge it up to business expenses. Miller can afford it. It's all for the glorious *New York Record,* anyway."

Bob had a hell of a time getting Valentina to see him. The troupe was due to leave within a few days and there were many things she wanted to do in Washington before she left. It was only through the intercession of the embassy secretary that he was able to get Valentina on the phone. He spoke for nearly an hour before he could get Valentina to agree to have dinner with him the following night. He made the date for the Penthouse Room, a fashionable spot in one of the hotels. The choice was no accident, for Bob had taken a room on one of the lower floors and ordered a supply of champagne to be kept on ice after eight o'clock.

Valentina was even more lovely than Bob remembered. She wore a simple dress that made her figure look even more startling than the ballet costumes or the glamorous dress she had worn to the embassy party.

She smiled warmly as she extended her hand. "I really don't know why I came, Mr. Davis, but you are so persistent. You know, of course, I am being followed. I noticed your eyes dart behind me when I walked from the elevator."

"I can't blame your Government for not letting such a lovely creature go about our city unguarded. Should I ask your bodyguard to join us?"

"No, please don't. That would only embarrass him. You aren't supposed to know he is there. He's new on the job, though, so don't discourage him."

"Good, shall we go in? The table's waiting." Bob guided Valentina to a table in the corner. He watched as the short man following her took a table near the door where he could watch them leave.

"What is it you wanted to speak to me about?" Valentina asked when they were seated. "You said you wanted to speak to me about Mr. Clayton."

"Can't that wait? You know I've never forgiven Mr. Clayton for taking you away from me that night at the embassy party. Can't I have a few moments with you before we start speaking about him?"

"But that's why I came. I thought you had a message from Mr. Clayton."

"Let's order first, then we can talk."

Valentina's lips were compressed into a hard line, then she smiled. "Since I have no choice we might as well. I have to confess I love American food. In Russia we have the best. By that I mean the ballet company has the best of everything, food, wines, clothing, everything. But first we will eat, then we will talk."

"Bring us a magnum of champagne," Bob said to the waiter when he finished ordering their food. Valentina hid a laugh behind her napkin.

"Are you sure Mr. Clayton didn't tell you anything about me?"

"Mr. Clayton doesn't speak to the proletariat. What could he tell me?"

"The proletariat? Is that you? Perhaps I should call you comrade?"

"I'd rather that you called me Bob."

"Not Mr. Davis?"

Bob shook his head.

"All right, Bob. What is it you wanted to speak to me about, Bob?"

"Here's the champagne. Let's have a toast. The Russians are great for toasts, I hear. Let me make a toast to you. To the fairest flower of all Russia, may you continue to spread your radiance over America for a long time."

153

"We're leaving day after tomorrow."

"But you'll be back."

"Perhaps." There was a wistful note in her voice that almost made Bob regret his plot.

"Let's drink to other tomorrows, then. Let's drink to your return to America."

Valentina drained her glass almost before Bob had finished his first sip. Clayton was right. She certainly could drink. He'd have to watch himself and that little bodyguard, too. He resisted an impulse to wave to the man as he reached across and refilled Valentina's glass.

The first magnum was finished before the main course was served. With each glass Valentina's face became more flushed, her manner warmer, but there was no indication that she wasn't in complete control of herself.

When the second bottle was opened, she smiled archly across the table at Bob. "I think you are trying to get me drunk. Are you sure Mr. Clayton didn't tell you anything about me? He tried to get me drunk once, but he was the one who got drunk."

"Must we always talk about Clayton?" Bob injected a trace of annoyance into his voice.

"But I thought you wanted to talk about Mr. Clayton."

"I only said that so you'd have dinner with me. I know you're leaving in a few days and I just had to see you again. I think I have a chance to go to Moscow as a correspondent and I wanted to know if I could see you, perhaps, if I did?"

"In Moscow it would be very difficult. We do not mingle much with foreigners there. We all live together and we are always rehearsing. Believe me, this trip has been a vacation, not work for me. I'm glad, though, that you wanted to see me for myself. I thought Mr. Clayton might have told you about some pictures."

"Pictures? Motion pictures? Don't tell me he promised to get you into motion pictures? That's the oldest gag in the world. I'm surprised he would use it."

"No, not motion pictures," Valentina said with a laugh. "It does not matter. Let us not talk about Mr. Clayton, then. Tell me about you."

"You are beautiful, you know," Bob said almost absently. His resolve was weakening, he knew. Valentina reminded him so much of Diane. Only she was blonde, more sure of herself, more worldly, more beautiful, perhaps, harder. He wondered if he had taken enough mineral oil. His head was beginning to feel strange and his stomach was tied up in knots.

"There are many women in Moscow more beautiful than I. We are not muscular and ugly."

"I never thought Russian women were muscular and ugly, but I don't see how they could be more beautiful than you."

"Ah, the food," Valentina said happily breaking the spell as the waiter arrived.

Bob was crushed. "Yes, the food. I trust it is as desirable as you are." Valentina was too busy eating to acknowledge the compliment.

By the end of the meal, and the third magnum, Valentina was humming softly to herself, moving her hands and her arms in the subtle ballet cadences. The bodyguard was visibly disturbed that the girl was getting drunk. Bob smiled over at him as if to reassure him everything would be all right. The man hid behind the menu, pretending not to have seen Bob's broad acknowledgement of his presence. Bob felt sorry about Valentina in a way, because she did seem at last to be feeling the liquor.

"I think we'd better go," he said. Valentina merely smiled. She swayed against him as she got up and he held her arm firmly as he steered her to the elevator. The bodyguard had called for his check long before and was ready to go when Bob and Valentina passed him. Bob studied the man in the mirror on the elevator door. The man made a great production of lighting his cigar as he watched tensely, straining to catch any words that might pass between them.

"Are you all right?" Bob asked solicitously as the pointer

on the elevator approached the penthouse mark. As the elevator arrived, he stepped aside to let two other couples get on first, then said to the operator; "Go ahead, we'll take the next one."

He could see the bodyguard relax and continue to light his cigar. The operator pushed the button to close the door and Bob thrust the girl forward and then squeezed into the elevator as the closing door clutched at his topcoat.

"We made it," he said smugly, smiling at the others in the car. Valentina wasn't aware or didn't care that they had given the bodyguard the slip, "Please stop at nine," Bob said.

Valentina didn't object when they got off the elevator. She demurred only slightly when he opened the door to the room. "What are we doing here?" she asked. "And where's Alexis?"

"You mean your bodyguard? He's still upstairs on the roof. I thought we could have at least one drink in private without Alexis listening to every word. Do you mind? You're not afraid, are you?"

"Afraid?" she said, peering into the room. She spotted the champagne bottle and the glasses. "You don't have a camera, do you?" She began to laugh as Bob closed the door and followed her into the room. She walked to the ice bucket and picked up the bottle. "Ah, this is not a magnum. Good. You did want to talk to me only a little. Did you want to make love to me, too? Perhaps just a little?"

Bob grinned sheepishly. He wouldn't mind making love to her and not just a little. He didn't think the scene would be a good one, though, with Clayton and a minister in the next room. "Have a drink and let's talk. We can talk about love and then later, perhaps . . ."

Valentina walked to the love seat and curled into the piece snugly. "It is good to put your feet up after a long day," she said, resting her head on the backrest and closing her eyes briefly. Bob stood over her with the two glasses, his heart pounding, his mouth suddenly gone dry.

"Here take this. Perhaps you'd like to rest after you drink it. I could throw a blanket over you."

Valentina took the glass and held it to him in a toast. "To love and sleep and warmth. They all go together, don't they? In Russia that is all the people think about and some of them don't have any of the three; it is very sad." She tossed the drink off and smiled at Bob crookedly. Suddenly, the smile faded and her face became blank. Her eyes closed as she slumped down on the love seat, the glass slipping from her hand and rolling across the carpet. The knockout drops Bob had slipped into the drink had worked faster than he had thought. He was glad it was over, he was rapidly losing his nerve. He walked to the door of the connecting suite and turned the key in the lock. "You can come in now," he said dully.

Clayton bounded into the room followed by a short bald man in a Roman collar. He held a Bible in one hand and a large handkerchief to mop his moist brow in the other.

"You did it, Davis, goddamn it, you did it," Clayton exulted.

"The knockout drops did it, not the champagne."

"What the hell, all's fair in love and war. Let's get on with it, Max."

Bob picked up his coat and started walking toward the door.

"Where are you going?" Clayton called. "Don't you want to stay and be a witness?"

"I've witnessed enough already. I'm going back to my apartment. I'll read all about it in the society columns of *The New York Record*. Columnist Weds Ballerina. It should make quite a story."

Clayton detected the sarcasm in Bob's voice. "Don't be getting riled up, Davis. After all, this was your idea, wasn't it? This marriage has got to be signed, sealed and delivered before this beauty wakes up. Come on, Max, let's go, we don't need any witnesses."

Bob closed the door slowly behind him. He felt sick and tired and old. He knew, too, that it wasn't the mineral oil, although his stomach was knotted in cramps.

The next morning Web came into the office with a black eye and several scratches down his face. That made Bob feel better and he had to hide a smile as the bureau chief went into his office without saying a word. Almost immediately Web's secretary came out to tell Bob he was wanted.

"It looks as if the lady doth protest," Bob said as he sat in a large easy chair beside Web's desk.

"Protest! She was like a goddamned wildcat, which is about what I expected. I didn't mind that so much, but then she started to cry and said I had ruined everything."

"I take it she wasn't happy that her little blackmail plot was turned upside down."

Web bit the end of a cigar and spat it upon the floor. He rubbed the stubble on his chin, reflecting that he still had to shave before the White House news briefing.

"No, not the plot. Well, yes, she was concerned about the plot, but there's more to it than that. She said she was a C.I.A. agent and. . . ."

"Valentina Blatinkoff, a C.I.A. agent? I don't believe it."

"Well she sounded damned convincing and I have a call in right now to check it. She said she's been working for us for years and they have been encouraging her to get deeper into her work as a Russian agent so we could learn as much as possible about Soviet espionage. She felt this job on me would put her in solid with the Kremlin brass and she would start to move in the inner circles. At last she'd be able to get the kind of stuff the C.I.A. is looking for. Now, she says, she won't be able to go back to Russia and she won't be any use to the C.I.A. either."

"It sounds preposterous," Bob exclaimed. He still couldn't believe Valentina was an accomplished Russian agent let alone a double agent.

"She cries pretty well," Clayton said doggedly. "I don't think even a damned good actress could cry that much. No, I think she's telling the truth. I'll know in a little while, at any rate."

"Did you tell her about the annulment and the divorce?"

"I tried to, but then she started to cry some more. 'The Russians won't want me, the C.I.A. won't want me, and not even you will want me,' she said. Besides, she said that as long as we were married and she had no job or anything she might as well be Mrs. Webster Clayton. She thinks I'm rich because I go to all those damned fool parties."

Bob began to relax. Perhaps things might work out after all. "Is that why you're worried? Are you afraid you're not enough of a capitalist to support your Russian bride?"

"No, I'm not worried about Valentina. She'll be all right; she's really quite a girl."

"Something is bothering you, though, I can tell from the way you're smoking that cigar. What is it?"

Web took the cigar from his mouth and studied the ash reflectively. Suddenly he ground the cigar into the ash tray savagely. "The thing that bothers me is who was out to frame me, the Russian K.G.B. or the C.I.A.?"

Chapter Ten

VALENTINA TOOK to being Mrs. Webster Clayton as easily as she drank champagne and she found the experience almost as stimulating. She had clothes, furs, and jewels in abundance, though everyone in Washington wondered how Web was able to afford it on his salary and his alimony payments. Web, of course, had always been circumspect about his finances, but he had parlayed some of the information he had picked up in search of his columns into large and profitable investments. He always could afford the things Valentina demanded, but none of his previous wives had blossomed forth in either the style or the speed that Valentina did. It was almost as if she was a little girl turned loose in a store with an unlimited charge account. The strange part was that Web was too happy to care; Valentina, as he had told Bob, was really quite a girl.

Her first time in the office was embarrassing to Bob at first, but she soon put him at ease. Valentina was being shown into Web's office by a secretary when she saw Bob bending over some copy. Web was waiting in the doorway of his office for her, but Valentina detoured to Bob's desk and planted a kiss on his cheek.

"Oh Bob," she said, "You have made me so happy. I don't know how to thank you."

"Valentina, er, Mrs. Clayton," Bob said, getting up from his chair. "I thought you might be angry at me. I've wanted to send you a note of apology, but I didn't think it was right."

"Apologize? What for? If it hadn't been for you, I'd be back in Moscow with those ten hours of rehearsals a day and that plain food. Really, I should thank you."

"Yes and I think Mr. Webster Clayton is very angry that you are not rushing into his arms," Bob said, stealing a look over her shoulder. Clayton was sending up storm clouds of cigar smoke.

"Angry, why should he be angry? Coming Webster, darling," she called across the room. The reporters bent over their typewriters to keep from laughing. The men on the desk smiled broadly at Bob, who was trying gracefully to send Valentina on her way.

"Let me show you to the office," he said, taking her arm and guiding her to the doorway where Web stood chewing angrily on his cigar. Web kissed Valentina lightly on the cheek, grunted at Bob, and then walked into his office and closed the door. The next day Web recommended that Bob be transferred back to New York. The recommendation was couched in the most laudatory language. In essence it said that Bob was restricted in the contributions he could make to the paper in the Washington Bureau. It was the bureau chief's opinion, the recommendation said, that Bob had a firm grasp of the Washington situation and could be counted on to perform in an excellent manner no matter what challenge presented itself on the paper.

When Web told Bob of the recommendation, Bob was surprised but happy. He knew of the trouble Boland had caused Web and Bob recognized that Valentina's approach on her visit to the office had seemed like a parallel situation. Bob knew Web would never forget what Bob had done for him; it was only yesterday, he said, that he only hoped he could forget.

Zugsmith was pleased to have Bob back. Clayton's report was more than anyone could have hoped for since Web did not give out praise easily. Zugsmith didn't know of Bob's role in Web's latest marriage, but he did know Bob had impressed the bureau chief highly and in no sense could Bob have been rated a failure in his Washington test. He seemed more eager about the paper than before, more willing to settle into his job and to be less bored. Actually *The New York Record* had little to do with Bob's new attitude.

Bob was in love, hopelessly and helplessly. All doubts

about Diane were removed the first week after his return from Washington. It was like a homecoming, far different from the weekend visits he had managed to steal away from Washington. There was always so little time then and now suddenly he felt as if he had all the time in the world and he wanted to spend every minute of it with her.

"Darling," Bob finally said one night. "I know I haven't been fair to you, but I did a lot of thinking in Washington, too. I want to marry you, but I can't right now."

"You can't? Why not?" Diane's eyes widened in anger. "Did you get married to Edith Miller while you were in Washington?"

"I hardly saw her. She came down twice in the four months I was there, but, that's my whole point."

"I don't understand," Diane shook her head, her anger melting into bewilderment.

Bob shifted on the couch to face her. "Let me explain. At one time I think Edith Miller wanted to marry me, but that's because she's impulsive and always gets what she wants. But then when she found I wasn't jumping at the idea, she sort of cooled off. She began to look at the situation more logically. She knew her father would never be happy if she married a Gentile and . . ."

"Are the Millers Jewish? I thought they were German Catholics."

"No, they're Jewish and there has never been a mixed marriage in the family."

"But that wouldn't stop you if you were in love, would it? After all I'm Catholic and you're a Protestant. That never entered my head. Do you think Edith Miller thought about that, too?"

"I don't know. Edith is very modern and very liberal, but I think when the time came she wouldn't want to get Daddy or Mother angry at her choice of a husband. But let me get on with my explanation about why I want to wait to get married."

"I thought that was it, because you're not Jewish."

Bob bent over and kissed her. "Not Edith Miller. You, you dunce. I want to marry you, but not now."

Diane perked up noticeably. "At least that's something, but go on with your story. You lost me for a minute."

"Well, my friendship with Edith could be very important at this time. Zugsmith liked the way I handled the Washington assignment and I think he's looking for a spot for me doing something other than editing."

"A promotion? Will you be a writer?"

"I don't know. It might be writing, but I'm not sure. At any rate, if I married you now, before Edith Miller realizes she no longer wants me, Zugsmith will think I turned her down and then I'll never get the promotion."

"Couldn't we keep it secret? Would they have to know on the paper?"

Bob shook his head. He took her hands in his and kissed them gently. "I don't want to go sneaking around corners. When we get married I want every body to know it. I want to put your picture in *The New York Record*."

Tucker was the only one on the paper Bob told of his plans. He was surprised to find him unenthusiastic.

"It seems a shame to do that to such a nice girl," he said somberly as they sat in Curry's.

Bob thought he was kidding. "You mean marrying me? I'd have to agree with you there."

Tucker shook his head sadly. "No, I mean marrying a newspaperman. Maybe you can make it work, though."

"You seem to have done all right."

"I've never mentioned it to anyone, but my wife has a drinking problem. It's not unusual for a woman left alone night after night with only that damned TV to look at. A lot of them do a lot worse things than drink. That's why there are so many divorces on the paper."

"I'm sorry to hear about your wife. I don't think Diane will have any problems, though; she doesn't drink. Besides, she wants to work for a year so we can buy a house in the suburbs."

Tucker rubbed his chin reflectively. "My wife didn't drink, either, but that's besides the point. With Diane's working hours you should be in pretty good shape, but when you move to the suburbs, that will mean another hour commuting time each way and another two hours your wife will be alone with all the problems the kids bring home . . ."

"Kids?" Bob said with a laugh. "Aren't you moving a little too fast. We're not even married."

"Even so, I'm telling you what you'll be up against. Sure, it's fine when the kids are small, because you can play with them in the mornings and the early afternoon, when they're running around, but then when they start to school, you lose them. You're in bed when they go to school and you see them on your days off. The wife has to be father and mother most of the time and it's pretty hard."

"I think a lot of fathers forfeit the raising of the kids, even when they work so-called normal hours; it's the way our society is constituted. But with all that and knowing Diane, do you think it would make a difference to her or to me?"

Tucker sighed wearily. "No, it's useless, I know. In fact, I'm not sure if I would do things differently if I had to do it again. Sure, she'll wait up for you the first couple of weeks, but after that you're going to find that she just can't stay awake that long, that's when the loneliness of a silent house starts to gnaw at you."

"What do you mean?"

"Sometimes you don't get to make love to your wife for weeks. She's asleep when you get home and you don't like to wake her. And . . ."

"There's always the morning and the afternoon, too."

Tucker grinned. "Damn it, Bob, I keep forgetting, you're a lot younger than I am."

Father Tim Reilly was the only one Diane told of her plans, but she always told her brother everything. It wasn't long before Father Tim met Bob and they hit it off at once. Tim was a little older than Bob, but they had many things in common. Tim had played football at Fordham, served in the Navy during the war and then entered the priesthood as he had always intended. He was still a sports fan and enjoyed talking with Bob about football and baseball.

He made a point to get to Curry's after he met Bob because he wanted to know the midwesterner better. He had a lot of Diane's warmth and charm and some of her stubborness, particularly about *The New York Record.*

"Why do you work for that Communist paper?" Tim asked one night in Curry's while Bob was waiting for Tucker.

"Communist paper? *The New York Record?* I know there used to be a lot of Communists in the Newspaper Guild at one time, but the Guild has cleaned house now. There might be a few Communists still on the paper, but I don't think you could call it a Communist paper."

"If you were an unbiased outsider, you'd be able to see that it's a Communist paper, right out of the Kremlin. Who do you think got us to recognize Russia? *The New York Record.* Who wants us to let Red China into the U.N.? That's right, you know it yourself."

Bob shook his head stubbornly. "But that doesn't make the paper Communist. Liberal, perhaps, but not Red."

Tim grew more serious. "Honestly, Bob, there are an awful lot of Communists on the paper. I wondered about it for a long time. The boys in the chancellory have said it for years and I used to think that it was all church talk. But after a while you start to read the *Record* with a new slant. It is really a revelation. Ideally, I suppose, the aim is to be objective, but that's my principal quarrel with *The New York Record.* It holds itself out to be the paragon of objectivity, but you know yourself the dispatches can be slanted and frequently are."

"But you have to remember," Bob argued, "that many of our dispatches from overseas are filed under censorship. Sometimes the reporter has to write what he does to get a dispatch past the censor. But any good copy editor should be able to sense it and to take out the propaganda or at least present it as such."

There were others, though, who shared Father Tim's belief as Bob soon learned. Less than a month after Bob's talk with Tim, Congressman Arthur Bayard launched an investigation into Communist infiltration into the press, with *The New York Record* his number one target. To many people, including Bob, the investigation was launched primarily because of Bayard's love of headlines. Besides, the paper was fair game in an election year and Bayard knew his hearings in New York would guarantee him television coverage and enough front pages across the nation to make his election a safe bet. Bayard was only a mild reactionary; he didn't see a Communist under every bed, but he saw a vote in every barb he could launch at the "Red conspiracy."

As Bayard expected, he got the front page treatment, even in *The New York Record,* at least for the first day of the hearings. By playing up some weaker foreign stories, Zugsmith was able to shunt the hearings to an inside page each day, which Bayard duly noted at the opening of the next day's session. There was no doubt he was after *The New York Record.* Some one remembered an endorsement of an opponent in some long forgotten campaign and the feeling was that Bayard remembered, too. The number of witnesses from *The New York Record* outnumbered the other media by ten to one, but after all the paper had the largest staff. Eliot P. Lowell, as expected, was at the top of the list of witnesses. Webster Clayton was on the list and so was Bob Davis.

"How did Bayard ever get the idea that you and Clayton were Communists?" Tucker asked in Curry's over their lunch hour drink.

"It's probably because of Web's new wife, Valentina Blatin-koff."

"The ballet dancer?"

"Yes, Valentina. Web and I got into trouble over her because she was an American agent who was acting as a double agent. The Russians thought she was working for them, but she was really working for the C.I.A. The story never came out, but the Russians were mad at us for getting their star ballerina to defect and the C.I.A. was furious because we ruined years of planning for them to infiltrate the Soviet espionage system. Web thinks we were put on the list because of that."

"A ballerina a double agent? That sounds a little too much, but then it's also a little much to think of Webster Clayton as a Communist. Clayton had a column a month ago saying what a good idea Bayard's investigation was. Of course, that was before he knew he was going to be a witness. He must be burning up."

"What do you think, Tuck? Are there really that many reds on the paper?"

"I think the list they have, what is it twenty-two? Well, I'd say yes that at least half of them have been or still are Communists. The funniest thing of all, though, is that Eliot P. Lowell is probably not a Communist. I told you that when Leche told him he was going to turn the country into a Communist state, Lowell darned near had a heart attack. His speeches in City College were just oratory. Lowell liked to hear himself speak."

"What about the rest of them?"

"As I said, I think about ten of the boys had or have ties to the party. Remember what you told me about Diane's brother, Father Tim? Well, you know, there was no one on that list from the foreign desk, except you. How does that make you look with him?"

Bob smiled at the thought. "He said a copy editor would have to be tired, dumb, or a Red to pass some of the stuff that appears in the paper. I can always say I was dumb, and I guess I was. I thought *The New York Record* was too pompous to be the haven for even ten Reds."

Tucker's estimation was precise, or at least it seemed so. Five of *The New York Record* witnesses admitted to having been Communists at one time. Five refused to answer anything about their past, taking refuge in the Fifth Amendment. All five were summarily dismissed, with the five admitted former Communists retained.

"I don't get it," Bob said to Tucker at the post mortem in Curry's. "The ones who refuse to answer are fired and the ones who say they were card-carriers are kept. Don't you think the others were entitled to the benefit of the doubt? Maybe they really did object to Bayard's prying into their life."

"But don't you see? They had cast doubt on the paper. All right, their refusal might have been based on the fact that they had principles, but they also might still be party members and therefore liable to perjury charges if they said no. That nagging doubt would remain with the public as well as the brass on the paper; they had to go."

"But, hell, the ones that admitted to being Communists could have been responsible for some of the reputation the paper had about being Red. Why were they retained?"

"They were the penitent sinners. They admitted their own guilt, but they wouldn't testify about any others in the party. So therefore they had principles, too. I don't say that's the right analysis, but at least the paper showed it had faith in their honesty. I'll bet, though, there'll be some changes. Three of the writers are on the political beat so I don't think it would be politic for the paper to keep them in so sensitive a position. The others are on the national desk and I don't know if anything will happen to them. I think they, too, might be doing something else pretty soon."

Again Tucker's judgment was flawless. The by-lines of the

three reporters who had admitted Communist affiliations disappeared from the paper. One was sent to rewrite, another was assigned to write obituaries and the third was assigned to the house organ "Off the Record" put out by the personnel department. One of the former Communists from the national desk was assigned to write home improvement articles for the Sunday section and the other switched to the obituary desk, where he handled all the local deaths, the obituaries of any government official or any foreign dignitary being given to some one else. *The New York Record* can't afford to take chances, Zugsmith explained to the head of the desk when he worked out the details of the transfer.

In effect, *The New York Record* emerged from the investigation unconquered and only slightly compromised. Congressman Bayard was re-elected by an overwhelming majority after a campaign in which *The New York Record* was strangely silent about recommendations for office in his state.

The public forgot about the number of Communists on the staff of *The New York Record,* but the staff itself never did. There was no open warfare, but the lines of difference that had always been apparent on the paper were more sharply etched. It wasn't strictly a matter of cliques, since the party ties cut across the ins and the outs, the possibles and the impossibles. It was more like an Argentine primary campaign, with every shade of opinion represented from far left to far right, with support or opposition for each of the men involved in the investigation. Zugsmith, Bob knew, was a moderate. It was said that it was he who counseled the publisher on the course to be taken with those who admitted membership in the party. Manley wanted to fire all of them, but Zugsmith's views prevailed, as they usually did when compared with Manley's ideas for running the paper. Miller didn't think Zugsmith had the personality to meet the social obligations of being managing editor, but he knew his judgment was more sound than Manley's in dealing with men and in the practical aspects of getting the paper out each night. The only thing he lacked judgment about was Alice Blaine, the successor to Helen Crawford as his favorite companion.

Alice was new to the paper, another recruit from Zugsmith's class at the university. She was younger than Helen Crawford, with little of Helen's warmth or charm. She was more calculating, ruthless, and dangerous than the most ambitious man on the paper; Alice was going to get ahead and she wasn't going to let anyone or anything stand in her way. Helen Crawford couldn't have been ruthless if she tried. She was more like an aging den mother to the men in the city room, who first were attracted to her by her easy-going morals and then came to respect her for her sense of humor, her kindness and her ability to handle difficult assignments.

Alice Blaine was assured special treatment from her first day on the job. Zugsmith had decided that Alice's skills could best be used on the foreign desk. He had wanted to develop women copy editors as a hedge against the future, when there might be another manpower shortage because of a war or the supply might be exhausted by the attrition of public relations, radio or many other more interesting and better paying jobs. Magazines had done well with women copy editors, Zugsmith told Miller, why can't we give it a try?

Miller understood. The publisher liked his executives to have leeway in hiring "friends." It made them more loyal, tied them closer to their jobs. Besides, perhaps Zugsmith was right; the lower salaries paid to women copy editors might be helpful with next year's earnings report, too.

Because she was operating in a man's sphere, Alice adopted everything masculine except the trousers; her clothes were so severely tailored, though, hardly anyone would have noticed if she had worn trousers. Her speech was rough and liberally sprinkled with profanity as if she was determined to show the men on the desk that she belonged. A plain girl, with a wide farm face, she wore a severe hairdo that was shorter than some of the copy boys'. Her figure was ample, but not as coarse as her clothes made it appear. Her nails were dirty as often as they were polished and manicured for Alice gave the appearance of a somewhat unkempt and unhappy masculine female rebelling against the strictures of primness, delicacy and neatness that usually bound most women in the business world.

Despite her appearance, Alice could be soft and womanly when she wanted to and most of the time it was when she was near Zugsmith. It wasn't coincidental, she arranged it that way at his suggestion. "Whenever you don't understand anything," he said, "ask me, I'll straighten you out."

Alice made use of the invitation to point out errors in the paper and to suggest changes in headlines. She adopted the I-want-to-learn attitude, but Zugsmith recognized the same approach Tom Crum had used earlier. He was right about Alice; she'd made a fine copy editor: she had the killer instinct and the determination it required.

With Alice on the foreign desk, Tom Crum would be her wall of insulation against any egregious mistakes. There was no need to train Alice any other way but under fire. On the foreign desk, Zugsmith could keep an eye on her, too. It was easy for him to suggest to Tom that she should have only early hours so she could get home before it got too late. Tom didn't know for almost a month that Alice's early hours coincided with Zugsmith's hours and it was easy for them to leave together for a drink or anything else they might have in mind.

All Zugsmith's personal choices were suspect in the eyes of the other men on the desk. Bob had survived the resentment because of his horse-playing; Alice didn't have that to fall back on and her brand of femininity was considered more of a threat than an attraction. She had the best hours, the best days off and the easiest to handle dispatches. When Alice was given a story that would change just as she was about to go home, Crum would give the changes to Bob to make; anyone else would have had to stay to handle the late material themselves.

At first Alice had trouble with the headlines and the editing. Bob had seen Crum ridicule men mercilessly for mistakes similar to those made by Alice, but Crum seldom spoke harshly to the girl. It wasn't only that she was Zugsmith's protege; Crum liked Alice, too. She played up to Crum shamelessly, often having lunch with him in the cafeteria and spending the whole time talking about ways to improve her work. Alice was eager to prove that Zugsmith was right in giving her the chance. She knew Zugsmith's help could take her far if she mastered copy editing. She took down everything Crum told her in a large notebook and spent her free time on the desk reading Zugsmith's old memos or thumbing through the cards carrying the names of the thousands of political, social and scientific figures in the foreign news. The cards were open to everyone on the desk, with each man, or woman, assigned to a certain number of countries. Those in charge of a set of cards would add new names as they came up in the paper, change the cabinet lists and add notations about any honors or titles held by the person on the card.

The cards, of course, were invaluable aids in checking the accuracy of dispatches from the correspondent and also for correcting the spelling of names garbled by the transmission clerks or those receiving the material at *The New York Record*. Yet, most of the men on the desk, Bob included, preferred to put off the updating of the cards as long as possible. The chore was looked on as a bookkeeping one and few men were willing to spend the time needed to maintain the files at peak efficiency.

Alice Blaine, of course, included the file cards in her learning program. She was assigned only three easy countries, although most newcomers to the desk were charged with maintaining the most difficult sections of the file with the most number of names. Bob still had a hangover of that policy with his assignment to maintain the Far East cards, covering seven nations, including Korea. The Korean cards were the only ones where modern history collided with ancient custom. Half the cards had been entered before the Korean War and the rest were of the war period or thereafter. Consequently, Bob found in going through the file that there were frequently duplicate cards, with General Koo Hee Shung, appearing as General Koo, General Hee, and General Shung, as well as with all three names. No one was able to figure out which of the three Korean names was the family name and as a result all three were used everytime in the copy.

No one questioned the system until Alice Blaine used the Korean cards. She insisted first to Bob and then to Tom Crum that the cards were all wrong. Koo Hee Shung was not correct, she maintained, the card should read Shung Hee Koo. The change came about, Alice said, after the Korean War when the country moved more securely into the Western camp and the politicians and others in South Korea Westernized their names.

"What about the North Koreans?" Bob asked, obviously enjoying what he thought was a ridiculous argument.

"They should be the same," Alice said firmly. Then she bit her lip. She realized the North Koreans had moved farther from the West and more into the sphere of China.

"But suppose they don't want to be the same?" Bob was enjoying her distress. Alice seldom got into an indefensible position. All her moves were logical, all her explanations valid, at least to herself.

"It doesn't matter to them anyway. The ideographs they use probably can't be translated into English anyway."

"But we've been doing it right along. To stop now and go to a different system would be stupid."

"If the President of the country Westernizes his name, shouldn't that be good enough for us?"

Bob thought for a moment. "I don't know. If John Fitzgerald Kennedy suddenly decided he wanted to be called Kennedy Fitzgerald John, I don't know if I'd change my name to Davis Bob."

"Now you're being silly," Alice pouted, growing angry that the exchange had lasted this long. She had thought her great discovery would be accepted with less argument and she would score points with Zugsmith and with Crum. "The President of Korea and the President of the United States are two different things. We're talking about translations and transliteration, not merely name changes."

Bob, too, was growing tired of the by-play. "Frankly, I don't care what the names are, but I'm not going to change all those Korean cards. I think we should be consistent, that's all. If we change, we'll be different from the other papers and the wire services, too."

"The New York Record doesn't follow, it leads," Alice said with all the haughtiness of Zugsmith. Bob knew he was beaten, but he wasn't giving up easily.

"Okay," he said, "but you've just taken over Korea as one of your countries, because I'm not going to change them."

He really didn't feel badly about it, but Diane became angry when he told her about the incident that night.

"That bitch," she said, with unusual fervor. Bob realized Diane hadn't seen Alice and her reaction was typical of any of the women he mentioned on the paper after his experience with Edith Miller.

"Don't you hate these women who know so much?" she continued.

Bob smiled. "What about the women who know so much about other women?"

"Meaning me?"

"Present company excepted, of course," Bob said innocently. He squeezed her hand across the table. "Maybe she does know what she's talking about. I could care less. If she wants to change the cards that way, it makes no difference to me."

"Why don't you ask Lee?"

"Lee who?" Bob searched his memory for a clue to the name.

"Lee, the dishwasher here. He used to be a big shot in Korea, or at least that's what the waiters say. They treat him with a lot of respect."

"In this club, a Korean?"

Diane shook her head. "He's right out in the kitchen, why don't you ask him?"

The dishwasher was a wizened Oriental with a bland, smiling face creased with age. Bob had seen many of the same types of faces in Seoul and along the backroads of the Korean countryside. Only the little stove pipe hat and the long-stemmed pipe were missing to complete the picture. The man looked up from his work as Bob and Diane approached.

"Lee, this is my friend. He's a newspaper man. He wants to talk to you."

Lee ceremoniously wiped his hands on his apron, bowed and extended his hand. "It is a great honor to meet a friend of the beautiful Miss Diane," he said in a flawless English.

"Is Lee your right name?"

"Yes sir, Lee."

"That's all, Lee? I thought all Koreans had at least three names."

"Sometimes we have as many as five or six names, but the average is three. My full name, as I am honored to say it has appeared many times in the American newspapers is Shu Lee Cho."

"Shu Lee Cho?" The name rang a bell in Bob's memory. His mind raced through the card file in the office as he tried to recall the connection. "Were you a professor? Weren't you the Premier of a revolutionary government that toppled a military regime and then was driven out in a counter-revolution?"

Lee smiled and nodded. "You do know your Korean history, do you not, my son. Yes, I was a professor, but I am not the Shu Lee Cho of whom you speak, our beloved Premier. I was a colleague of his at the university and I did hold a small post in his most temporary government. In Korea many names are similar if not exactly alike. Our names were often confused, so much so that when the Premier was forced to flee, I, too, had to leave Korea rather hurriedly."

"You were a professor, but not the Premier?" Bob wanted to make sure he understood.

"That's right my son. I am only the premier dishwasher of this club. Like your President Jackson of beloved memory, I have a kitchen cabinet, but my rule is only over pots and pans."

"But you knew the Premier? That's wonderful. Let me buy you a drink. You must have a fascinating story to tell." Bob took the old man by the arm and started to guide him to the dining room.

Lee held back. "I regret I am not suitably attired. I cannot go in there in these soiled clothes."

"Don't let it bother you," Bob insisted. "Put on your coat, we can sit in the back and no one will see us."

Lee turned to Diane. "Do you think it will be proper, Miss Diane?"

"Certainly," she said reassuringly. "The boss has gone home already anyway. There aren't many customers out there and the show is about to start. I don't think too many people will be watching the back tables while I'm singing."

"Only fools and old blind men," Lee agreed, shuffling off to get his coat.

Bob was fascinated by the old man's story. He knew many of the names from the Korean card file and he spoke of his days in Seoul with warm good humor. Everything he told Bob was off the record, though; Lee had entered the country illegally, and was still sought by the old military junta. That was why he couldn't seek better employment, something more in line with his talents.

"But our Government would protect you," Bob said.

Lee smiled. "The man who lives in protective custody is not truly free. Here it is true that I am a lowly dishwasher, but I am free and I am happy. I have my books and my pipe at night and your city in the daytime. I can walk where I want; watch the children, feed the pigeons, sit in the sun, and day-dream. I have quite enough; at least I am free."

"Did you ask him?" Diane asked as she returned to the table after her number. She was dressed and ready to go home.

"Ask him what?" Bob said, the hassle with Alice gone from his mind completely.

"About Korean names. How do they go?"

"Oh yes. Professor Lee," Bob said, turning to the little Oriental. Then he stopped. "Professor Lee? If your name is Shu Lee Cho, how are you called Professor Lee?"

"Because I Westernized my name, my son. Lee was my family name, Shu the name of my beloved mother and Cho my own name, given me at birth. My friends would call me Cho."

Bob shook his head to clear away the confusion. "I am sorry if I'm confused, Professor, but I'm not alone. *The New York Record,* the paper I work for is confused, too."

"You work for *The New York Record?*" Lee was obviously impressed. "It is a fine paper, but too much leaning toward the Communists."

Bob ignored the remark. He didn't want to get off on another tangent when he was zeroing in on the name problem. *"The New York Record* is trying to Westernize the Korean names in the news, but it is being done differently from the way you have told me. They are turning the names around so that your name on our cards now would be Cho Lee Shu and you would be Professor Shu. Are you sure your way is the correct way?"

Lee smiled through the dim light and the cigarette smoke. "As I told you, my son, I taught at the University of Seoul for twenty years. My specialty was languages, so I am certain I would know my own name and the customs of my country even in your language and in your country."

"She's wrong then, isn't she?" Diane put in happily.

Bob nodded, smiling to himself. He wondered how the most capital could be made out of his discovery. He didn't want to do anything until Alice had converted all the cards to her system of names; that would make his maneuver more telling.

177

"Professor Lee, could you write a letter to *The New York Record* telling them about Korean names, just as you have told me?"

"For what purpose, my son? I have told you I do not seek publicity; I do not think it wise in my circumstances. I arrived in your country under a cloud of trouble. Why should I come to the surface now and write to your exalted newspaper?"

"It would mean an awful lot to me," Diane said. She bit her lip nervously; she hated Alice Blaine without ever having seen her.

"It would be only for the eyes of my superiors, not for the public," Bob said. "You would be helping to straighten out a great wrong being done to your countrymen. They are being called by the names of their mothers instead of their fathers. Would that not cause them to lose face?"

Lee smiled. "I have been too long in the West, too long washing dishes to be concerned with face. It is a silly Oriental custom, I am afraid."

"It would help to straighten out a bad woman," Diane said.

Bob shot her an annoyed glance. "She's bad only in a professional way, Professor. She is one of those women who knows everything. I am sure there must be many like her in your country."

"Ah, yes, a shrew."

"A bitch," Diane put in heatedly.

"Miss Diane, you surprise me with your language. Your cheeks, too, are enflamed. She must truly be a bad woman if she arouses you so. If that is the case, I will surely write the letter, but I count on you, Mr. Davis, to protect me from the public; the letter will not be printed."

Bob waited a month before drafting the letter for Lee. He enjoyed talking with the old man on his trips to the club and he pointed out the changed style when Korean stories appeared in the paper. Alice's changes were hardly noticed. Zugsmith went along with the shuffle of the names, but he insisted that all three had to be retained, regardless of the order.

As a result, there was nothing in *Editor and Publisher,* scant notice in the other papers, and hardly a ripple at the U.N. over the switch. Both the north and south Koreans at the U.N. had long despaired of trying to teach Western journalists anything, especially those from *The New York Record.*

The letter mentioned Lee's university service because Bob knew the awe a string of degrees created on the paper. He was also hoping that Manley's male secretary, who normally handled such correspondence, would get Professor Lee confused with the Premier, thus adding weight to the stricture on the order of the names. An address had to be given and Bob suggested using the club address so Lee would not be disturbed in his rooms if a reporeter was sent around to check the letter, which was sometimes done in policy matters.

Bob was off when the impact of the letter was felt on the desk. Alice's reaction was understandable: she had just finished getting the Korean cards into the form she wanted and now she faced the task of putting them back into a different style. She fell into the same trap Bob had in assuming that Professor Lee was the former Premier.

The edge was taken off Bob's triumph, however, when the proof of the editorial page was put on the desk for checking on his next night back at work. Bob read the editorial related to the story he handled, then glanced at the letters to the editor column almost idly. Lee's letter was the first one in the column. It was complete with the club's address and a footnote telling the readers that Professor Lee was the former Premier of Korea. Bob froze in his chair. He had been confident *The New York Record* would not acknowledge in public that it had been wrong on the Korean names, but there was the letter for all to see. It was a precedent, but a shattering one for Bob; he had betrayed the Professor and exposed him to danger. Suddenly Bob sensed that there was some one standing over him. It was Howard Tucker.

"What's the matter?" Tucker asked. "You look as if you've seen a ghost."

Bob got up from the desk and motioned Tucker to follow. He sat down by Tucker's desk and quickly told the rewrite man the whole story.

"That's not so bad," Tucker said soothingly. "I'd think you'd enjoy a bigger laugh on Alice after the paper comes up."

"It's not that, it's the old man. I told him the letter wouldn't be printed. I never thought they'd use it. Besides, it was sent to the Foreign Editor, not the editor of the editorial page."

"There obviously was a slipup, but there isn't a lot you can do about it."

"If the State Department or the Immigration Department sees that footnote about the former Premier, they're liable to give the old man trouble."

Tucker ran his tongue over his teeth, his thumbs hooked in his belt loops. "How would it be if the footnote and the address didn't appear? Would that help you?"

"It would be something. At least the old man would not be bothered at the club. I could explain about the letter, but the footnote and the address could be real trouble."

"Okay, I can take care of it, but it will cost you a bottle of booze."

"What are you going to do?" Bob asked, puzzled.

"I know a lot of printers," Tucker said archly. "I'll go up and have them pull the address and the footnote. The booze is for the printers; they like to drink."

"But suppose the page has been matted?"

Tucker smiled. "That's the trouble with you bright young men, you know too much. If the page has been matted I'll go down to the press room and have it chiseled out of the form. We used to do that all the time with obscenities. In that case the press men will get the booze; they like to drink, too."

"I don't care if it takes two bottles. Get out that address if you can."

Bob turned quickly to the editorial page when the paper came up. The letter was still there, but the address and the footnote was missing. He turned and smiled broadly at Tucker, who was just returning from Curry's. Tucker walked to the desk.

"Did everything come out all right?"

"Fine, I'll pick up the bottle tomorrow," Bob said.

"Were you serious about two bottles?"

"Certainly, why?"

"Well, my friend in the composing room is an old-timer. He loves that whisky. I think for another bottle he might manage to lose the letter for the second edition."

"Do you really think he could get away with it?"

"Sure. Enough weird things happen in the composing room by accident. It would be no trick for him to drop the type. He can slip in another letter. No one ever checks the editorial page after the first edition, anyway. There are so few changes that no one bothers. If anyone picks up the change, he can always say the type was pied."

"In that case, let's go for it."

"Two bottles?"

"No, three, one for you. It means a lot to me to show the old man it wasn't my fault."

"Okay, three bottles, but only on one condition."

"What's that?"

"That you bring that gorgeous girl of yours up some night and help us drink it. You can even bring the old professor, if you want. He sounds like a fascinating guy."

"I can't guarantee the professor, but Diane and I will be there. I'll try to get the professor, but he doesn't like to meet people."

Everything worked to perfection. The letter disappeared after the first edition and no one on *The New York Record* was the wiser. Bob had forgotten that five hundred thousand copies of the paper had gone out with the letter in the first edition, though. The first edition had the greatest circulation outside the city and it was long after Lee had accepted Bob's explanation that the repercussions were felt.

Another Korean letter appeared, this one expressing gratification that Professor Lee was alive and hailing him for his efforts to install a reform Government. This elicited another letter attacking Professor Lee for having abandoned his country and soon a virtual missive war was being carried on on the editorial page.

Tucker's interest in the story caused him to keep close check on the situation. "Your Korean friend is going to be interviewed," the rewrite man said on one of his luncheons with Bob in Curry's.

"Lee? When?" Bob was concerned. He had watched the build-up of fear in the old man as the controversy was fanned in the letters to the editor. It would have been impossible for Bob and Tucker to keep out all the letters, not that Tucker wasn't willing to try.

"They're working on it right now," Tucker said. "They know the adddress was that of the club, but they couldn't get any information because the professor was off. You'd better warn him to lay low for a few days."

"But he has to work. I don't know if he has any friends he could go to. Of course, I could put him up in my place for a few days, but it would be pretty tight."

"You say he's a dishwasher; can he cook?"

"I don't know. Yes, he can, too. I remember Diane was sick one day and he made her some Korean soup. It was pretty good, too. Why?"

"If he can cook, his troubles are over. I have a friend who has a big place up in the Catskills. He's seldom up there and he wants a caretaker and a cook for when he does go up there. This guy is pretty well loaded, so I'm sure he'll pay well. Do you think the old man would go for it?"

"In the Catskills? I remember the old man telling me how he missed the mountains of Korea. I think he'd go for it, at least until the heat dies down. He's unhappy as hell about the publicity and I'm sure he'd welcome a chance to drop out of sight again."

Diane was visibly upset when Bob arrived at the club.

"Bob, all sorts of people have been here looking for Professor Lee. They had a fellow from your paper and then there were men from the television stations and the other papers. There were also a couple of F.B.I. men and then two different groups that appeared to be Orientals. Charlie, the Filipino busboy, said they had guns. Bob, I'm scared. If anything happens to Professor Lee I'll never forgive myself."

Bob put his hands around her shoulders and patted her reassuringly. "Don't worry, honey, nothing is going to happen to Professor Lee. Did the owner tell them where he lives?"

"No, Nick is home sick, and the manager said he didn't have access to the employee records. The F.B.I. man didn't seem to believe him, but they said they'd be back tomorrow."

"Do you know where the Professor lives?"

"I could find out, why?"

"I think it would be a good idea to get him out of town. I have a job for him up in the mountains. Do you think he'd take it?"

"I know he wants to get out of here. He's really frightened. He said there might be some people looking for him and I could see he was worried. Oh Bob, if anything happens to him because of that damned bitch on the paper, I'll die."

"Don't worry, baby, nothing is going to happen to Professor Lee. Come on, let's get his address and let's get going."

Bob didn't have to do much talking to convince the Professor that a trip to the country would be beneficial. His usual serene manner was gone and he was nervous and disturbed by Diane's story of the men who had been at the club.

"It seems that the old military clique did not fade away as I thought," he said with an air of resignation. "In that case, Mr. Davis, I must agree with you completely. It is best I fade away myself."

They packed so hurriedly and then checked the room so thoroughly for anything of value that it appeared the place had been ransacked. *The New York Record* reporter and the rest of the press who arrived with the police the next morning agreed on that conclusion because it made good copy. The reporter was young and imaginative and the signs of a struggle that leaped out at him and the club owner's account of the Oriental visitors of the previous day blended perfectly into an adventure tale that moved the story up close to the foreign news. Of course, the tabloids went all the way and the foul play that was hinted at in *The New York Record* account was proclaimed boldly on the front pages of the sensational sheets.

Bob read the stories with a feeling of smugness as he relaxed at the desk after the long drive with Professor Lee and Tucker. Suddenly he bolted from the desk to speak to Tucker.

"Howie, how do you know this friend of yours won't turn Professor Lee over to the immigration officials or the F.B.I.?"

"Forget about it. He's a friend of mine, isn't he?"

"I know, but it might hurt his business if the Professor is found there. What does he do?"

"He's a gambler. I guess you'd call him a gangster. He's in the country illegally, too, so I don't think he's about to contact the immigration officials."

That made Bob savor his coup even more. He thought of the Professor enjoying the mountains while under the protection of a gangster. He was laughing to himself when Alice finished reading the article on Professor Lee. The implication was clear; the Professor had been shanghaied and taken back to Korea or he had been murdered and dumped into the river.

"I feel sorry for the Professor," Alice said loudly. "But it's his own fault. Everything would have been all right if he hadn't disagreed with me about those Korean names. I'm glad I didn't bother to change them back."

Chapter Eleven

BOB WAS surprised at the power of the bottle on the paper. Zugsmith had driven most of the high-powered drinkers off the paper, but there were still some men who kept a bottle in a desk drawer or a locker. Mostly, though, the paper was put out on coffee. The drinkers did their best work at Curry's when martini lunches were consumed each night. By that time, though most of the work had been done and the after-lunch chores for most of the men consisted of checking earlier stories. Some of the liquid lunchers were too bleary-eyed to do much checking, but the system of checks and balances prevented most of serious errors from getting by. If the mistake wasn't caught by the desk itself, it might be caught by the proof room or a man from another desk who was reading the paper merely to kill time on a late shift or for interest in some particular story.

Whisky had an almost status appeal for some men, particularly if they didn't buy it. In this, many of the man on *The New York Record* represented throwbacks to the old school of anti-journalism that contended you could buy most newspaper men for a drink. Many of those who took bottles or other gifts from news sources or publicity men weren't being bought, but some of them had arrangements, either tacit or explicit, with the givers of gifts. Each Christmas, the reception desk would be piled high with baskets of liquor, fruit, and other gifts for delivery to the top editors or the writers. The men on the desk were virtually ignored, for they had little to say about what stories would get into print. There were exceptions, of course, since the desk head in certain departments could put through copy on his own and the make-up man could always see that a particular article was printed rather than put on the overset. The business news department attracted the most number of gifts, but sports, real estate, drama, and transportation—any dealing with news of a service or product for sale—also came in for their share of Christmas getting.

The publisher frowned on the system, but he was powerless to stop it. Each year he would put a notice on the bulletin board stating that the paper was opposed to the acceptance of gifts, but the packages would continue to arrive for those not discreet enough to have supplied their news contacts with their home addresses. One top editor made sure his Christmas cards were mailed the first week in December with his home address on the envelope. Then he would leave a note on his front door that all packages were to be left in the garage. That way, he never saw the package being dropped off and he always could tell the publisher that he really did believe in Santa Claus if he was ever challenged. Some of the men, of course, respected the publisher's wishes and some gifts were sent back. Although the newcomers on the paper didn't know it, in doing so they were recalling Byron Guilfole, the former real estate editor, whom the old-timers called the man who shot Santa Claus. Guilfole was responsible for the prohibition against taking gifts.

Each year Byron would receive so much liquor that he couldn't carry it home. To turn the bulky bottles in to more easily manageable cash, Byron would hold a pre-holiday sale for the men on the desks or the liquorless departments each year. His prices were far better than Curry's or even the lowest discount store. There was no bargaining because Byron's sales were annual sell-outs; they had to be before his staff arrived back from vacation. That was one of the keys to Byron's success as an unofficial liquor dealer. Each year he would give the three men in his department the holiday week off. The men appreciated it at first because it gave them time at home with their families, but they began to realize that Byron was keeping all the Christmas packages for himself.

Guilfole felt that the bottles and the occasional checks were all part of his job. It was the same way with junkets arranged by builders, complete with all expenses and attractions, including women, if he desired and Byron usually did. In fact, Byron's constant money troubles were attributable to the alimony he was paying three ex-wives and the money he was lavishing on his latest flame from some chorus line. Byron's weakness for women and a fastidious bookkeeper for a prominent builder led to the ban on the acceptance of gifts by employees of *The New York Record*. One of the items Byron had accepted on a junket was the services of a "model" over night and the facts were properly documented in an investigation of the builder for improprieties on a state contract. Byron wasn't alone on the list of witnesses at the investigation, but he was the only one from *The New York Record*. The publisher's prohibition against accepting "gifts of value" followed almost immediately. When it became impossible to define a "gift of value," the ban was broadened to include all gifts.

No one on the paper resented the fact that Guilfole was responsible, however. He was probably one of the most charming scoundrels who had ever worked on the paper. You couldn't help liking him even though if you were in his department he could very well be cheating you. A graduate of a small college in the South, Guilfole had an ante bellum graciousness combined with the scruples of a carpetbagger. Christmas wasn't once a year for Byron, it seemed to come every day. Because of the vastness of the market he covered, much of the loot came from publicity men for builders. The arrangement was a happy one for Byron since he could keep his men working as rewrite men all week and he could charge the publicity men, or the builders themselves for whatever material was used. It wasn't a hit or miss proposition with Guilfole. He had definite rates, which were about half the advertising rates, so therefore a bargain for the publicity men. He always reasoned that the readers would believe the news columns before they would believe the advertising columns and he was right.

Small items were twenty-five dollars, larger ones fifty, pictures one hundred. The builders were happy to pay and would have gone on paying if that builder's bookkeeper hadn't been so careful. For the payments to Guilfole came out in the same investigation that disclosed his junket adventures, but the story was never printed in *The New York Record*. Nor was the story of Guilfole's changed status reported, although the paper's policy of never firing anyone was sorely tested. Zugmith, realizing the discharge of the editor so soon after the investigation could prove troublesome to the paper, finally worked out a solution that Miller accepted.

"If Guilfole is such a damned good space salesman," Zugsmith argued, "Let's promote him to the advertising department."

Miller knew Guilfole would be the paper's highest paid space salesman, but he was happy with the plan. It was in keeping with a long-standing policy on the paper: botch up one job and you get promoted. Tucker and the rest of the rewrite men laughed about it, but it was true enough. A demotion would indicate that *The New York Record* had been wrong; a discharge was unthinkable, so the only way to go was up. Some of the best executives had failed either as editors or writers; some of the worst executives had been excellent writers or editors.

Guilfole was long gone before Bob joined the paper, but he knew Sellers Warrenton, the drama critic, just as did everyone in America. Tucker had told him a story about Warrenton that was even more amazing than Guilfole's.

Sellers Warrenton was strictly a creation of Zugsmith, who not only gave him the job as music critic but even picked out his name. Warrenton was another example of something that could happen only on *The New York Record*. He had no training in the newspaper business, but for years held the life and death say over hundreds of musical productions and then later stage presentations. His introduction to *The New York*

Record was as a pit violinist from a Broadway theater who was befriended by Byars Wallington, the *Record's* famous music critic of the Twenties.

Wallington was a throwback to the Nineties. He dressed in elegant style, always wore an evening cape to the openings and was seldom seen without a huge black silver-headed cane. To him, music was everything; the criticism of it was something he had to put up with in deference to the fine living it provided, but it was not truly art. Despite his disdain for journalism, Wallington was unquestionably the most astute critic of his day. It was only his methods of getting his reviews into print that were so hard on the paper and on Zugsmith, particularly with his sensitivity to the deadlines, the demands of the train schedules and all the hundreds of gears that had to mesh perfectly to perform the daily miracle of turning the huge rolls of newsprint into a product to be admired, quoted, and damned equally in all sections of the country.

When Wallington first met him, Warrenton was playing violin in a cheap restaurant in the Village. His name was Anthony Spartoffi. He was darkly handsome, charming, and articulate, but with no more ambition than to some day have a trio of his own that would play in the larger, better clubs uptown. Wallington took to Spartoffi at once, as much for his charm and wit as for his skill with the violin. The critic would drop into Tony's club several times a week just to hear him play the songs of his youth or the latest arrangements of the classics. Wallington had started to drink heavily about that time and he found more and more a need for alcohol and stimulation when it came time to write his reviews. It really wasn't writing, since he had never learned to type and he was too temperamental to sit down with a pad and pencil to commit the words that came pouring from his consciousness about an opera, a concert or some other performance he had attended. The *Record* provided him with a secretary who reported late at night whenever there was an opening. The secretary would take down the rapid-fire delivery of Wallington and then transcribe the notes hurriedly so that the review could be set in type.

Zugsmith put up with that only because the system had been in effect before his rise to power. There were many things about *The New York Record* he would like to have changed, but he, too, was thwarted in many cases by the glacial movement about the place, the deeply rooted tradition of how it was done last year. Wallington began bringing Tony Spartoffi into the office to play his violin while the critic paced up and down spewing forth his review. That's when Zugsmith began to get uneasy. He knew the old man was drinking more heavily than usual and he feared that allowing Wallington to have his own musical court jester would prove too much for others on the paper. Christ, for all he knew, the movie critic would have to have a young starlet in to inspire him while he was writing. Things were bad enough.

There was no mistake about it, though; Tony did help Wallington a lot. He'd play some of the passages of the piece they had just listened to and the old man would close his eyes and nod his head as the memories of each false note and each perfect octave came flooding back and loosened the dam of words at the end of his tongue. It was only when the pieces were very bad that Wallington had trouble and that Zugsmith worried. On the bad pieces, the critic didn't want to remember and his head shaking would soon become nodding as he slipped off to sleep.

Tony would try to rouse him, nudging him gently and then at last he would give up. Turning to the young secretary, he would say, "What was the last thing he said?" The girl would read back the dictation and then Tony would supply the rest of the phrases he knew Wallington loved to use when the music had not appealed to him. Wallington never knew the difference and Tony had the critic's style down so pat that no one else on the paper knew the difference except the secretary.

Zugsmith's restlessness, though, was Tony's undoing, or his

making. Zugsmith arrived one night when Tony was trying to arouse the critic.

"What's going on here?" Zugsmith demanded, furious that Wallington was asleep.

"Mr. Wallington doesn't feel good," Tony explained, nudging the critic once more spiritedly.

"Feel good? I think he's feeling too good. I can smell him from here. He's drunk."

Wallington came awake, his pride bristling that he had been caught in such an embarrassing position. "Who's drunk?" he demanded heatedly, his lips moist, his eyes rolling. "I merely was deep in thought trying to recall a particular passage in the performance we heard tonight. Drunk, certainly not, I'm insulted, Mr. Zugsmith."

"I don't give a damn if you are insulted, Mr. Wallington. Where is your review? We're already twenty minutes late for the edition and we'll be lucky to make the last edition at the rate you're going. How much more do you have to cover?"

"How much more? How much have I written? Miss Perkins, what was the last thing I said?"

"Don't wake me up, let me sleep," the girl read from the pad innocently.

"So," Zugsmith said triumphantly, "you weren't asleep. What do you call that?"

Wallington drew himself up to his full five feet six inches. "I call it a gross insult to the most famous critic in America. I don't have to take your insults, sir. I am highly respected in music circles. I can buy and sell your kind every day."

"What about your review, sir," Zugsmith cut in sharply, his eyes on the clock, his mind racing with calculations about his chances to make the final edition.

"Damn my review, sir. Damn *The New York Record* and damn you, sir," Wallington retorted. He picked up his silver-headed cane and started toward the door. "Coming, Tony?" he called.

"Just a minute," Zugsmith said. "Is this the young man that

has been appearing on your expense account as a violinist?"

"Yes, sir, I guess that's me," Tony said meekly.

"Then you have been paid by *The New York Record* to attend these various concerts?"

"Yes, sir, I have."

"Could you finish Mr. Wallington's review?"

Tony looked at the secretary and motioned her to be silent. "I think I can, from what he told me in the cab coming over here."

"Tony, you wouldn't," Wallington called from the door.

"I'm just trying to be helpful, Mr. Wallington. I don't want you to lose your job."

"Hang the job. Come on, boy, let *The New York Record* go to hell."

"We can make it well worth your while," Zugsmith said, his eyes still on the clock. "If you do a good job, we might even make you music critic."

"Don't listen to that damned nonsense, Tony, come on," Wallington begged from the door.

"Music critic, me?" Tony's eyes lighted up. He knew the power that the critic of *The New York Record* enjoyed. Suddenly the held-back ambition burst forth. "I'll do it, sir," he said. "I'm sure I can."

"Zugsmith, you are a bastard," Wallington said heatedly, brandishing the silver-headed cane.

"But, Mr. Wallington, you said you could buy and sell me. I should think you wouldn't want to be troubled by such insignificant people. Oh yes, before you go, I think you should know that the review in tomorrow's paper will be signed, not by Byars Wallington, but by Sellers Warrenton. I think that is a nice name, a *New York Record* name. I'll like it all the more because it will always remind me of you."

Tony did well; in fact, he did better than well. He even learned to type and the time for getting the reviews into the paper was shortened until there was no question about making the second edition unless a concert or performance ran extra late. The saving, of course, was more than in time. The secretary was no longer needed and Tony, or Warrenton as he was called from that first night, needed no violinist to get him in the mood. His knowledge of music was deeper than Wallington's, perhaps, and his technical insight greater, but he lacked the full appreciation of the classics that the old man had had. This was no handicap for years, but it ultimately led to his switch to dramatic criticism. That change, too, could happen only on *The New York Record*.

Warrenton was in Salzburg at the music festival, which the publisher had included on his European itinerary that year. They met after a performance for a drink in the hotel bar.

"Excellent performance, don't you think?" Miller asked enthusiastically.

"Yes, excellent," Warrenton agreed with little emotion.

"What's the matter, Sel, don't you like Wagner?"

"Oh, Wagner is fine, but I think sometimes we emphasize the classics a little too much. I think we should pay attention more to the new sounds in music," Warrenton said, Tony Spartoffi fighting beneath the surface to emerge.

"You mean the new jazz, rock 'n' roll?"

"Yes, that, too, but more specifically, the contemporary music. The music of Broadway. I think that type of music is trying to say something today."

"Don't you think the classics say anything?"

"Yes, certainly, but it's all been said before. How many ways can you interpret Wagner or Bach or Beethoven? If you go too far, then it is not classical, you are saying something yourself, not what you think someone else said or meant to say."

"And you say that this new expression is found on Broadway?"

"Yes, many of the musicals are trying to say something. In time we might recognize some of these musical comedies as the beginning of American opera. I think we should do everything we can to encourage that."

Miller drained his glass and motioned to the bartender. "Did anyone tell you that I'm unhappy with our drama critic?"

"No, are you?" Warrenton asked, genuinely surprised.

"He's a fine critic, but I think his tastes are a little too, what should I say, a little too *New York Record*. I think his standards are probably too high. Perhaps he'd be better off with your job; the trouble is he doesn't know a thing about music. I sometimes think that's why he seldom raves about a musical show. You know he hasn't liked a helluva lot of shows that have turned out to be hits. You know what Merrick has done to him and, well, it's getting a little embarrassing. Some of the shows he's panned I've enjoyed. I don't know what the matter is, but the answer is, yes, I am unhappy with our drama critic. His score on straight plays hasn't been bad, but he has been death on musicals. Some of my best friends have put money in shows that have closed in a week because he didn't like them. Others have survived despite him and the number of corpses that are rolling up big grosses and staying around to haunt him are growing. I think it's time for a change. What do you say? Do you think you'd like the job?"

"Really, my roots are in the theater," Warrenton said, remembering his days in the pit. "I think I could understand the problems of staging musical plays and perhaps be more sympathetic."

"Don't get me wrong," Miller said hastily. "I'm not telling you what to like and what not to like. I'm just certain that a fresh viewpoint is needed. You say the music in the theatre is trying to say something and should be encouraged; all right, let's encourage it or at least that portion of it that is promising."

"There's one thing, sir," Warrenton said meekly, hardly daring to spoil anything so wonderful as the publisher's offer.

"What's that?" Miller asked testily.

"What's going to become of Mr. Brownster, the present critic?"

Miller smiled, perhaps Warrenton would be all right; he

didn't have that go for the jugular philosophy of many of the men on the paper. "No one gets fired on *The New York Record,* you know that. We'll just make him critic of the arts. That way he can review serious dramatic works or he can do whatever he wants. The big thing is to get him out of there, don't worry about it."

Warrenton did well as a dramatic critic. He was a positive critic, liking most things, but never failing to give an unfavorable notice when it was deserved. His former association with the theater stood him in good stead. He knew the pit band members and the stage managers in many of the shows he reviewed. That didn't influence him in any way, of course, but he never failed to find out if any of Sanford Miller's friends were backing the show before he decided the proper temperature and tempo for writing his revue: Sellers Warrenton was a *New York Record* man from the first night Zugsmith spoke to him.

Zugsmith didn't create the legend of *The New York Record;* he only helped to perpetuate it. In many respects, the mold the paper forced men into was a handicap for Zugsmith, who was responsible for bringing about some changes and improvements in the paper. Zugsmith was the great technician, striving constantly to brighten the appearance of the paper, to lighten the stories, get in more humor, and broaden the coverage to something warmer than the world-shaking events of the day. He knew he had to go slow, though, since the publisher, the hierarchy of the paper resisted change and fought many of the changes Zugsmith wanted to institute. That's why the legend was as much a bane as a banner to Zugsmith. He could not move the men he favored fast enough because of the great stress on seniority, the chains of old loyalties, or the boundaries of the fiefdoms of the management.

To Zugsmith, the typical *New York Record* man should be fiercely devoted to the paper, abundantly talented and highly tractable so his energies could be directed along the lines

Zugsmith thought best. Zugsmith would be the first to admit he was the supreme egotist; but he was an egotist among egotists. Many men on *The New York Record* would have been happier, more prosperous and even healthier if their egos had not convinced them there was no other place where their talents could be so fruitfully employed. Because they thought they were working on the greatest paper in the world; they saw themselves as the greatest newspaperman in the world. There were some who were convinced the paper could not publish without them. These men played out this ironic charade with all their strength, frequently working while ravaged with illness, and boasting of their attendance records with a sense of pride that never acknowledged the paper would still be around to publish their obituaries.

Unfortunately for Zugsmith, the typical *New York Record* man came in assorted shapes, sizes and degrees of intelligence. They had that fierce loyalty in common, but the legacy of free and easy hiring from the days when manpower rather than talent was paramount left Zugsmith with a maze of moves that would baffle a chess master. And once he had chosen a man, he never relented, even though the choice was a poor one. Many men were promoted constantly and changed from job to job in a futile effort to find a niche for them because Zugsmith had decided they were talented and would not admit he had made a mistake.

Those who were not favored by Zugsmith, the unbelievers who thought *The New York Record* was a false god with a cult they could never embrace, were banished to the far reaches of the city room if they were on the reporting staff, or sent to the sports or financial departments if they were copy editors. In the cavernous city room, some of the men would be so far away that the editors would call them on the phone to tell them they were needed for rewrite or to go out on an assignment or to go home. Bob always wondered why the man stayed or why they were kept on at all.

Except for their immediate friends or fellow workers, these

men, and some women, too, would go virtually unknown. If they lasted long enough for retirement, they would be given a small party and an even smaller gift while the speakers strove to recall some humorous incidents about the guest of honor. If they didn't last, there would be a properly respectful item in the office notices and everyone would say to himself: "Oh, that's who he was." Often, the notice would elicit something such as: "He was the fellow who always wore the eye shade and the arm garters"; or "He was the one who would only drink distilled water he brought to work with him in a jug." The reason was that many of these undistinguished and indistinguishable nonentities affected outlandish garb, habits, dress, or manners to seek recognition in the great mass of humanity that made up *The New York Record*.

Sammy Sailer, a fat dwarf who found a mistake in a baseball schedule and received a lifetime pass from the National League, wore a baseball cap and slippers in the office. Vic Rand succeeded Joe Herman as the head of the sports desk and ate and drank himself to death on the largesse of promoters only because it was free. George Bergen, the last copy editor on the city desk to wear arm garters and an eye shade, swore that the writers and the printers were in league to get obscenity in the paper and he spent hours waiting for papers to make sure they didn't succeed. He never let a writer speak of the puck in hockey, changing the word to disk so the substitution of an f for the p would not shock the old ladies in Scarsdale. When an i was substituted for the o in shots on the goalie in another hockey story, George was sick for a week.

Of course, the news room did not have a monopoly on the colorful characters. They were found in the business departments, among the mailers and the printers, too. One printer was known as the Italian phantom because he would go on periodic binges and every other line off his machine was "Etaoin shrdlu," the automatic signal for an error that was cast by the linotype operator by running his fingers down the first two rows on his keyboard. The drunk did not have a monopoly on the practice, but for years after he left the paper when the line "Etaoin shrdlu" appeared in a proof, the editors would say: "The Italian phantom has struck again."

One of the wildest characters in the composing room was a make-up man who had been discharged from a veterans' hospital with a certificate attesting to his sanity. The make-up editors bending over the forms to check the type would look at him oddly after he had slapped their hands with the long lead column rules and screamed: "Don't touch the type, you ain't a printer." Then he'd smile and say, "I got a paper that says I'm sane, do you?"

The technicians on the paper were perhaps the largest group and these men formed the backbone of the copy desks and were the shock troops of the reporting staff. Old enough to have judgment tempered by experience, this group was rated neutral by Zugsmith. He knew they were necessary, but they were not "his" boys. They were courteous to him, of course, but there wasn't the same obeisance Zugsmith noticed in the men he had hired. He supposed it was only natural, but it disturbed him somewhat, but not enough to move any of the technicians to the outer reaches with the living exiles.

Finally, Zugsmith's table of organization took in the extras, the copy boys, the clerks who were too new on the paper to be graded and sent either upward, downward, or outward. Everyone was on a six-months trial; the device was a convenient one for getting rid of any misfits or potential boat-rockers. If any of these were to show up, it would have to be among the extras since they were the only ones Zugsmith hadn't rated or screened. It was an odd situation, for the extras included college students awaiting their big chance upon graduation or college graduates still awaiting their big chance. *The New York Record* was obsessed with degrees and many of the copy boys had Ph.D's. They lived on hope and eighty-five dollars a week, filling paste pots, stripping the news service machines or picking up copy from the wire room for distribution to the desks, sending the edited material to the composing room, and then distributing proofs and papers when the editions came up. They were errand boys—going out for coffee and sandwiches or copies of the *Tribune,* racing across town to pick up exposed photographic plates from the scene of a news event, or even taking home a reporter when he had too much over in Curry's. Most of the boys were waiting for a chance to go out on a story and fearing that they might be declared misfits by their section chief, Solly Schwarz, who had never graduated from high school.

Solly was a misfit himself. He had been born with a fast brain, fast hands, a sharp tongue, and a clubfoot. He never grew much over five feet and the college students he bossed unmercifully towered over him until Solly cut them down to his level. His clubfoot was never a handicap from his earliest days of running away from the police or running with the neighborhood gangs in his youth. The clubfoot, though, gave him an opportunity to use his brains and his hands since he got into countless fights where he would outpunch or outthink his opponents.

Solly bore the marks of many battles when he walked into *The New York Record* during the wartime manpower shortages. Zugsmith was desperate for copy boys and the cocky air of the youngster who sailed across the room so fast despite his clubfoot caught his eye. Solly became a copy boy without equal. He was on top of the reporters almost before they shouted for him and he scooted back to the desk like a shot, only a slight lurching of his shoulders betraying the built-up heel in his left foot.

After the war, it was all attrition. No one else wanted to be a copy boy except Solly and he was soon chief copy boy. That meant he got more money than the others and he supervised their activities in running to the various desks. He also got to control the expense fund that was kept at hand for purchasing other papers or for cab fare when the copy boys had to go on errands. Solly turned this windfall into a steady profit by lending copy boys money between paydays. His rates were usually six-for-five, meaning that he would get back six dollars on paydays for five during the week. Solly's keen eye also saw possibilities for other profits and he would sell advance copies of the Sunday sections to reporters and desk men for a nickel a section. The nominal fee enabled the buyers to get started on reading the massive Sunday edition and it was surprising how fast and how high the nickels built up. To Solly though, the extra money became meaningless as his salary increased as the editors found him more and more valuable. He had time and money to travel extensively and to live well. In his mellowness, he contributed the accumulated nickels and his loan-sharking profits to the annual Christmas fund as a gift from the news department.

If Solly mellowed so far as money was concerned, he never let up on the other copy boys, invariably collegians, who were flayed into action by his sharp tongue.

"Come on, Harvard," he'd scream, "get off your ass." He'd cock his head to the side in a challenge, waiting for the copy boy to respond. Usually the boy would move reluctantly with a protest, but Solly would smile broadly, his sharp nose and pasty face giving him the appearance of a theatrical mask.

"You came here to work, didn't you?" Solly would scream at his troops.

Some of the boys working under Solly decided quickly that if this was the newspaper business, they wanted no part of it. Others enjoyed the sharp banter with the little man and still others existed merely for the day when they would get their big break to be a reporter and then have the chance to order Solly around. As with most jobs on *The New York Record,* it was a matter of timing. Some copy boys were serfs for only a few months before openings beckoned; others served for years under Solly's lash or gave up and sought work on other papers, lying outrageously about what they had done on *The New York Record* and frequently succeeding in deceiving the editors of other papers to whom *The New York Record* was legend.

For those who stayed on the paper, there was a training routine of sorts. Some of the boys would work on the desks as clerks, getting a chance to move up as a full-time clerk if an opening developed. On weekends, there were sermons to cover, giving the copy boys a taste of reporting.

Solly was in charge of the assignments for the sermons. He took special delight seeing that the Christians were assigned to the Jewish services and the Jews to the Christian churches. Of course, there weren't enough churches to go around, but he refined the process by sending the Protestants to the Catholic masses or holy hours and the Catholics to the Protestant services.

"*The New York Record* isn't paying you guys to go to your own church," Solly explained to the copy boys when they protested about the switches. "Any body can cover a sermon in his own church; we got to see what you can do in unfamiliar circumstances. Besides, it's all part of the brotherhood movement. You go to my synagogue and I'll go to your church, maybe."

Not all of the sermons got into print. Some were too badly written or too inconsequential for that. Others were forced out by the space problem, always present and unrelenting. Regardless of whether it appeared, the paper paid five dollars for each sermon.

"What are you complaining about?" Solly would ask when the boys turned through the pages of the paper and failed to find the sermon. "It's an easy five bucks. You don't want to do it, we got lots of guys that do."

When a sermon was published, it would be clipped reverently and filed away in the wallet of the boy who had covered it. The others would crowd around and read the item over and over, trying to analyze why the changes were made by the copy desk, understanding some changes and then blaming themselves for not having seen the obvious approach to the article in the first place. No one could recall when a well-written sermon had been the direct cause for promotion and that seldom happened. If a boy turned in a good sermon, Zug-smith would ask who had written the piece and then keep tabs on the boy for any future signs of promise. One sermon did not make a *New York Record* reporter Zugsmith knew. It was up to the sermon-coverer to persist in his efforts and to convince Zugsmith the first was not a fluke.

There were a legendary number of old copy boys around, but legends often sprang up about newcomers, too, including the copy boy who was sent to the *Herald Tribune* to borrow the non-existent type stretcher and never returned, and, of course, the richest copy boy in the world.

Bob helped the copy boy get his job. The boy was Larry Finnegan, the son of one of the richest contractors in Indiana. The boy's father had known Bob and sent Larry to see him about a job on *The New York Record*. Fresh out of graduate school at Yale with a Ph.D., Larry wanted to learn the news-paper business.

"My father said if I liked it he might buy the *Fort Wayne Item*," the youngster said with a smile as he sat with Bob in the reception room of the *Record*.

"That's the best way to start in the newspaper business," Bob acknowledged. He knew the father had more than enough money to buy the paper and that Larry wasn't just making conversation. John Finnegan was always direct and honest and his son was no different. Larry was clean cut and handsome in a shy sort of way, with intense blue eyes. He had done some writing, but he agreed with Bob that the best way to start, in fact the only way available at that time, was as a copy boy under Solly Schwarz.

"One thing, Larry," Bob cautioned. "I don't think it would be a good idea to let Solly or anyone else know about your fa-ther and his plans to buy a paper for you if you like the busi-ness. It's bad enough that you have a Ph.D. I know how this place operates and I think it would be better all around if you kept it to yourself about your father's money."

"I wasn't trying to use his money or his position, Mr. Davis," Larry protested.

"I realize that, but this Solly Schwarz can be a son of a bitch in riding a copy boy. He's the one who will determine your work hours and will assign you to write sermons, which will be the showcase you'll have for your writing. You're hitting the paper at the wrong time, since quite a few promotions were made in the last six months and now everything is being sort of held down in anticipation of a strike. Being a copy boy will give you a look at how the paper operates, though, and it might help you make up your mind."

Larry took Bob's advice. When Bob introduced him to Zugsmith, the name Finnegan with Indiana seemed to ring some far-off bell, but Larry assured him it was a very common name in the state. Solly Schwarz liked the shy young man because Larry learned quickly and worked fast. He was willing and eager; Solly had to concede grudgingly that there was hope for some of these Ph.D's.

"What do the men mean when they ask for a two-dot edition?" Larry asked Solly on his second night on the job.

Solly smirked, as if the task was distasteful, but actually he didn't mind explaining. He took a paper from the desk and pointed to the dots after the volume's Roman numerals. "You see those periods?"

Larry nodded.

"That shows what edition it is. Usually the two-dot is the last edition. That's why they always want the last edition to see what late stories were made the night before."

"I thought we just had two editions, the City and the Late City. I know the paper goes in again after the Late City Edition, but I don't think they call it the Latest City Edition, do they?"

Solly smiled. "Actually we have four editions, just like the tabloids, but we don't put stars on the ears the way they do. The first Late City goes in at midnight, right; well that has four dots after the volume number. The next one goes in at one-thirty and that has three dots. The final goes in at three and that has two dots."

"Is there ever a one-dot paper?"

"Lots of times. I've had to rout the men out of Curry's a couple of times when late stories have broken. We've even gone in as late as five o'clock in the morning. That was with one of the Russian's first space shots, I think."

"That must have been quite a night."

"I got a one hundred dollar bonus for that one," Solly recalled proudly. "Plus the overtime."

"They don't put on all the pages late, though, do they?" Larry had a keen mind. He was taking his apprenticeship seriously and was already figuring cost factors in the running of a newspaper.

"No," Solly said, turning the paper to an inside page. "You see that?" he said, pointing to a plus sign next to the large L near the page number. "That means that this page has been postscripted; in other words, it has gone in once beyond the Late City Edition. If it had gone in twice, it would have two plusses and so forth."

"I noticed the plusses before, but the dots are too small. That's very interesting."

"One thing," Solly warned. "When you hear anybody say rush this for postscript, get your ass moving. They have to stop the presses to get that plate on and time is money."

Larry knew that better than Solly. He was keeping a notebook about all his observations on the paper. For a copy boy, he seemed to be everywhere, something that did not escape Zugsmith.

"What is that kid hanging around the make-up table for?" Zugsmith asked Solly on his way to the washroom one night.

"He wants to learn. He's a real eager beaver; not like most of the young kids we get these days."

Zugsmith looked at Larry leaning over the shoulder of the make-up man, trying to puzzle out the moves of plotting the stories to fit the layouts. "I don't mind him trying to learn the business," Zugsmith said sourly, "but see that he doesn't disturb the make-up men. Get him away from there."

The encounter was the first of many Larry had with Zugsmith, who was around later than usual because of the tension about a strike. Perhaps the tension was part of it, too, since ordinarily eagerness was looked on favorably by the assistant managing editor. Larry's particular brand, however, seemed especially irritating. Sometimes it was pointing out a typo in a headline, raising a question about vagueness in a head, or even pointing out a broken headline, which was frequently taken for granted by other copy boys when they were assisting the editors to sort the proofs in the composing room.

It was Larry's self-assurance more than anything else that irritated Zugsmith; that and staying around later than usual. "He acts as if he's going to buy the paper," Zugsmith complained when Bob asked how the young Hoosier was doing. Bob said nothing. He wondered if Zugsmith had made the connection, but he quickly discarded the notion, for Zugsmith was a great respecter of wealth and power. If he knew Larry's father was almost wealthy enough to buy the paper, his attitude toward the boy would have been far more friendly.

Solly liked Larry, although he couldn't figure him out; he was different from the other copy boys.

"Here's a dollar," Solly said to Larry before sending him on one of his errands. "Get six copies of the *Tribune* at the corner stand."

Larry left without a word, for it was a usual chore. When he returned, though, he turned the papers and the forty cents change over to Solly.

"Keep the change, forget about it," Solly said.

Larry shook his head stubbornly. "No, it's part of my job, I don't want the money."

"Look," Solly said, annoyed, "Mr. Miller has a lot of money. He can afford it. All the other copy boys keep the change, why can't you?"

"I'm sorry, Solly, I just can't take it."

Solly put the change back into the jar he used as a safe. "You're fighting the whole system," he said.

He had a similar argument the following week, when Larry turned back a dollar he had received for cab fare to the Associated Press.

"The traffic was so bad I walked," he explained.

"Are you crazy?" Solly almost screamed. "If you get a dollar for expenses, you take the dollar for expenses. Do you think the reporters are honest when they fill out their vouchers? They ride two or three to a cab and each one charges full fare. They free load for meals and they put down the full amount for breakfast, lunch, and supper. Wise up, Larry, the world isn't on the level, you know."

Larry shrugged and walked away, leaving the dollar on the desk as Solly gaped.

When Larry started to cover sermons, he looked on the task as his big chance since he knew that all of the copy boys' efforts were reviewed by Zugsmith even if they didn't get into the paper. Zugsmith was always the schoolteacher, always on the lookout for talent, even in Larry's case. The problem was that Larry had too much talent for covering sermons in the routine way *The New York Record* demanded. He wrote his report like a critique, disagreeing with the logic of the preacher and criticizing his delivery and presentation. The critique was extremely well done, Zugsmith had to admit, but first of all a writer on *The New York Record* had to learn to follow orders and to observe the formula, especially "that damned Finnegan kid." He sent Larry's effort back through Solly, with a note that said: "Don't criticize, just report."

To Solly, that meant that Larry had not done a satisfactory job. As a result, Finnegan's name was removed from the roster of sermon-coverers and he was assigned to the late shift, the traditional exile for the newcomers and those who were being by-passed either permanently or temporarily. Larry would get another chance, of course, but he spent his time in exile most profitably. He had more time to visit the museums and get to know the city. His late night duties allowed him a clearer look at the operations of the paper as the number of bodies thinned out and the rapid-sequence slowed to a more understandable pace.

One of the duties of the late shift he enjoyed most was taking the news bulletins to the paper's annex where a huge electric sign coursed around the building carrying the message of *The New York Record* to the heart of the city. Enos Jones, the custodian of the annex would tap out the bulletins on a perforated tape and then feed the tapes into a machine that activated the electric circuits in the sign. Enos was an eccentric, a scholar who had been with the paper for thirty years. He was looking forward to retirement, he told Larry as they spent the lonely night in the cold drafty tower as the reflections of the lights in the sign swam around the room like tropical fish.

Enos was a dried out scarecrow of a man whose lonely job gave him ample time for reading. He had read Plato and Aristotle and all the Greek classics, which Larry had majored in at Yale. The young millionaire and the old man spent many enjoyable moments talking about Greek philosophy each night until Solly would get uneasy and call to inquire about Larry's whereabouts. Along with the bulletins, Larry would bring Enos coffee to take the chill off the tower room. Sometimes the old man would take a bottle from the locker in the back of the room to add a few more degrees of warmth.

Enos was the only one on the paper, except Bob, that Larry spoke to at any length. Larry would report to Bob each week, but he saw Enos virtually every night. He told Enos of his ideas on sermons and the old man thought they were great. Probably the old man didn't really get Larry's point, but the youngster was pleasant company and he did bring that coffee every night.

When Larry's exile ended, he covered a sermon in a matter of fact way that impressed Zugsmith so much that the sermon appeared, in an abbreviated form, in one edition. The same thing happened the next week and Solly felt that Larry was making the most progress of any of the would-be reporters. On the third week, Larry was back in the office after attending the services when Solly saw him.

"Hey, hot-shot, did you turn in that sermon yet?" Solly called not unkindly.

Larry shook his head wearily. "No, the rabbi really didn't say anything."

"What do you mean?" Solly almost screamed. "That's one of our most important synagogues. The publisher's father used to go there. We have to have a story on whatever the rabbi said. That's a must, M-U-S-T."

"But it was the same old platitudes. If we write that, the rabbi will look bad. It's all right if he says it from the pulpit, but in cold print, he'd be laughed at."

Solly pulled nervously on his cigarette, his eyes on the clock and his mind calculating the time left to make the edition. "Look, Finnegan, this is one sermon we have to have. Now you've got a half hour to get your ass moving. It doesn't have to be long, but we have to have something. Now get on the stick."

Larry spread his hands helplessly. He smiled sadly. "I'm sorry, Solly, I'm not going to do it. He was pathetic."

"Still the goddamned critic, eh? You better go see Mr. Zugsmith. You tell him what you told me and see what he says."

"I'll be glad to tell him," Larry said brightly. He felt Zugsmith was beginning to feel more kindly toward his writing.

"Mr. Zugsmith," Larry said as he entered the editor's office, "I'm Larry Finnegan. Solly told me to come to you to explain about the sermon assignment I was on."

Zugsmith shifted the long cigarette holder to the corner of his mouth. So this is the critic, he thought, taking in the determined chin and the resolute air about Larry as he tilted back in his chair. "What assignment was that?"

"The Temple Nathan, sir. I . . ."

"Temple Nathan? That's one of our musts. The publisher's father went to that temple, you know. We have to have a good story from there, but that should be no trouble. I know the rabbi. He's a wonderful speaker, don't you think?"

Larry shifted his eyes from Zugsmith's face. He could feel his mouth starting to get dry. "Yes sir, he's a wonderful speaker, but the truth is, sir, he didn't say anything. It was just a lot of platitudes about love thy neighbor and all that; it was just a lot of corn."

"Are you sure you went to the right place, Temple Nathan? Rabbi Lyman?"

Larry nodded. "Yes sir, I spoke to the rabbi before the service. It was a fine sermon for a temple or a church, but it wouldn't read right."

"Don't you think you should let our readers be the judge of that, young man?" Zugsmith tried to conceal his annoyance. He stole a glance at the clock and realized the sermon was unlikely to make the first edition. If it didn't make it at all, there would be a call from the rabbi to Miller and then a note from the publisher to Zugsmith.

"Why don't you just write it as simply as you can and we'll get it in. It doesn't have to be long."

Larry shifted his feet uneasily. He hadn't been so uncomfortable since his oral examination for his doctorate. "I couldn't do that, Mr. Zugsmith, it would be dishonest."

"Dishonest?" Zugsmith fairly shrieked, the cigarette holder popping from his mouth. "What the hell do you mean dishonest? Now damn it, boy, you get on that typewriter and knock out a few quick paragraphs or your days on *The New York Record* are numbered. Dishonest? I never heard of such a thing."

"I'm sorry, Mr. Zugsmith, I just can't. That's one thing the rabbi got across to me: be honest with yourself. I've always tried to be that and I can't change now. I've enjoyed working on *The New York Record,* but I don't think my talents are appreciated. I . . ."

"Talent? Appreciated? What the hell do you think you are, a Pulitzer Prize writer? You're just a copy boy. I know you've got a Ph.D., but so what? You can't write a simple story about a sermon. Christ, boy, the world is full of platitudes. *The New York Record* is full of platitudes. Did you ever read our editorial page? Yes, you would. Well what's wrong with platitudes? 'It's dishonest,' you say. Isn't that a platitude?"

"Not to me it isn't, sir. That's why I wrote that first sermon that way. I feel that if we are to find the truth, we have to look for it everywhere. We have to cut through the verbiage and the window dressing and say what things really are, what they really mean."

Zugsmith picked up the cigarette holder from the desk. He placed a fresh cigarette in the end and then lighted up casually, the break giving him time to regain his temper.

"Mr. Finnegan," he said, not unkindly, "we've had some great writers on *The New York Record.* Some of them are still on the staff; others have passed on and others have gone to other papers or to other successes. Those that left, I'm sure, weren't really cut out for *The New York Record.* Yes, I think you have talent; you'd have to have some to get a Ph.D. from Yale. But I don't think you'll ever be a true representative of *The New York Record.* You might find some other newspaper that will appreciate your talents, but frankly, I think you'd be better off in some other line of work. Good night, sir."

Larry was surprised and relieved. He felt newspaper work in New York was not for him, even if his father owned the paper. The deceit, the scores of men in ruts and the projections of how much further he might get in another city had dissolved some of the interest he had when he arrived.

"Are you leaving tonight?" Solly asked when Larry reported on his conversation with Zugsmith. Solly was wondering who would cover the late shift for him.

"No, I'll finish out the week. I want to say good-by to Enos in the annex, anyway."

The farewell to Enos turned to be more hectic than Larry had planned. He bought a bottle of whisky to take over to the old man and he could hardly refuse Enos's pleas that they have a farewell drink. He had two drinks in all, large and straight in a paper cup, just enough to give Larry a slight glow.

"Well, I might as well tap out my last message," he said to Enos, who had neatly killed most of the bottle and was falling asleep in his chair.

"Go ahead, Larry," Enos said, waving a thin arm limply. "Don't forget the kicker."

It was the same thing Enos had said every night that Larry worked the stiff old keyboard of the tape puncher. The kicker was the break between the last news item and the start of the recycle. It read: "Buy the *New York Record*. Only The Truth."

"Don't forget the kicker," Larry echoed as he tapped out the bulletins on unrest in India, the city's latest scandals, the weather forecast. "Don't forget the kicker," he said again as he reached the end of the bulletins. He held his breath, laughing to himself as he tapped away.

By the time he reached the street, the weather forecast was just flickering across the board as Larry looked up. There was a string of lights and then the kicker started to run for the first time. It said: "Fuck *The New York Record*. It Lies, Lies, Lies."

Larry turned to the few people in the street, a broad smile on his face, expecting the score or so of people in the square to stare up at the sign in disbelief. But no one noticed and no one seemed to care.

Chapter Twelve

ZUGSMITH BLAMED Bob for Larry Finnegan. Bob didn't find out at once, but he began to suspect that something was wrong when the assistant managing editor no longer stopped at the desk to chat after the big push of copy. At first Bob thought it was the talk of a strike, which had everyone on edge with a sort of hopped-up gallows humor about how long the paper would be shut down. Of course, there had been strike threats before in the time he had been on the paper. In the past, the negotiations had gone down to the wire and then the publisher had settled, his pride in keeping *The New York Record* on the newsstands as much a factor as his sense of fairness or economic beliefs.

"Don't count too much on Miller's pride to prevent a strike this time," Tucker warned in Curry's.

"I know," Bob said. "Now that the *Record* is part of the publishers' group, the other papers will be putting pressure on Miller to hold out."

"Do you have a job lined up?"

"No, I really hadn't thought about it, but it might not be a bad idea. A lot of fellows have parlayed a by-line into some pretty good spots on Madison Avenue; maybe I'll be able to do the same."

"But you've never had a by-line."

"No, but *The New York Record* has a mystique that opens a lot of doors."

"I wouldn't count on that mystique in a strike, either. The reason so many men go from the paper to Madison Avenue is because the connection gives them an edge in getting stuff into the paper. When there's no paper, though, forget it."

"I understand Zugsmith has been talking to some of the men about working during the strike. They figure they'll put out a paper if they get enough people to cross the picket lines."

Tucker looked angry. "I don't like strikes and I don't know anybody that does, but damn it all, you have to be a real son of a bitch to cross a picket line when the guys you work with are out marching."

Bob nodded. "I remember a couple of times when I was a kid my father was on strike and he used to say about the same thing when my mother asked him why he didn't go to work."

"I can probably fix you up with a job at one of the television stations, Bob. I know a lot of people at both CBS and NBC. In fact, you could probably swing something permanent if you like."

"On television? Doing what?"

"Writing and editing news shows, I guess. They're the jobs that are usually around, at any rate."

"It would be a relief not working nights."

Tucker smiled. "There's no guarantee you wouldn't be working nights, you know. In fact, some of the men I know go to work at three in the morning for the early morning shows. The big thing is it's a job. You'll have something coming in if there's a strike."

"*If* there's a strike. I wonder. We'll know before long, though."

The talk of the strike added to the tension that was normal on *The New York Record*. The production department, which had gained in stature in recent years as the paper grew and prospered, became more demanding that the deadlines be met. The distribution system depended on catching trains and planes and meeting the quotas and schedules of dealers in outlying regions. Six copies went out to the White House each night and the President was never without his copy at breakfast. To meet the demands of the enlarged circulation, the deadlines had constantly been changed.

When Bob started on the paper, he would report at 6:00 P.M. for a paper that went to press at ten-thirty. Then the copy deadline was nine-thirty, but now it had moved to seven-thirty for a nine-fifteen press time, with the men starting to work at four P.M. For Bob the earlier starting time meant only that he had more time to kill before picking Diane up at the club. For some though, the new time was oppressive. Some of the men found the extra pressure too much to take. Nervous breakdowns increased and more nervous stomachs were prevalent. In the main, the copy desks responded to the demands, but the composing room, more bound by union regulations, found the earlier volume of copy hard to handle in the allotted time.

To speed the process, and to hedge against the strike, new systems were introduced; including teletype settings, TTS, which called for the use of a typewriter keyboard for the punching of tapes that would be run through linotype machines to produce the lead lines that would be cast in the mold of the pages. The age of the computer had arrived on *The New York Record,* but it dawned with considerable travail. The new operators on the TTS machines were so inexperienced that the number of errors in the paper propagated, bringing forth a groundswell of letters threatening to cancel subscriptions unless *The New York Record* returned to its old standards of excellence. With accuracy in typography sacrificed in the name of speed, Zugsmith ordered that only grievous errors, those involving statements that might be libelous or those containing vulgarities, were to be corrected. Both profanity and vulgarity appeared in print more often as the regular printers took out their frustrations about the threat they saw in the TTS system by making errors either consciously or subconsciously.

Etaoin Shdrlu, the Italian phantom, made a major comeback in the composing room as the printers set about harassing the publisher into acceptance of the wage demands made by their leaders. Whole pages of type were pied and union meetings were held in the composing room to cut down on production time and to make the paper late. The make-up men contributed to the confusion by losing inserts, transposing paragraphs and biting off important statements on colons so the reader was left frustrated and mystified about what had been left out. The pressmen joined the movement by arranging for the paper rolls to break shortly after the presses began to roar, causing shutdowns that were costly in money and time lost in getting the paper out. The ink feeders to the presses were sabotaged, too, and the usual fine mist of ink thrown off by the presses became a drenching rain that made the men demand slower runs and ruined thousands of papers with ink smudges and blots.

The errors, the slowdowns, the strike threat and the general increase in tensions were hardly noticeable under the icy calm Zugsmith maintained. Bob had no way of knowing how much of a turmoil the assistant managing editor was really in or he wouldn't have gone to see him. If he had known that Larry Finnegan was still bright in Zugsmith's memory, Bob would have started looking for a job on Madison Avenue right then.

"I hate to bother you, Mr. Zugsmith," he said, walking into the little cubicle after the first edition. Usually Zugsmith was home before the paper came up, but then it was a Wednesday that Helen Crawford was working.

Zugsmith looked up from the paper briefly and then let his eyes go back to the page. "Yes, what is it?" he said, the annoyance in his voice clear.

Bob was uncertain whether he should sit down. "It's about the strike, sir. I . . ."

"If there's a strike, it won't be any of my doing. It will be the fault of the Guild. You are a member, aren't you?"

"Yes, I am." Bob couldn't understand why he felt guilty.

"Do you know you're getting one hundred dollars a week more than the top minimum the Guild is asking?"

"Yes sir, I do."

"So why do you belong to the Guild? You don't need it."

"No sir, I don't, but perhaps some of the men do. That's why I belong, to help the others."

"You have to learn, Davis, that the only one you have to

help is yourself. You'd be a lot better off than getting jobs for people like that Larry Finnegan and . . ." Zugsmith bit down on the cigarette holder to regain control. Bob was shocked. Zugsmith hadn't called him by his last name in years and to bring up Larry Finnegan must have meant that something deep was troubling him.

"Yes sir," Bob mumbled and started to walk out of the office.

"Where are you going?" Zugsmith demanded. "You said you wanted to talk to me; what about?"

"I thought you might be a little upset, sir. I'll talk to you some other time."

"Upset? Who's upset?" Zugsmith almost shouted, the cigarette holder dropping on the desk and rolling under a chair. "You want to talk to me, go ahead. There's no time like the present."

Bob took a deep breath. He wished he hadn't come in, but it was too late now.

"I think I've come to a turning point and I'd like to know where I'm going. The strike threat has sharpened the focus on everything. I've been here nearly three years now and . . ."

"And you've done very well in that time."

"Yes sir, I have, but if you remember, you told me, or at least you led me to believe that I wouldn't always be a copy reader, that I . . ."

"I told you writing is out of the question. If that's what you want to know, the answer is still the same."

"Well, it isn't really, but it might help. You see, sir, I think there's opportunity for me in advertising or in broadcasting."

"Do you think you'd be happy working any place except *The New York Record?*"

"I don't know. That's what I'd like to find out from you, Mr. Zugsmith. You told me, or at least indicated I was going to be one of your assistants some day and I think I should know now how much longer I have to wait."

Zugsmith started to laugh, a bitter, hollow laugh that made

the hair on Bob's neck stand up. "You've been here three years and you're impatient. Isn't that awful? There are men who've been here twenty years and they aren't making the money you are. Yes, you've done a good job, but so have a lot of other people. You're not irreplaceable you know."

Bob's face flushed as if he had been slapped by a huge hand. Zugsmith's manner softened when he saw the expression on Bob's face.

"Now don't get me wrong," he said. "You're a good desk man, but . . ."

Bob recovered his composure. "Did you ever hear the expression 'good men die on the desk?' I don't intend to do that, Mr. Zugsmith, I assure you. I had the idea that you had something else in mind for me, but perhaps I was mistaken, or perhaps you were."

"I never make a mistake," Zugsmith spat out. Bob had hit a nerve. Zugsmith had perpetrated and perpetuated some of the worst promotional policies on the paper by his refusal to admit he was wrong about a man. He knew he wasn't wrong about Bob, but he could never forgive him for Larry Finnegan.

"You simply made a wrong assumption," Zugsmith said, fighting for control of himself. "You're not used to the way we do business in the big city; it's understandable."

"Yes, I see," Bob said, his mouth dry, his stomach in a knot.

"You're perfectly welcome to continue what you're doing on *The New York Record,*" Zugsmith said, stealing a glance at Bob from behind the paper that he had picked up again. "But I wouldn't count on doing anything else, if I were you. There are certain levels you reach and then you can't go any higher. We can't retire people in wholesale lots just because of the eagerness of younger people. You have to learn to be content in your job."

Bob was silent as he looked at the obviously uncomfortable assistant editor seeking to appear interested in the paper.

Larry Finnegan! Bob could understand the young man a lot better now. He started to smile in spite of himself. "Thank you, Mr. Zugsmith," he said, turning to search out Tucker and that job at NBC. His smile only made Zugsmith more furious.

The newspaper strike started before Bob could make his television connection, but he was hired by the network the next day. His good looks and his easy manner attracted the attention of one of the senior producers and Bob was assigned to a news crew as an interviewer.

"I was right about you being star-crossed," Tucker said when they met in Curry's to swap rumors about the length of the strike. "You seem to click wherever you go."

"I think it was the midwestern accent. It seems the producer is from Indianapolis and he wanted to give a fellow Hoosier a break. What are you doing about a job?"

"Not a thing. I come down here once a week to collect my strike benefits and to walk in the picket line. Truthfully, the strike is a blessing in disguise to me. I was pushing a deadline for a science-fiction book I have under contract and I'd never been able to get it done if I had to work. I'm writing at home and driving my wife crazy."

"I thought I'd have a lot more time to spend with Diane, but she quit her job at the club because her mother's very sick. She's nursing the old lady and I've only seen her once all week."

Tucker smiled. "I guess you're meeting all those television actresses and models now, aren't you?"

"I've met a few, but if you're not a producer or a director who can do them some good, they don't want to have anything to do with you."

"Couldn't you tell them you'd get something in *The New York Record* about them, when it starts publishing again? That might help."

"I'm really not interested. I've been going to a lot of movies and catching up on all my reading with this new found night-time leisure. It would be great if Diane didn't have her mother to take care of."

Tucker cocked his head and looked at Bob impishly. "It sounds like you've got it pretty bad. I guess absence does make the heart grow fonder."

Bob shook his head in agreement. "I found that out when I was in Washington. We really should have gotten married then, but I thought I should string Edith Miller along until Zugsmith delivered on that job. Now I realize what a fool I was."

"Well, you could still use your influence with Edith. You haven't officially left the paper, have you?"

"No, but I'm looking forward to marching in to Zugsmith the day the men go back and interview him about any attrition in the employee ranks."

"There could be quite a few. It looks like a long strike. It's two weeks now and they're not even talking."

Tucker was right. The strike dragged on as the weaker papers refused all efforts at settlement. In some cases, the shutdown was cutting deficits and the publishers of the weaker papers felt that the losses the strong ones were sustaining now would narrow the gap between the weak and the strong when publication resumed. It was a specious argument at best, but Sanford Miller's hands were tied by his commitment to the group. Shutting down *The New York Record* was contrary to everything he believed in and he suffered for it.

January was cold and windy, ripping at the picket signs of the marchers in front of *The New York Record* building. February was snowy, with the pickets returning from their tours with snow covered coats that turned the Guild headquarters into a gigantic puddle. March was wet, but the sun was threatening to shine as the negotiators finally seemed to be approaching some sort of an agreement.

Bob had made a commitment to himself to walk an hour of picket duty each week, just as did the strikers from out of town. He wanted the men from the news room to know he was supporting them even though he was working. Some of the others never showed up at all, working at public relations jobs that were mainly payoffs for past favors or prepayments on expected favors or filling in on some of the weekly papers that had gone daily to fill the news vacuum in the city. Usually Bob walked the picket line with Tucker, but Tucker had a conference with his publisher that day and put in his hour in the morning.

It was raining and it would have been easy for Bob to go home and forget about the whole thing, but he knew he couldn't. When he met Alice Blaine on the picket line, he was sorry that he hadn't.

"Bob, how are you?" she cried with a sincerity that surprised him. "I've seen you on television; you're really great. You seem so at ease as if you were doing it for years."

"Thanks. It's really just like reporting, but instead of taking notes you're holding a microphone."

"Do you like it? Are you coming back to the paper or are you going to stay in television?"

A truck passed by and splashed the curb water all over Alice. She stood for an instant holding her umbrella and looking down at her dripping coat and stockings.

"Shit!" She exploded. "Look at me! I had a date tonight with a guy who promised he'd speak to his boss about a job. He's in publishing and they're looking for editors."

Bob could hardly keep from laughing. Alice had been almost coy while she was talking to him and now the toughness had come out again. "Can't you go home and change?"

"I live way out on the Island. I look a mess. I usually wear slacks when I'm picketing, but I wanted to make an impression. I'm wet clear through."

"Maybe you can go over to Curry's and dry off, or the Guild hall . . ."

"No, forget it." The deep frown on Alice's face eased into a smile. "Wait a minute, Bob. Don't you live in the Seventies someplace?"

"Yes, 72nd Street, why?" Bob began to feel uncomfortable. He should have gone straight home from the studio.

Alice's eyes were alight now as she reached back in her memory for the facts she needed. "And didn't I hear you talking on the desk once about how comfortable your fireplace is, even though it's a fake."

"Yes, but . . ."

"Then why don't I go up to your place and dry out. I can wash my stockings and press the coat dry. You do have an iron, don't you? And I can keep my date after all."

Bob nodded, dumb struck by Alice's reversal of roles so quickly. He had always regarded her as a woman who would get what she wanted, but he never expected to get such a clear demonstration.

"Well let's go then," she said. "Call a cab."

Alice didn't look bad in Bob's robe. She was no Diane, but she wasn't as unattractive as she had seemed in the office.

"This is a nice place," she said, sitting before the fire and looking around the apartment. "I'd think it was great even if it was a hole in the wall. I was wet right down to my girdle. I don't know what I'd have done without you, Bob."

"Forget it. I hope you get the job. Can I mix you a drink while you're waiting for the stuff to dry?"

"I'll have rye and water, if you've got any. I know everybody in New York drinks Scotch, but I prefer rye."

"Rye and water, coming up." Bob mixed himself a double Scotch. "Out in Fort Wayne it's bourbon, but I've taken to Scotch since I've been here, that's true."

"Here's looking at you," Alice said, touching her glass to his. She took a deep pull from the glass and snuggled down into the cushions of the couch as the warmth of the whisky crept over her. "You know, this is the first time I've really looked at you, Bob. You're handsome."

221

Bob blushed inspite of himself. "You mean the last eight months in the office you never looked at me? You've spoken to me almost every night."

Alice shrugged. "But in the office, you're just like a piece of the furniture. You're another machine, turning out the copy and headlines and never really coming alive."

Bob looked into the fire, the scene in the city room coming into focus as he thought of Alice's words. He nodded slowly. "You're right. It is sort of a dehumanizing situation. I remember when I was first there, no one spoke to me. The sound of a voice in friendly conversation was startling. You're different out of the office, too."

"I know." Alice clutched the robe around her with one hand as she tilted her head back and drained her glass. "You don't like me in the office, do you?" She turned to look at Bob squirm.

"I wouldn't say that. I know you're a hard driver and won't let anything stand in your way. Where I'm from, we take things a little easier."

"But you're in the big city now. You have to play by the rules of the jungle. If you're going to make it in this town, *The New York Record* or any other place, you have to be ruthless. You can't be worrying about everyone else all the time."

"That's what Zugsmith told me just before the strike."

"Did you have a fight with Zugsmith by the way?"

"Why?" Bob was surprised. He didn't think anyone knew, although the rumor factory on the paper was unrivalled.

"He used to kid with you a lot, but I noticed he wasn't doing that lately."

"I thought you said you didn't notice me?"

"I didn't. I noticed another copy editor Zugsmith talked to, but I didn't notice how red your hair was or how blue your eyes are. That's what I mean. The personal things. Could I have another drink, please?"

Bob got up and poured another drink. He looked at his watch as he handed Alice the glass.

"Don't worry about the time," she said. "I'll be going as soon as I finish this drink. The stockings are just about dry and other stuff is good enough to wear."

"I don't want to hurry you, but you have that date."

Alice smiled. "What would you say if I told you I don't have a date, that I made the whole thing up just to get up to your apartment?"

"You don't have a date? You . . ."

"No, I do have a date, but what would you have said?"

Bob thought for a long time before he answered. He didn't know what she wanted him to say.

"I would have said that it was out of character for you. If you wanted to come up to my apartment you would have come right out and asked. You believe in getting what you want."

Alice hugged herself in delight, then held her glass on high in salute. "Here's to you, Bob, you're one hundred percent right. You know me even if you don't like me."

"I never said I don't like you. I . . ."

"Not even after that Korean thing?"

"What Korean thing?" Bob wondered how much she knew.

Alice smiled, the drinks were beginning to make her feel very warm, very cozy. "Come on, Bob, I met your printer in Curry's one night and he told me about pulling out the letter. I figured the rest out for myself."

"Letter, what letter?" Bob realized that his best course was to deny everything.

Alice shrugged, getting up from the couch and standing with her back to the fireplace. "All right. You screwed me on that and I was determined to get even, and as you said I always get what I want."

Bob looked at the silhouette in the robe. "What is it you want?"

Alice uncrossed her arms and held the robe open. "I want you to make love to me," she said, dropping the robe and throwing herself on him.

"Wait a minute," he cried, fighting her off. He held her wrists and pushed her back. She certainly looked different from the way she did in the office. "Let's go in the bedroom," he said.

She's no Diane, Bob mused as he lay on the bed after the act. Still, she wasn't bad, much more tender than he had a right to expect. But then he wasn't expecting anything, or anyone and when his bell rang he couldn't image who it could be. He slipped on his robe and went to the door in his bare feet, slipping the chain lock on before he opened the door. It was Diane.

"Have you heard the news?" she said, still breathless from the two flights of stairs. "Open the door. I came down as soon as I heard."

"News? What news?" Bob knew he couldn't keep her in the hall waiting. He closed the door, took three quick steps to his robe before the fireplace and put it on over his first robe before opening the door.

Diane kissed him as she came in. "Isn't it wonderful? The strike's over. I heard it on the radio. I was hoping you hadn't heard because I wanted to be the one to tell you. Why are you wearing two robes? Are you cold?"

"I got a little chill out in the rain." His mind raced in search of a way to get Diane out of the apartment long enough to get rid of Alice. "I was going to take a couple of aspirins, but I don't have any. Would you run down to the drugstore and get me some, please?"

"Aspirin? But you've had a drink, I can smell it. I don't think you should take aspirin when you're drinking." She started to take off her coat, but Bob shook his head.

"There's nothing wrong with taking aspirin with Scotch, that's the best thing for a cold. Please, darling, the store will be closing in a couple of minutes."

She was just about to go when Alice walked out of the bedroom naked. "I'm sorry," Alice said, walking back into the

224

room and peeking out through the door. "I didn't know you had company."

The fire leaped into Diane's eyes, wide with disbelief. "It's that girl from the office," she said incredulously. "That lesbian."

"Alice Blaine," Bob said numbly. "But I can explain everything. She got drenched."

"Don't bother," Diane snapped, her eyes blazing. "I left my sick mother to come down here tonight so we could celebrate. That's why you wanted to get me out to get aspirin. You might need aspirin, Mr. Davis, but I've just got rid of a headache. Good night." She slammed out the door, fighting off her tears down the stairs and out on the street, breaking down only after she had hailed a cab and settled into the back seat.

Bob was still standing in shock when Alice came out of the bedroom in her slip. "Girl friend, eh?" she said. Bob nodded unbelievingly.

"I'm sorry, Bob, honestly I am. I didn't want this to happen. What did she say?"

"The strike's over." He shuffled across the room and dropped onto the couch.

"The strike's over? We're going back to work?" Alice's depression and remorse disappeared instantly. Bob nodded unhappily. He still couldn't believe it.

"Cheer up," Alice commanded. "Have a drink and pull yourself together. She'll be back. You could get any girl you wanted. You've got something, Bob, I mean it. I'll write her a letter. I'll go to see her, if you want."

"Would you, really?" He snapped out of his lethargy. Perhaps that might work.

"Certainly, but not tonight. The strike's over so that means I won't be needing that job in publishing. There's no need to keep that date I had either. Come on, Bob, cheer up. Let's go back to bed."

Chapter Thirteen

ONE OF the biggest stories in *The New York Record* on the first day publication resumed was the notice of the death of Sanford Miller, the publisher. Miller, convinced he had betrayed all the tradition of the paper by letting it be shut down, drove himself unmercifully during the bargaining sessions, which continued almost uninterruptedly for three days at the end. He was determined to get the men back to work, but unwilling to agree to something the other papers would not be able to afford. The strain was telling and Miller suffered a heart attack a half hour after the final agreement was reached.

There was a full page obituary of the publisher that had been prepared when his plane was overdue on a world flight and there was also a promise to present within the next week a capsule account of the news of the three months while the presses of *The New York Record* were silent. That had been Miller's idea: to keep the *Record* complete by filling in the gaps since the last publication before the strike. To him, history itself would be incomplete without the opinions of *The New York Record*.

During the official period of mourning, there was no talk of a successor to Miller, although the rumors were flying as usual. There was no son-in-law to take over for the first time in three generations and everyone agreed that an era had ended when *The New York Record* had gone on strike.

Sanford Miller's widow was in her late fifties and mentioned as the most likely candidate to be the new publisher, at least on an interim basis. She now controlled the stock in the company because her father had carefully bought her sufficient stock in the *Record* to assure her leverage in the event of marital difficulties. Edith Miller was regarded as the most unlikely choice to be the publisher, although the grapevine expected her to finally settle down to choose a husband and the man who would eventually be in charge of the paper. Beau Manley and scores of executives from various departments were mentioned in the publisher sweepstakes by various factions who had the usual hard to refute arguments on why their candidates could not miss. The only trouble was that the experts figured that sentiment had died with Sanford Miller.

Bob had given Zugsmith two weeks' notice when he returned after the strike. He knew things would be chaotic until the operation smoothed out again and he didn't think it right that he simply not come back at all. He had four days to go when he received a notice to report to the executive offices. He took the elevator up to the tower where Sanford Miller had maintained a combination office and apartment that afforded a dramatic view of the city. Bob was surprised that Edith Miller was the only one there when he arrived.

"Thank you for your lovely note about my father," she said quietly, shaking Bob's hand and motioning him to sit down.

"I didn't really know your father personally, but the old-timers liked him, so my impression of his being a nice guy must have been about right."

"I really think the strike broke his heart. He didn't want to close the paper, but he was forced to."

"I know," Bob said uneasily. He looked around the rich furnishings and wondered why Edith had summoned him.

"I don't know whether you know it yet, but I'm going to take over as publisher. I . . . ."

"No, I didn't know. Congratulations."

"Thank you. No, I guess you couldn't have known it since it was only arranged a few hours ago, although my mother and I have known it for a couple of days now. In the past it has always been the husband of the oldest daughter who has been the publisher, but since I have no husband, I'm going to do it myself. It will probably be only for a little while, until I find some one I can live with and who can live with me and the paper."

"That won't be hard. You're a very attractive girl."

"Thank you, Bob. You know, it's funny. I don't think I ever told you, but you could have been the publisher right now, do you know that? You know I liked you an awful lot, still do in fact. But when I saw the way you looked at that singer, Diane, isn't it? I knew there could never be a feeling like that toward me and I wasn't willing to settle for the kind of marriage my parents had. You were honest, though. I realize you must have known how I felt and you could have used me if you wanted. That's why I called you here tonight. I have to speak to someone I can trust, someone who won't tell me things just because he thinks I want to hear them or because he thinks he has to say them because I'm the publisher now."

"I'm flattered on several counts, Edith. I can still call you Edith, can't I?"

"I certainly hope so. I don't think Miss Miller would be right except when there are others around and I really don't like 'boss.' "

Bob smiled. She was going to be all right. "What I wanted to say is that I'm flattered that you liked me and that you feel you can trust me. But didn't you hear I'm leaving?"

"You're leaving?" Edith was shocked. She bit her lip nervously, then smiled wistfully. "I might have known. I guess you'll be staying with NBC. You were very good on the few programs I saw. You should do well in television."

"I hope so, but frankly it seems sort of superficial to me. There's nothing you can point to and say I did that or this is my work. Everything is of the moment, it's so transitory."

"I'm surprised to hear you say that. I guess the money is good, though."

"Right now, I'm not getting as much as I was here, but I guess that will change, too."

Edith shook her head. "I don't understand. If you really aren't crazy about the work and it's less money, why are you leaving?"

Bob wondered how much he should tell her. He thought

any mention of Larry Finnegan would be absurd, even though he was convinced that lay behind his trouble with Zugsmith. "I wanted to get off the desk and Mr. Zugsmith told me I was doing work at my skill capacity and I shouldn't expect to do anything else."

"He said that? Uncle Zach? I always thought he regarded you as one of his bright young men. He had you marked for big things."

Bob smiled sheepishly. "I thought so, too, but I guess we were both wrong."

Edith looked out of the window at the skyline, her mind whirling as he tried to fit the pieces together. She turned back to Bob, her face grim. "If I asked you to stay on the paper, Bob, would you? Don't answer yet until I tell you why I called you up here. I need some one like you to talk to and to give me advice. I wanted you to start training under Uncle Zach, Mr. Zugsmith, for an editorial position. I still do and if you stay, you can do that or you can write if you want to. What do you say?"

"Does Mr. Zugsmith know of your plan?"

"Perhaps not actively, but he knew that's what I had in mind for you for some time."

"But he doesn't know now that you invited me up today, when I'm supposed to be leaving the end of the week?"

"No, would it make a difference?"

"Not to me, but how will he feel?"

"You mean you'll stay?" Edith's face lighted up with a smile. She reached over and placed her hand on Bob's arm. "Don't worry about Mr. Zugsmith. If he objects, I'll tell him I'm grooming you to be the next publisher. That will keep him quiet."

"There's only one thing. I'd like to make one condition on my staying."

"More money? Things are going to be a little tight because of the taxes, but you'll have to get that as Uncle Zach's assistant."

"No, not money. I'd like to be there when you tell him that I'm going to be one of his assistants."

"You can if you want, but there are a lot of things involved with my taking over as publisher."

"I wasn't serious. I would like to know how he reacts, though."

Edith studied Bob closely. "Very well, but now let me see how you'll react to something. Lewis Lexford is going to be the new managing editor."

Bob was surprised, but only mildly so. Beau Manley's power had been obviously getting weaker for some time. "That's nice, but is that what you wanted to measure my reaction on? Why?"

"Well, after all, you were responsible for Lexford's Pulitzer Prize, which really made him. He was just an ordinary correspondent before that and I guess he still is."

Bob looked straight into Edith's eyes. "That's what the desk is all about. But tell me, what's going to happen to Beau Manley?" Bob thought Beau would be a valuable ally for Edith to have during her transitional period.

"Beau's going to be sort of an executive overseer for me, watching that I don't stub my toe. Actually, Beau is being kicked upstairs because of his age and his drinking, but my mother likes him and he will be helpful. Lexford's a much younger man and I think the change is important for the paper at this time. He's handsome and well-spoken and creates a favorable impression wherever he goes. I know some of his dispatches still give the desks trouble, but he's the charming type of front man we need as managing editor. There's more to this business, I've found out, than just writing and editing. Lexford had a good war record, too, so he might fill the bill."

"I wish him the best of luck. I know Beau has slowed down a lot and that a change is needed, and I think it's smart that you make these changes right at the start. It will show a directness and a purposefulness that will cause the staff to sit up and take notice."

Edith leaned over and impulsively kissed Bob. "You always know the right thing to say, don't you? I can't tell you how happy I am that you've decided to stay."

Bob stood up. "I guess I'd better be going."

"Don't go yet, have a drink. I want you to drink to your new publisher. You're the only one who knows it outside of the editorial board, Beau, and Uncle Zach. It won't be announced until next Monday's paper."

"Just one drink, I really have to be going."

Edith walked to the huge bookcase at the side of the room and pushed a button. The bookcase swung back to reveal a compact bar. "This is where my father used to do a lot of entertaining. I remember as a girl coming up here and going crazy looking for the button to make the bar come out. What will you have?"

"Scotch, please, with just a little water."

Edith filled the glass almost half full, then put in just a dash of water. "Here's to *The New York Record,*" she said as she handed the glass to Bob, "May it have as bright a future as it does a past."

"I'd rather drink to you," Bob insisted, "I think you've got just enough guts to do a helluva job."

Edith put down her glass and started to cry. "Oh, Bob, I'm so scared. I talk big, but I'm frightened to death. I need your help, Bob. I need you."

She moved close, putting her arms around his neck and her head on his shoulder as her body melted into his. "Just tonight I need a man's shoulder to cry on. Just tonight, Bob, please?"

Bob could feel the flush from the Scotch sweeping over him. Reflexively he began to respond to the nearness of her body. He put the glass down and tilted her head back for his kiss. "Just this once, only this once, boss."

231

Bob was the lowest in the pecking order of the five men who worked under Zugsmith. Only three worked at one time, with the two others filling in on days off and allowing for a rotation of shifts. Normally, the lowest man was put on the latest shift, although there was often more to do and more decisions to make. For the past year, Zugsmith had been using some of the desk heads as fill-ins for his assistants, particularly during vacations. For the first few days, Bob merely went through the motions, watching the others carefully and trying not to get in the way. About the only things he learned were the location of the button to signal a shutdown of the presses in the event of a news break of major importance and the names of the lawyers who were to be called in case a question of libel arose. The lawyers, too, had a pecking order, with the least senior to be called first and latest at night. Bob smiled when he looked at the lawyers list with their comparative listing of importance; he thought that if all four of the lawyers were in at one time, they would probably be just like the men in the bullpen: watching each other carefully and trying not to get in the way.

The pecking order among Zugsmith's assistants was more than figurative. Bruce Jamieson, the number one man, was a huge Texan who commanded everyone in the city room except Zugsmith. Since Zugsmith usually went home at seven o'clock, Jamieson's word was absolute on the first edition and the planning for the second edition. The number two man, Chauncey Burnside, was a proper Bostonian who served as a buffer between Jamieson and the desk heads or department chiefs who would come to the bullpen with a question or a headline or a story for approval. Burnside, like those below him, never made a decision. If a question was asked, he would relay it to Jamieson, who, afflicted with the same lack of authority, might walk into Zugsmith's office for the most trifling decision.

Bob had observed this on the foreign desk and in other departments of the paper. Among Zugsmith's assistants, however, the system was basic, although it sometimes worked in reverse, with Jamieson referring a query posed by Burnside to Del Chapin, a converted Californian, or to Les Cohen, the number four man and the only native New Yorker in the bullpen. Cohen, as the late man, liked to make decisions and had no compunction about offering opinions if they were solicited. He made sure, though, that he never volunteered ideas unless they were sought.

There were many other unwritten laws in the bullpen. One involved the clipboards that each of Zugsmith's assistants carried with all the verve of an ancient coat of arms. The boards were used to keep news bulletins, summaries or headlines available at the men's desks or usable when they went to the composing room each night for the making up of the pages. Bob regarded the clipboards more as a badge of rank since Jamieson's was aluminum with his name on the clasp in metal, Burnside's a higher grade of wood than was ordinarily available in stationery stores, and Cohen's of fiberboard.

Bob saw no need for the boards except for setting the men in the bullpen apart from the others in the city room. The clipboards made the bullpen men instantly recognizable as they moved through the room. Bob saw no need to get one, but he was told by Cohen the second week, "Better get a clipboard; fiberboard. You can get them in Woolworth's."

Bob was going to say he didn't need one, but decided he was still too new in the job. When he went to Woolworth's, he found that the boards came in two sizes—standard, the size used by Cohen, and small, just about big enough to hold a small note pad. He bought one of the standard size clip boards and twelve of the small ones. When the men on the foreign desk came to work that night, there was a clipboard at each place. Tom Crum walked over to Jamieson with the board as if it were a new toy.

"Look what I've got," he said with all the joy of a small boy at Christmas. "Everyone on the desk got them, too."

Jamieson looked over his glasses. "Hmpf," he snorted.

"I got the boards for the boys on the desk," Bob put in from his seat behind Jamieson. "I've found out how important it is to have a clipboard. It makes headlines come out easier and keeps all your papers neat. Really, Tom, I thought it would be a little remembrance of me."

Jamieson turned around, his face growing redder. He opened his mouth to say something to Bob, then turned back to the pile of copy on his desk and continued to leaf through it.

Crum could see that Jamieson was not amused. He waved the clipboard at Bob in salute. "Thanks, Davis," he said. "I'll tell the boys what you said."

Zugsmith was in his office and overheard the whole exchange. He tried to stifle a smile; he had long been amused by the clipboards and the regard Jamieson and the others had for them. Having Bob in the bullpen wouldn't be so bad after all. It will be a welcome change, he thought, from the more or less stylized exercises of servility of the others.

Of course, the clipboards were not the only thing Bob questioned. He thought the system called for too much duplication of effort, with each man going through all the copy that would appear in the paper or be rejected by the editors as too insignificant, too dangerous, or too dull. The aim was that all of the copy would be seen by the men in the bullpen, but there was too great a volume to achieve this goal except on a rare night. The stories filed by the correspondents would be read completely, with the major stories of the wire services afforded the same treatment. The minor stories would be covered if possible, which was seldom with the great volume that poured into the paper each night.

Cohen never took his eyes from the copy he was reading. He continued to leaf through the stack. He regarded Bob as a rival for the advancement he saw mapped before him and he did not intend to encourage Bob to bring up any ideas. Bob respected Cohen. As the late man, Les was charged with handling any late breaking stories and frequently had to make decisions. Bob knew he would be getting late shifts, too, and he was looking forward to seeing if some of the routines could be made more meaningful. Everything was too formal to suit him. Jamieson seldom spoke directly to anyone except Burnside, even if he wanted to speak to Cohen or Bob, who were sitting only a turn of the head away. Questions would be passed up or down the chain of command regularly, with Zugsmith being rung into the procedure where a decision was concerned or when the question was being referred back to its source after making the complete tour of command. This was true even when the lower echelons did not originate the question.

Jamieson, for instance, might toss a piece of copy to Burnside saying: "What do you think of that?"

Burnside would read the material, usually unexpected and therefore in the position of having to dislodge something that had been scheduled if it were to be used. After he was finished, Burnside would say, "Well . . ." His inflection was different each time, depending on what he thought Jamieson wanted to hear. Then he would toss the copy to Cohen, or, early in the night to Bob, saying "What do you think?"

Bob was thus cast in the position of being forced to make a decision even though he was the least experienced of Zugsmith's assistants. But Bob had the confidence the others lacked and unflinching faith in his instincts.

"I wouldn't get excited about this," he'd say. "The wire service stringer in that area isn't too reliable from what I've heard. You could play it as a short with reservations."

"Yes, that's what I thought, too," Burnside would say. Turning to Jamieson, who in the best traditions of the charade, never heard or pretended to hear Bob, Burnside would say: "I think you could play it as a short, with reservations, of course."

Jamieson picked up the paper again and glanced at the lead as if he were seeing it for the first time. "Yes, that's what I think, too. Let's do that," he said.

Jamieson wasn't always so mild. Sometimes he would bluster and bellow, puffing himself up to his full six feet two inches. Many times he forced things through not by logic, but by sheer will and Texas lung power.

"Who the hell wrote that head?" Jamieson snorted one night when Bob was new in the bullpen. The Texan was convinced Bob had written the head, which had been set in type and proofed as part of the nightly routine. Jamieson and his aides had to check all heads on page one. They also would go over the other heads when the paper came out, but page one was their particular concern early in the night.

Zugsmith was just leaving for the night when Jamieson let out his bellow. He stopped at Jamieson's desk to read the headline the Texan was holding out to challenge. Zugsmith took the cigarette holder from his mouth. "I wrote that head," he said. "Why?"

Jamieson blushed beneath his tan. "It tells the story," he said meekly.

When the paper came out, Jamieson and his two aides would go through it page by page. Any major changes were dictated by the importance of late breaking stories and what had been done by the *Herald Tribune* , the only paper rated a rival of *The New York Record*. The tabloids didn't count, for Zugsmith believed the tabloids appealed to a different public. The *Tribune,* though, had been a rival from the earliest days of *The New York Record* and the respect for the paper lingered long after the *Tribune's* circulation and advertising began to slip as *The New York Record* pulled away to make its superiority, or at least its appeal for readers and advertisers, perfectly clear.

The *Tribune* was published only a few blocks from *The New York Record* and went to press earlier. As a result, Jamieson and the others had read the first edition of the *Tribune* before the *Record* came out and their thinking was colored accordingly.

Jamieson would sit at Zugsmith's desk leafing through the

paper, with the others following while sitting in the low over-stuffed chairs. Burnside and Cohen would have their clip-boards on their laps for taking notes. The routine seldom changed and would go something like this:

Jamieson: "Page one looks all right, I think, but maybe that picture should be a little bigger. I think we should indent that Washington story in column two."

Burnside: "Remake the picture to get it bigger, indent Washington story in column two. You got that Les?"

Cohen: "Remake picture bigger, indent column two story on Washington, check. What about that story on the relief requirements; the *Tribune* has a box on it on page five."

Burnside: "Only a box, eh? That could be an overplay at that. Maybe that doesn't rate page one after all. What do you think Bruce?"

Jamieson: "The welfare story? Only a box, eh? They had that Jersey story out front, didn't they? Why don't we put the Jersey story out there and move the welfare story inside. I guess we could cut it, too. How much overset was there?"

Burnside: "Overset? What's the figure, Les?"

Cohen: "Ten columns."

Burnside: "With ten columns of overset, we could certainly cut that welfare story. Maybe we could use a box on it."

Jamieson: "That's right, a box would be just right."

The same weighing of what the *Tribune* had done with the various stories was carried out page by page and shifts were made accordingly, with no thought that the *Tribune* editors were doing the same thing as they went through the *Record* in their offices. This frequently saw the *Tribune*'s late editions with a story on page one that the *Record* had featured earlier, with the *Record* dropping the story in favor of one that ultimately would be replaced on the *Tribune*.

When the post-mortem was completed, Cohen would make the rounds of the desks calling for the changes or space trims being called for by Jamieson and Burnside. Aside from being the low man in seniority, Cohen had this task because the late man would be able to check on the changes later to see that they had been made. Bob inherited the same role when he took over the late shift as the newest man on the job.

Bob approached the assignment with a more relaxed air than Cohen, who was pressing hard to impress the copy editors and rewrite men with his importance. He knew that Zugsmith, a perfectionist, was angry when the overset was too large and he was reluctant to make any late changes that would build up the amount of material set in type but not used in the paper. There was no thought in Cohen's mind for economy in this, for he would frequently order pages killed —an expensive hobby for a late man—to have a headline rewritten or some minor error corrected. In some cases, Cohen would be bucking the system for many of the errors were in items of particular interest to the paper, such as the announcement of Lexford's promotion to managing editor.

All items of this type were "must use," meaning that space and prominent position had to be found for them at all costs. Other lesser important items were "please use" and some were just "use" although no one could figure out the relative power of any of the designations. To the compositors, though, the "must use" and "please use" categories seemed to be red flags that called out the worst in each man. Accordingly few of these extra important items were free of errors. Lexford's promotion notice stated that Lexford Lewis was to be the new managing editor, the printer either purposely or inadvertently transposing the names. The error was caught on a proof, but the correction didn't appear before the first edition had gone to press under the pressure of missing trains or planes. *The New York Record,* the paper of the record, had become a victim of forces beyond its powers to control so that record was often distorted by errors and omissions.

The stories themselves were written to describe every possible facet of the event being covered. The aim was to leave no questions unanswered, which made the stories long and the overset longer. This also tended to crowd out the shorts each night, which Zugsmith considered important for full coverage and also to break up the long columns of type. Each night the make-up desk would inevitably ask for more shorts and each night the editors would just as inevitably kill the shorts after the first edition to keep their longer stories intact and to reduce their overset. The death and the dearth of shorts were attributable to the build-up of ads that frequently created odd-sized holes in the paper that could be filled only by a long story wrapped around several columns or under a multicolumn headline.

"Watch the *Trib*," was the standard instructions from Jamieson and Burnside as they left each night and turned over control to the late man. The control was only nominal, for Cohen made it clear to Bob in his breaking-in period that he was to call Burnside if any unusual stories broke. If Burnside thought the story warranted it, he would call Jamieson, who might call Zugsmith if the news was really extraordinary. Of course, there was one other guide available to the late man: the lesson of precedent. Many times Jamieson or even Zugsmith would ask: "How did we do it last year?" Then Bob or Cohen or the least senior man would go to the files to scan the paper containing the answer. Bob had no idea how long the system was being followed, but he knew the back issue file was seldom not in use.

After his first night on the late shift, his first when he had been in charge of the editorial operation of the paper for even a few hours, Bob felt good. He was still full of adrenalin when he arrived home at four in the morning. The glow lasted until he went to work the next night. Zugsmith had an odd smile on his face as Bob greeted him.

"How did it go last night?" Zugsmith asked almost archly.

"Fine, no trouble at all," Bob replied brightly.

"I see you moved some stories around. Cut some back, too."

"Yes, the *Trib* had a little different play on some of them so I thought we could afford it."

"What happened to that Albany story we had on page one?"

"I moved it inside. I thought the fire story was bigger and better. Three people killed, you know."

"A fire's a fire," Zugsmith said with a shrug. "The *Tribune* only had a box on it."

Bob knew the *Tribune* had only a box because it went to press earlier and was not able to make more details. He thought he had done damned well in shepherding the story through the city desk at that late hour. He learned before many more nights, though, that the late man would be second-guessed no matter what he did.

His first resolve was to stop playing games with the *Tribune*. He saw the latest editions of the paper and realized that the same indecision that existed in *The New York Record* city room was prevalent at the *Herald Tribune*. If anything, the *Herald Tribune* editors were more desperate, for the strike had hurt their paper far more than *The New York Record*. The circulation and advertising lineage gaps were widening still more. Let them do the following, Bob said to himself, refusing to change a story the *Tribune* had played off its front page.

Strangely enough, Zugsmith's comments were more limited the next day than at any previous time in Bob's tenure as late man. It was two weeks before Zugsmith indicated he noticed the change.

"You must be doing something right," Zugsmith said grudgingly. "The *Trib* seems to be conforming to our news judgment more and more."

"I noticed that, too," Bob said.

"You're really getting the hang of things, aren't you?"

"I think so, but it all goes back to something you told me the first day I was here."

"Oh," Zugsmith said, obviously pleased, "What was that?"

"You said *The New York Record* was the greatest newspaper in the world; that there are many *Records,* but only one *New York Record*. Well, I thought about that and I asked myself why the greatest newspaper in the world should follow the lead of a formerly great paper that is losing out because it hasn't been able to keep up with the times."

"That's right. I never thought of it that way. By God, Bob, you just might make a *New York Record* man."

Bob smiled. "There's only one thing wrong, sir."

"What's that," Zugsmith asked, a note of alarm creeping into his voice.

Bob turned to make sure Jamieson was listening and then he replied: "That's not the way we did it last year."

Chapter Fourteen

THE AGE of the writer arrived on *The New York Record* with the naming of Lewis L. Lexford managing editor. Lexford never considered the work of the copy editors too important and the carefully nurtured philosophy of Zugsmith was in danger from the first week Lexford took over. Basically, though, change would have come anyway; it was more of a coincidence that it arrived with Lexford.

Bob met the new managing editor at one of a series of get-acquainted luncheons Lexford arranged at Sardi's. That in itself was a departure, for none of the previous editors or executives had bothered to break bread with the staff. Lexford's Oxford training and his long years of doing business and getting interviews over lunch inspired the suggestion and Edith Miller eagerly went along. The competition of television and the impact of instant news broadcasts were weaning the public away from the traditional newspaper, Edith thought, and she was interested in bringing the paper, her paper, more up to date. For that reason, the ascendancy of the writers was as much Edith's idea as anyone. She had never understood the workings of the desk, possibly because her articles had been lovingly and lightly edited because she was the publisher's daughter and she also happened to be a good writer. It was impossible for anyone to know exactly how talented a writer was, Bob thought, without having seen the writer's efforts in the raw, his syntax jumbled, his transitions muddied and his points obscured. Lexford didn't make it any easier.

"Weren't you on the foreign desk?" Lexford asked when he was introduced to Bob.

"Yes, I've only been off a few weeks now."

"Yes, Bob Davis," Lexford said turning the name over in his mind. "I've heard of you."

Bob wondered if Lexford knew how many of his stories had been put together and patched by his desk. Lexford was mainly making conversation. Sure, he had heard of Bob through mentions in Zugsmith's memos or as a name signed to the daily report to the correspondents as the late man on the foreign desk, but Bob knew Lexford had never heard of him as the copy editor who had won him the Pulitzer Prize.

Lexford's British background and his years of watching the sun set on the empire uniquely qualified him for the job of managing editor. He could be firm and decisive when he wanted to be, but his long experience with the people of backward countries gave hm a sort of paternalistic approach that fitted in perfectly with the very model of the old-time managing editor of *The New York Record*. And yet there was a ruthlessness about him, too, that warned against any false sense of security from the outwardly kindly appearance. Lexford regarded it as the strangest kind of a fluke that he was an Englishman with a great deal of say over the most important and influential paper in America, but he was determined to make the most of it.

Edith had chosen Lexford to be managing editor because her mother had been captivated by his charm when she met him in London and because the new publisher wanted to end the death grip Zugsmith held on the editorial staff. Only by bringing in someone who was not one of "Zugsmith's boys" did Edith expect her ideas for brightening the paper to be carried out. Lexford filled the bill admirably: he had charm, a proper sense of his role as a subordinate of the publisher, and a stubborness that would enable him to stand up to Zugsmith and fend off his suggestions for maintaining the old, proved, reliable formulas that had worked so well on the paper in the past.

"I was really shocked at the size and the inefficiency of the office," Lexford said to Edith at one of their private luncheons soon after his installation in Beau's old office. "I haven't been back to New York in five years now and the place has certainly grown since then. I guess there must be nearly a hundred more reporters."

Edith smiled over her cocktail. "Probably you were here in the daytime, before the full staff started working. Yes, we have put on quite a few more reporters, but I don't think it's anywhere near a hundred."

"Do we really need that many? British papers cover just about as big an area with only half the staff and I understand finances are a bit strained now."

"What can I do?" Edith said, spreading her hands helplessly. "The policy of the paper is that no one is ever fired. We still have some men who remember when we needed that big staff to cover the Titantic sinking or some other big disaster."

"But that city room is so large, how in heaven's name do you keep track of them all?"

"They have a public address system on the city desk to page the men when they're needed. That helps a lot."

"Have you ever thought of closed circuit television?"

"For the city room?"

"For the whole plant. That's the big thing in industry abroad these days. It enables a manager to keep track on all departments. It helps a lot with efficiency, I hear."

"It seems so much like Big Brother is watching you. I think the men might resent it."

"Oh, they would, at first, but it does give you a big edge in management. You can spot trouble before it starts and move in to head off strikes and labor disputes."

"I suppose we could give it a try," Edith said without much conviction. "I know one place it would be helpful, between the art department and the city room. Frequently, I've seen where time could be saved if we had instant communications between an artist and a copy editor for instance. That might be where we could try it first."

"That's all right, I suppose, but I was thinking of a console in my office. I could keep closer touch with the operations that way, but of course, it's up to you." Lexford had become huffy like a small boy denied a toy.

"Don't get me wrong," Edith soothed. "I'm all in favor of electronic aids and all that, but we wouldn't want any of the staff to think they were being spied on. I think I read of a case in Britain where something like that was done by installing closed circuit TV cameras in the wash rooms. I think that was going a little too far."

"Oh, I agree wholeheartedly. You do have unions here, don't you? Perhaps we might try out the map idea first at that. That one camera could take in a great deal of the city room and then we could expand the coverage if necessary."

"Is there anything else you think we should be doing that we aren't?"

Lexford smoothed down the corners of his mustache. "There is something I've been meaning to talk to you about, but it's a little awkward."

"Don't be silly. There shouldn't be any barriers between us. Just because I'm a woman, don't let that stand in the way. We're both interested in the paper. Speak up."

"Well, it seems to me our employee policy doesn't back up our editorial policy. We speak of more rights and more opportunities for Negroes, but we have very few on the staff. I'm sure you must have heard about this before."

"We do have one Negro in the financial department and another as a clerk in the news room. They're both light-skinned; perhaps you've overlooked them."

"That may be so, but you have to have been out in Africa to learn how important that is for us. The new nations look on *The New York Record* as their friend and many of the leaders have mentioned to me that they are impresed by the way we have fought for civil rights in America. I think we have to do more than have two light-skinned Negroes in minor jobs, though, if we are really to keep the faith with what we are trying to do."

"I agree, but this is something I hadn't given much thought

to. I suppose there must be qualified black reporters on some of the black papers in the country. We could certainly recruit some of them. I think it would be a good idea."

"Yes, but we really should do more than that. The rising sense of blackness the African nations have given the American Negro is like the winds of change that swept away colonialism. We should put into practice the programs we espouse: training more Negroes to be reporters and copy editors."

"Fine, agreed, but we have to start some place and I think it would be wise if we could lure a good Negro reporter from one of the black papers. That would dramatize what we're trying to do and also serve as a showcase for the reporter and his stories."

"Incidentally, it might provide an entry for him into places where a white reporter can't go. There was a black fellow from Pittsburgh who was welcomed to sessions of councils in Africa where no other western reporters were allowed. I think it makes good sense philosophically and business-wise."

Edith frowned. "I wonder if some of the old-timers on the paper will be able to stand it. You know change terrifies some men and now they have a woman publisher, an English managing editor, and they'll be getting Negro reporters. Some retirements might be accelerated."

"From what I've seen in the few weeks I've been here, half the staff could retire without slowing down the operation one bit."

"I've often thought that, too, but I've never been able to figure out which half it should be."

Jefferson Davis Gray was a revolutionary figure on *The New York Record* in more ways than one. When he was hired, at much more money than he expected, he insisted on keeping the same by-line he had used in Pittsburgh: Jeff Gray.

"No one would know who Jefferson Davis Gray is," he argued with Zugsmith. "I have a following of sorts among Negroes and I think it important not to change my by-line."

"But we've never permitted the use of nicknames, even in sports. When I heard we were going to hire you, I thought your name would look impressive on the page, but Jeff Gray seems so informal."

"When I spoke with Mr. Lexford, he didn't have any objection to my by-line."

"Did Mr. Lexford know you intended to use the by-line Jeff Gray?"

"Yes, he said that was fine, the paper needed brightening up. It had grown too stodgy."

"Did he say that?" Zugsmith's eyebrows arched.

"I'm not sure if he used the word stodgy, but that's what he meant, he made that clear."

"Well, if Mr. Lexford said it's all right, there isn't anything I can do about it. I do think it might be a good idea, though, if you did start in sports. That way we could get our readers used to the idea gradually."

"Sports? I had the impression Mr. Lexford was talking about doing straight reporting. He even mentioned something about there being a possibility I might be sent abroad. I don't mind sports, understand, I've done a lot of that in my time. I'll work anywhere I'm told."

"You do have an athletic background and that might be the way for you to break in. I think you'll find *The New York Record* different from the *Pittsburgh Call.*"

Jeff looked out over the sea of white faces in the city room, the nervous knot in his stomach growing a little larger as he realized the pressure he would be working under. He turned back to Zugsmith and rubbed his moist palms together for emphasis. "Well," he said, flashing his magnificent white teeth, "the pay is a lot better for one thing."

Jeff Davis, the son of an Ohio mechanic, had parlayed the ability to run with a football into a college degree from U.C.L.A. He was a star on the Coast and might have gone on to professional play if he hadn't injured his knee in his senior year. The injury left him with little of his old mobility and less of his speed. He could still sprint for a bus if he had to, but he had to be careful of his footing since a sudden turn or a shift of his weight would double him over in a hot stab of pain from his knee.

Jeff had gone to college because of football, not for football. He amazed some of his teammates by his ambitious schedule of courses and he surprised his instructors with his high intelligence and his fluid writing. Jeff Davis was no football bum and he didn't have to rely on pro football for a better life than his father had. Jeff was confident his talent for writing would take him far; the closed doors he found on graduation were more of a crushing blow to him than his knee injury. The newspapers, the magazines, radio and television weren't ready for a top-flight black reporter. They never said that, of course; the doors were closed politely, but firmly: "We're not hiring, just now. Leave your application with the girl at the desk. If anything opens up, we'll contact you." But the contacts never came and the year Jeff promised himself he would spend on the *Call* stretched into two, then three, then four. He was famous in the Negro press, but that wasn't good enough for Jeff; he wanted to be famous in the whole lily-white stinking business! His job on *The New York Record,* he knew, could lead to that.

Bob recognized at once that Jeff would be under a strain. The whispers he heard in Curry's: "They sure hired a black one, didn't they?" convinced him that Jeff was going to need a friend. Bob wandered back to sports where Jeff was serving a week on the desk to get acquainted with the styles and procedures of the paper.

"Hi," he said, walking up to the huge giant laboring over a piece of wire service copy, "I'm Bob Davis."

Jeff scrambled to his feet. He was half a head taller than Bob, broader through the shoulders with a strong, rugged face, an incredibly thin nose and wide brown eyes that moved rapidly over the person being met.

"Jeff Gray," he said with a smile. "Aren't you the Bob Davis who played for Notre Dame?"

"Yes, I am, but I was nowhere in your class. Were you on the U.C.L.A. squad in '50?"

"I was just a sophomore. I played only a few minutes. I remember you came through the line and faked me out of my shoes. I missed the tackle and then the coach took me out."

"Was that on that touchdown?"

"Yes, I think you ran about fifty yards. The score must have been twenty-eight to zero then, that's why they sent me in. It taught me a lesson I never forgot, though."

"What's that?"

"Always look at a man's eyes. That's one way of telling which way he's going."

"Evidently it works because if I remember you were all Pacific Coast or something, weren't you?"

"I was all-Conference, but none of the other teams had much that year."

"How do you like it in sports?" Bob sat down at the desk and looked at the copy Jeff was handling. "Still got you handling shorts, I see."

"Man, I'll say. I must have had about twenty of those one paragraph stories. What do you call them? A heads. By the time I get up to the Z heads I should be an old man."

Jeff looked at a piece of copy unhappily. "It's hard to edit these things down. I wanted to use the typewriter, but I was told that's not allowed. There must be a million rules on this paper. They have the style book, that's about two hundred pages, then they have a bound volume of memos. There must be two hundred of them or more. How do you ever remember all that stuff?"

"Don't be discouraged. I know how you feel. I worked in sports when I first came here. They figure this is the junk yard. If you can pick your way through this stuff, you'll do all right no matter where they put you on the paper. I understand you're going to be out covering the Yankees next week."

"That's what they say. I guess they figure if the team finally got integrated, the press box might as well, too."

Bob smiled, Jefferson Davis Gray might never be a *New York Record* man in the old sense of the word, but he was going to be all right.

Bob's assessment was perfectly correct. Jeff's copy was crisp, fresh, and knowledgeable. He knew baseball intimately and his breezy approach stirred wide notice. His reception in the press box was a trifle stiff from some quarters, but the other reporters were not biased enough to overlook talent. Jeff soon was just another one of the working press, just as he always wanted to be.

Jeff's hiring by *The New York Record* seemed to signal the start of a new manhunt by leading corporations throughout the country. Suddenly bright young Negroes were in demand. The two light-skinned men who had been on the staff when Jeff arrived departed for more lucrative jobs, one for a position in government, the other as a news broadcaster on a radio station. They were replaced from among the flood of Negro applicants that were sent to the paper when the by-line Jeff Gray started to appear and it was realized that one of them had made it, and made it big.

Jeff Gray's instant success was something *The New York Record,* under its new management, was not reluctant to capitalize on. Guest appearances on television were arranged for him, promotional ads featured his picture and Zugsmith's memos cited his leads as different and praiseworthy. Edith wanted to move him to the regular reporting staff after a month, but Zugsmith argued, and Lexford supported his contention. To take Jeff off baseball in the middle of the season would seem like an affront. The rapport the paper was seeking with its liberal audience would deteriorate into mistrust and misunderstanding. Jeff was a captive of his own talent, his own ability; he would stay in sports at least until fall.

The Yankee ball players, especially the Southerners were hostile to Jeff at first, but he soon won them over as he had the sports writers.

"How the hell did you get the name Jefferson Davis Gray?" one of the players asked after the freeze had broken somewhat.

"I guess my mother must have know that some day I'd be doing what I'm doing right now. If you remember, the team really started to take off when I started covering."

"So does that mean you're our good-luck charm?"

"Hell no, man, but it's like my mother used to say, if there was ever anyone that could get the Yankees running, it was Jefferson Davis."

Undoubtedly, the pennant run by the Yankees and the assault on Babe Ruth's home run record by Roger Maris added drama and excitement to Jeff's articles. But he would have stirred notice with even a dull subject, for he had the ability to get behind a story and make it come alive with humor or pathos if needed. In three short months, Jefferson Davis Gray had become a celebrity, a mark of success for himself and the new liberal policies of *The New York Record,* but Jeff was too smart to be deceived or duped by success.

"I know I'm a whore," he said to Bob at a World Series press reception. Jeff had been drinking with some old friends from Pittsburgh and he seemed to resent Bob's advice to call it a night and go home. "Don't think I don't know the paper's been using me," he continued. "I've been using them too. If I wasn't black do you think I would have walked in and started to cover the top assignment in the department? It's all part of the game. *The New York Record* needed a black man to put in front of the public and I filled the bill. Just a goddamned whore, that's what I am. But let me tell you, I'm not selling myself cheap."

"I know, Jeff," Bob said in an attempt to quiet him. "I don't blame you a bit. I thought the same thing when I saw those ads, but what the hell, you have to roll with the punch."

"Sure, that's easy for you to say, but what about me? I wanted to make it on my own and I could, too, I know damned well I could. I showed them, didn't I?"

"You're making it on your own, aren't you? Who the hell is writing that stuff for you if you're not doing it? Why buck the system? Sure you might have breezed through the preliminaries because you were black, but now that you're in the bigtime, the main event, you're staying up there with your own talent, your own writing. There must be thousands of readers who don't know if you're black or purple and they don't give a damn. All they care about is that you're doing a good job. You're telling what happened each day and you're writing great inside features that have never been done before. I think Maris talks to you more than he does any of the white reporters."

Jeff snorted over his drink. "That's because he's a loner, an outcast just like me. He must recognize a kindred spirit."

"Bullshit. You have the knack of getting to him that the others don't. They consider him a stupid jerk, but you've found his human side. That shows talent."

Jeff was silent for a minute. He finished the last of his drink and then looked down at Bob in a strange way. "You know, Bob, that's how I feel about you. You never patronized me and you never gave me any crap. You treated me just like another guy from the first night you came back to sports when I was struggling with those shorts. I started to say you've really been white to me, but that's a contradiction to the way I feel. Human is more like it, yes, human. You've been a real human to me, Bob, thank you." He grasped Bob's hand roughly and slapped him on the shoulder.

Bob steadied Jeff as he seemed to stumble. "We midwestern boys got to stick together in the big town," he said. "What do you say we call it a night. The bar's just about to close anyway."

"Just one more drink, Bob, come on."

"I really don't need another drink and I think you had enough."

"Come on, what the hell, it's free isn't it? That's one of the benefits of being a member of the working press, you can free-load off all the promoters. They think we're a bunch of whores anyway."

"You going to start that again?" Bob chided gently. "If there's one thing I can't stand it's a drunk who repeats himself."

Jeff was taken back for an instant and then he saw Bob was only jesting. He put his arm around him and pulled him toward the bar. "Davis, you're a good old son of a bitch even if you haven't got natural rhythm. Come on, have a drink. We'll drink to the good old *New York Record,* the Midwest, or anything you want, even whores."

"But only high-priced ones," Bob said lightly.

Jeff grew serious for a moment. "You're goddamned right. I'm not going to sell myself cheap; they're really going to pay."

That was in October. By December, Jefferson Davis Gray was no longer on the staff of *The New York Record.* Another raise and a Christmas bonus—something unheard of for years on the paper—weren't enough to keep him. Jeff knew the reputation he had made with his coverage of the Yankees and Maris was a transitory thing. He was a hot commodity at this time and he could cool off quickly. He had received scores of offers from businesses to enter public relations and many from radio and television stations eager to have their liberal images enhanced by one with Jeff's talent and charm. In the age of television, one offer was too attractive to turn down. He stopped by the bullpen to tell Bob about it on his last night.

"I had no idea whoring would prove so profitable in this town," he said, a touch of irony in his voice.

"Don't be silly. If you didn't have the talent, you wouldn't have got the chance. Don't feel guilty about it, enjoy it. After all, you'll be a national figure on television."

"Yes, I can just see some of those cats back in Akron when they see me on the screen. 'Look, there's old Jeff without a football,' they'll say."

"And they'll probably say, 'He looks great; I always knew he could do it black or white.'"

"What do you mean, 'black or white,' man? I'm going to be coming over in color. Jefferson Davis Gray in beautiful living color."

Edith Miller's influence and desire for change were felt on the business side of the paper, too. Beau Manley's kick upstairs wasn't entirely wasted since among other things he indicated to Edith that the dead wood was stifling the advertising end of the paper, too. The circulation had been doing fine under Seymour (Si) Levy, a tough East Sider with the paper for thirty years. Si was never one to be complacent, though, and he was always pushing the truck drivers and the deliverers to meet timetables and to fill quotas. Si was probably the best known man in New York. He was the friend of the Mayor, the Police Commissioner, and virtually all the labor chieftains. He had an expense account that enabled him to take care of the policemen who overlooked the parked trucks in the street around edition time, the union leaders who overlooked some of the stickier points in the contract around negotiation time, and the newsdealers who always gave *The New York Record* preferred positions on their stands.

Si was a fighter in his youth, on the streets at first and then in the ring. He knew he had to fight for everything he wanted out of life and it was the same with his paper: he was never satisfied with the circulation figures, always pushing the roadmen to open up new territories and the subscription department to try harder. When he found that returns were running higher than normal, Si called on both the police and his underworld friends to investigate. The underworld came up with the answer: large numbers of papers were being stolen each night by the employees and then being turned over to newsdealers, who would cut off the masthead and the date for credit as a return. Si stopped that by centralizing the point where the employees would pick up their papers and by stamping "Free Copy" over the date of all papers for employees, thus cutting off any credit on unpaid for papers.

"Si Levy is the kind of man you need at the head of your advertising department," Beau told Edith as she puzzled over the cost sheets in her office. "Our advertising department has been stagnant for years. There's no push there, no drive. Most of the ads that come in are unsolicited and plenty are turned down by puritanical relics like me who have been on the paper for thirty years."

"That's the whole trouble," Edith said. "The advertising manager has been here too long, but you know one of the sad things is that he was a child prodigy, I guess, because he still has several years to go before retirement."

"Couldn't you kick him upstairs, the way you did me?"

Edith looked up in surprise. She hadn't realized Beau's sharpness had caught the subtlety of his promotion, even though he had proved more valuable than Edith had imagined. She patted his hand across the desk reassuringly. "Now, Beau, you know I need your advice. You were a friend of my father and I feel secure with you to count on. You were being wasted in that managing editor's job. Zugsmith was really running the paper anyway."

Beau dropped his eyes and nervously tugged at his tie. "Yes, I know. I guess I was drinking a little too much, too. I appreciate your confidence in me, Edith. I think you should put Si Levy in charge of advertising if you could possibly do it. He's a terrific promoter."

"Promoter? Perhaps that's the answer. We could make him a vice president in charge of promotion and that would include advertising and circulation both. Harry Bellows would be under him, but he'd still have his title of advertising manager. That might work."

"It might be a lot for Si to do. It's a tough job handling both circulation and advertising."

"I wouldn't expect him to continue as circulation manager. He could name his own replacement. The title would just be a subterfuge to mollify Bellows. It might work."

"I know Si has always been unhappy that our advertising

hasn't moved with our circulation. He says circulation opens the doors for advertising, but the department hasn't been delivering. I wonder how he'll like the assignment."

"Let's ask him," Edith said, reaching for the phone on her desk.

Si liked the idea at once. He was eager to start and had many ideas to increase the advertising revenues.

"The first thing we have to do," he said, gesticulating with his cigar, "is to get rid of our censor. I've seen page after page of ads turned down that the *Tribune* was glad to run. I don't recall anyone being scandalized by them."

"Just a minute, Si," Edith said. "I don't want to turn the paper into a girlie magazine or anything like that. I agree that some of the censor's moves may have been stuffy, but I'm not familiar enough with his work to say for sure. If you say so, it must be so."

"I'm telling you. Times have changed, but too many men on *The New York Record* will never admit it. Look at fashions. They're more daring than thirty years ago aren't they? And the movies, they're more frank, too, right? Well if we're dealing with fashions and movies in advertising, it follows that we've got to change, too. We can't impose Hays office censorship on movie ads today. I'm sure sensible censorship, nothing really gross allowed, of course, could bring in nearly a million lines more of ads a year."

"A million lines? That's an impressive figure."

"Look, Miss Miller, let me handle the whole thing for six months my way. If you don't like it, I'll go back to circulation or even resign if you want. We've just about reached the saturation point in circulation and there are just so many things I can do. The challenge has gone out of the job for me, but this new one is something else. I think I can do a helluva job for you and *The New York Record*."

Edith looked him over. He was a short man with about a dozen hairs in a forelock that he rationed sparsely over the rest of his head. He had thick lips, fast-moving brown eyes behind his thick glasses, and a restless manner that made him seem to be moving even when he was sitting still. "All right," she said, extending her hand across the desk. "You have six months. Either *The New York Record* starts to make money or starts to lose friends. I'm not sure your ideas will work, but we might as well give them a chance. Too many things have been played safe around here. If they're a success, it will mean a lot to both of us. If they fail, all people can say is 'What did you expect from a woman? She should have known better to put a circulation man in charge of advertising.' "

Si came out punching. He shook up the advertising sales staff completely, riding the men until they made more calls on advertisers to get Si off their backs. He instituted a system of check-ins that enabled him to know where all his salesmen were at all times. The passive role of accepting advertising was discarded completely as Si and his staff went out and fought for ads with all the fervor that he had fought for circulation. The tricks, the deals, the contacts he had made in circulation were modified to serve the advertising department. There was no clear threat to neglect any news of a product or a company in the paper if an ad was not forthcoming, but the message was clear: the free rides are over; it costs money to put out a paper, advertise, or be banished. The only difference from the old days was that Si's crews carried rate cards instead of blackjacks. The strong-arm was being refined, but it was being applied strategically, subtly, and effectively: the lineage figures zoomed not in six months, but in only two months.

Part of the record was achieved through the annual review of the year, traditionally a money maker for the paper. But Si exploited this feature to the skies, breaking the review down into sections and then getting the world network of correspondents to dun news sources and governments for expensive ads to run in the annual review.

Edith was impressed, but she vetoed Si's idea to fatten the golden calf by running a winter review and a summer review.

She did agree to expand other seasonal features and to turn loose Si's sales force on the advertisers in such lines as home building, garden supplies, home improvements, automobile shows, and boat shows.

"The important thing to remember is that we have to give a little to get a lot," Si explained at a conference with Edith and Beau. "If we run these special sections, we can use some junky story about how great this company is provided we get a big enough ad out of them."

"We still have to keep our sixty to forty ratio of news to advertising, though," Edith warned.

"Sure," Si said through a cloud of cigar smoke, "but in this case the sixty is for advertising. The forty per cent can be 'news' about the products, which is really advertising, too."

"Do you really think it will work?" Beau asked. "It would seem that a company might not be willing to take an ad just to get a couple of paragraphs into a special section."

"Beau, you're a helluva newspaperman, but a lousy salesman. Don't you realize what these companies do? They take that small item that appears as news and they reprint it with a credit line to us. The people who see that don't know it was in a special section so they say to themselves if *The New York Record* says this is a good company it must be so. Don't worry, these big outfits aren't advertising for nothing. It's just about time we realized we shouldn't give away anything we can sell."

"What about the ethics of this?" Edith put in, feeling a trifle unsure of the implicit sandbagging in Si's plan of attack.

"Ethics? To me, the only ethics I was brought up on was the survival of the fittest. You know yourself, Miss Miller, the newspapers in this town are sick. They're all pushing for ads just as hard as we are. Thank God, we're not as badly off as some of the papers, but we got to fight for ads just like they do. The circulation is there and if you build up a backlog of demand for these special sections you can raise the ad rates.

Like I say, everybody's doing it and the ethics of it should be pretty clear. It's the businesslike way to do things."

Edith turned to Beau with a wan smile. "I always try to think how my father would react to all these new things that are going on, but when I think of my father, I think of the inheritance taxes that have put the paper in a hole. I don't think there is anything else we can do. We need the revenues so I guess that's your answer, Si."

Si smiled. "That's the way it's always been. I remember back in the old days when I was just starting on the paper. Your grandfather was the publisher then and believe me it was rough. We had to fight tooth and nail for every newsstand and just about every sale. I remember we used to carry blackjacks, black paint, and sugar. The blackjacks we'd use on the newsies who were reluctant to give us good position on the stands, the black paint we'd smear over the other guy's papers, and the sugar we'd put in the gas tanks of the trucks taking out the papers for the opposition."

"I read about those days," Edith said, "But I never knew my grandfather had anything to do with what was going on. He always seemed so upright and dignified."

"Oh, he was, make no mistake about it, but he was in a fight for his life. He didn't know all the details, of course, but he measured things by results. The paper was two cents at the time and you had to keep selling or your advertisers would drop out. The best thing that we ever did was with the help of some German chemist who arrived after the war. He gave us some stuff that we put into the ink supply of the *Trib*. It kept the ink from drying and everyone who bought the *Trib* had ink-smeared hands for days. Their circulation went into a real tailspin then and they started with the circulation contests that they ran until they went broke."

"I guess my asking about the ethics of pushing for advertising seems a little silly in light of what you've told me about the old days, doesn't it?" Edith asked, biting her lip.

"Not at all," Si said, shaking his head. "We're not going to use blackjacks and the paper is established now. We've just been sitting on our duffs too long and getting fat, dumb, and happy. We'll operate within the context of today, but you're damned sure we'll operate. That's the only way to make a buck."

The energy of Si Levy was amazing. He was everywhere at once, keeping old friends happy and making new ones as he moved into the executive offices of the large corporations to pin down advertising contracts and make new contacts. The censor wasn't removed completely, but Si was given the final word on whether ads would be run or not. The Sunday supplement of the paper blossomed forth with full color ads featuring lingerie, beauty aids, and fashions. The advertisers were selling sex and *The New York Record* was not backward about showcasing it. Many of the old-timers considered the supplement pornographic and blasphemous, the pornography related to the scantily clad models in the ads and the blasphemy charged to the articles authored by some of the new writers on the paper.

"The Emperor's getting gayer," Tucker said to Bob as they leafed through the Sunday supplement in Curry's one Saturday night.

"Well no one could call the paper the old lady any more," Bob agreed.

"I remember the old days when the paper was accused of being dull, the managing editor, I think it was Carter Bergen then, said; "We'd rather be dull than flippant.' The tide seems to have changed now, though. Some of these new fellows are really hip with their leads and styles. Slang, fragment sentences, just about everything goes now."

"But some of it is still deadly dull, at least to me. I've read through plenty of stories by Guy Latrec and thought what a waste of space. The words flow and all that, but I read paragraph after paragraph looking for the point to the story and

260

then I get down to the end and there's none. What he says in a column or more could be told in three paragraphs, if you're speaking of substance. It's like eating a piece of lemon meringue pie and finding out there's no lemon, only meringue. Latrec may be brilliant and the best of the new breed on the paper, but it seems like a lot of feathers to me."

"My, haven't you become the cutting critic now that you've moved into the executive circle," Tucker said in mock seriousness. "Do you have any complaints about my work, sir?"

"Knock it off," Bob said, pushing Tucker gently. "I noticed your by-line on a couple of pieces last week. How did that happen?"

"Well, Edith, Miss Miller, wanted to know why one of my anonymous pieces wasn't signed. There was no good explanation anyone wanted to give her, so she left orders that I was to get a by-line in the future."

"That's great. After how many years? Now maybe you can get off that rewrite dead-end."

Tucker shook his head mournfully. "I could, I guess, if I wanted to, but I can't afford it. I've got too many commitments. I'm supposed to do another space-age book and the magazines are gobbling up everything I turn out. I'm trapped, Bob, just as I told you that first year you came. I guess the same thing will be happening to you, too."

Trapped? No I'm not, Bob thought, I can always get away. But the seeds of doubt were there, he knew. He found himself agreeing more and more with Zugsmith and even Jamieson these days; so much so he was beginning to wonder and worry. "I don't think I'm trapped yet," he said to Tucker, downing the last of his drink and picking up the moist bills from the bar, "I'm going to get a chance to do some writing and after that I don't know. I still don't know if I'm right for this place or if it's right for me."

There were many others on the paper who experienced the same fears that Bob shunted to the back of his mind. Some of the men were talented and had no reason for concern, but others recognized that the new searchlight being turned on the writers would show up their efforts as clumsy, or at the best, merely workmanlike. The accent was on youth and Guy Latrec—called La Trick by those who objected to his success in getting all the top assignments—was the newest of the new breed. He had been a copy boy who might have been lost in the shuffle in another era on *The New York Record*. But he had the luck to be there when the styles, the tempo, the emphasis and the paper itself were changing, sending many of the old standards, the strictures blowing in the wind.

The old system of coverage by suffocation still existed, but the methods of smothering the story were different, amounting to an almost sneering irreverence on the part of the writer. Reporting in depth is what Lexford called the system, but the line between analyses and opinion was a difficult one to hold, especially when the desks had been warned that changes made in the stories of certain writers would have to be explained in duplicate, with one copy of the explanation going to the author and the other to the managing editor.

Like most rulings, the dictum had exceptions; not all writers were covered or included in the memo on copy changes. Latrec headed the list, of course, but Webster Clayton and many of the old-timers were there, too. Bob was convinced the memo was another manifestation of the legend of the Emperor. He conducted an experiment to test his contention, working closely with the city desk on the project, but keeping the details secret.

First, he retyped the lead of a story by Latrec, omitting the by-line at the top of the page. He showed the copy to Jamieson as the first step in his plot.

"What do you think of this feature?" he asked, "It was written by one of the copy boys."

Jamieson looked through the three pages of copy, commenting as he went along, "I don't get that lead. What's he trying to say? It certainly is long enough, isn't it? What's the point? I don't see any point to the story."

"That's the way I felt," Bob said. "I just wanted to get your opinion because I didn't want the kid to be discouraged on the basis of one man's opinion."

A week later, Bob got a copy of another story by Latrec. This one he submitted with the by-line intact. In Bob's opinion, the article was still vague and pointless. He had to concede that he conditioned Jamieson's response by asking, "Have you read this story by Latrec? It's pretty lively."

Jamieson started reading the first page. Half way through he started to smile and the expression was frozen on his face the rest of the way through the article. "He certainly knows how to use words," he said, with genuine admiration. "His sentences are full of imagery. It's the modern style all right: smooth and flowing. It's a pretty good piece."

"I knew you'd like it," Bob said archly.

Latrec had the widest latitude on assignments. Nearly three days a week he would write about anything that struck his fancy, his stories cutting across department lines, sometimes appearing in the news section, sometimes the feature section or even in sports or financial. Edith Miller encouraged this policy because she was toying with the idea of instituting a featured column of the sights and scenes in the city. Latrec was trying out for this assignment, although he didn't know it. There were men he was competing against, of course, and that made Latrec unhappy. Guy was a Latin and bitterly jealous, measuring the headline on his story compared to others, evaluating the play, the length, etc.

He was a small man, barely five feet seven inches, but in his mind he became a giant at the typewriter, playing the keys like a maestro to bring out what he considered rare pearls to be cast before the swine on the copy desk. His writing, his choice of words, his well-turned and well-honed phrases could never be faulted by the desk, or changed, for that matter, but the substance of his articles and his judgment were open to serious question. And yet, because he was Guy Latrec, boy genius, his copy was often edited lightly or passed unchanged.

Bob wanted to do his writing on the same beat as Latrec, and he could have if he had appealed to Edith. But Zugsmith, still holding to his belief that Bob didn't know the city well enough, arranged for him to work in the financial department, where he was assigned to turn out a series of meaningless pieces on the price of hog bellies, grain futures, and the like. It was Zugsmith's idea to discourage Bob from writing but Bob only tried harder to bring the dull material to life. He succeeded so well that he received an unprecedented by-line on a commodities exchange piece. He also received a free hand to write features on any aspect of the financial world he selected after only ten days in the department. The financial editor was convinced he had discovered a real find. He wasn't aware of Zugsmith's thinking and he was looking forward to keeping Bob. Perhaps he might have if Bob hadn't met Eleanor Wilson, a tall blonde publicity agent for a Wall Street broker.

Bob was ripe for something at that time; he hadn't seen Diane in weeks and he couldn't stand Alice Blaine now that she was working as Lexford's assistant and virtually shaping his judgment on much of the news. Eleanor was something special in financial publicity. She wasn't a writer; she was a placement specialist. When Bob first heard her say that he had to agree that everything was in the right place and in the right proportions. Even if his romance with Diane hadn't cooled, Eleanor would have rated a second look. Tall and willowy, she had the perfect pale complexion of the beauty ads, flawlessly perfect make-up on the eyes to give the right accent, voluptuous lips, an ample bosom, a thin waist, and the sexiest legs ever to be put under the table at a board meeting.

Eleanor and Bob hit it off at once. He was new, therefore malleable, she reasoned. More than that, he was handsome and he could write on anything he wanted. She had found that out at their first meeting; Eleanor never wasted time. If he hadn't asked her out, she would have pulled the canceled theatre tickets routine; it worked every time.

Their first date was mostly talk. Since Bob had been the aggressor, it never occurred to him that he was being used skillfully and subtly.

"I don't understand why you didn't stay in television instead of going back after the strike," she said over their after dinner drinks. Eleanor had the happy faculty of knowing her subjects and she had seen Bob on television during the strike.

"I might have, but I wasn't sure I wanted to be in television."

"The money must have been better. Doesn't money mean anything to you?"

"It means a great deal, but that's just it. I'm making more money here than I was on NBC. I guess I'm one of the lucky ones."

Eleanor arched her eyebrows. "I wouldn't say that. Perhaps you're making more in salary than some of the others, but I'm sure the incomes of many men on *The New York Record* are a lot higher than yours?"

"You mean they have investments?"

"Sort of. It's more like an insurance policy, I'd say. I'm sure you must have figured it out."

"I know a lot of the men write for magazines and some have written books. That's about the only way I know of that they could have extra income, though."

Eleanor smiled. "Writing a book is a lot of work. There are ways to make money without writing a book. I'm sure you can figure it out."

Bob was too honest to know what Eleanor was talking about. Besides, he was interested in Eleanor for a much different reason than she was interested in him. That never occurred to him until their second date, when Eleanor sprang her trap.

"You know, you've been so nice to me and I've never done anything for you," she said lightly.

"You don't have to do anything for me," Bob assured her, "just being with you is enough for me."

"No, I mean it. I have a way for you to make enough money so you could go back to Indiana or do whatever else you wanted."

"Not robbing a bank, I hope."

"No it isn't robbing a bank. All I want you to do is buy some stock."

"Buy stock? I have some now. Which stock do you have in mind?"

"It's a new electronic firm, but it's certain to be a great success. I can't tell you now, but I'd advise you to buy as much as you can."

"What's the name of the stock and what is it selling for?"

"It's Durren Computer and it's priced about fifteen. It should go much higher."

"All I could spare would be one thousand dollars. That wouldn't buy a lot of shares."

"It would be hard to make a big enough killing on one thousand dollars to make it worthwhile."

"Maybe I could raise two thousand dollars," Bob said, sensing that his first reply hadn't been too well received.

"That would be better, but, of course, I could lend you say three thousand, that would give you five thousand."

"But why should you lend me three thousand dollars? I don't know when I could repay you."

"Don't be silly, the stock would be my security. You could always pay me by selling the stock."

"I don't understand. First you want me to buy stock, then you want me to sell it. It's confusing."

Eleanor chucked him under the chin and smiled sadly. "You could pay me from the profits you make when the stock goes up. That's the whole secret; the stock is very underpriced and is bound to go up when . . ."

"When what?"

"When the public learns about the big breakthrough the company has achieved in the computer field."

"A breakthrough? What's it all about?"

"It's very complicated and I really don't understand it. It has something to do with memory storage. More information can be programmed into a computer in a smaller space or something like that. It's all hush-hush because this could play a big role in space exploration and premature publicity could hurt Durren Computer."

"What about mature publicity?" Bob asked, a great light beginning to dawn. It was hard to remember that Eleanor was a flack.

"You mean after you've bought your stock?" she said archly.

"Yes, after I've bought my stock."

"Well, that would be the time for mature publicity. That could make the stock go up and you could get back enough money to pay me the three thousand dollars."

"Easy as that, eh? Is that what they call wheeling and dealing? How high does Durren Computer expect their stock to go?"

"After your story?"

"Yes, we'll say that."

"About two hundred dollars a share is the target figure. They feel the demand is there and a story in *The New York Record* should easily make the stock worth that much."

"But will the stock really be worth that much, or will it just be a lot of crap kicked up by a story in *The New York Record?*"

"Well, that's hard to say. It's relative, I guess. If the people are willing to pay two hundred dollars a share, you'd have to say it's worth it, wouldn't you?"

"I'm not too sure. Let's see, with the price at fifteen dollars, five thousand would get me about 333 shares, right? And if those 333 shares were to sell for two hundred dollars each, that would be $66,000, right? Not bad for a newspaper story. That should make me the highest priced whore in town."

"Bob," Eleanor said, genuinely shocked. "You shouldn't talk that way. The story is going to come out eventually,

267

there's no reason why you shouldn't be able to make some money on it. If you don't, somebody else will. This isn't the first time publicity has been used to blue sky an issue."

"Blue sky, that's it. I couldn't think of the term. But if I'm going to make so much money, somebody has to be making a great deal more. Some of the insiders must have thousands of shares."

Eleanor flushed and lowered her eyes. "I suppose so, I really don't know."

"How many shares do you have for instance?"

She looked up, her eyes blazing defiance. "They said that if I could get you to write this story, I'd get a thousand shares."

"And what about the three thousand dollars? That wouldn't really be a loan, would it?"

Eleanor lowered her eyes again. "No, that was to come out of the expenses. I put it on a loan basis because I didn't know what you'd do."

"In other words, you weren't sure how big a whore I was, right?"

"Something like that. I guess we all have our price. If I were to offer you three thousand dollars, it would be an insult, I know. But if that three thousand could be turned into thirty thousand almost overnight, you might consider it. Would you?"

"I really don't know. There's something missing here, something I can't put my finger on. What I want to know is if there's nothing wrong in what you're trying to do or what you're trying to have me do, why is it necessary to go to all this trouble? Certainly publicity in the normal course of events would more than achieve your purpose."

"Bob, I'm sorry I've disappointed you, but I want to be honest with you now. You're right, there is something wrong. The unanswered question is whether this principle, this program will really work. Normally, these things are submitted to panels of engineers before they're evaluated for marketing. Durren Computer just doesn't operate that way. It doesn't belong to the organizations that do the testing and it doesn't want to submit to testing. They feel it might take too long or the secret might leak out or something. Their engineers are satisfied, that's enough for them. If it's enough for you and you could write the story I'd be deeply grateful."

"How grateful?" Bob said, his eyes narrowing.

"Ever so grateful," Eleanor said, looking deeply into his eyes.

Bob looked at her for a long moment. He didn't know whether it made him glad or sad to see her almost groveling. Money did funny things to people, he thought.

"From what you tell me, this is a complicated thing and it might take at least a week for me to get the information and to write the story."

"Oh I don't think it would take a week. A few days, perhaps, but . . ."

"No, it has to be a week. A week in some quiet hotel or resort, where I could talk to the engineers without being disturbed and where we could talk or do whatever we wanted to without being disturbed."

"We?" Eleanor asked, her eyebrows arched, a shade of fear in her voice.

"Yes, you and me. I think you would have to stay very close to me to make sure I got all the facts, all the background, everything that's coming to me."

"Everything?"

Bob's voice turned hard and his manner sharpened. "You're damned right, everything. You'd better learn that a whore's life can be pretty lonely. If I'm going to be one, you are, too; we can console each other."

Eleanor tried to control the hate she felt mounting within her. She realized it wasn't Bob she hated, it was Eleanor Wilson, the wonder of Wall Street. Bob was just a means to an end, but he was handsome and he could be fun. "When do you think you can write the story?" she said.

Bob looked at her in surprise. He thought his tactics would

be enough to shock her out of the idea. Her gaze never faltered as she looked at him, her mind whirling with the thought of a week away and all that money. Bob started to laugh.

"You certainly fooled me, but I guess I had it coming to me. I thought you had class. I guess Wall Street is just as bad as any other street in this town; they're all filthy."

Eleanor's eyes popped. "What do you mean? Do we have a deal or don't we?"

"I'm sorry, you picked the wrong man. In Fort Wayne it was the politicians who were always trying to bribe the newspapermen. I guess they succeeded in a lot of cases, too. But I never could be bothered. I guess I'm not constituted that way. There's a lot more dishonesty on this paper, I know, because it's bigger and the city is bigger, but I still want no part of it. I'm sorry, Eleanor, but the answer is no."

She gathered her purse and slid around from behind the table. "I guess there's nothing more to say, then. I better be going."

She was silent in the cab ride to her apartment, nervously biting her lip and looking out the window to avoid Bob's gaze. He was going to have the cab wait, but Eleanor insisted that he come up to her apartment.

"We can at least have a drink to what might have been," she said, turning on the charm again.

"I won't change my mind," Bob warned.

"If I thought you'd change your mind, I wouldn't invite you up. There'd be no point to it."

Bob was unconvinced, but he was sure of himself, too. "I want to warn you, though, if I come up to your apartment, I'm going to make love to you, or at least try."

Eleanor smiled. "Still being honest, eh? That's what I like about you. You're different in a very disturbing way. You made me feel cheap and low back there in the restaurant, but I'd feel worse if you didn't say what you did just now. I could be very fond of you, Bob, honestly." She kissed him just as the elevator door closed and they embraced hungrily as the car ascended. Eleanor could feel Bob growing tense as he pressed into her. She was even more desirable than he imagined. He'd miss that week in the hotel; he'd have to make tonight count for a lot.

"Here we are," she said as the car came to a stop. "I have a dog, so wait by the door until I lock him in the kitchen."

"Hurry up," Bob said, kissing her as she turned to go through the door, "You've got a tiger here, too."

She smiled as she whirled through the door and snapped the lock behind her. "Bob?" she called through the door softly, "How does it feel to want something really badly?"

He looked at the top of the apartment. The letters 8D were burned indelibly into his brain. He shrugged and walked back to the elevator. "Going down?" he said flatly as the door of the car opened and a fat matron edged to the back.

Bob was hardly surprised a few weeks later when he read a story in the financial pages about a new process perfected by Durren Computer. The story was under the by-line of Guy Latrec. By the end of the day, Durren Computer stock had climbed to $175 and the challenges to the story by leading scientists and engineers had started to roll in. The next day's paper explained that the process was still subject to review and Durren's stock plunged to fifty dollars, where it stayed merely as a tribute to the tenacity of those who had bought at one hundred dollars and above and refused to believe the fairy tale had ended.

Bob was back in the bullpen by then and he had time to figure out that Latrec had made better than fifty thousand dollars if he had received the same proposition from Eleanor. There was no assurance that she had to sell Latrec as much as she did Bob, though, since Guy seldom bothered to check out sources or to question information. "I wonder if he got the week in the hotel?" Bob mused.

The true story of Durren Computer never appeared in *The*

New York Record and an even bigger one went unpublished the same week. Si Levy rushed into the daily editorial conference brimming with excitement. "I did it, by God, I did it," he almost shouted.

Lexford looked up in annoyance from the summaries that had been submitted by the department heads. He didn't like the commercial side of the paper encroaching on the news conference.

"Well," Si said, almost breathless, "our Venus probe is going to land on that planet tonight. A flag will be ejected just before the probe hits the surface. The flag will be an American flag, but underneath the big flag will be a little pennant. What do you think it will say on the pennant?"

"I have no idea, old boy," Lexford said, his annoyance mounting, "What the devil will it say?"

"Buy *The New York Record*," Si almost screamed ecstatically. Suddenly, he slumped into a chair in the back row, away from the conference table, where the advertising director and other non-news sections heads sat.

"What the hell good is it?" he moaned. "Security won't let me tell anyone about the pennant because they'd want to know how it was arranged; and besides, who'd believe me, anyhow?"

"Let's start," Zugsmith said briskly. "Si, I'm surprised at you. If *The New York Record* said it was so, it must be so, but I don't think we can use the story. Besides, you haven't started circulation on Venus yet, have you?"

Chapter Fifteen

FATHER TIM was waiting when Bob walked into Curry's with Tucker. "Bob," he called, "I've been waiting to see you. How are you, boy?"

"I'm fine, Father, how are you? I think you know Howard Tucker."

"Yes, I do, how are you Howard? I haven't seen you in here in some time."

"I've been doing some reporting and feature writing so I haven't had a steady diet of rewrite," Tucker explained.

Bob ordered a drink and had another beer brought for the priest. "If you two will excuse me," Tucker said, "I see some one I want to talk to." He made his way to the back room, leaving Bob and the priest standing at the bar.

"He's a nice guy," Tim said. "He knew I wanted to talk to you."

"And I wanted to talk to you. How's Diane?"

Father Tim smiled. "That's what I wanted to talk to you about. She's well, but she isn't all right, if you know what I mean. My mother's been sick as you know and Diane's been taking care of her. A stranger might say Diane's sad because the old girl is ill and tired out from waiting on her hand and foot, but it's not that simple."

"Is there something wrong with Diane? What are you trying to say?"

"Look, Bob, I don't want to pry into your business, but I take it you two had some sort of a misunderstanding."

Bob snorted and took a deep gulp of his drink. "That's putting it mildly. She found a naked woman in my apartment."

Father Tim smiled. "Oh, that's what it was. I thought Diane was more broad minded than that. I'm sure you had a good explanation, or at least a good story."

"Father, I don't know how many years you've been hearing confessions, but I bet you never heard a story good enough to explain something like that to a wife or a girl friend."

Father Tim rubbed his chin. "I guess you're right, but that's not why I'm here. I don't want to convert you or hear your confession, Bob. I just want to let you know Diane is taking my mother to Florida for the winter and she'd like to say good-by before she goes, but she's too stubborn to admit it."

"To Florida? When is she leaving?"

"Next week. The doctors say the climate will be better for my mother and Diane thinks she might be able to get a job that will enable them to stay all year round."

"But how do you know she wants to see me? I called a couple of times and she wouldn't talk to me. I know she was hurt, but there's just so much a man can do, you know."

"Why don't you try one more time?"

"I'll call her right now," Bob said.

"No, wait. You're off tomorrow, aren't you?"

"Yes. Why?"

"I'm supposed to have dinner with Diane at my mother's apartment. You've been there, I know. Well, I told Diane I might bring a friend and she, of course, thinks I'm bringing another priest. How would you like to be that friend?"

Bob didn't need to be convinced.

Tim was right, Bob knew, as soon as he looked into Diane's eyes. She stood looking at him silently as Tim stepped out of the doorway in front of Bob.

"Diane," the priest said sharply. "Don't you know it's positively sinful to look at a man that way without kissing him?" He smiled as she rushed into Bob's arms.

"Darling," he whispered in her ear. "I'm sorry, I'll never be able to tell you how much I've missed you."

Diane stood back and beamed at him through tear-filled eyes. "Bob I don't care what you've done. I just couldn't go away without saying good-by. I'd have come down to the paper next week before I left or gone into Curry's, but I just couldn't go away cut off from you."

They kissed again fiercely until Father Tim coughed intrusively. "Now let's not forget that we're dinner guests tonight, Bob. I don't know what you came for, but this sister of mine is a great cook. I think you should save any kissing until after dinner, you might lose your appetite, or at least I might."

Four of the five days before Diane left for Florida were magnificent torture for Bob. He would knock softly at the apartment door and she would let him in for a few hours of passionate kisses and whispered talk on the living room couch while Mrs. Reilly snored peacefully away in her bedroom. The last night, when Bob was off, Diane had a neighbor sit with her mother while she went to his apartment. She was the seductive, desirable Diane once again.

Never had she been more tender, never had Bob been more effective.

He kissed her hungrily, his physical strength spent, his passion railing at his unresponsive body. "I want to marry you, only you."

Diane looked at the ceiling. "Now is not the right time to get married. I have to take care of my mother just as you had to take care of your job before."

"Maybe if you got pregnant, then you'd have to marry me."

"Bob," she said, "it's a simple enough problem: what would I do with my mother?"

He rolled away moodily. "I suppose we could put her in a nursing home or she could live with us, but not while you're in Florida and I'm working in New York."

"Well, then, why don't you work in Florida?" Diane said, only half in jest.

"*The New York Record* doesn't publish in Florida. Oh, I suppose I could get a job on a paper down there, but it wouldn't be the same."

"I certainly wouldn't want you to make any sacrifices for me," she said with a pout.

"That's the whole point. If it were only you, I'd say the hell

275

with the whole thing and chuck everything. But your mother stands between us just as surely as *The New York Record* did or does." Bob laughed bitterly as he thought of Zugsmith. "You know, Zugsmith never married because he has to take care of his mother. If it weren't for you and it weren't for Zugsmith, I never would have started on *The New York Record* and I wouldn't be here now."

"We'll be staying at my uncle's house in Coral Gables. He's a professor at the University of Miami. He's on a sabbatical in India now and he's due back next year. The plan is for my mother to stay with her brother and his wife, she's a nurse, if she still wants to remain there after the winter. With my mother getting that kind of care, I'll be free to do anything I want. Even to get married."

"Darling," he cried, "you don't know how happy you've made me, or your uncle's made me. I felt so trapped with no way out. I wouldn't want to hurt your mother, but I know it just wouldn't work out for us to plan on having her with us."

Diane smiled. "You don't have to be another Zugsmith, after all, do you? There goes your last excuse for not getting married, at least for another year. But let me warn you, Mr. Davis, this time I want it official. I want my engagement announced in *The New York Record.*"

Bob's improved frame of mind was apparent to everyone on the paper. He called Diane every night between editions on the special long distance lines the paper maintained and he was looking forward to spending his vacation in Florida. The strike had scrambled the vacation dates, however, and Bob found that he wouldn't be able to get away until early spring. Knowing that Diane was there when he called and that her mother was getting better was enough to tide him over until then he felt, and he threw himself into his work with even more fervor than in the past. Zugsmith noticed as much as the others. But Zugsmith's power was steadily being whittled away and neither he nor Bob knew or could guess if a Zugsmith recommendation would carry the weight of the past or even any weight at all.

The paper was changing, but in many ways it was unchanging because of the people on it.

Zugsmith acquiesced in the policies established by Lexford, who accented the obvious in Zugsmith's view. But Lexford was viewing the city with the eyes of a child or a foreigner and many facets of commerce, government, social life, and politics were being examined more closely and at greater length. This was in perfect harmony with the new talent on the paper, which had no background to erect taboos or to regard history as anything more ancient than last year. The result was a series of articles on the Fulton Fish Market, Ellis Island, the Aqueduct race track, and other familiar landmarks around the city. To Lexford, though, they were new and news: if he didn't know the history of the places and the writers were turning, for them, virgin soil, there must be others in the city who were in the same situation; therefore, the series not only were expanded but often were repeated to the point where some stories became standard jokes on the desks.

In some respects, Zugsmith was as much to blame for the repeaters as anyone. He wasn't fully satisfied with the direction Lexford was taking, but he wanted to show his interest by bringing up points overlooked in the stories or posing questions left unanswered. This served a dual purpose: the reporter was reminded of the Zugsmith school of journalism and Lexford was reminded that Zugsmith could still be valuable to the paper. Only Bob, Lexford knew, was not a personal selection of Zugsmith for service in the bullpen. And Bob, Zugsmith had now decided, was the best bet to see that the old policies were preserved or at least respected in some small measure.

Lexford wasn't concerned about the loyalty that was directed toward Zugsmith instead of toward the managing editor. He was secure in his position because he felt he had Edith's confidence. At one time, Lexford had entertained thoughts of wooing Edith and moving into the publisher's office after a perfunctory stop in her bed, but Edith made it clear her admiration for her managing editor was strictly professional. She had what she wanted: a growing paper with unabated respect; a husband wasn't exactly necessary, but he could be most convenient and that, too, would come in time.

Many people called Edith's marriage to Harvey Drake a marriage of convenience. He was the publisher of *Now,* a mass circulation news magazine whose goals dovetailed completely with those of *The New York Record.* Harvey recognized the need for both the magazine and the newspaper to diversify to meet the competition of television. It was that as much as his charm, good looks, and social position that convinced Edith he was the man to sit in the publisher's chair. She, too, recognized the changing world of the press and believed entertainment had become the primary function of *The New York Record.* The news was all there for any one to read, but the fashion story, culture, and the arts were being covered more than when her father took over as publisher. Everyone, including Edith, expected more changes when Harvey Drake was named publisher upon his return from a month's honeymoon.

To the men in the news room, Harvey had earned his spurs in bed, but Bob knew Drake had solid qualifications for his new job. He was a lawyer who had taken over *Now* when the magazine was in trouble. Through his management, *Now* had become one of the top new magazines in the country. It had not only increased its advertising lineage and its circulation, but it had also branched out into radio and television and book publishing. So the new publisher of *The New York Record* did not go to the bridal chamber empty handed as so many of his predecessors had; Harvey Drake represented everything Edith could have hoped for—at least almost everything.

"I hope you'll be very happy," Bob said when he met Edith in the city room after one of the news conferences. She still at-

278

tended the daily sessions on rare occasions and Bob hadn't had a chance to see her since the wedding.

"Thank you, Bob," she said with a wide smile. "Your note when I was married was wonderful. I'll treasure it always."

"I really think you've done an outstanding job as publisher. Your husband also seems to be taking command easily."

"He's a demon for work and brilliant. He knows more about financing than I could ever learn. I think he'll be good for the paper. We're merging some of the companies his magazine is affiliated with, as you know. That will mean exciting new things around here for all of us. Publishing, radio, television. There are so many things planned by the board under Harvey's direction they make my head spin. I could never do what he's doing. I might have kept the paper going, but he's showing me how the resources can be used better and made to grow. I feel as if I'm back in school again."

"All the same, I hope you'll be happy," Bob said, looking deep into Edith's eyes. She looked at him defiantly a moment and then lowered her eyes.

"I know what you mean. Yes, I think I love Harvey very much. He's certainly a handsome man and a charming one. Still, I appreciate your thought, Bob, I know it's sincere. I'll never forget how honest you were with me."

"Everything worked out, didn't it. Mr. Drake, your husband, is just what the paper needed and . . ."

"And you're engaged to that lovely girl. I saw her picture with the announcement. I wanted to write you a note, but I thought it would be better if I saw you. Congratulations."

"Thank you, Edith. I feel very lucky."

"Now that I'm married, and you're going to be married, we're sort of equal again, aren't we?" Edith teased only half in jest. "Maybe it wouldn't be so bad if you cheated a little as long as I was cheating on my husband at the same time. That way, neither one of us would talk."

Bob's mouth popped open as he searched for an answer. He

knew Edith was teasing, but there seemed an earnestness behind her remarks and her manner that made him uneasy.

"I have to be going," she said before he could speak, "Don't forget, I still consider you a very special friend." She winked as she turned away.

Bob was still uncertain what she meant when he was summoned to a luncheon with the new publisher about a month later. Drake had been holding informal sessions with the departments heads and the top editors in small groups to become acquainted with the personnel and their problems. When Bob received his invitation to the private dining room, he assumed he would be one of several men at the luncheon. He was surprised when he saw only two places set.

"Davis, I'm glad to meet you," the publisher said as he strode into the small dining room, taking Bob's hand and shaking it heartily. "My wife has told me a lot about you."

"I'm honored to meet you, sir," Bob said, wondering just what Edith had told her husband.

"Please sit down," Drake said, waving Bob back into his chair. "Will you have a drink? It's a little early in the morning for you night workers, I know, but how about a Bloody Mary?"

"That would be fine, sir," Bob said, studying the publisher as he called the waiter and gave the order. Drake was slight, pasty-faced, with a long thin nose and nervous brown eyes. He was full of electric energy, smoking nervously, and seeming preoccupied even when listening.

"I'm finding out that running a newspaper is a lot different from running a magazine."

"The deadlines come much more frequently," Bob put in.

Drake laughed nervously. "Yes, that's true. Fortunately, I'm not concerned with deadlines. That's up to you boys in the news room. I don't want to get involved in that. It's the quickest route to the graveyard as I see it. You must have to have an iron stomach for that: four editions a night. I think I'd go stark staring mad."

"It's all a matter of what you're used to, I guess."

"Yes, from what Edith tells me, you've been used to a lot." Drake seemed to pause as if he was testing Bob's reaction. "Flying in the war and all that."

Bob's relief was almost evident. "It's the same thing with flying, I guess. Then, though, I was too young to know any better. I don't think I could fly the planes they have today. Aviation has made such rapid strides in the last few years it has made old men out of a lot of former pilots."

"Old? You're hardly in your thirties yet, aren't you?"

"Thirty-two."

"And you've been on the paper how long?"

"Four years."

The waiter came in with the drinks and moved silently away.

"I've been on the paper eight weeks today," Drake said. "Let's drink to that. My eight weeks and your four years. Here's to a lot more for both of us."

He toyed with his glass after downing half the drink, his eyes avoiding Bob's. "As you know, I've been holding these meetings with the staff to find out what's going on. Are there any complaints you have, any dissatisfaction?"

Bob wondered what the publisher wanted to hear. "The only complaint I have is an unsolvable one: night work. There's nothing anyone can do about that so long as *The New York Record* is a morning paper. The paper has to be put out at night."

"That's true, I guess, but is that so bad?"

"It's hard on your social life. I guess it would be hard for the wife of a newspaperman, too."

"You're not married are you? No, come to think of it Edith showed me a picture of that very attractive girl you're engaged to in the society pages. Congratulations."

"Thank you." Bob was surprised Drake had remembered the picture and the item.

"Regardless of how attractive the girl is, I don't think I can do much about your hours. This is a morning newspaper, after all, and most of the work has to be done at night. Of course, if things develop right for you, your hours could change. I noticed you did some writing in the business section not long ago. Would you rather be a writer?"

Bob was silent for a moment. There were few writing jobs on the paper he really wanted, though he thought the writers had a better life, even if it was somewhat more irregular than the copy editors or the men in the bullpen. "I'm really not sure at this point," he said honestly. "I'd like to be in on all the big events, the important happenings, but I like to plan and to know what I'm going to be doing next week and the week after that."

Drake smiled. "I don't even know that. About the only one on the whole paper who does is Webster Clayton. I'm sure you'd like to have his job, but he's so independent and such an institution I don't think I could replace him or tell him what to do if I wanted to."

"I'm sure you could tell him what to do if you wanted to, sir," Bob said with conviction.

"I'm not too sure. I represent an outsider, you know, and Web is the old guard. Whether you know it or not, there's a helluva battle going on right on this paper at this very minute. Sides are being chosen and the lines drawn. I'm on one side with my plans for the paper and Web is on the other side with the traditions and the taboos against firing anyone and the past history of having promoted incompetents for God knows how long. That's the reason I'm having these little get-togethers with the staff. I'm trying to find out whose side everyone is on." He looked at Bob intently, waiting for some expression of loyalty, which would seem politic to even the rankest member of the opposition. Bob said nothing, nodding solemnly and waiting for Drake to frame a direct question.

The publisher seemed annoyed. "You know, Davis, my wife told me I could get a straight answer from you, which certainly would be a novelty around here. I've never heard so much double talk since the last political debate I covered. Everyone seems afraid to commit himself. I had Zugsmith up here for lunch and I swear I don't know what he said or what he meant and we talked for two hours or more. What do you think of Zugsmith, by the way?"

"He's a fine man and a great newspaperman. He was responsible for my getting the job here." Bob didn't bother to mention that he was also responsible for his near-exit from the paper.

"Don't you think he's too much of a precisionist, though?"

"You mean some of the things he puts in his memos? That I'd have to agree on. Having worked on the desk and seen how these things get by, I think the human side of the paper is sometimes overlooked. There are some people who think the whole thing is impersonal: that if no one showed up to work, the paper would still come out in some mysterious way. I don't hold to that belief. I think it's the plugging rewrite man and the silent copy editor who exert the magic. They're not Zugsmiths or Lexfords, but without them *The New York Record* would be lost."

"That's very interesting," Drake said impatiently. "What about Jamieson? What do you think of him?"

"Mr. Zugsmith thinks he's very qualified."

"Ah, that's what Zugsmith thinks. I want to know what you think."

Bob swished the drink around in his mouth playing for time. "Mechanically, he's a good newspaperman. He has all the moves; he knows his job."

"But what? I assure you, Davis, this conversation is strictly confidential. Edith, Mrs. Drake, suggested I ask you about the men in the city room, so please consider it is she who is asking the question."

"I think Mrs. Drake has seen them operate and knows them well. I wouldn't want to pass any judgments."

"That seems to be the usual thing around here, no one wants to make a decision."

Bob laughed. "I'm sorry, sir, but I think you've learned a lot about the paper in eight weeks. Everything is done on the basis of what was done last year; that's the easy way, the safe way."

"But how can you run a news operation that way? The news is constantly changing; someone has to make a decision."

"Oh the late men make decisions, but sometimes they're criticized for it. Then the next time they decide to call up their immediate superior who has to call up his superior and so on. I'm surprised you haven't been called about some decisions in your eight weeks here."

"But where does the buck stop?"

"I don't know, really. In the case of the late man, it comes right back to him because usually the message comes down from on high, step by step: do the best you can. The only catch is that puts the late man under greater pressure because now he has spotlighted that a change has to be made. If he's wrong, he catches hell; if he's right, nothing is said, for no one would ever suggest or acknowledge that a decision had been made."

"Is that what you think of Jamieson? He doesn't make a decision?"

"I wouldn't like to go into personalities. What I'm talking about is a general condition on the paper that Mrs. Drake is well familiar with. I'm sure she could pinpoint any of the personnel for you. She was a very good reporter and really enjoyed the confidence of the city room."

"I know, but she's part of the old paternalistic pattern here. Enough blunders have been made in the name of personnel relations. We have to make changes. I don't know where to start, frankly. The resistance to change is great and so many habits are so deeply ingrained that it's hard to convince people they have to change. I hope I can count on your help, Davis."

Bob wiped his lips with his napkin. "I told Mrs. Drake I'd be happy to help in any way I can. I hope I haven't been too devious in answering your questions, but I don't think it proper that subordinates be asked to evaluate their bosses. I wish you luck in your plans for the paper, though, sir."

"Would you like to hear what some of those plans are?" A dreamy look came into Drake's eyes as he seemed to look right through him.

"Yes, I would, if it wouldn't be out of line for me to know."

"I'm counting on you, Davis, to help make this paper the most powerful in the country, in the world."

"There are some people who say that's the role the paper has now."

Drake shook his head. "Any power *The New York Record* has is strictly an accident. Oh, I don't say the strings haven't been pulled to elect a Mayor, a Senator, or a Governor, but it was done so ineptly that it was all too obvious."

"When you say strings were pulled, Mr. Drake, what do you mean?"

"What do I mean? Come on, Davis, you know perfectly well what I mean. *The New York Record* might print all the news, but there's nothing to prevent it from printing it in such a way that its own ends are served. A favorable story can start on page one, an unfavorable story can be cut to a short and buried in the back of the paper. But it's all there and no one could point a finger. But you know and I know that even opinion polls can be influenced by the order of the questions and the questions themselves. Don't you think *The New York Record* hasn't done that in the past both in the news columns and in the editorials?"

"And you intend to change all that?" Bob asked eagerly.

Drake snorted. "You're missing the whole point, Davis. I said I want to make this paper into the most powerful in the world. That can only be done if the ineptness of the past is overcome. If we're going to slant the news, then let's do it right, subtly and forcefully. If we want to see changes in this country, and changes that are long needed in social legislation, in politics, and in government, we have to work toward that goal with all the weapons at our command."

"But isn't that what government is for? Do you really think it's the role of the press to usurp the powers of government?"

"I don't know that I'd accept the word usurp. Challenge, yes. That's what *Now* has been doing and the people love it. But with a news magazine you lose the effect because of your publishing schedule. Things you want to hit on are no longer news by the time you get into print. With a daily newspaper and a newspaper with the built-in prestige of *The New York Record,* you can be making your points and scoring your gains every day. You know yourself, Davis, the President reads our paper the first thing in the morning. All right, we're going to really give him something to read, because we're going to make clear the road he should take if he expects to be re-elected or if he expects to have a friendly Congress. It's not what *The New York Record* wants, it's what the people want, don't you see?"

Bob shook his head in disbelief. "But how do you know what the people want?"

"We'll take polls and we'll do interviews in depth, en masse, and every other way. We'll talk to the blacks, the young, the protesters, the dissenters, the whole spectrum roiling the country, then we'll go to press."

"But," Bob protested, "you said yourself polls could always be slanted. How . . ."

"You're catching on," Drake said with a smile. "I knew Edith thought highly of you and now I know why. I'm counting on you, Bob. Shall we eat?"

Bob was still numb when the waiter appeared almost before Drake stopped talking. Bob looked at the publisher, peering earnestly at the menu and at the antiseptic, aloof waiter with pencil. "I think I've lost my appetite," he said dourly.

Bob's luncheon did not go unnoticed. Zugsmith, of course, knew that his assistant had seen the new publisher alone, but he was surprised that Lexford knew, too.

"Do you think there's any significance to Davis's seeing Drake alone?" Lexford asked, dropping into the chair across from Zugsmith's desk.

The assistant managing editor stifled a smile. He knew Lexford was wondering about his future, just as were all the other members of the hierarchy except Beau Manley.

"I don't know," Zugsmith said guardedly, "Drake knows Edith was very high on Bob and he might be trying to find out what sort of a man he is."

"He could be measuring him for bigger things, eh?"

Zugsmith bit down on his cigarette holder, which rose like an exclamation point to the lift of his eyebrows. "I wouldn't be surprised. Davis is pretty sharp and he's new enough to suit Drake's purposes."

"What do you think those purposes are?" Lexford's nervousness was apparent.

"I think he wants a brighter paper, primarily, a fresher paper, and he feels he can get it with a fresh team, perhaps."

"And that's where Davis comes in?"

"He may. As I say, he's probably the brightest of my assistants and his standing with Edith can't hurt him. He's a funny fellow, though, and a lot depends on what he wants. He's very independent."

Lexford shook his head. "You know, I really think I was better off as a correspondent. This office intrigue never was for me. In the past I could smile about the shake-ups, but now I'm right in the middle of choosing up sides. It's an uncomfortable position."

Zugsmith smiled, enjoying Lexford's discomfort. "Oh, I wouldn't worry if I were you. I don't think Drake plans to change managing editors." He paused to allow Lexford an instant to relax and then plunged home the knife: "Not just yet, at any rate."

Lexford jolted in the chair. "That's what's so damned annoying about this whole situation. Certainly, Drake plans to make changes, but the question is which way will he jump.

More to the point, the question is which man should we back so that we'll come out the best. You say that Davis appears to be the logical candidate, but I think it will be one of Drake's own men. After all, why should he favor Davis?"

"There are several reasons: he's young, he's bright, he's popular with the men, he's a favorite of Edith's, and he would be both something of the new and something of the old. Frankly, I think you should back Bob Davis if you're going to choose up sides."

Lexford snorted. "It's easy for you to say that; he's your boy. From what I heard, you've brought him along from the first day here; in fact you invited him to join the paper."

Zugsmith nodded. "That's right, but I was also happy when he was going to leave once and now I'm glad he changed his mind. I think the paper needs him and I think you should do everything you can to help him."

"Why Davis? Why not one of Drake's own men?"

"Did any of Drake's men have anything to do with your Pulitzer?"

"Of course not, why?"

"Do you know who did most of the editing of your stories for the time covered by your prize?"

"No, I truly don't. Tom Crum, I supposed."

Zugsmith shook his head like the traditional schoolmaster. "It was Bob Davis. I thought you knew that. Virtually everyone in the office does; I don't see how you could have failed to know."

"You know, Zach, I fail to see the point of all this. All right, Davis was the editor on my dispatches, but isn't that what he was getting paid for?"

"Yes, but you have to remember that I see the dispatches before they're edited and then I see what comes out in the paper. Did you ever compare the two?"

"Hell, man, I stopped reading my published dispatches when I was working for the *London Times*."

Zugsmith could see that Lexford was lying. "Very well,

that explains it, but take it from me, I seriously doubt if you would have won the prize if it hadn't been for the work Davis put in on those dispatches. It was really brilliant. I haven't seen anything like it since the war, when we had real craftsmen on the desks. It's really hard to believe that you never knew."

Lexford shrugged. "I'm sorry, but that's the way it is. I suppose, though, from what you've told me, I should be grateful to Davis after all. Perhaps he might make the best man to back at that."

Zugsmith smiled. "I was sure you'd see it my way," he said smugly. "We'll just have to play it close to the vest and make our moves when we think Drake is ready."

The changes Drake sought came slowly and not without travail. His goal was a long-range one, though, and he could afford to proceed cautiously, working for change on every aspect of the paper so that his philosophical changes would be lost in a welter of detail. Some of the resistance he met was built-in, some because there was a widespread belief among the old-timers that a magazine man didn't know anything about running a newspaper. Some of the programs, other than those dealing with news treatment, were self-defeating, with no hope of success.

Typesetting meant money to Drake and he was determined to cut down on the overset. Each desk had to keep a complicated log of material sent to the composing room, material used, and material killed. Drake's natural bent for statistics meant the keeping of flow sheets, with the time of the movement of copy and heads recorded faithfully at each step of the operation so that each step could be checked and held accountable for a sales loss, a missed train, or a late press run. When errors were made, the writers, the copy editors or the make-up men had to submit written reports explaining why the error had slipped by. Some of the old-timers when asked to submit such explanations wrote merely: I quit.

So Drake's program was working, but whether it was succeeding was debatable. The news was becoming softer and the paper was doing things it would never countenance in earlier days: espousing causes. A poll service was hired and many questions of the day surveyed, with properly loaded questions to provide fuel for an editorial or a series of articles. *The New York Record* ceased to be the paper of record, although its readers still swore by everything that appeared there. In one instance, this vunerable reliability came back to haunt Drake and Lexford.

A story on a prominent political figure appeared that cast doubt on the politician's honesty. The article was retracted, or at least denied the next day, but within the week *The New York Record* was citing an article that appeared in the politician's home town paper as evidence of the truth of the original story. Unfortunately for *The New York Record, Editor and Publisher* investigated and found that the home town paper had picked up the article from *The New York Record,* which therefore was quoting itself as a source to authenticate one of its own questionable statements.

Fortunately, the paper could sluff off or overlook such instances, for the new breed of writers on the paper never let facts stand in the way of a good story. This was a rather common characteristic of the younger writers, but none was more guilty than Guy Latrec, who was sardonically referred to as the best writer and the worst reporter on the paper. Latrec was the unchallenged fair-haired boy not only of *The New York Record,* but of all of New York. He wrote unceasingly, turning out articles for all the departments of *The New York Record,* selling stories to magazines and even publishing books. An odd thing was that Latrec never gave up on a story. The story he wrote for the sports department would turn up on the feature pages in a longer form and then in the magazines in still a longer form. His books were made up of articles that had been in print at least twice before, in most instances.

Latrec represented the conflicts that existed on the paper in more ways than one. It wasn't only his writing, which had broken out of the newspaper mold through the use of delayed leads and verbatim quotes or profanity; it was the man himself. He was a loner, though he tried to give the impression that he was reaching out his hand to the whole world. He wore his hair long and was one of the first to adopt the extremes in clothing that made their debut in the Village. In Guy's opinion, his clothes were part of the over-all picture of the new image of *The New York Record:* his appearance allowed him to communicate with the young, the Negroes, the Puerto Ricans in the city and to talk their language. He was from *The New York Record,* but man, he really dug what was happening and was ready to tell it like it is.

Telling it like it is meant many things to Guy. The one bad habit he had inherited from the old-guard on the papers among the assignment editors was a preconceived notion of what the story was about, what the leading characters should say. Consequently, his quotes were masterpieces, summing up the philosophy of a rejected people, a downtrodden people, or a people in revolt with a pithiness that made the words leap from the paper. Guy's writing was almost literature and well it should have been, for it often was fiction.

It wasn't always Guy's fault that he wrote stories that were never wholly true. After all, he was young, and there were sophisticates among the people he was dealing with who recognized his malleability and bent it to their will and for their profit. Bob was suspicious of some of the quotes and some of the facts that Latrec used and his suspicions were shared by others on the paper, including Tucker.

"I swear," the rewriteman said, "those quotes he uses are right out of the pulp magazines. Only stereotypes talk like that, but he makes it sound so natural and weaves the dialogue in so skillfully that the over-all effect is hypnotic."

"I know," Bob agreed. "But there's something about it that doesn't ring true. He was a copy boy, as you know, in the sports department when I was there, and, when the news got around about Lexford's Pulitzer, he was one of the kids that came to me for advice. I told him he just had to hang in there and keep writing and that proved good advice. I didn't know he had so much on the ball, but I think he's really being wasted on a newspaper. I know the men on the desk have a lot of trouble checking out his facts and a lot of his information is wrong. The public evidently thinks he's great, though, judging from the letters sent in to the paper."

"I think he makes up the quotes if that's what you mean. A lot of reporters don't take shorthand and they fill in blanks in quotes when they miss something, but Latrec seems to supply the whole quote. I remember one time when I wanted to check on a quote because I had to write a radio tape for the broadcast desk and I went over to Latrec to make sure that it was right. I asked him to check on his notes. He made a big show of looking for it in his notes, but then he said he had thrown away some of his notes and that was why he couldn't find it."

"Mr. Latrec will bear watching, then," Bob said, not unpleased that his suspicions were confirmed.

Bob challenged Latrec on one of the biggest frauds to be carried in *The New York Record* and after that Guy started to carry a tape recorder to authenticate his quotes. The fraud story, though, was merely an instance where Guy was in over his head. He had a habit of talking down to people and received his comeuppance when a group of youngsters told him of a secret murder society that was supposed to be operating in the city. The story was splashed across the front page on the first day and was still prominently displayed on the second and third days as the police and the social agencies began checking and commenting on the secret society. The final admission by the leader of the gang that the secret society story was a hoax was almost a secret in itself. It didn't appear in *The New York Record* at all, and only the *New Yorker* pointed out that the story, which had been allowed to die an unnatural death by Zugsmith and Lexford after they learned the truth, had never been a story in the first place.

"You're leaving yourself wide open for criticism, Guy," Bob said to the young reporter after the furor about the secret society had died down.

"How do you mean?"

"Well, a lot of people think you zing your quotes—make them up without really checking with the speaker. After this secret society thing, they're going to think that you're concentrating on fiction writing and not being concerned with truth. If I were you, I'd start carrying one of those small recorders with a lapel mike."

"That might not be a bad idea. The only thing is that when the people know they're being recorded, they freeze up. They try to be proper and all the local flavor is lost."

"With a lapel mike, you don't have to tell them you're recording. You're not going to use the material on the air so I don't think there would be any invasion of privacy so long as you told them you were a reporter in the first place."

"Sometimes I've gotten stories by pretending that I wasn't a reporter. What do you do in a case like that?"

"I don't think it would be fair to use a recording if the people think they're talking to a plain citizen rather than a reporter. At least identifying yourself serves notice that what they say could appear in print. Without the notification it's too much like eavesdropping."

"I think you're right," Latrec said. "I don't think I have to justify myself to any of these bastards in the office, but using a recorder could make things a lot easier for me. The interview could cover a lot more ground and I wouldn't have to take time out to make notes. I think people might be ready and willing to talk to a reporter just because they know he's a reporter. As soon as they see you taking down their words, though, their reaction is different. They become different people."

"Which ones do you quote, the note-supported ones or the memory-backed ones?" Bob asked narrowly.

Latrec's eyes twinkled. "Suppose we start using a recorder and then we can find out."

The system worked perfectly so far as Guy was concerned. His freedom from note-taking gave him more latitude and enabled him to explore more intimate subjects with those being interviewed. The microphone he used was inconspicuous enough not to be noticed by those he reported on and his stories continued to have the flavor of the pre-recording days.

"You've got to hand it to Latrec," Tucker said grudgingly. "Since he's been using that recorder his stories certainly sing with the true flavor of his subjects. That was a good idea of yours."

"Thanks, but Guy is the one who deserves the credit. I used to think he was zinging those quotes, but now other reporters are using recorders and I think the language is more believable than in the past."

"Of course," Tucker said with a smile, "They all could be faking their quotes, too."

"You're too damned cynical," Bob said. "Let's have a drink at Curry's before it closes."

In walking to the locker room, they passed Latrec's desk. The drawers were half open and the lapel mike was visible in the top drawer.

"You'd better put that away or one of the cleaning men will have a nice toy," Tucker said as Bob moved toward the desk and picked up the combination microphone and earpiece.

"These are pretty good little gadgets," Bob said. "Have you ever used one?"

"Not like this, but I have a recorder at home. I dictate story ideas when I'm too tired to type. It's like psychiatry. I lie down and things seem to come easily to me."

"With one of these, you could talk to yourself on the subway, if you want. Listen." Bob pushed the play back button and the voice of Latrec started to come out of the tiny microphone. The tape sounded like this:

Latrec: "Would you say that the city has been negligent in its attention to the Negro problems in your area?"

Second Voice: "It's bad, man, bad."

Latrec: "Yes, but what is your specific complaint against the city? Would you say that the white power structure has prevented the filtering of funds down to the level where they are really needed?"

Second Voice: "It's bad, man, it's really bad."

Latrec: "But you have to really be more specific. If I'm going to help you, you have to give me something that will make a headline. You have to say something more than it's bad. How is it bad?"

Second Voice: "What you want me to say, man? It's outasight."

Latrec: "Never mind. I know what you can say. I'll take care of it."

"I'll be a son of a bitch," Tucker said incredulously.

"I will, too," Bob agreed, "But a quiet one." He pushed the erase button on the recorder and watched the spool of tape spin back to the rewind reel. "Come on," he said, "I think I could really use that drink."

Chapter Sixteen

DRAKE'S CONTROL over the paper tightened relent-
lessly. He moved new men, his men, into key positions, under-
cutting the established editors and stymieing others Zugsmith
had marked for advancement. Edith was withdrawn from the
actual operation of the news room, but she insisted the transitions be made as smooth as possible, the displacements
marked by a dignity in keeping with her father's and grandfather's policies. There were some early retirements as those
displaced by Drake's executives declined to accept reduced
authority after being in control of departments for years. For
others, though, there were vertical shifts and kicks upstairs,
with the amelioration of a title and an entry into a new stock
option plan Drake introduced. The corporate image was
changing and so was the product; the imperiousness was still
there, but it was less grand, less benevolent, more intellec-
tually oriented.

Where the men being superseded remained in their old jobs,
their powers diminished, their ambition crushed and their initiative restricted, Drake called on his Madison Avenue advisers to resolve the problems of tables of organizations. Executive editors were placed over editors whose authority had been
unquestioned in a department. Suddenly, news directors,
chiefs of correspondents, and assistant managing editors were
almost as numerous as the scores of reporters at the desks in
the city room. Everyone, it seemed, had a title, but few of
those superseded by Drake's men had any clear-cut duties. In
addition, Drake's men, being new to the operation, were reluctant, in many cases, to exert positive control; they seemed unsure of their new powers. As a result, the paper drifted along
almost by itself, the men on the desks meeting the deadlines,
the reporters covering their usual beats and the public being

only slightly aware of the struggle going on behind the mast-head.

What Bob called "sneer journalism" became the vogue, with every facet of the news being treated critically in search of lightness, scandal, or ineptitude. How much Edith was responsible, or how much was attributable to Drake Bob could not determine, since the trend seemed to be an extension of Edith's irreverent treatment of the society matrons while she was reporting. Everyone knew where the power lay, though, and the lesson Sellers Warrenton learned about reviewing plays the publisher's friends had interest in permeated all departments. No friend of Drake's was ever treated with anything less than obeisance in the society pages or in whatever area he made news. Edith's designer, for she was now moving in more fashionable circles than those of a reporter, was always hailed on the fashion pages and even a prominent manufacturer who had a better than fair race horse was made a minor deity by the sports editor because of his links to the publisher.

Drake reveled in his new power. His magazine had never given him an identity, but now he was sought out as the speaker at civic dinners, a board member by leading banks, and a candidate for honorary degrees by leading universities. Everything, of course, was *quid pro quo,* the civic causes that Drake embraced, the banks, the universities all being assured of ample coverage in the future for the honors they had accorded the publisher. The Mayor, the Governor, and even Cabinet officers were frequent luncheon guests in the publisher's private dining room, and the staff always knew when the party had been particularly grand by the left-over hors d'oeuvres that were set out on the appetizer counter in the employees cafeteria, only a few feet and a few million dollars away from the inner sanctum.

Like his predecessor, Drake began to take people on tours of the building, but Bob had to acknowledge that Edith was always in the party. She never failed to stop to exchange a few words with him, something that never escaped Drake's notice.

The publisher began to realize that Bob would be a perfect compromise candidate to head the newsroom operation. He was young, loyal to Edith, talented and respected by the old-timers on the paper. He could be most useful, even if only as a transition.

"How are things going?" Drake asked Bob on one of his tours.

"Everything's quiet, tonight, sir."

"No, I don't mean tonight. I mean generally. I'm hearing a lot of good things about you. You've handled a couple of late breaking stories very nicely, from what I've heard. That riot last week made a lot of trains and we picked up a lot of news-stand sales because of your decisiveness. I've been meaning to thank you."

Bob recalled the incident easily because he had killed one of the special stories one of Drake's men had ordered to make room for the riot article and had to write an explanation for his actions the next day. "It's all part of the game," he said.

"Well, I want you to know I appreciate it. Remember our luncheon talk, do you? I'm counting on you, Davis, we need men like you here."

"Nothing ever changes," Tucker said to Bob over some drinks at Curry's when Bob explained how he had been commended by the publisher after one of his subordinates had criticized Bob's news judgment. "With Drake touring the place like old Sanford Miller used to do, the only thing different is the faces. It's just like the Army, or at least the World War II Army. When I look back, I wonder how we ever won the war with all the foul-ups we had in uniform. Here I wonder how we ever get the paper out with all the doubledomed thinkers around here. It's lucky that they have a doer on late in the bullpen. At least you're not afraid to act."

"I don't know what you're complaining about," Bob said. "You're writing features about three times a week. Your by-line is always in the paper."

"I know, but it's just like that science-fiction stuff I write. It has no guts, no touch with reality. We're supposed to be reporting in depth and to be objective, but every time I want to really start digging into a story, I'm warned away by one of the new editors. They want only bullshit, they want it by the yard, and they want it to meet their preconceived notions. That's no way to operate."

"And yet, the paper's making money. It's having its best year from what I've heard."

"But that's because the market is shrinking. There are five fewer papers in New York now than when I came here. If you consider there are more department stores and more people to read the paper, you have to figure on any of the surviving papers having great years. It's small credit to the quality of the paper, it's merely a matter of being alive."

"You know," Bob said, taking a long pull on his cigarette. "I think Edith Miller was doing better than the clowns they have in charge now. Certainly there have been some changes since Drake took over, but from what I see, the men he has put in charge are too timid or to inexperienced to move. He told me the paper was going to be much more positive a force than in the past."

"Did it ever occur to you that Drake doesn't have a free hand? You know Mrs. Miller still controls a big block of the stock and she may be resisting some of the moves he wants to make."

"That could be, but the result seems such a hodge-podge. They've changed the front page layout and the inside pages a lot, but basically, these are only frosting. The product, the accent on 'if it's long enough, it's good enough,' the tendency to look down our noses at everything seems to be more apparent than in the past. We're grinding a lot more axes now and the news is being slanted more than ever. I don't know whether it's the men or the paper. Do the men corrupt the paper or does the paper corrupt the men?"

Tucker snorted. "Boy, aren't you in a black mood. That's

what that late shift does to you, I know. What's got into you, Bob? I thought you had finally accepted the idea that you'd be a forty-year man."

"I'm not too sure. I miss Diane more than I ever imagined I could miss any one. I want to marry her and have a real life with her, not this upside down life we lead."

"We agreed long ago there's no cure for that. Unless you're really married to your job on a newspaper, you're going to be unhappy in the real world. That's why Zugsmith was always so insistent on getting 'real' *New York Record* men."

"That's it. I'm not married to my job and the relationship seems more unattractive under the new management than the old. Besides, I just got a letter from Larry Finnegan. Do you remember him?"

"The Ph.D. copy boy who rigged the electric sign?"

"That's right, but he wasn't an ordinary Ph.D. copy boy. His father was one of the wealthiest men in Indiana and he's just bought one of the Miami papers for Larry to run. Larry wants me to be managing editor."

"Managing editor, in Miami? What time does the next plane leave?"

"That was my first impression, but I want to think about it. The money is right and the climate, too. I think it would be exciting to take on the challenge the job represents, but I want to talk to Zugsmith first. Being a big duck in a small pond might not be for me, but at least I'd have a lot more freedom of action."

"What does Diane say?"

"I haven't told her yet, but she'd say I should do whatever I want to, which is what she has always said. Candidly, though, I think she'd like me to get away from *The New York Record*. And I'd see her a lot sooner than I thought."

"When do you have to decide?"

"Larry said he'd like to know by the end of the month. That gives me about two weeks. I should know pretty much then which way I'm going."

"Forty years or a commuted sentence. I wish I had that alternative."

"You do, you know. Larry said I could bring anyone along I wanted. If I decided to go to Miami, I was thinking of asking you to come along as city editor or something."

A long dreamy look came into Tucker's eyes and then they misted over. He shook his head sadly. "No, Bob, I couldn't do it. I'm honored you'd think of me, but I'm too deep in the rut. The kids, the mortgage, the college educations, you know. If I was twenty years younger, I'd go in a minute, but thanks, no. I'm not trying to influence you in any way, but if I were you, I'd be out of here tomorrow."

"That's one thing about you," Bob said, masking his smile as he turned to Tucker and punched him on the arm affectionately, "You'll never be a *New York Record* man."

Bob had trouble seeing Zugsmith. Things were happening that Bob didn't know about until four days before the deadline for his decision on the Miami job. He learned about them from Zugsmith as he sat in the assistant managing editor's office waiting for him to finish page one for the first edition.

"I guess you've heard about Web Clayton," Zugsmith said, taking the long cigarette holder from the desk and lighting up with marked nervousness. "I guess that's what you want to see me about."

"Web? No, I haven't heard anything about him. Is he ill?"

"I don't suppose he's feeling too well right now. Drake wants to replace him as bureau chief in Washington."

"Web Clayton?" Bob was shocked. The campaign was being stepped up. "I know he's pushing sixty, but why would Drake want to do that? Web is still one of the most respected columnists in America."

"Oh, Drake knows that and the idea was to have Web concentrate on his column while Childs took over the bureau. He . . ."

"Joe Childs? The fellow from *Now?* He's only been on the

301

paper about a month. I don't see where his experience could come anywhere close to Web Clayton's."

"It's not a question of experience, it's a matter of control. Web is a rugged individualist as you well know. He hasn't changed a bit for any publisher and he doesn't intend to now. He runs that department with an iron hand, you know, and Drake thinks the iron hand should be relaxed so different direction can be applied. You've seen it in the city room, you know what's happening."

"But the people in the city room are behind the scenes. If Drake undercuts Web, I don't think Web would stay on the paper. He always talked of having enough money to retire anytime he wanted to. This might be the time."

"This is the time. I thought you knew. Web is coming to New York right now with his resignation in his pocket. Not only that, he has the resignations of the four top writers down there with him and several of the editors on the desk."

"Mass resignations? I didn't know so many of the Washington staff knew Childs."

"He worked in Washington at one time and I don't think he created too favorable an impression. It's not so much a case of knowing Childs as respecting Web Clayton. The men evidently feel he represents something in journalism they don't want to see change."

"Web was a hard man to work for, but he had a lot of talent. I'll be sorry to see him go."

"He's not gone yet. He wants to see Mrs. Miller to explain his resignation to her. I don't think she'll let him go. She always liked Web."

Bob looked out the window at the worn brick of the theater across the street. He remembered his first day in the office and his interview with Zugsmith. It seemed so long ago.

"What is it you wanted to see me about if you didn't know about Web?" Zugsmith said. "I thought you wanted to ask for his job."

"Could you have got it for me? I thought you said Childs was all set for that spot."

Zugsmith puffed nervously at his cigarette. Bob's analysis was perfect. Zugsmith's power had been lessened with the rise of Drake's men and even Lexford was no longer secure. The patterns of power were changing and Zugsmith's lines of communication to Mrs. Miller were frequently blocked.

"I don't know about the column if Web quits," Zugsmith said, "But I was thinking of you as sort of a compromise candidate to head the bureau. I know the men down there liked you when you were there and your friendship with Edith Drake could help. I was thinking of suggesting you to Drake myself because he's upset about Web's threat, too."

Bob sighed, spreading his hands wearily.

"I once thought I'd like Web's job, but I don't think so any more. I can see what the men on the desk and the reporters mean when they say that management is killing all the old dedication, the old pride that made this place work. When they start going after an institution, and a damned good one like Web Clayton, that's the time to quit. I've made up my mind; that's what I wanted to tell you: I'm leaving *The New York Record.*"

Zugsmith looked as if he had been slapped. His face turned ashen and the cigarette holder fell to the desk as he gaped at Bob in disbelief. "Leave *The New York Record?* You? I've counted on you, Bob, you know that. I expect you to take over for me some day. And it won't be long either. I'm past retirement age the way Drake figures and I know Edith would let you move in. You know what he's trying to do to *The New York Record;* you could stop him if you went to Edith."

Bob shook his head stubbornly. "If I wouldn't ask Edith for help before, I wouldn't ask her now. I don't think it should be a matter of friendship or who you know or cliques or anything like that. That's the whole trouble with this paper. There's too much cronyism. It was bad enough in the past, but when a new broom comes in you have a right to hope that some constructive changes will be made. When you see the same old patterns developing, it gets too discouraging."

"Discouraging?" Zugsmith almost shouted. "What have you to be discouraged about? You've come up faster and farther in a short time than anyone since the war. You've . . ."

"Except Joe Childs."

"All right, Childs I can't control. But Edith will listen if I talk to her about you. Don't do anything hasty, Bob. There's a great future for you on *The New York Record*. Where would you go? Back to television?"

"No, I have an offer to be the managing editor of a paper in Miami. It's an afternoon paper and the hours would be more like a normal working day. The money is good and the challenge is attractive."

"You mean to say you've been looking for a job while you've been working for me? Sneaking behind my back, using *The New York Record* to further your own ambitions?" Zugsmith was working himself into a fury. Bob's departure would mean that Zugsmith's last hope for his philosophy to be retained on the paper would disappear. Jamieson had already been replaced by one of Drake's men and the circle was drawing tighter around Zugsmith's empire.

Bob looked at Zugsmith in disbelief. He had no idea his decision would affect the assistant editor so deeply. He knew Zugsmith had been unnerved by the recent changes on the paper, but Bob had never seen him lose control before.

"I didn't look for the job, it came to me," Bob said defensively. "Do you remember Larry Finnegan, the copy boy who had the argument with you about the sermon?"

"That young idiot who put those obscenities on the electric bulletin? Yes, I remember him well, why?"

"He's the one who offered me a job. His father bought the paper in Miami and he wants me to be managing editor."

"That, that spoiled brat is going to be the publisher?"

"I suppose so. It's his paper, at any rate."

"Come, Bob," Zugsmith said soothingly, "You know you can't work for a fellow like that. Anyone who did what he did is too unstable. You'd never know where you stood from one week to the next."

"Do you know here? It seems to me the players have been changing so rapidly lately that you need more than a score-card to keep up with them. If I remember correctly, the last time you mentioned Larry Finnegan, I was out of favor then; who's in favor this week? Childs? All right, what happens if Mrs. Miller backs Web and she tells her son-in-law to go to hell with his bright young man? No, it's getting to be a dog fight I don't want any part of. I don't know if Larry Finnegan is stable or not. I do know he's honest, though, and that means a lot to me."

"What?" Zugsmith shrieked, rising from his chair, "Are you implying *The New York Record* is not honest. I . . . ." Suddenly he clutched his throat and fell to the floor. Bob bounded from his chair and lifted Zugsmith to the small sofa in the corner of the office. He loosened his tie and propped his head up on one of the sofa cushions.

"Burnside," Bob screamed through the door to Zugsmith's assistant. "Get a doctor," he said, as the New Englander trotted into the room followed by Chapman and Cohen.

"What happened?" Chapman asked, dialing the medical department as Bob tried to get Zugsmith to take some water.

"He collapsed while he was talking to me. Hurry with that doctor."

Zugsmith opened his eyes and smiled wanly. "What are you getting excited about?" he asked weakly. "My doctor told me excitement can kill you. I'm beginning to think he's right."

"Don't talk," Bob ordered. "The doctor will be here in a minute. Just relax. Take a little water." He turned to the door, which was crowded with reporters and desk men looking in to see what had caused the sudden evacuation of the bullpen. "Chapmen, Cohen," he ordered, "Get those men back to work."

The two assistants shepherded the crowd away from the door, but Tucker slipped by and knelt at Bob's side. "Anything I can do, Bob?" he asked.

Bob shook his head. "I wish the doctor would get here."

Zugsmith's eyes flickered in recognition of Tucker. "Howard, how are you? I always wanted to apologize to you for keeping you on rewrite for so many years, but I never got around to it. I . . ."

"Don't worry about it, Zach. I never minded it, really. It doesn't really matter anyway, does it?"

Zugsmith shook his head sadly. "No, nothing much matters any more. Only the paper. Promise me, Bob, you won't leave. Now there's no longer any waiting, the job can be yours. You can do things your way."

"Don't talk about it. Just relax. Where the hell is that doctor?"

"He's on his way," Burnside said, hovering over the sofa helplessly.

Zugsmith turned his head in the direction of the voice. "Chauncey," he said, "I want you to tell Mr. Drake and Mrs. Drake I said Mr. Davis was the one I would recommend as my successor. I want you to tell them . . ." The words were cut off as a sudden hot thrust of pain sank deep into Zugsmith's chest. He grimaced and then his face seemed to relax. He opened his eyes and put his hand on Bob's arm. "Don't leave, Bob, don't," he said, the hand slipping down Bob's sleeve as the shallow breathing stopped and the eyes started to glaze.

Bob got up from the sofa and turned to Tucker, spreading his hands in resignation. Just then the doctor sprinted into the room.

"Where is he, what's the matter?" the doctor rasped in a voice hoarse from his efforts to hurry.

"It's too late, doc, he's dead," Bob said, suddenly feeling tired.

"Dead? Who says so?" the doctor persisted. He went over to

the sofa and listened in vain for a heartbeat. "Yes, he's dead," the doctor conceded. "It looks like a heart attack to me. Was he one of our reporters?"

Most of the thousands of workers on the paper outside of the news room had no conception of the operation of *The New York Record*. Everyone to them was a reporter. "No," Tucker said to the doctor, "He was Zachary Zugsmith, the assistant managing editor."

"Zachary Zugsmith," the doctor repeated, writing in a little notebook. "Assistant managing editor, eh? I never heard of him."

Bob watched numbly as the doctor walked out the door.

"It looks as if you're in charge now, Bob," Burnside said. "What do you want to do?"

Bob stared at Burnside and then turned to Tucker.

"Come on, Bob," Tucker urged, "It's your decision."

Bob shook his head to clear it. "Get out the files," he said, "And see what we did when Zugsmith's predecessor died. I'd say it should go on page one, with a picture. If we have a prepared obit, we should make it for the first edition."

"I'll knock out an obit in time for the edition," Tucker said. "That's the least I can do."

"Thanks," Bob said. Turning to Burnside he said: "Count on it for a two-column head down at the bottom of the page. What do we have to move off to make the room?"

Burnside went to his desk for the dummy layout of the page and returned almost instantly. "It's another one of the features that Joe Childs has been pushing."

"Move it inside or hold it over if you have to; Zugsmith deserves to be on the front page."

Burnside nodded and walked out of the room. "That was nicely done, Bob," Tucker said. "I like that. I better get hopping, but we'll talk it over in Curry's. Will you be able to sneak away?"

Bob nodded. "I need a drink and there's something I want to talk to you about. But go ahead, I'll see you later."

Tucker left and Bob walked out to the cluster of desks where Burnside and the other assistants sat. He smiled to himself as he noticed that Burnside had moved down in the order of progression, leaving the number one desk for Bob. He was inside with the ambulance attendant watching the removal of Zugsmith's body when Drake arrived and held a whispered conversation with Burnside. The publisher walked into the inner office after the body was carried out.

"It's a terrible shock," he said, sinking into a chair and lighting a cigarette.

"Zugsmith meant a lot to this paper and the paper meant everything to him, it was his whole life," Bob said.

"They don't make men like him any more," Drake mused, lapsing into the clichés of the funeral parlor. "I understand he told Burnside he wanted you to be his successor."

"Yes, he did, but, of course, I know you have your own plans. I took over only because the others seemed so shocked. I'll let Burnside run things, if you wish. It's entirely up to you."

"No, no, not at all. That fits in with my plans exactly. I think you're just the man for the job. In fact I've been thinking that way for some time. I know my wife would approve and Mrs. Miller, too."

Bob could feel himself blushing in spite of himself. "Thank you very much, sir, I appreciate your confidence."

"There's only one thing," Drake said, pausing noticeably. "I don't think Zugsmith's obituary should go on the front page. Particularly I don't think it should replace that article on the hippies that Joe Childs ordered."

Bob could feel his temper rising and struggled to control it. "Zachary Zugsmith gave his life to this paper. For forty years he ate, slept, talked, slaved for *The New York Record*. I think he deserves to be on page one. I think the paper owes him that much loyalty."

Drake waved his cigarette impatiently. "You'll find, Bob, that when you're at the top, loyalty is a one-way street. It comes up as it should, but it doesn't have to go down. There are other factors involved. Now you can't start out by knocking off one of Joe Childs' favorite stories. He's touchy enough these days, God knows."

"I don't see how you can equate a feature story about hippies which we could hold over to a tribute, if you will, to a man like Zugsmith. He's responsible for a lot of honors this paper has won. I think we could at least do this for him."

Drake smiled indulgently. "You're letting sentiment cloud your judgment. The hippie story will sell more papers and there are other considerations to be weighed. Joe Childs was very upset the last time one of his stories was moved off the front page and he told me that if it happened again he'd quit. Now Joe is a good man, and I wouldn't want to lose him. I wouldn't want to lose you, either, Bob, because you could be managing editor some day and I don't mean too long in the future. Lexford has never captured the loyalty of the men and I know Joe Childs is too much of a newcomer to ever do it either. You'd be the perfect choice, but I don't think I could say that if you're going to let sentiment influence you. Be smart, Davis, you've won. You have before you what millions of newspaper men have dreamed of. You'll be famous."

Bob's mouth was dry and he swallowed hard to ease the constriction in his throat. "I have some standards of my own, Mr. Drake. I have to face the facts and do the best I can."

"That's fine," Drake said, cutting him off and getting up from the chair. "I knew I could count on you." He shook hands with Bob, who stood numb for an instant after the publisher left. He was still looking out the doorway when Tucker entered the room.

"I'm finished, Bob. Would you like to read the dupes?" Tucker said, holding out the carbon copies of his obituary on Zugsmith.

Bob took the papers and began to read. It was one of the finest stories Howard had written, full of the warmth and the humor Zugsmith had worked so hard to bring to the paper.

"It's great," he said, "It catches the man perfectly. You must have been a great admirer of Zugsmith's. Now there's something I want you to do for me. I want you to follow this story right through. Go up to the composing room and see that it gets into the page and then that the plates are made and the presses started. I want to make sure that Zugsmith is page one."

"Is there any doubt about it?"

"Drake said that Joe Childs would quit if we took his story off page one and that Zugsmith didn't warrant page one."

"The son of a bitch," Tucker ejaculated. "What are you going to do?"

Bob looked at the rewrite man, pleased at his anger. "I told you what to do. Don't let anyone change anything in the composing room or on the stereotypes. You get on that and I'll keep Burnside and the others here. I think we should put it on the electric sign, too."

"But what are you going to do when Drake sees the obit on page one?"

Bob smiled. It was the first time all night he had felt relaxed. "I'm going to do just what I told Zugsmith and what I was trying to tell Drake before he cut me off: I'm going to Florida."

Tucker beamed. "If Drake finds out that I rode shotgun on this obit, I might join you at that. Is that offer still good?"

"Anytime," Bob said. He shook hands with Tucker warmly. "I'm going to get out as soon as the paper comes up. I don't want to wait around for Drake's phone call. We'll get together at Curry's some other night. Tonight I feel awfully tired. I think I'll go home and call Diane."

Tucker went out to start his supervision of the typesetting and the make-up and Bob began a line by line discussion of the obituary with Burnside and the others. He had one eye on the clock while they labored over the article and he timed himself perfectly, finishing just as the last light went out on

310

the electric board denoting that the last page had gone to press.

Bob got up and went to the locker for his coat. He walked out through the city room and down the stairs without talking to anyone. Outside, the night air was cool and fresh and almost clean smelling. Bob walked moodily to the corner and stared up at the electric letters racing around the annex. "Zachary A. Zugsmith, assistant managing editor of *The New York Record,* dies at sixty-two," the sign said in banks of bulbs three feet high. It was the last item, Bob knew and the "buy" line followed, with the paper's motto at the end: "Only the Truth." The electric bulbs winked down on the great city. Bob smiled as he ducked into the subway.